The Wild Time

The Wild Time

THE MID-WORLD OF THE TRUCE
BOOK ONE

STEVE DOUGLAS

For my family and their longstanding support and love.
For my wonderful wife, Pamela, inspiration, and proof-reader.
For Chris, our brilliant son, editor, and publishing manager.
For our daughter Sara, who radiates energy, intelligence and
encouragement.

Contents

ONE SIDE OF

The Game of

THE MAN AT ARMS

THE MID-WORLD SPY

THE ILLUSION

THE APPRENTICE

THE CHARMED KNIGHT

THE PRINCESS

THE TALISMAN

THE WEB OF FATE

THE GREY COUNCILLOR

THE MAGI

THE ARMED HOST

THE GREAT SPELL

THE WIZARD

THE MASTER

the Masters

THE
APPRENTICE

THE
CHARMED
KNIGHT

THE
ILLUSION

THE
MID-WORLD
SPY

THE MAN
AT ARMS

HE
CIAN

THE
CAPTAIN

THE
SENDING

THE
MID-WORLD
WEAPON

THE
ARCHERS

THE
MID-WORLD
POWER

THE
ANCIENT
SECRET

THE
SORCERER

THE
FORTRESS

ALANTÉA

The Forerunner

Far Avalon
(Goblin Market)

Nemesis

Bizere

Erivan
Forest

Varaj

Piranus

North
Haven

Wizards League

River Bariloch

Amalric

Cities, towns, villages

Wizards towers

Greenway

Boundary of The
Wizards League

Sea's
Edge

Khiva

Chapter One

The Slayers and the Slain

NIGHT WAS COMING. SENTAURIS sped through the darkening forest then paused, peering through a tangle of brush, shoulders heaving slightly until her breathing slowed. Anger and tension surged through her body, though she kept her eyes focused on the scene before her, where an evening watchfire smoldered in the slight breezes of an early dusk. Subdued murmuring sounds echoed softly through the forest glade. All seemed peaceful from a distance, but she had arrived too late, and the scene before her radiated grief and death into the somber, rainy skies of early spring.

As she crept closer, Ghorm, her Familiar, made whispering, strangled noises, trying to drug their horse with spells, while at the same time struggling to keep Sentauris back. She waved him to silence, and they moved like hushed ghosts through a thicket of grey birches. Faces could be seen as she neared the camp — white petalled brush strokes lit by dusk, framed against a dark, oncoming night.

Anger was surging inside her, and she struggled to control it. Mad dog raiders sent by Dark Gods had again attacked her people. This time they would pay — despite Dark-Souled Set or Arioch the Malevolent, or Mallegro the Insane. As they drew closer, Ghorm became completely quiet, anxious not to alert their foes. Night was settling over the forest and its darkness deepened. Laughter came from the camp as raiders shared the possessions of the dead. Soft weeping sounds could be heard from refugees captured by the raiders, helpless people destined for slavery or human sacrifice.

Sentauris edged forward and drew her bow. Ghorm's small feet danced in frustration.

As she opened her mind, the powerful Seer's Sight within her flooded her senses with images:

She was among horseriders and wagons as they raced over forest trails, harried by raiders on three flanks. One by one arrows and long lances struck down the armed defenders of the refugees....

She entered a dark temple filled with smoke and the smell of burning flesh. Massive walls of stone rose on all sides — and they were grey with ash and soiled with grime. The chants of priests and acolytes echoed through the rising smoke that surrounded them. Just behind the procession, weeping captives were being led before the throne of a Mid-World Power, an enormous being who claimed Godhood, and demanded the worship of lesser beings. Sentauris peered through her vision quest and beheld Moloch, Fire-God, and fearsome slaughterer of innocents. Moloch seated in his place of power sat three times man's height and vastly greater in bulk. Face greyish dark and swarthy, his thick goblinlike features were fixed in a gloating smile that vanished as he perceived the intrusion of Sentauris. Moloch snarled grey smoke through bloated, fleshy lips. Eyes huge as saucers darted back and forth, reaching for her....

She tore herself free and sank back, struggling for breath. Part of her wanted to cry out loud. A God! Moloch! Again, Ghorm tugged at her, but she clenched his hand until the worst of her fears slipped away, then she began inching forward again, always more cautiously as she neared the campfire. As she drew closer, she probed with her Sight, though now more carefully, more briefly and focused....

Grey and brown shapes moved over green as a horse's head nibbled on long grasses....

Pale tears of a youth seeped down his face as he tried to comfort his mother....

Thick, fleshy hands of a guard picked among the dead, searching for gold, hidden weapons or talismans, and the dead had no privacy as his searches became always more intimate....

More light flared over the camp as the watchfire was fed...firelight was passing over more than forty raiders...with perhaps three times that number held as prisoners....

Light flashed over a grey beard that framed a lean, cruel face, with a mouth that whispered and eyes that searched for her —for Sentauris!

Again, Sentauris pulled back. They had sent a Priest Mage with their raiding party! And the Mage was aware of her! She crouched, and slipped an arrow into her bow, whispering into Ghorm's mind, *No, I'm not going to hunt them all, not this night. But one of them has the power to summon his God-King, and he will not be permitted to do that!*

Sentauris shifted from her crouch to stand beside a broad oak, one with a trunk more than twice her thickness. She pulled back on her bow and peered into the future.

A Gateway was forming, an enchanted passage to the kingdom of Moloch, with crowds of armed men pushing through the glade toward that Gateway. She shifted, seeking the Mage.

The camp stirred as the Priest Mage called out orders. Men raced toward weapon racks.

Lights were gleaming through the glade, and Sentauris watched as her own helpless form was slashed by two arrows. Pain was radiating through her body as guardsmen leaped at her with bright flashing steel. She muttered a snarl and shifted. Beside her Ghorm was whispering spell words, struggling to match his own small powers against the force of magic surging from their enemies' camp.

Words of power spilled from the Priest Mage's lips. As the air grew bright all through the glade, captives began crying for help, sobbing in fear. Sentauris shifted, face fixed in a grimace, and she peered.

And met only a vacant darkness, the emptiness of death. Sentauris snarled a curse and released her shaft, drawing another in one swift motion.

Within the glade, the Priest Mage took two tiger-swift steps from his watchfire. An arrow passed to his left as he cried out more words of power in a voice touched by triumph. Five guardsmen sprang from the glade, racing toward the dimly perceived figure of Sentauris.

And then a second arrow surged out of the darkness — and it filled the left eye socket of Moloch's Priest Mage. Enchanted lights flickered once then fell dead as their fashioner toppled, clutching his dying features. More men blundered into the shadows, stumbling and tripping over root systems as their eyes struggled to adjust to the lack of light. Sentauris took three steps back, then another three. Only one of the guardsmen had managed to track her. Growling with anger at his own night fears, he rushed at her out of the darkness, sword slashing through tangles of brush. Sentauris drew her own blade, slipped past his outthrust weapon, and slashed though the mail covering his throat.

Then she stepped back, searching future paths from the surrounding darkness while milling guardsmen made thrashing, growling sounds all around her. Most of her futures led to deep wounds or death — but not all. With great caution, she chose a path that led to her own survival, then slipped silently from the glade into the dark stillness of the nighttime forest.

·)(·

Tallus pounded on his anvil, with the red light of his forge pit gleaming over his dark Tanu skin. Beyond the half-opened shutters of his armory, the pale light of an overcast morning was beginning to slip into his armory, and Tallus frowned. Some work at the forge was best done in darkness, depending on the force of magic needed, depending on each weapon's purpose. Would this weapon still have power? He whispered spell words over the dagger and watched as its rune inscription caught fire, symbols gleaming in the muted darkness of his armory. He allowed a faint smile to flicker over his face: the weapon he held might one day prove a deadly surprise to one of his Mid-World adversaries.

Tallus straightened when he heard the sentry's call and he was out of his armory in a flash. Ten steps were taken before his mind fully registered that his sentry warned of a lone rider and not the feared war party that would force Tallus and his war band back into the hills. He reached the gate post still holding the gleaming dagger in one hand and his powerful dark hammer in the other. A second guard joined them; these two formed the gate watch. Standing beside the taller of the two humans, the Tanu-born Tallus stood only a hand's breadth higher, but the Tanu's bulk was more than twice that of the humans.

A lone rider hurried up the ravines, easily avoiding the pitfalls and slides that marked the passage of the unwary and unwanted. *Sentauris*...his mind recognized the dark-haired figure urging her mount up the hillside. By pure logic, she should have been killed long ago during the border warfare that surged back and forth at the edges of the Wizards' League, but Tallus was only mildly surprised at her survival. Was she, as she claimed, a Seeress? A Weapons Master? At any rate, she was a figure of mystery, always accompanied by that useless Ghorm, some stepchild of hobgoblins.

Sentauris reached the outer walls and banged hard at the heavy wood of the gates, calling, "Tallus! Send for Tallus!"

At a signal from their Tanu leader, bars were lifted to admit the Seeress. In reality, their gates were little barrier to any determined invasion, intended only to check night stalkers, or to provide a brief delay so that their band of renegades and mercenaries could vanish into the forested valleys that lay beyond the upper hillside.

Sentauris entered, pulling at the reins of her grey, weary gelding. Ghorm trailed a step behind, having paused to examine the rusty gates with a smile, as though amused by their crudeness.

"Send for Tal —" Sentauris broke off, as she found herself only a few paces from the Tanu smith.

"A new gate warden," Ghorm said to Sentauris in a mocking, partial whisper. "Big as a gate he is, and as thick."

Tallus stared down at the waist high Ghorm with little affection. "You might use some bulk yourself, stepchild of rats."

"Quiet, Ghorm," Sentauris cautioned. "There's no time for insults. Tallus, I need a score of fast riders — men skilled with bow and sword, and none of the chicken hearted or the double dealers with their shifty eyes. You will be paymaster. I have left sufficient gold sealed in a place less than a morning's ride from here."

Sentauris was in obvious haste, but with slow deliberate motions, the Tanu placed the cooling dagger in his belt and folded his arms, one great hand still grasping his forge hammer. "I do not doubt payment," he said, studying Sentauris. "Indeed, you overpaid me for your last venture. What I doubt is your life, child of short lived, mayfly humans. With every step, you create more enemies among the Great Dark Gods. Those Gods have been seeking your death ever since you were born. Your Wizards and their League seem a frail alliance, like a bank of clouds hanging over the South of Alantéa, ready to be blown to sea by the hot, wrathful breath of Dark Gods.

"And you, Sentauris, even should your Wizards survive for a time, they do not even support you; indeed, they no longer even *acknowledge* you. If war is coming, what is it to be — Sentauris and a few ragged riders against the whole of the Mid-World of the Truce? Why should I permit my followers to join in such an unequal contest?"

Sentauris flinched, like a child recoiling from the wrath of an elder. She glanced for a moment to the hillside, where mists were hovering over the rough dwellings of the ragged band supporting Tallus; they were greyish mists, drifting slowly in the still air. Then she folded both hands together, closed her eyes and let her mind search. After a moment of silence, she spoke in low, trancelike tones.

"The Wild Time is coming to the South of Alantéa the Forerunner, a partial war of raids, and confrontations of many different forces, with swift riders racing over forest trails. Both the Wizards and their foes have hidden resources. Most of the Mid-World of the Truce is aligned against the Wizards...though not all the Greater Gods oppose the Wizards and their League. The struggle appears unequal, yet its outcome is far from certain."

Sentauris took a deep breath and looked up. "Though the outlook is dark, we are not doomed. And so..." Sentauris trailed off. Both her own eyes and those of the Tanu smith were drawn to the dagger at Tallus' side, which was radiating a reddish gleam like blood in the pale light of an overcast morning.

"That blade, that weapon," Sentauris said softly, "has something of your own fate woven into it. I will study it if you wish, though neither of us may take pleasure from the message my Farsight brings."

Tallus turned to his silent guardsmen and to Ghorm. "Leave us for a moment; we have a small matter best spoken of in private." The guardsmen turned away and left, their interest dulled by the fatigue of a long night's watch. Ghorm followed with greater reluctance, though he took some pleasure in providing the guards with a critique of their rough village: a dozen or so poorly maintained dwellings of stone and timber had been built up against the hillside, landscaped only by wild grasses, and brush, and slides of cracked stone. But beyond Ghorm's view, on a rough plateau above the village, horses grazed on slender grasses and wildflowers.

Cautiously, Sentauris reached out and took the dagger from Tallus. In her hands, the metal's red sheen shifted to a silvery, pale star shine. Again, she closed her eyes and invoked her powerful Seer's Sight. Tallus watched on intently, in silence.

"It is night," she said in hushed tones, "pitch dark. You lie in a place far from here, against a back shield of cliff rock, holding this blade before you. Your body seeps blood from wounds...some are made by weapons and some by sorcery so that you feel the pulse of your life slipping away. Horns are ringing in the distance...are these the Horns of Elfland? I cannot be certain. Yet another, darker being, much closer, is coming for you, and it is powerful, much stronger even than your mighty Tanu form...and it is evil..." Sentauris shuddered and broke off. "Beyond that, I cannot see. I wish my visions had shown me otherwise...."

Tallus barked a short, bitter laugh. "I should cast this thing from me and choose a different fate. Your human brethren are mayflies, breeding and dying like maggots in sacks of flour. Already I have seen six of your generations rise and fall, while even now my own forebears consider me little more than a wayward child. Why should I concern myself with the affairs of your mortal brethren, and so endanger my own life?"

Sentauris handed the Tanu smith his dagger with some caution, wary of the strange blade. "I often turn from Fate or Destiny, so I would not counsel you to do otherwise. Yet I will say this about your future: you were not destroyed in my vision, only in great danger. Your blade was rising to protect you, while allies sought to rescue you. Further, there seemed within that

Tallus of the future, such strength of will, such purpose, even satisfaction, that I do not think you will allow yourself to turn aside. The elders of the Tanu may be unhappy with you, but I will guess that you serve others of the Mid-World who are not the enemies of my cause, and it may be that you have been placed to the north of the League to influence events during the coming Wild Time."

Tallus stared hard at Sentauris for a moment, then he lowered his voice and spoke more softly: "We have come to a critical moment. I have learned more about you since the last time we did business. You must speak to me of your Uncle Vlasoff, that so called 'Firebrand'."

Sentauris sighed and looked away. "If you know his 'Firebrand' nickname, you will also know that my uncle is only partly sane. Both my parents were killed in the early border wars, and so Uncle Vlasoff raised me — and he raised me as a fighter. More than seven months ago, Vlasoff was struck down. A Dark Sending took him —"

"Hold for a moment," Tallus interrupted, almost gently. "Mortals have thousands upon thousands of tragic stories, and there will never be an end to their sorrows. I need only to know if Vlasoff can be found and if there is any way he can betray you."

"It is most unlikely that Vlasoff will be discovered and trapped," Sentauris said. "He lives in hiding, surrounded by a pack of fierce dogs, and he is always armed. As for betraying me, my uncle knows nothing of my plans or deeds. Indeed, only rarely is he able to recognize me or speak my name, so I am not concerned —"

"That is enough," Tallus again interrupted. The Tanu turned toward his waiting guardsmen, calling instructions that would bring more than a score of paid outriders to serve Sentauris. As he left her to return to his forge, Tallus murmured in low, bleak tones, "Some of your enemies, at least, are also my foes. Guard this truth closely. Do not let yourself be taken alive."

·)(·

The raiders serving Moloch had struck the refugee party in the wild, unsettled country that lay three days march from the League's northern border, in a place almost equally distant from Piranus and Rigal. Lacking a Priest Mage to open a passage to the kingdom of their God, they pushed hard toward Rigal, where the Servants of Moloch maintained a large temple supported by many servants and worshippers. At Rigal, the Raiders hoped to deliver their prisoners into the short-lived service of their Fire-God and be themselves well rewarded.

Sentauris and her mercenary allies followed more than a full day behind, but moved more swiftly, burdened neither by captives nor by the need to move refugee wagons over rough roads. On the first afternoon of their pursuit, they found an elder lying dead at the roadside's edge, cut down for some small act of defiance. On the second day, they encountered the body of a young mother, who lay not thirty paces from the road, with three arrows in her back, with her dead daughter beneath her. Even the most hardened of the mercenaries rode with greater purpose after that encounter.

Sentauris had chosen three as scouts and outriders. She followed twenty paces behind, with the balance of their war band strung out behind them. They were riding hard on horses that were no longer fresh. Ghorm rode behind Sentauris, and as always, her Familiar grew pasty faced and ill when jostled and shaken over rough roads.

Sentauris felt Ghorm's nausea and the slow withdrawal of his mind into a private place that allowed him some escape from his discomfort. Her own sharp senses brought flashes, images of the forested lands all around them, stands of green trees, some with white or pale green flowering tips, flocks of birds lifting from clearings, a stag with broad antlers slipping over a low thicket of brambles, while wolves slipped away from the passage of armed men.

The air she breathed was filled with different fragrances: the flowering forests of Alantéa, streams running hard from snowmelt rushing down hillsides, sweating horses, and the smell of unwashed men riding beside her. She could sense also, something of the minds of those that rode before and behind her — confused half thoughts, a strange mixture of emotional fragments: fatigue, a dull hatred for the servants of Moloch, lust for her own body, fear of their Tanu leader, Tallus, a desire for rest, for easy wealth, and dark, cold ale. One even desired the mind of Sentauris, no doubt for its ability to seek out hidden places. She searched for thoughts of betrayal, of double dealing, but these were stray, jumbled, unfocused: nothing but daydreams of lust and wealth easily fulfilled using swift violence.

The lack of a traitor, of an enemy among her riders, seemed to Sentauris a reason for worry, even fear.

Something was blocking her sight, and it seemed to be moving along with her as she passed swiftly over rough roads. She could see into the next few hours, through the afternoon, evening and into the night. But beyond that time, her Farsight brought her nothing but a blurred, grey darkness, one that suggested a single, blind moment, followed by death.

Once before she had traveled with a traitor, an assassin bearing a concealed, enchanted talisman, an ornament with enough power and purpose to block her own sight. But the assassin's mind had reeked with treachery, and so others loyal to her had confronted him before his plot had ripened. Her would-be assassin had fled, howling curses and threats on behalf of his dark master.

Now danger once again surrounded her, but without any particular focus. She reached out and touched her sagging Familiar: on this night of all nights, she would need allies, and only Ghorm could be completely trusted. *Sleep, Ghorm, sleep.* Her thoughts brushed his resting mind. *Rest your hidden sorrows, your small powers, and sharp though dark wit. Sleep, for I will need you later.*

Through the long afternoon, the gap between Sentauris and the servants of Moloch steadily narrowed. No more deaths were discovered, but a trail of castoff clothes, and strongboxes, and sacks of grain marked the passage of the raiders as they lightened the weight of their spoils.

Two hours before sunset Sentauris led her war party over an even rougher track, a more northerly passage through hilly country. Without baggage or captives, they continued moving at twice the pace of those they pursued and could expect to intercept the Dark God's servants sometime late the next day.

Their pursuit came to a halt at nightfall, and they made camp close to a hill stream that still ran icy and chilled from the snowmelt of early spring. They were shielded from the raiders by distance and a range of hills, so a watchfire was kindled, but it began as a halfhearted effort, a slight, dampened thing that sent wreaths of smoke into cloud-streaked skies, into a night that only hinted of starlight.

Sentauris set a watch then lay back, eyes closed, trying to peer into the future. When she looked for a score of images showing so many future choices, she found only thick fog, a place where dull blurry masses shifted like icefloes in a dark, unsettled sea. Fear lurked in that fog too, along with the distant groaning sounds of ice breaking in the darkness.

She passed let the first portion of the night quietly, letting Ghorm slowly recover. The little Familiar's breathing deepened, and he slept a brief, healing sleep, free of dreams. While Ghorm rested, Sentauris fed the watch fire until it crackled, radiating greater light than smoke. The moments counted down; twenty or thirty minutes away, a fog of the unknown clouded her Seer's Sight. Sentauris strolled away from the fire and casually, gently, stirred Ghorm.

"...so stupid," he sputtered. "Riding, bouncing with me just like baggage. Let me be, leave me alone...."

"Ghorm," she whispered intently. "Ghorm, I need you. Look what's to come...." She opened her mind, showing him the fog of unknowing that clouded their future. Ghorm scrambled to his small, slightly furred feet.

"Then let's get away!" the little Familiar cried. "No force in Alantéa is worth the loss of your life, not those captives, not those stupid Wizards, not the evil of the Great Dark Gods, none of them!"

"Hush, Ghorm. We have faced danger, you and I, so many times before. Once we begin to run, we will never find a hiding place or safe haven. Our own fears and the malice of our foes will clutch at us for every moment of our brief remaining lives."

Ghorm drew a deep breath into his slight frame and steadied himself. "How much time do we have?" he asked in hushed tones.

"In about twenty minutes, a thick fog settles over everything, and my Sight fails me."

"First things first, then," Ghorm muttered. He stepped quickly around the forms of sleeping mercenaries and relieved himself against a thicket of winter deadfall.

When he returned, he joined Sentauris at the camp's edge, where they sat, backs against the trunk of a towering cottonwood. Fifty paces from them, their watchfire threw light and shifting shadows over the darkened ground before them.

"Now," Ghorm said quietly, "take me through the minds of those around us. One of them, at least, must be a deadly threat to us. Try not to spare their private thoughts as you so often do."

"A survey," Sentauris murmured, "how strange yet fitting. I will move from left to right." She nodded at a form lying thirty paces to her left. "This one is deep in dreams. He walks beside his father on a riverbank where —"

"Next," Ghorm interrupted.

"His comrade sleeps a dreamless sleep, while the one to his right dreams of an inn, where he sits consuming a rich dark ale while wondering if others have noticed that he wears no trousers or even undergarments. He —"

"And next to him?" Ghorm prompted.

"The man to his right lies half awake, stomach in turmoil, wondering whether his food was tainted...."

"What food?"

"Cured mutton. He —"

"Forget him."

"The next is at the edge of sleep, but fear stirs in him, fear of the fire pits of Moloch. He considers that flight is preferable if events do not turn out as we've planned. We should be wary of this one when we fight."

"Worry at daybreak if we survive this night. Time runs short. Leave the sleepers or near sleepers. Whomever, whatever, should be awake at this point."

"Yes, and next to him one lies awake, thinking of...me. He greatly admires my powers of sight and wishes to see matters through my eyes. Yet he bears me no ill will, considering me as part goddess almost...hmm...."

"An ally, perhaps," Ghorm muttered. "What else?"

"The guards by the watch fire speak in muted tones.... One speaks a rumor that after each foray I choose as a bedmate the one who performs the greatest feat of arms. Ha! But the other contends that I do not mix business with pleasure. The second, of course, is correct, but for each of them, it is idle chatter. Some distance from them, another lies awake, mind filled with dreams filled with lust, in which I figure prominently...hmm...he is most inventive. Pity that a great darkness will fall over us in seven or eight minutes."

Ghorm spat into the darkness. "Are these just dreams, or has he a plan?"

"Yes, a plan. He has a potion...undetectable in wine, a substance that will inflame me with desire."

"The scum." Ghorm sprang to his feet and stared across the camp at a figure lying on his back, face turned to a cloud-streaked night sky. "No doubt his potion is pure poison, though he may not realize how he's been used against you. Any moment now he will rise and offer you tainted wine. Make him drink it instead."

"He has no wine; he waits until we reach an inn, several days from now...and he is the last one awake."

"No wine!" Ghorm began pacing. "Then it's not him. Maker curse this whole adventure! Let's ride then, you and I, far from this place." Sentauris shook her head gravely, and stood, stringing with effort her powerful longbow, a weapon reinforced with thin strips of bony matter.

"Why am I not surprised at your answer?" Ghorm grumbled, then stopped his pacing. "Wait. Think, Ghorm, think. What of the other, your admirer, who desires not your body, but your mind? Has he a plan?"

"Yes, a plan," Sentauris said, staring into the distance. "He still wishes not to possess, but to share my visions...he has been given a talisman and told to ingest it while holding my image in his mind...and then he will share my thoughts for as long as I am near him.... Now he takes the talisman and raises it toward his lips...."

"That's it!" Ghorm snarled, then called out, "Stop, you, stop! Spit it out, you fool!" His eyes searched for one awake among the sleeping outriders. Only one stirred, his slumped form recoiling in surprise. From fifty paces, the man's throat seemed to quiver as though he had gulped some slight object, and it had passed down his gullet.

"Too late," Sentauris muttered. She notched an arrow to her longbow and walked deliberately forward.

"Maker curse me for a fool!" Ghorm snarled: Sentauris would not turn aside. The little Familiar scurried in front of her and raced toward a young man who was rising, hesitantly, to meet them.

"Cough it out!" Ghorm yelled at him. "Spit it up, you fool!" As Ghorm sped around the watchfire, he drew a slight dagger from his side. For any well-armed man, Ghorm would seem a figure to be scorned, except that the little Familiar's eyes were blazing with both fear and anger.

"I mean no harm!" the man called, backing from Sentauris and Ghorm. "See, I will leave if you think it wise." As Sentauris closed with him, she noticed as though for the first time, how finely sculpted the young man's features were, how soft his eyes seemed, more like those of a poet or bard than a wayward mercenary living in the wilderness.

"You fool," she murmured, "you poor young fool."

"I would never harm you, nev—" His protest broke off as the first level of the Transformation Spell struck him: spasms shook his body; his head and neck thickened, and something like silverish green scales began forming over the back of his hands. Still vaguely human, he stood under overcast skies, with firelight casting a menace of shadows all around him. A few of those close to his transformation woke and began to scatter.

"Kill him, Sentauris," Ghorm snarled. "He's becoming a Sending, a thing launched against us."

"Go far from here!" Sentauris cried. "Seek the Gods! Only they can change your fate —" A second transformation shuddered over him: The Sending grew larger, drawing bulk from the magic of Alantéa. Huge shoulders burst through its clothing; and these were also layered with silverish green scales. A few pale rays of moonlight began to investigate this forest confrontation. More men woke; a few of them began fumbling for weapons.

"Get up! Have you dung for brains?" Ghorm yelled at the remaining blurry eyed men still sleeping around the watchfire. He hurled his slight dagger at the Sending and began whispering spell words.

"I —" the Sending mumbled through thickening lips; but then all its old human willpower slipped from its form as the third level of transforming sorcery swept over it; and now its form glowed yellow and silverish green as though drawing moonlight from the night skies.

A bowshot from Sentauris caught the creature fully in the place where its heart should have been. It stood as though untouched, thickening, with scales growing larger, saber teeth forming from beneath its ragged jaws. Almost idly, the Sending turned to Sentauris.

"Sentauris, Sentauris," it sang in a falsetto voice from deep in its throat. "How I longed for thee, my little Sentauris. Come now and join your transformed lover in the darkness."

"That voice belongs to Arioch the Malevolent," Sentauris said slowly, "Arioch the Cruel." She began backing from the Sending: the thing loomed above her, half again her height, more than four times her bulk, and it glowed a greenish silver into the night. Power was gathering in its open palms, shallow and green pools of force. Behind the thing, the tiny Ghorm readied himself for one last desperate and futile act of magic.

But now, at last, the fog of unknowing was clearing, and she could act.

"Sentauris," the Creature sang, "How I loved thee, Sen —"

"Fight this thing!" she cried. "Listen to Ghorm!" A blast of power sprang toward her, but she had danced away from it on quicksilver feet. A second blast was avoided, but the blast's concussion hurled her from the fire and her allies. Sentauris rolled, twisted, and leaped up. She no longer held a single weapon, but her powerful Sight was alive as never before.

"Ghorm, hold back," she cried again and leaped aside. "Fight this thing!" She called again to her allies. "We will make a plan! Listen to

Ghorm!" She turned and raced into the darkness, leaping easily over moss covered, fallen logs, sliding past clutches of brush, her Seer's Sight replacing vision as it guided Sentauris through tangled passages into the future.

The Sending still followed behind her, still singing in Arioch's falsetto voice of its love for Sentauris. Saplings and smaller trees were crushed or brushed aside by the creature's bulk. Blasts of power shook the young forest's network of branches, shattering tree limbs over the fleeing form of Sentauris. Moonlight seemed to be drawn to the silver and green glow of the Sending, so that the cloud cover above them parted, shining brighter light over the pursuit.

"Sentauris, my lovely Sentauris," came the voice, not far behind her, and again she dodged, barely avoiding falling branches that smashed at her shadowy form like clubs wielded by blind Storm Giants. She slipped over a ridge of rock and halted, drawing deep, shuddering breaths. Blasts struck the shelf of rock behind her, but the stone held. Below her lay a streambed, water running fast and chilled from spring runoff. The sky above was filled with moonlit cloudbanks. The hillside below was treeless so she would no longer be battered by falling branches. She rolled over and peered out, still breathing heavily. The creature was striding directly toward her, as though lured by a beacon. *And above it, a raven shape seemed to float, a ghostly image with the wingspan of a Griffin. What was it?* She dropped back, just as another blast of force shook the rock shelf.

Ghorm.... She reached for the mind of her Familiar.

Sentauris! Stay far from here! I and a few others will track this thing, but flee, deeper into the forest, run away!

Sentauris slipped farther down the rock face, then raced to her right along a ridge that lay above the stream. As she ran, she sent bursts of thought out to her Familiar. *Good. Some are listening to you. Gather the others. Ghorm, all paths leading deeper into the forest end in my death.*

Forget the forest. But! We have a chance — here is the plan. She ran further along the ridge, stumbling only once as her feet sped over rubble, sending debris splashing into the stream bed below. Moonlight and her own Seer's Sight guided her to an upward passage, one with clefts for handholds. She climbed and peered back: Arioch's Sending was lurching toward her along the ridge, still crooning.

"Arioch! I still live!" she called out in triumph, unable to restrain herself. In response, a blast of green power hurtled toward her, but instead of dropping back, Sentauris spilled over the rock's surface, rolled once, then again as rock chips splintered over her. Now, as she headed back toward their makeshift camp, she danced through pools of darkness, slipping behind thick tree trunks to shield herself from the Sending's blasts of power. As always, her wind steadied, but the fall of thick branches clubbed at her, one numbing her left shoulder. Sentauris danced on, leaping, sliding, back toward her camp, all the while calling instructions to Ghorm.

Behind her, the Sending sang on endlessly, mindlessly, like the monstrous toy of some insane watchmaker.

Firelight glinted in the distance then faded, as she again sheltered from the Sending's violence. Then, closer, greater light flared as she neared the camp. She raced into the firelit clearing: it seemed deserted, except as a futile gesture her sword had been left beside the fire. She swept it up, sped beyond the watchfire, then turned as though to face the creature.

She paused, ready to leap aside. Arioch's Sending lurched into the clearing, still chanting mindlessly. The blazing watchfire lay between herself and the creature. Above it, the same raven shape loomed again, but no time was left to investigate her ghostly vision. She backed, gauging the movements of her attacker, watching red flames throw light over the Sending's green and silver glow. Now that she no longer fled, its blasts of power subsided, and it advanced, arms outstretched, as though preparing to embrace a lost lover.

But as it passed just to the watchfire's right side, the Sending stepped through a thick coil of rope — a snare made by her allies. Sentauris leaped to one side then sped forward. The rope around the Sending's leg tightened and tugged. The thing staggered, turning half aimlessly, as its tormentors appeared. Sentauris sped forward, lashing a second rope around its right leg and then she pulled with all her strength. Nothing would move it. Blasts of force ripped into the surrounding forest. Men cried aloud; their horses rose in panic.

But then, strong arms took the rope from Sentauris and lashed it to a team of wild-eyed packhorses. Another team of her allies grasped the second rope.

The Sending toppled face first to the ground. Blasts from its outstretched hands rocked the forest's ground. Crying aloud with fear and defiance, men leading horses dragged the Sending into their watchfire. It bellowed, blasting the ground all around it. Flames, a blue and green venting of magic, surged over its scaled form. On fire, it writhed, groaning, and shrieking in agony. Sentauris darted toward the flames, hewing at the thing with her long sword, but her blade left only shallow wounds.

And as though restored to purpose, the Sending burst from its bonds and rose, still burning blue and green with the flame of incandescent magic. With its last strength, it sought to embrace Sentauris, and again she dove, crying for Ghorm.

The little Familiar hurled the full force of his small sorcery at the creature: a column of black smoke formed about the Sending's head and upper body. Blinded by black smoke and in an agony of burning, the creature lurched from the watchfire, blasting at unseen foes who scurried from its path.

"Axes!" Sentauris called out, moving swiftly toward it. "To me the ax men!" Six men swarmed around her, one handing her an ax. They swept over the Sending, hewing arms, and legs from the creature, until it toppled, helpless, the power of the construct reduced in stages as its force of its magic power shriveled in waves of blue and green fire.

As it stilled, Ghorm, too, froze then toppled backward, completely exhausted by the strain on his slight powers.

The Captain of the Outguard stared out into the overcast night sky. He was not alone: just to his left and behind him, other servants of Moloch also stood staring into the distance. A magic, liquid moonlight was pouring over the far ridge of hills that rose over the left side of their forest trail. Sounds came from a distance, the sounds of some great being or beast creature raging at the agony of its own death. And almost, at the edge of the Captain's vision, a greenish glow could be seen, as though a distant watchfire had been lit to signal the end of some strange being.

Again, came the sights and sounds — death cries from some night monstrosity, accompanied by hints of green. Even the strongest wolf pack or the most confident pride of lions would avoid that place. Was his Master, the Great God Moloch, settling accounts with an old adversary? Were two different Gods locked in conflict? So many deities shared power in Alantéa that events in the hill country above him might have nothing to do with the Outguard's attack on those feeble Maker Servants.

Sounds dwindled into those of the normal night forest: whispers of leaves rustling, owls hooting, and vague croaking sounds from the distant malice of night ravens. He returned to his sleeping roll with a touch of fear: the night's events might have nothing to do with his service to Moloch, the

Fire God, except that their luck had turned bad ever since the witch woman destroyed their Priest and leader. An arrow in his eyesocket while he was moving, not even standing in place! And after, almost casually, she had cut down Haseen, one of their better swordsmen.

More than a year ago, word had been passed to the Outguard Legion, telling of an archeress seeking to defend helpless refugees, but what warrior would fear a lone woman in the wilderness? Later, sitting around a table covered with beakers of wine, some beverages touched by dream spices, the Priests' warning had been the stuff of drunken humor: *Beware of the shadows! Or Sentauris and her Hobgoblin will leap out at you!*

He turned on his side and tried to force himself to sleep. Perhaps the Great God Moloch had trapped the witch woman and the sounds from the hills above were her death cries, as the last drop of malignant sorcery was drawn from her poisonous body.

And then, perhaps some other confrontation caused those sounds.... He was sleepless until deep into the night when the cloud cover descending over the far hills muffled all sight and sound.

· X ·

At daybreak, the winds shifted, leaving only patches of fog that hovered briefly over the forested hillside. Above them, rising layers of distant clouds still obscured a red sunrise, and the day seemed as bleak as his mood. The Captain rose and began calling out orders. It was time to move — and move quickly.

As always, their captives whimpered, or rather the old men groaned and the women began their endless weeping, sounds that always set his teeth on edge. He stifled a snarl. All the captives were as dead as last year's Fire-God Sacrifices. If only they would stop their squirming and squealing! Lately, he had begun lying to them, telling their elders that their cooperation would reduce their time of service. And several times, he had sworn an oath on Moloch's honor! The Captain laughed aloud. What oaths could bind him to such weaklings, people who prayed and begged and pleaded to their Maker, some long vanished deity who listened to no prayers, never gave guidance, never intervened. Ridiculous! One never trusted Moloch or could predict his actions, but at least he was a God, one with power and the malice to make His will felt.

The Outguard was moving now, but too slowly: Rigal lay more than seven hours before them, and their passage ran through rough country. Much could still go wrong. He called to the two outriders serving him, and they, in turn, carried his words to the seven sub-tier leaders serving under him. The seven joined him, holding their horses back for a moment until their caravan of captives and wagons and Outguard riders passed a little farther toward Rigal.

He studied his sub-tier leaders for a second; one day one of them would try to replace him, to push him aside through cunning or strength, but for the moment, none stood out. All seven were silent, waiting for his word, hard faces held expressionless as their eyes followed the caravan's passage, or the slow motion of horses nibbling on slender grasses.

"So, noises in the night," the captain began, speaking softly, "but to what end, to what purpose? Do any of you know?" Almost furtively, their eyes flashed together, then they began shaking their heads: none knew.

"Come now, come now," the captain continued, "this is a matter for the Guard, and no concern of our Priests. A sign, any sign, might guide us."

One called Quarm cursed under his breath, then muttered, "In my early years four times did the Gates of Dreams open before my sleeping eyes. Last night there came a fifth time, but I will say no more until you bond yourselves to me." Without hesitation, the Captain drew his dagger and opened a small cut on the meat of his hand. Others performed identical rituals, then they reached out to smear the blood between them, each taking care to share blotches of red streaks with the other seven.

"So, we are one blood," the Captain said solemnly. "What follows is to be shared with no others, through death and beyond." Privately, he doubted that the matter could be shielded from the jealous Priests' Guild and their persecution of all those with even the most remote magical powers.

Quarm stared at them with shifty, dark eyes, then muttered, "All that I beheld was twisted and distorted as though I was looking at it from a broken mirror — yet the witch woman survived. A great Sending was launched against her not by our Master the Lord of Flames, but by some other greater or lesser God. Not only did she survive, but she called others to her side and together they fought that Sending, then destroyed it — not with witchery or even mageical force, but by fire and the strength of their own weapons. Wild magic surged all around her, yet somehow the witch woman kept one step or two swift steps from destruction. She danced with Death but was never embraced by that mighty entity."

"These events may be to our advantage," the Captain said evenly, "if many of those following her were dispersed or destroyed."

Quarm smiled: a dark, twisted grimace. "Both those who fought and those who fled gathered quickly to her in the battle's aftermath. Only the dead could not rally to her side; I suppose we should gather some satisfaction from their failure to rise."

More furtive looks flashed among the leaders of the Outguard as the tails of horses flapped swirling flies into new patterns of flight.

"Captain," said another man, "forgive me for saying this, but our luck has been bad since we first met the witch creature. Why do we not simply kill these weak vermin and make great speed to Rigal? Let the Priests or even the Fire God deal with Sentauris."

"Have you ever taken part in such butchery?" asked the Captain shaking his head calmly. "Had you done so, you would know that with all the squealing and screaming, biting, and scurrying, that it always takes much longer than you think. And besides, what would be our tale when the Priests call us before the Great God Moloch? That we fled from Sentauris and her Hobgoblin? At best we would be mocked all our days; at worst we would be consigned to the flames.

"Now, here is my sober counsel: firstly, we will set a great pace for Rigal — lie to the scum sucking Maker Servants, tell them that they are to be released at the City Gates. Secondly, plan to use these human vermin as a flesh shield if we are attacked. Should they assail us, they will find themselves killing many of their own people and be forced to give way. And thirdly, I must show you this." With some caution, he pulled apart the ringlet of armor shielding his upper torso and revealed an amulet made from nephrite, on which the Fire God's insignia was inscribed in lines of meticulously crafted silver.

"This," he said in low tones that were almost a whisper, "this will summon the Great God Moloch, but it may only be used, *must* only be used in a time of the greatest peril." A few bowed in reverence while others looked on with an awe that was mixed with relief.

"Go," said the Captain. "Get this mass of two footed dung lickers on its way to Rigal." They spurred their horses on, some calling out commands to nearby Outguard riders.

Slowly their pace picked up. As their captives surrendered to hope, additional food, and water, and later, even wine, was released to them. Wagons rolled, sometimes bouncing over rough roads. At midmorning, the day brightened, with shafts of sunlight beginning to sweep over damp hillsides. Rigal was only three hours away, and in less than two hours they would be in more open country, less vulnerable to hidden strikes. Gauging the angle of the sun, the Captain decided they might make it.

Great God and Master, the Captain prayed silently, *Lord of the Pits of Flame, forgive me for those times when my sacrifice was too slight, or my sword hand raised on your behalf too light. Recall only my numerous gifts of blood and treasure....*

Without the slightest of warnings, their swiftly flowing caravan became a jumble of wheeling wagons, and stiffening reins, with men crying aloud and horses rising in fear or fury. Then captives and captors all came to a confused halt.

Their Captain pressed forward, venting his rage: "What are you doing? Where are the archers? If it's an ambush, form a shield wall!" Two of his Outriders were pushing back toward him, striving to reassure their leader.

"Captain, it's no trap, but a mess of fallen trees. Look before you — no signs of ax work, no fresh horse hooves." It was obvious that the two trees straddling the road showed no sign of ax work and lay with roots exposed... but freshly exposed, and there had been no wind...and yet in the trees' upper reaches, the bark was scarred, likely by thick ropes.

He turned, raging at the Outrider, but the man was toppling, one hand clutching an arrow shaft that had plunged neatly into his throat.

"Fools!" he called out, spurring his horse, pulling away from the fallen trees. "Horse archers draw your weapons!" Hooves pounded as he raced back from the ambush. An arrow struck him but skipped away from the metal shielding that he wore. Outguard archers were launching arrows haphazardly against well concealed foes. A half score broke ranks and sped back along the forest trail. Lines of outstretched rope took their horses down, then Outguard men were slain as they lay groaning.

As the Captain bent lower in his saddle an arrow passed not a handsbreadth from his head. Bewildered guardsmen were wavering, dropping by ones and twos, hands brushing at arrow shafts. His mind raged at them: *This is so stupid!*

He reached the first of the captive wagons and slipped from his horse. One hand drew a dagger while the second grasped a young woman, forearm locked around her neck. One choking squeeze stopped her shrieking. He backed from the roadway, holding her as a shield. Two of his sub-tier leaders had managed to join him; one held a gibbering old woman, the other a pale faced boy. A third leader was racing toward them, but he fell forward, revealing three arrows in his back.

Clutching hostages, the three backed from the forest trail, watching as lancers emerged from the far side of the road, wielding bright spears against the remnants of the Outguard. A few of their men fled through the clearing and passed into deeper woods. None seemed to get far.

They backed into the adjacent meadows, each with a dagger pressed against a hostage. Fifty paces away, a tall, raven haired figure sheathed her sword while slipping from her horse in one motion. Regarding them with unblinking, sea grey eyes, she drew back her bow, an arrow pointed at the captive just to her left.

"Witch creature!" he called to her. "You will destroy your own people!" Her bow sang once and the man to his left toppled, arrow centered neatly in his forehead. The boy he had held scrambled away, crying out in fear.

He shifted his dagger to the hand holding his captive and began to fumble with the locket that lay just within his chain mail.

"Moloch!" he called out. Nothing. He scratched at the amulet's surface, breaking its seal. The other Outguard survivor stiffened, then fell dead. The old woman he had held pulled away from him, then toppled to the ground either from wounds or fear.

"Moloch! Aid me now!" Again, nothing. But without the slightest warning, the young woman he held wrenched at the arm holding his dagger with both hands, and then bit down hard on his wrist. *I'll kill you dead!* his mind shrieked.

As he stabbed at her, an arrow took him in his shoulder and his body recoiled in shock. Both his hands scrabbled at Moloch's locket. A second arrow struck, chest-centered, passing just below his fumbling fingers. His body shuddered with pain and his sight dimmed.

Moloch lied to me, lied to me, lied to me, lied to me!

He raged on until a soft, clumsy darkness collapsed over him like the shadows of a nightfall that would last forever.

Chapter Two

Evening at The Weasel's Feast

"WE DID IT, UNCLE," Sentauris said to Vlasoff in her softest voice. "Just two days ago we managed to free more than a hundred of our people and get them safely over the Saugus River. Most went south toward Gravengate, while a smaller party travels east to Stone Mountain. But you taught me how to deal with those raiding parties, and that's the reason we won the fight."

Vlasoff said nothing, only sitting warily on a stump, staring out into the forest as though searching for foes. Five of his seven wolfhounds stood watch, sniffing the air, and searching for shadows in the forest's depths, while the other two dozed. They were hidden in a valley, close enough to the Wizards' League that they could flee back into lands protected by the Wizards in a short time. Water flowing from intersecting streams helped turn aside probing magic.

"One thing you could help me with," Sentauris continued, "if you're able to. Before we dealt with the raiding party, we had to fight off some sort of creature. It took shape as a great lizard, but above us, in the night an image flickered — a vision of a large raven shape with fierce red eyes. What can you tell me about that, Uncle?"

"The Sending," Vlasoff whispered, and then as he always did when his mind stumbled, his eyes began to seep tears. His two sleeping dogs woke, and then all seven of them began to whimper.

"Hush, hush," Sentauris said softly to the wolfhounds, embracing her uncle. "Don't worry. Over time, I can usually solve mysteries. This afternoon, we are off to *The Weasel's Feast,* and we'll learn how things are going on both sides of the League's border." Vlasoff's eyes again lost focus, though the tears on his cheeks began slowly drying.

Ghorm sighed. Wary of powerful, heavyset wolfhounds, Ghorm had perched himself on a stony hillock that was covered with moss, some twenty paces distance from Sentauris and Vlasoff. He watched them with interest but also detachment. Ghorm had never met the parents of Sentauris — they had been killed in battle years before Ghorm had been born into the Mid-World of the Truce and then joined Sentauris.

So as Ghorm grew up, he had to deal with Sentauris' uncle and guardian. When he was younger, Ghorm had both feared and hated Vlasoff because of the violence that stirred inside their leader with his grim face. Behind his back, his fighting force referred to Vlasoff as "The Firebrand," though none dared to use those words in his presence. And yet whenever Vlasoff struck down their enemies or devised some cunning plan, something like awe, and something like love, began to fill Ghorm's small heart.

Now, as Ghorm watched Vlasoff from a distance he remembered that fear was still his strongest memory. Twice, Vlasoff the Firebrand had stormed toward Ghorm with murder in his eyes. Both times, Sentauris had stood in front of Vlasoff, forcing him back with her own strong body, crying, "You will not, not *ever,* bring your violence against my Familiar, Ghorm! Not ever!"

Now, Ghorm felt an entirely different emotion, something almost human. What was it called? Pity, he felt something like pity for the ancient, almost mindless "Firebrand."

· ⚭ ·

After about two hours ride east and south of Vlasoff's hidden valley, Ghorm felt himself relaxing. Nightfall was coming and there was no hint of their foes. He took a deep breath; this particular inn was usually entertaining, peaceful, and the food was always better than good.

"*The Weasel's Feast,*" the little Familiar muttered with considerable relish, letting the phrase roll from his lips. Then he tried it for a second and a third time. "A strange though intriguing name for some long-forsaken river inn. Still, imagine its menu selection! Baby hedgehogs boiled in brine. Stuffed lizard tongues, with a garnish of rat tails...."

The sun had set only moments ago, and a chilly dusk was gathering around them as they approached a river settlement too small to be given a name. Nearly two days had passed since Ghorm had collapsed after the exhaustion of his slight magic, and the little Familiar had finally recovered. Now he was taking considerable pleasure planning menu selections for *The Weasel's Feast.*

"...slugs in sparrow sauce.... My! How delicate they are, yet still chewy! Stewed batwings...maggot soup — a flavorful, yet hearty fare...."

More than a day had passed since the captives had been freed and escorted toward League lines. The refugees were safe now: nothing but a slow time of healing lay before them. Before parting with them Sentauris had spoken seriously with their elders, telling them that the Wizards seemed preoccupied with the construction of their mighty fortresses.

However, warfare flared over the borders. Those refugees who were skilled in arms, or tracking, or hunting game should try to help with the border skirmishes and clashes that lay to the north.

Now, she turned from the river to stare into the distance: those she had freed had passed from her sight, moving toward Gravengate and Stone Mountain, adding their numbers to others serving the Wizards and their League. A few perhaps would help with the struggle to the north.

"...tiny mouselings on toast," Ghorm rambled on with obvious relish. "Freshly severed snake segments still twitching as they died."

"Stop it, Ghorm," Sentauris muttered, "you know that we'll have to eat sometime. And besides, there's good reason for the inn's name. A score of years ago, river men founded an inn called *The Lion's Den*, and shortly after, *The Griffin's Aerie* rose to compete with it. Both inns, despite their pompous names, were ratholes frequented by the worst scum — bandits, procurers of slaves, backstabbers, river pirates — and had never been a haven for the unarmed or the unwary. *The Weasel's Feast* was so named to mock the pretensions of the other two, and it keeps an excellent wine cellar, brews fine ales, and boasts a menu selection far different from the items you have listed and will *not* repeat."

Ghorm muttered something under his breath in which a reference to "crushed toads" might have been heard.

"Five years ago," Sentauris continued, her voice rising slightly, "the river rose beyond its previous flooding zones and carried away both *The Lion's Den* and *The Griffin's Aerie*. Perhaps some rough justice does exist in this world, and now only *The Weasel's Feast* remains, ready to supply us with an evening of...."

She peered down a range of paths to the future and began to laugh softly. Amusing, entertaining events lay before her: somewhere over a far hill their frequent companions, Danger and Death had grown weary and lay sleeping the sleep of exhaustion.

With great care she turned off her future vision: it was time for her inner being to be refreshed, renewed, to not know events beforehand; she would even let herself become surprised.

"Now what are you doing?" Ghorm asked as he felt the shift in Sentauris' awareness.

"An evening's holiday." Sentauris reached out and touched Ghorm lightly. "We have nothing to fear on this night, especially with you as my brave and resourceful sentinel."

"Sweet words; where's the gold?" Ghorm muttered, as he always did, then he fell silent as they drew closer to the Saugus. Even with the full partial darkness of dusk gathering about the river, deepwater foam caps from the river's surge were still visible, though shadows over the river made the coils of dark water seem like snakes that surged toward Gravengate and the coast. And as the light failed, the air grew noticeably colder; Ghorm hunched down against the evening's chill, while Sentauris clutched her cloak more tightly around her.

A muddy horse track led them to the river's edge, then the track ran parallel to the water. Only two hundred paces away lights were emerging from a hilltop crowned by *The Weasel's Feast:* a ramshackle cluster of buildings that descended over four levels from the hill's peak. Lamps were shining from many windows with different shapes — circular, square, oblong, pentangular, as though *The Weasel's Feast* had been created at a gathering of builders impaired by strong drink and many incompetent craftsmen.

As they neared the inn, the light faded completely from the Saugus, so that only lapping, rushing sounds marked the river's presence. Though now, over the river noises, Ghorm thought he could hear the sounds of soft, flapping wings, and seconds later, an owl's outline flew across the glowing lights framed by the inn's beaming windows.

"Squint!" Ghorm called into the darkness, then added in lower tones, "And if the Owl-being is here then Wylar is waiting for us at the inn. But what's the reason?"

"Yes" Sentauris murmered, "and why would Wylar venture beyond the borders of the Wizards' League? If the League ever creates a real border, it will be set on the south side of the river. And if Wylar travels beyond League lines, is it likely that he would journey alone?"

Ghorm stared up at the inn's glowing lights with a mixture of scorn and expectation. "The Wizards would never dare to pass beyond their borders, so they've sent their two Adepts to meet with you — Wylar, the dark, lean stoat, and Orantes the bloated hedgehog with his red beard. Well met at *The Dead Rat's Gargle,* or whatever this forsaken place is called. Ha! All we need now is a brace of troll —"

"Seeress..." came a soft, almost hissing sound from a place just at the river's edge. Ghorm's dagger flashed from its sheath; the hand of Sentauris gathered to her sword hilt but did not draw her weapon.

"Sentauris, mighty Seeress," the voice said, hissing quality more evident — and it spoke from a greater distance, as though some wary creature was backing slowly into shallow water.

"Speak," Sentauris said, one hand held out to hold Ghorm in check. "You need not fear us."

"...Sssssss...fear of sharp metal chases away all the glistening words I was taught so carefully...." Something weighty was tossed onto the horse track in front of them, splattering mud into the shadows. "A gift for you, Seeress," the voice hissed, becoming more distant, "in balance for the unwitting traitor's betrayal...or was it 'witting traitor'? No matter." With a soft splashing sound, the messenger vanished into cold, dark, and swift waters.

"Ghorm, you frightened the poor thing," Sentauris said, dropping lightly to the ground, but Ghorm was there before her, slight hands extended into the darkness, feeling for a parcel that was covered in muck.

"Cloth and twine cover a thing of metal," the little Familiar murmured, lifting it by its binding. "Also, it reeks of magic. Is it another of the poisoned devices sent by Arioch? Enough of those."

"Thank you for your caution, Ghorm, but relax — tonight our old adversaries Death and Danger are lying in the darkest alley of a distant city, dragged down by a heavy weight of wine that's been laced with opium. Bring that thing with you, and we'll let the Adepts play with it." Again, Ghorm hefted the package by its binding, noting how its bulk was greater than its weight. One squat foot was placed in the stirrups of their horse, and Ghorm rode the last hundred paces with one arm clutching the package, the other holding the leg of Sentauris.

They passed from a shadowed darkness into pools of light that spilled from *The Weasel's Feast*. As though waiting for them, two grooms emerged from adjoining stables and took their horse. Warmth, and lights and smells, and the muted noise of soft music began to sweep over Seeress and Familiar as they passed into the inn: platters of roast fowl, and suckling pig, and broiled freshwater fish were being carried from a kitchen on their left into the lower tap room. Flames leaped up from three small fireplaces clustered along the right outer wall. Lute and muted horn instruments provided a background tapestry of soft music, while lights from vat-candles and flickering torches threw shadows into every corner.

"We've been in the field too long," Sentauris said softly, drawing in all the sights and smells and sounds. It seemed that they were expected, not only by the outside grooms: porters armed with brushes and soft cloths first took Sentauris' cloak, then began struggling with layers of old and new mud. As they brushed, she studied the taproom on the inn's first floor. This section of the inn had lower ceilings so that a tall man might reach up and touch the plaster overhead. Panels of dark, scented wood covered the taproom's inner walls. Some panels were obscured by woven hangings, while others held small paintings done in oil on treated wood. Perhaps seventy could be served around a score of wooden tables, though on this night only half that many were in use.

As her eyes reached the far side of the taproom, two figures rose and bowed gravely to her: one was dark-haired, tall, and lean, clean shaven except for a fringe of beard that arced down to his chin; the other bulked larger, with a rust-colored beard, and as he straightened, one hand toasted Sentauris with a flagon of wine. These two were Wylar and Orantes, servants of the Wizards. Each was known as an Adept, a Magician, though many wondered if they had real power.

Sentauris gave them the most casual of waves, as though recognizing remote, almost forgotten cousins, then she turned from them, seeking to arrange for a room and a bath.

"A nice touch," Ghorm muttered under his breath, "but I do not think you will escape so easily." And yes, from the corner of her eye, Sentauris could see both Wylar and Orantes sliding past tables and chairs as they made their way toward her. But first, a room and a bath. Yes, the porter assured her, a room had been set aside for her, but the bath was more difficult, with a staff committed to the evening's food and drink.

"Sentauris, magnificent Sentauris," Orantes' voice rumbled from just behind her. "Come, join us. We are your hosts for the evening. Fine beverages and superb food await us."

She turned to regard Orantes, with his red beard, an enthusiastic lover of life. Just behind him stood Wylar, with dark hair, a more sardonic, detached observer.

"At our last meeting you two were so very different," Sentauris noted dryly. "I remember how you both stood silently behind Thorian as he exiled me from Stone Mountain forever."

"A misunderstanding only." Orantes waved his hand as though brushing aside the slightest of insects. "If the Wizards are sometimes rash, they —"

"The Wizards still do not love you," Wylar interrupted, "but that was then, and this is now. Come, Sentauris, share wine with us, then dinner. We have much to discuss."

"And besides," Orantes added, somewhat more seriously, "recall our faces as Thorian thundered against you. Did we share his anger, his indignation?"

"You did not," Sentauris admitted. "You stood downcast like two small boys who had lost a playmate — something that I will never be."

Sentauris took a deep breath before continuing. "But tonight, I will share wine and a few tales with you, though you must take care not to get too close or downwind from me, for Ghorm and I have been in the field far too long."

"Then I will seek my colleagues," Ghorm said to the three, "the aptly named Squint and Whisper. We Familiars have a saying," he added, staring openly at Orantes' largish belly, 'While the great ones consume, the small ones must fume'." With this, Ghorm stepped back to the door, while the two Adepts led Sentauris to their table.

"They won't 'fume'," Orantes said, pouring wine into three deep goblets. "One of Whisper's few pleasures involves the exchange of lies with little Ghorm."

"But Whisper's greatest pleasure," Wylar added dryly, "is upbraiding his overly joyful master."

"Ah, but not tonight." Orantes raised his glass to Sentauris. "On this night, the nagging Familiars have passed to one side, and the gloomy Wizards roam alone through dark and dismal fortresses, while we are gathered at *The Weasel's Feast*. To Sentauris! May she confound our enemies and not our masters!" He drank deeply, eyes twinkling with amusement and pleasure.

A naughty lad, Sentauris thought, *and much more entertaining away from his grim Wizard masters.* She leaned back in her chair, sipped, then drank more deeply: the wine was excellent.

Wylar set down his half-filled goblet. "Now, before my esteemed colleague becomes overly eloquent, I should tell you how we came to join you at this so strangely named inn."

Sentauris poured more wine. "Of course, the Wizards sent you. They love me now and all is forgiven."

Wylar shook his head somberly. "Would that it were so."

"You should never have told them that their mighty fortresses would one day be reduced to rubble," Orantes added seriously. "Gravengate and Stone Mountain have been under construction for so many years now, and those fortresses are the Wizards' most precious possessions."

"All that is by the by." Wylar held up his palm to forestall Sentauris. "Thorian and Balardi remain most annoyed with you, though Merlin shows a flicker of detached amusement whenever your name arises. Here, in short, is the reason that we sought you: though we lack your power as a Seeress, by Divinations and Auguries, we can clearly see that a grim time is coming for our League, and its foundations tremble."

"The Wild Time is coming," Sentauris interjected, "as I told you many moons ago."

"Just so," Wylar continued. "A conspiracy of hidden powers arises. That alliance intends to crush us completely or to scatter our peoples again to the four corners of Alantéa. Against these shadowy alliances, only a few, scattered forces may be engaged in the League's defense. Orantes and I now have permission to seek aid from any quarter, for terms that will not completely compromise us."

"And so, we sought you, the lovely Sentauris," Orantes added. "We were careful not to mention your name, although the Wizards must have suspected that we would turn first to you when seeking allies."

"So, I am 'She Who Cannot Be Named,' to be counted among other allies such as mangy Trolls and demented Hobgoblins," Sentauris said dryly. "The honor is almost too great. Still, in your quest for confederates, you may have inadvertently come to the right place." She felt down underneath the table, and pulled up the muddy parcel, holding it gingerly by its binding before placing it in the table's center. "Advise me first about the nature of this gift, then after I will tell you how it came to me."

Orantes leaned forward, frowning, and his eyes lost their sense of mischief. Whispered words slipped from his lips and the parcel unbound itself, revealing a corselet of fine chain mail, light and strong. The bearded Adept ran his hands cautiously over this gift of light armor, all the while chanting, almost singing under his breath. Then with a start, his hands drew back, as though seared by a sudden fire.

"Interesting," Orantes murmured, "it repels magic as well as sharp metal. But this thing of magic could not completely disguise its origins, so I can say —"

"Not just yet," Wylar interjected. "First before speculating on origins and potential allies, we should seal ourselves from the Mid-World's prying eyes and ears, whatever their intentions." With less flamboyance, but with equal power, Wylar spoke seven crisp words in an undertone, and the three were shielded from sorcerous intrusions, both those from afar and those nearby.

·)(·

Just a short distance away Ghorm snarled a curse when the sound faded from his Divination image. Moments later the image also vanished, so that their small storage chamber became noticeably darker.

"I should have left the telltale on Wylar or Orantes," Ghorm muttered as he looked up at the Adepts' Familiars. "My connection might have survived if I had linked it to one of your two masters." The three sat in an upper cone-shaped tower used by the inn's proprietors to store old paintings, ceramics, curtains, musty bedding, and overly elaborate, though tarnished silver bowls. A slight candle had been allowed to extinguish itself, so the room was lit only by the remote glow of torchlight that rose from the courtyard beneath them.

"You will have to tell us the tale yourself," Squint said with some resignation. The Owl-being Squint stood a little more than half Ghorm's height, though his fluff and feathers made him seem bulkier than the slight Familiar. From a distance, little separated Squint from other owls, but closer, his shrewd eyes radiated wit and intellect; also, his feathers showed unusual patterns of deep brown and dark grey.

"A tale, a fine story for an evening's rest at a dilapidated lightless inn," Ghorm said, with just a trace of malice, staring at their third companion, Whisper. Orantes' Familiar bulked much larger than the other two but was far less substantial: Whisper was a Shade, a Wraith with a human's height, but able to conceal itself within the slightest pocket of darkness.

Ghorm began telling of their struggle with the Servants of Moloch, and of the sorcerous snare plotted by Arioch. At every step, Ghorm subtly enhanced his own role, until at tale's end, it was Ghorm's magic that triumphed, and even Ghorm's weapon that dealt the death blow. As he finished, he stared expectantly at Whisper, as though awaiting a response from the Shade. A dark quiet filled the tower, disturbed only by remote river sounds and noises in the courtyard made by local residents stumbling home from the tavern.

"I have hunted for the youth who pursued Sentauris, and as an unwitting servant of Arioch, he became a monster," said the Shade, after a time. "He looks at me from Death's Dream Kingdom and struggles to speak, but his lips form a language I do not understand, and no sounds are coming from his mouth, but only a dry rustle, like snakes passing over several year's fallen leaves. You two cannot understand the mind of a Shade such as I have become: one part of me regards the Kingdom of Life, the other the Kingdom of Death. On the other side of life, in a vast Empire of the Unliving, hordes of dead beings shuffle listlessly about, performing hidden tasks, yet I can understand neither their motions nor their speech. It is said that only when a Shade's death is upon him is he able, although briefly, to understand the speech and actions of the dead. My time is not yet come, but I believe that one day I will understand at last the language of ghosts, and seconds later, I, too, will be dead."

Both Squint and Ghorm stared at Whisper for a moment, their eyes filled with skepticism mixed by a touch of disquiet.

"It is usually left to me," Squint said in his dry voice, "to adjudicate this contest of untruths. I must declare it a draw. Ghorm's lies were unusually clever, weaving portions of the truth with strands of inventive distortions. Had he a sorcerous weapon, capable of injuring a construct formed of magic, I might have believed more. Of Whisper's tale, I might be tempted to believe only a trace, except that the Peoples of the Shade have an unusually strange origin. But now, hard as it may be for two such competent taletellers, let us have a little of the truth."

"Yes, my own lack of a magic weapon," Ghorm conceded, "is an obvious flaw," and he went on to tell them the true tale, or most of it — he was unwilling to acknowledge the extent of his weakness following the casting of spells. "So, in the end," he finished, "the Sight of Sentauris aided by my own small magic together with bright fire and heavy metal brought about the death of the monstrosity sent by Arioch.... Now, what of Whisper's tale, of seeking Ghosts in a Kingdom of Death? What portion of his fiction is true?"

"Not a single word," the Shade said easily. "No being can truly see the aftermath of life. My tale was utterly and completely a fabrication."

Sharp, bitter words formed on Ghorm's lips, but instead, he leaned back and laughed the laugh of a giant.

·)(·

"...its metal was forged in Elven smitheries," Orantes was saying, still studying the metal corselet, "enhanced by Tanu sorcery and later cured by Sidhe mage craft. Most unusual."

"As Sentauris told us," Wylar added, "this Tanu smith may well be among our hidden allies, but we should proceed with caution when exploring this matter. These three, Tanu, Sidhe, Elves, may call themselves 'The Kindreds' but are by reputation vastly different in appearance. I have seen only one — an Elf Mage, greatly daring as he journeyed through enchanted passages to Stone Mountain, wishing to speak privately with Thorian. I caught only a glimpse of this being, but he was as tall as the Wizard, lighter skinned, with hair almost albino white."

"The Sidhe bulk larger," Sentauris said. "Most are brown haired, though a few are golden crowned, and all with skins colored a light grey or brown. Somehow, I doubt that the Sidhe have ventured into your League: they are easily the most martial of the Kindreds, often found on distant battlefields, and most unlikely to slip by stealth into places forbidden by the Powers."

"Not so with the Tanu, for I have seen them at Sea's Edge," Orantes said, eyes still staring at the metal corselet. "Two came seeking some device from Merlin to aid them in their work at the forge. Certainly, they seemed overly cautious, though it was hard to disguise their bearing: both were dark skinned, with twice the bulk of Wylar here, and even taller. Yet I wonder how all our discussions of these beings can alter their status: the Elf-Lords and the Sidhe and the Tanu all maintain embassies with a wide range of the Powers of the Mid-World. Who among the Kindreds would assist the Wizards and their League and thus offend the Gods?"

Sentauris frowned. "Let us try to peer into the heart of this matter. Tallus describes himself as a 'Tanu rebel.' But *if* the Tanu, or the Elves, or the Sidhe — those loosely calling themselves the Kindreds — *if* they wished to aid us without attracting the malice of the Gods, then they might well insist that those acting on our behalf distance themselves from their own peoples, so that if the leaders of the Kindreds were challenged, all their efforts might be dismissed as the work of exiled hotheads."

"As I feared, these are false friends only," Orantes murmured, pulling back from the metal corselet, his right hand seeking a nearby goblet of wine.

"Partial friends," Wylar corrected, "and while better than no friends, they will certainly not greatly assist us in the coming challenges to the Wizards' League."

Orantes leaned back and gulped down a half goblet of wine. "Yes, our time of troubles," he murmured as his eyes drifted into the distance. "This 'Wild Time' as our colleague the Seeress has called it — so messy, so difficult, with all pleasure squeezed from our own lives. Sentauris, lovely Sentauris, why do we not together, you and I, depart from this inn, from this dark river, and leave Alantéa the Forerunner to its own devices. In the Far Lands along broad seashores lie pockets of the same sorcerous energies that power this land. There, in those warm, sunlit lands, we can spend our days in delight, far from overbearing Wizards and gloomy fortresses and nagging Familiars. Come." One of Orantes' arms made as if to push himself from the table, while the other raised his goblet for another long pull of wine.

"So you have suggested several other times," Sentauris replied gently, "and as before, I am unable to accept. My Seer's Sight is often blind when I consider my own future — mysteries await me. I sense, though, that I will not be able to choose one mate, one person to be with forever. Still, your sunlit lands sound most tempting, here at the edge of spring."

"Another time, far from here," Wylar said to Orantes. "I, too, would seek refuge in flight with the lovely Sentauris, but perhaps those thoughts are best left to dreams and visions at the edge of sleep."

Orantes nodded sagely, though his eyes flickered with a touch of self-mockery. "Such is the truth, and we three here have the virtue of all heroes, of placing the greater good ahead of our own desires. Besides, Whisper would never let me escape so easily.

"So, my utterly enchanting yet unavailable Sentauris, one of my tasks is to describe or portray the travails of our League of long time Servants." Orantes began clearing the largest part of the broad table before them, then murmured, "A longish, dry presentation is forthcoming, best suited for ale." He signaled to surrounding waiters, and as he cleared space in front of him, dark ale was placed on a side table, in a tankard so large that Ghorm might have lifted it with both hands.

A generous portion of that dark ale passed down Orantes' throat in one long swallow.

"So," the Adept continued, "what I conjure before us is the League, or what it wishes one day to become." Once more in hushed tones, he invoked words of power. Glistening mists seem to gather on the table before them, but around them, large candles and torches began to dim, as though magic was drawing power from the inn's light sources. Seeing the beginning of magic, nearby tables began to slowly empty, though a few watched on from a distance with narrowed, speculating eyes. Sounds of stringed instruments and muted horns diminished and then stopped completely. As other noises faded, Sentauris thought she could hear the distant bark of Ghorm's laughter.

"Fear not," Wylar murmured to Sentauris, "that our kind hosts will lose currency on this night. It is not gold that we lack, but power." He pulled his chair around to sit beside Orantes. Sentauris did likewise, so that the three of them sat with backs to the taproom's farthest wall, facing out toward the few patrons remaining in this suddenly quiet section of the inn.

On the table before them, glistening mists began to coalesce until Sentauris watched as an image formed showing the shoreline of Southern Alantéa — which was also the southern border of the Wizards' League. With every passing second, other details became more distinct. Towns and cities were shown as small points of blue. Rivers such as the Bariloch and the Saugus flowed with tiny streams of clear water, while three pools of deeper blue formed around the League's three strongholds: Sea's Edge, where Merlin dwelled, Gravengate, ruled by Balardi, and Stone Mountain, where Thorian's stronghold looked out over an expanse of whitecapped ocean.

Sentauris and the two Adepts sat staring at a contoured map that began at the League's southern border and encompassed the whole of the League together with a small portion of the lands beyond. The League's Northern border seemed formed by the Saugus on the northeast, then a rough line bounded the League as though running from North Haven in the west to a point where the Saugus turned sharply south toward Gravengate.

Orantes ceased his spellcast and spoke softly to his two onlookers. "Before us lies the dream of the three Wizards...while here," he paused to take another long pull at his tankard, "here is the reality." The League's northern border pulsed, flickered, tried to reassert itself then faded. Points of red fire drifted down along the League's northern border, while other darting red lights flickered all along the coastline, and other pulses of red seemed to appear from nothingness in the midst of lightly populated spaces within the League's border.

"As you may have guessed," Wylar said quietly, "the red lights reveal the warfare waged against us, both along our borders and within league lines."

Sentauris studied the shifting patterns of light for a moment then murmured, "Your League is not winning."

"All too true, yet worse is to come," Orantes continued somberly. "Behold the League as we foresee it a little farther into the future." Thousands of red sparks seemed to sweep over the tables' images; for a time, amber lights seemed to rise in defense of the blue, but in the end, blue lights faded as did the League's borders. In the end, only three small points of blue remained: at Sea's Edge, at Stone Mountain, and at Gravengate, and the radiance of these three points seemed to diminish as they watched.

"Reduced to three small strongholds," Sentauris said shaking her head, "and even these will one day be demolished. No one has believed me, though I have seen those future events in the clearest of visions. Yet your current difficulties seem no less deadly. No wonder the tepid Wizards seek outside aid!"

"Here I must defend the Wizards," Wylar said. "You will have noted that I lack my Adept colleague's flamboyance, while, on the other hand, you have heard few unmeasured words from me. The Wizards are 'tepid' because much of the Mid-World of the Truce is allied against them. If the Gods could simply 'will' the League's death, our alliance would have failed long ago."

Sentauris shrugged. "An old puzzle, why the Gods permit the existence of the Wizards' League. Yet there's no secret as to why the Gods dislike our peoples so much: we are Maker Servants, followers of the God of Gods, the Activator of Demon Princes and Creator of Seraphs Powers. Perhaps the truth of their origins restrains the Gods."

Orantes shook his head solemnly. "That truth has never stopped the Powers before, nor has the threat of Judgment Day when the Powers of the Mid-World will stand before the Maker. That day of reckoning seems impossibly distant, while on this dark evening, our foes seem numberless and overwhelmingly powerful."

Wylar spoke more low words; Sentauris could feel the spell shields all around them deepen and close around the three of them, so that all the distant clattering sounds of the nearby kitchen faded, the seeping hiss of shimmering embers in fires that had been recently tended grew still, and even the deepwater sounds of the flowing Saugus trickled into silence.

"Our adversaries," Wylar continued in low tones, "though they are many, are not exactly 'numberless.' While the Wizards do not even mention their names, they have allowed us access to various scrolls and tablets, so we've learned that the Dark Gods who plot constantly against us include many notorious and fearsome Powers: Ahriman, Arioch, Bael, Hecate, Kali, Mallegro, Moloch, Quarezokziil and Set. No doubt this is only a partial list, and since I know little of their rankings in power, I have listed them in order of their names."

Orantes swallowed another large mouthful of dark ale and shook his head. "We should not overlook the three so called 'Renegades': Un-Maurag, Mordred and Haeglin. These are called various names, but the term 'Renegade' has been applied to them because they defy The Mid-World of the Truce, some sort of pact agreed to by the Gods. But these 'Renegades' have even less love for us than those other Great Dark Gods."

Sentauris took a deep breath and sat upright. "With such a formidable list of adversaries," she said, searching the eyes of the Adepts, "you must at least have at least a few friends among the Great Gods, the Powers of the Mid-World."

Neither Wylar nor Orantes would meet her eyes. "The Wizards have failed to mention any of these possible 'friends,'" Wylar finally said in a quiet voice.

"By all the Nine Billion Gods!" Sentauris muttered. "How has your Wizards' League managed to survive?"

"There is the Truce," Orantes said, again looking away from Sentauris. "This pact seems to prevent alliances among the Gods so that all the Great Dark Gods are not able to join together with the Renegades and come against the Wizards' League in force."

"Forbidden alliances may well be among the Truce Terms," Wylar said, and now his dark eyes studied Sentauris closely, "rules that are at the heart of the Mid-World of the Truce, a series of commandments that are only vague rumors to those of us in the League. Without knowing the exact nature of those rules, do you wonder that the Wizards tread most warily?"

"It doesn't matter," Sentauris said, drawing a deep breath. "Any single one of those Gods you named is powerful enough to destroy your League."

"That may not be precisely true," Wylar said carefully. "Should any one God, even a Greater God, come against the three Wizards, that Power might not prevail."

"What?!?" Sentauris sat up straight, struggling to clear the wine fumes from her mind. "Let me see if I understand this matter. Let us say that Arioch, a Dark God, and master of enormous power and malice, were to emerge suddenly from the Mid-World and assail Gravengate. What then?"

"Arioch would most likely be defeated," Wylar said flatly. "The Wizards would join together and expel him from the League."

"No wonder the Gods hate the Wizards and their League!" Sentauris said, struggling to keep her voice down. "Still, how can you be so certain?"

"For the purpose of testing these balances," Wylar said evenly, "the Mid-World of the Truce has produced *The Game of the Masters*."

"Ah, now for further explanations," Orantes said, rubbing his eyes, "such thirsty, dry work, and time for more ale."

"No, it's time for dinner, old friend," Wylar said. "Otherwise, this night's work will pass far too early into dreamland." Wylar signaled to an attendant at the far edge of the taproom, and the kitchen was prompted into a whirlwind of final preparation. With a second gesture, Wylar waved aside Orantes' construct showing the League: the map shimmered, drifted into segments, then vanished like mists drifting into the morning air. As serving dishes began arriving, Wylar also murmured a slight Charm over the three of them, so that a fresh chilled wind swirled about them, and some of the weight of wine and ale was lifted from their bodies.

Almost too easy being an Adept, Sentauris thought. *Yet if I exchanged my Seer's Sight for their powers, I would be blind again, and that I could never live with.*

Food was set before them with new dishes emerging every few moments: grilled freshwater crayfish seasoned with sharp spices, legumes on a bed of wild rice, breasts of roast pheasant, steamed bass, medallions of lamb, and two other dishes that Sentauris could only vaguely identify. Having been long in the field, she ate — as did the others — with a hunger that was difficult to control.

After a brief time, it was clear to Sentauris that they could never finish all that was set before them. She took a deep breath and murmured, "I was never fed like this at Gravengate or at Stone Mountain. Have the Wizards suddenly become epicures?"

"Would that it were so," Orantes said, wiping his hands on a napkin, then reaching for a goblet of red wine. "So, the appetizers having been fairly begun, I now become toastmaster." Orantes struggled to his feet, wobbling somewhat, and raised his glass to Sentauris. "First, to the radiant if field weary Sentauris, may she bring greater confusion to our foes than to our allies! And secondly, to the legendary Weasel for whom this inn was named. If that creature indeed feasted as we have, that being was far closer to Godhood than to beast!" Each of them drank deeply.

Maker's Touch! Sentauris thought, staring at the mass of food before them. *If servings in front of them contained only "appetizers," then the main course hasn't even been served!*

· X ·

"It was a good theft, as such things go," Squint said, watching Ghorm gnaw at a leg of roast pheasant that was only slightly charred. "Whisper wrapped our dinner in folds of darkness, then shifted it into the shadows. From those shadows, I flew it back to our stronghold."

Squint himself picked at a wing of the same pheasant Ghorm consumed, while Whisper watched on with some amusement, consuming nothing himself. The slight candle in the cone shaped tower had been relit, so the two Familiars dined on stolen dinner in a faint light that was well suited to a den of thieves.

After he finished, Ghorm belched aloud then rose to wipe his small, greasy hands on a set of old curtains that hung in a corner of the tower.

"So, what happens next?" Ghorm asked Whisper. "Is the Fat One going to drink himself into oblivion? Will you let him?"

"We are on leave, all of us enjoying a brief rest," Whisper said, his shadowy body drifting to the window overlooking the courtyard. "Soldiers have leaves as do Familiars — even Wraiths."

"Yes, but leave from what?" Ghorm said, his voice dripping sarcasm. "Have the Adepts been judging too many flower pageants? Grown weary relieving so many maidens of their flimsy bodices? Meanwhile, Sentauris and I have been fighting the battles of your League in the wilderness."

"No, we too have been active in the League's defense," Whisper said in his soft voice. "Militias have been formed to handle most incursions, yet when those raids are accompanied by a force of magic, they must be countered by my master or by Wylar."

Ghorm laughed out loud. "Yes, I can picture Orantes, the Fat One, bouncing along rough roads, riding in a fury!"

"He has ridden hard at times," Whisper said, his voices growing more intense, "and into great danger."

"With Wylar at his side," Squint added.

"Bounce, wobble, bounce," Ghorm murmured. "I suppose I can imagine The Fat One riding hard with Wylar at his side. Now tell me about what happens when the two arrive at the battlefield — tell me about the radiant blasts of power, the surge of transforming energies."

Squint and Whisper were silent for a moment, then Squint said quietly, "The Adepts can do much, and yet there are at present no radiant blasts of power."

"Nor surges of transforming energies," Whisper added.

Ghorm stared at his two friends for a moment before speaking. "So, either your Adepts are less than powerful, or the Wizards don't trust them fully."

"Perhaps a little of both," Whisper said.

"And yet, *I* think there's something else," Squint added, "something we don't yet understand."

Ghorm stared at his two friends in silence for a while; this was the first time the other two Familiars had been willing to discuss the Adepts and their shortcomings. He pulled up a stool and sat closer to them. Their tower grew darker as torches outside the inn gradually burned lower.

"So, what's going to be decided below us at the inn?" Ghorm asked, watch the two Familiars closely. "Are the Adepts and the Seeress going to ignore the Wizards and join forces?"

Squint and Whisper glanced quickly together. "Something like that," Squint said.

"The Adepts believe," Whisper added, "that the Wizards will turn a blind eye to their temporary alliance with the Seeress."

"They *hope* for a blind eye," Ghorm muttered, shaking his head. "How the Wizards will truly react is another matter." He took a deep breath and readied to leave.

"No, don't go," Squint said.

"We know how unhappy you are when we speak about the Adepts," Whisper added, "but stay, stay and talk with us."

Ghorm laughed his short bitter laugh. "So, this is a time when the diplomats reveal their dark, sinister secrets. All right, I will begin the exchange. Uncle Vlasoff has a nickname, what was he called?"

"Vlasoff the Firebrand," Squint said, after a pause.

Ghorm nodded. "And his most recent name?"

"Vlasoff the Ember," Whisper said, "referring to his diminished intellect, and it is not a name we have ever used."

"So that we understand each other," Ghorm continued, "the Adepts are not widely loved and have their own nicknames. And they are called...?"

Squint sighed. "They are known as 'The Replacement Adepts' and are regarded far less highly than those who preceded them."

"They are growing stronger," Whisper added. "As Healers and Conjurors, they continue to improve, but like all humans that have not started out well, they have a long way to go. Neither Wylar nor Orantes were born into happy circumstances."

"Imagine Sentauris," Ghorm muttered, "losing her parents at an early age, brought up by that someone known as 'Firebrand'."

"Wylar and Orantes had different, though equally unhappy beginnings," Whisper said.

"Have either the parents of Wylar or Orantes emerged?" Ghorm asked. "What about the famous sister of Orantes?"

Whisper shook his shadowy head. "Spirella, who spent most of her waking life devising torments for her older brother. Orantes still delights in discussing her perverse plots and how stunned she was when she discovered that Orantes had the Gift — and she did not. Orantes' father left the League some time ago. I doubt that we will ever know the name of his father's real master. Mother and daughter have moved to Khiva on the south coast, where Spirella has become a jeweler with some small talent. Orantes no longer mocks her craft. The less heard about that family the better."

"The same is true of Wylar's parents," Squint added. "They simply vanished into the Mid-World, leaving Wylar's unloving grandparents to raise him. He still sends the grandparents silver each month, with short notes, but he does so only out of duty, without any sense of affection."

"Sentauris still cares for and loves her crazy uncle Vlasoff," Ghorm said, shaking his head, "while he is only dimly aware of her."

The three Familiars sat in silence for a moment. Many other things were better left unsaid. Squint and Whisper understood that their masters drew strength and purpose from Sentauris and that Ghorm was unsettled when the three were together.

Ghorm finally changed the subject. "Enough of the Adepts. What of your Wizards? Your mighty founders seem to have settled into remote and cranky retirements."

"Ah, the Wizards," Squint said quietly. "We would not speak of them, except late at night with a close friend and ally. The Wizards endure the endless hatred of the Gods; currently, their malice is expressed by untraceable Sendings of great cunning and power, so as to test each Wizard's strength. Several times each month, one Wizard, at least, is confronted by a construct of power, forcing him to turn from his work and contend with a creature bent on that Wizard's destruction. Balardi destroys such Sendings with a fury that sends concussions booming over the Plain of Gravengate. Thorian is colder, less prone to rage: he imprisons each construct, then dissects the thing to learn the nature of its force of magic. Lately, Merlin has taken a different approach: he reenchants those constructs then frees them."

Whisper breathed out what might have been the thinnest of laughs. "Even now, ridiculous but harmless and untouchable ghostly sendings drift through Varaj, or Far Avalon, or Grave's End, crying, 'Where lurketh Merlin? I have been sent to destroy that Wizard, Merlin! Woe unto this mortal conjuror!' It is rumored that a few of the Powers even find these twisted Sendings somewhat amusing."

"A nice touch," Ghorm conceded, "all that elaborate mockery without any direct challenge to the Gods."

· ❇ ·

Sentauris groaned aloud, "I may never eat again," she said, pushing herself back from the table. The lean Wylar had long since retreated from the field of food, and even Orantes had slowed measurably.

"So," she continued, "now that the Jolly One is almost sated, will the Dour One continue his dry discourse?"

"I am not quite so 'dour', Sentauris," Wylar said, wincing, "and to avoid overlong dryness, tell me what you know of *The Game of the Masters*."

Sentauris shrugged. "A board game with pieces of carved jade, supposedly featuring archetypes of various forces. To those of us struggling in forest and field, the *Game* seems mostly a conceit of those frequenting ornate palaces — or gloomy fortresses."

Orantes laughed aloud and beamed at Sentauris: a huge, demented grin. "How I wish the Wizards were forced to deal with you on a daily basis!" He drew a napkin, wiping his hands and mouth with surprising daintiness. "Still, the *Game* is more than a pastime. Let us say you are a...Sidhe Warlord, born with a decent force of magic and have been troubled by...a lesser Dark God. Should you invoke your Board, from any place in Alantéa or the Mid-World, you might challenge that Dark God into *The Game of the Masters*; and so, your relative strength of power and wit might be tested without recourse to weapons."

"Others, such as the Wizards," Wylar added, "play the *Game* not to challenge, but reveal their place in the hierarchies of Power. All we hear are rumors," and here Wylar lowered his voice and glanced around. "What we hear is that Merlin is rarely defeated."

Orantes pulled himself unsteadily to his feet and hauled a smaller but cleared table toward their overburdened one. "Images, always images, rather than words," he muttered to himself. As before, he began chanting, and if some of his words were slurred, still the force of his magic was great enough to overcome any flaws in his spells.

Images appeared on the table: large jade pieces on an even larger board. The first rank seemed to hold lesser pieces: warriors, armed knights, lesser workers of magic, slight creatures of the Mid-World. On the second rank stood pieces of greater power: a Magician, what seemed to be an enchanted weapon....

She jerked wide awake: to the weapon's left lay a creature with a raven's shape — the same image that had lingered at the edge of her vision just two nights ago...*The Sending*...an archetype of the force sent against her by Arioch the Malevolent.

And now, as though activated by some hidden power, the raven shaped image of the Sending grew lifelike, quivering with motion and color, then launching itself with a tiny, remote cry, toward the center of the board. As it settled, a second piece, showing a row of archers, also shimmered, became fluid, then moved out to counter the raven-shaped Sending. The inn was completely still; all the faces of those around them were frozen in shock.

What were these Adepts doing! She glanced at into their faces: Orantes was backing away in surprise, while Wylar was whispering low, intense words. On the table's center, both the raven-shape and the clustered archers slowed, then grew still, frozen, with all the colors drawn from them as they became again nothing more than images of carved wood.

"What strange potion has the Jolly One consumed tonight?" Sentauris asked, drawing a deep breath. "Have them bring me a goblet of that same brew."

Wylar shook his head, frowning. "Somehow, *The Game of the Masters* is aware of you, Sentauris. Perhaps your contest of two nights ago, of Sending against Archers, has made it seek you out."

"Whatever power has just intervened, it was not my doing, or my choice." Orantes pulled back, fumbling for his goblet. "Magic has failed me before, but never in the past has some outside force taken control from me." He washed away the sour taste of failed magic with one quick gulp. "Let me close down this ridiculous *Game* before its silly pieces find some way to poison our wine."

"One moment," Wylar said. "Sentauris, you should know of the three ranks of the *Game*: lesser, greater, and greatest. On the third rank centermost lie the most powerful of forces: the Mid-World Power, showing the Gods;

the Master, representing the player of the *Game*; and the Ancient Secret, reflecting all the hidden, unknowable forces that lie buried within the Mid-World of the Truce. Yet note how Wizards and Sorcerers are also placed in the last rank, though farther out on its wings."

Sentauris stood and stared down at the table: were all those other pieces beginning to shimmer, or was it the wine? "Yes," she whispered, "what lies before us is truly far more than any 'game.'" Almost unbidden, her hand reached out into the images of carved, strangely fluid wooden pieces. "Before me, within this construction...."

Her senses jarred. Suddenly, in her mind, she stood alone, far from the inn. A Power, a dark, cloaked, and cowled wraithlike figure loomed before her. Arms extended from its cloak; one was covered with beast fur, the other that of a fleshless skeleton. As though from the greatest of distances, the skeletal hand reached out and touched her on the forehead with fingers conveying an immeasurable cold.

"One day," she heard herself saying, in a voice that belonged to another being, "one day, far from this moment, the Wizards will face a second, even greater challenge. Then they will learn far more of the Contest of the Powers, and then even *The Game of the Masters* will be confronted with its own doom."

· X ·

As the night deepened, banks of clouds rolled south, and moonlight began to pour through the broad windows of the inn's cone shaped tower. Gradually the conversation of the three Familiars flagged, then dropped into a restful silence. In the soft quiet, Ghorm's eyes drooped with fatigue, while Whisper and Squint began staring at the moonscape outside of their aerie with a barely concealed longing.

Aside from Sentauris, Ghorm thought, *these are my only real friends, and each of them is as strange as I am. Sad to think that one day the politics of the League might keep us from seeing each another ever again.*

Ghorm broke the silence with a loud yawn. "It's very well for you creatures of the night to admire the moon and its phases, but now it's naptime for little Ghorm the Goblin."

"Be wise, Ghorm, and care for yourself," Squint said. His wings flapped, lifting him to the tower's windowsill. "Next time we meet, perhaps I'll tell you some of my own lies." Then the Owl-being swooped down toward the forested groves that lay just three minutes flight from *The Weasel's Feast.*

"Farewell, Ghorm," Whisper said in his thin voice. "Tomorrow I'll be busy organizing my talented but imperfect master. Any day after that, seek me again for a new contest of lies." Then Whisper too, passed from the tower: a shifting coil of shadows that floated slowly to the ground.

In forested, moonlit glades, Squint floated in the silence of an owl in flight, hunting his true dinner: night foraging kit foxes, stoats, weasels, and their own prey.

Some distance away, Whisper shifted through pools of moonlight, studying the interplay of light and shadow on the forest floor.

And instead of sleeping, Ghorm also stared out at the moonlight. As always, an ocean of longing and sorrow lay before him, ready to drown him, if he let it. On this night, he let a little of that sorrow — like the foam of an ocean wave — wash over his gnarled, squat feet.

·)((·

"...the spellwork of idiots ends in flatulence!" Orantes finished his curse. "From now on the Wizards can play with their silly *Game* by themselves."

Despite the wine consumed, Orantes' face had grown sober. *The Game of the Masters* had been banished from the taproom, but not from their minds. Sentauris nodded in agreement both with Orantes' curses and his sentiments. Then she pushed her chair back, ready to speak polite, farewell words and so end the evening.

"Wait, hold for a moment," Wylar said, tugging gently at her chair. "Let's not end our time together on such a sour note."

"Stay," Orantes urged. "It's not often that Whisper leaves me to my own devices. And besides, we have not yet discussed our true reason for seeking you out."

"Yes, I was aware that much remained to be spoken," Sentauris said, rising. "It does not take Seer's Sight to know that you are losing your war and that you desperately need counsel on military matters. We will deal with that tomorrow." Wylar and Orantes glanced at each other, then rose reluctantly to bid Sentauris good night.

"For now," she continued, "it's sleep for me, though a squalid, grimy one, with no bath to be drawn at this hour."

"There is the river," Wylar said with a trace of a smile.

Sentauris laughed aloud. "Frigid waters surging south! My wisdom and insight won't help you much if my lifeless body is carried to the ocean like frozen driftwood."

"The currents don't have to be swift," Orantes said, glancing to his fellow Adept.

"And the waters need not be cold," Wylar added, now smiling openly.

"Are you not the naughty lads!" Sentauris said, laughing. "And will the two Master Magicians swim themselves?"

"We will," Orantes said, offering his arm with ponderous gallantry. "To the river! Let it beware of our mighty if somewhat wine addled powers!"

"In my role as the 'Dour One'," Wylar said, "I must think upon the aftermath of our adventure. While you two are busy taming the waters, I will seek soft cloths and sandals for our return."

As Orantes and Sentauris stepped outside the inn, bright moonlight swept over them, while the night's chill struck them like a blow. They recoiled, forcing a laugh. A distance of only two hundred paces separated the hillock's base from the water's edge, but Orantes moved ponderously, then seemed to slow as though sobered into doubt by the clear night air. Sentauris tugged him forward.

"Come now," she said cheerfully, "the stuff of heroes and all that."

"Yes, heroes...born with mostly dead brain matter — the lovely Sentauris, of course, being a wonderful exception." They veered to the right of the docks that lay beneath *The Weasel's Feast*, heading toward an island of sand and gravel that formed a rough beach. Above them a three-quarters moon beamed down on them, revealing much of the moon's landscape: patchy seas of dust bordered by crumbling mountains. As they neared the water Orantes glanced about as though seeking a convenient exit. None was available, so at the river's edge, the Adept drew a deep breath, waded knee deep into icy waters, and splashed chilly water over his face.

He returned to Sentauris muttering, "Don't tell Whisper that I chose discomfort without his nagging." Shivering, the Adept began to chant. As he worked his magic over the great river, Wylar appeared, carrying an armful of broad cloths, material once intended either for baths or for rough bedding. Leaving his burden on high ground, Wylar stood beside his fellow Adept, nodding as though following a pace in music. Then the two were chanting in near harmony: Orantes, flowing, melodious in tenor tones; Wylar a low, rumbling bass, a counterpoint, and framework, focusing their power.

The air about them grew warmer. Slowly the river's surge became sluggish as crosscurrents and counterflows formed a nearly still pool of water by the shore. Lights seemed to emerge from the pool's depths — a phosphorescent silver mingling first with tarnished gold, then with a churning blue and green. Finally, with the appearance of pulsing copper surges in midwater depths, their pool warmed, with steam rising into the night air.

Orantes turned to Sentauris with an elaborate bow. "Your bath, madam."

"I can array you in a cloak of darkness if you wish," Wylar added.

"Ha!" Sentauris took ten paces from them and kicked off her boots. "We care little for such niceties in the field. A moonlit darkness is dark enough." It took only seconds for her to slip from layers of clothes, then she took swift steps toward strangely glowing waters, and dove headfirst into the Saugus.

The water's surface was as warm as a lake on a summer's day. Swift strokes took her to the pool's center, where she dove down in one smooth motion. From a distance she could hear one discrete diving sound — Wylar — then a second, much larger splash as Orantes hurled himself into the water, striving for maximum impact.

In the pool's depths lights still flourished. At upper levels, waves of silver and gold sent a gentle warmth surging slowly outward, while in the middle, seething aquamarine waters threw out greater heat. In the depths, pulsing copper fountains provided water that was much warmer.

She rose to the surface through layers of warm and cooler waters, drawing a deep breath, then she dove again to explore the perimeters of the pool. Perhaps fifty paces from the pool's center lights dimmed and the water cooled. A wall of churning waters marked the boundary where the Adepts' magic fought off the river's surge. Here at the pool's edge, freshwater trout and bass and river pike poked their way through walls of churning water, drawn by warmth and strange lights. Heat and the sight of a naked Sentauris drove them back, their fish faces flashing a comical alarm.

And now at the edge of her vision, a much larger swimmer loomed: Orantes. Vaguely like a walrus and surprisingly agile, the Adept was swimming in mock pursuit of Sentauris. She laughed, air bubbling to the surface, then rose for one quick breath.

The chase was on. Taking care not to outdistance Orantes, she led him through the length and breadth of their shielded portion of the river, hearing the Adept alternately laugh at intruding fish, or mutter a curse as he brushed against pulsing, hot waters.

A few moments of energetic pursuit were enough for Orantes, and he lay for a time at the surface, drawing deep breaths, staring at a night sky where the moon's brightness crowded thousands upon thousands of stars. While Orantes recovered, Wylar floated toward Sentauris. His eyes, too, held mischief, though he was careful not to approach her too swiftly, nor to stare openly at the lithe form of Sentauris that floated beneath the water's surface. It seemed enough, or almost enough, for Wylar to stare into the eyes of Sentauris.

"So, we kept our word," Wylar said, "fine food, excellent wines — now even a bath. Be kind to us and overlook our failed spells and false alarms."

"Those are forgotten," Sentauris replied, dismissing them with a wave of wet hair, "but I cannot think of a time when I will forget this night."

Orantes drew a deep breath and paddled toward them. As he neared Sentauris he turned, and spewed water at the looming moon: with wild eyes and a matted red beard, Orantes seemed like an ancient woodland God, hurling defiance at some unnamed lunar adversary.

One of these, perhaps even both, seem destined to be my lover, thought Sentauris. *But which one, and when? Now is certainly not the time, though the waters about me are rich with sensual undertones, and both these lads seem prepared for a frolic.*

Sentauris laughed aloud at herself. Part of her mind had been paying too much attention to events beneath the waterline. She turned, took one great breath, and dove again in one smooth motion. Pausing briefly to investigate all the many gleaming lights and pockets of warmth, she swept like a porpoise to the edge, then burst through into the River Saugus that flowed so freely in the night.

Cold and swift dark currents surged over her. Behind her, the Adepts were calling out in warning and alarm. Sentauris coiled and hurtled back into the pool. Carefully she rose in an area outside of their vision then made her way almost silently to shore.

Wylar and Orantes were still staring down the river in search of her, speaking hushed words together, when Sentauris rose into the chilled night air. She covered herself and her long dark hair with soft cloths, then turned and called back to the Adepts,

"Well met at *The Weasel's Feast!*"

Her room looked out over the moonlit docks and the Saugus beyond. Just to the right of the docks lay the slight inlet where their pool had been formed; nothing remained of it now except the dim glow of fading lights.

Sentauris lay back and released her Seer's Sight from the prison within her mind. As it returned, it brought visions...Ghorm was sleeping peacefully on a loose bed of curtains in an upper storage room, while Orantes was holding forth in the taproom — somehow the Adept had found an audience and was regaling them with tales of the Wizards, jests at the expense of unnamed Powers, and stories of his own, mostly ridiculous adventures.

And Wylar...the Adept lay at the edge of sleep, wondering if Sentauris would come to him. Not this night, though perhaps one day, sometime when her own destiny became clearer...She closed her eyes, composing herself for sleep.

— ! — What was that? She stood up in one fluid motion, then turned... nothing stirred for leagues, but somewhere far from the inn to the north, a thing of menace was leaking malice into her thoughts. Could she learn more of it from a different location? Almost before her thoughts were complete, she had changed into her traveler's garb, choosing only shoes of light leather rather than riding boots.

As she descended to the inn's lower levels, she glanced into the taproom, where Orantes was surrounded by nearly a score of travelers and porters and stable hands. And he was mimicking...the Wizards! Surely that was Balardi's gesture of pounding the table, and Merlin's airy wave of his hand. Orantes winked openly at her, then continued his performance, now showing the hulking countenance of some jealous Dark God.

Sentauris passed from the taproom into the last hours of moonlight, slipping easily into a loping run that could carry her for leagues. Her Seer's Sight and her own night vision guided her effortlessly around tangles of brush, and dew sliding over brush, and rotted logs. A hovering three-quarters moon lay at her back and sounds of the river gradually grew dim as she passed further into winding forest trails, seeking a path that gradually led to higher country.

Less than a league from the inn, she found a hill that provided a far greater overview than the hillock supporting *The Weasel's Feast*. She climbed swiftly to the top, though the hill's crest was treacherous with deadfall and rubble so that she was forced to be cautious.

Moonlit countryside lay all around her, though the Saugus was only a remote ribbon of water, and the inn was obscured by a rise of trees. Those pulses of power had come from the north, she decided; far from this place some powerful being filled with menace had allowed its shields to slip, if only for a moment. From time to time such remote echoes reached her when the Gods fought, or one of the Powers forced its will upon lesser beings. Often, she could link the sensation with its cause only months or years after when news of the conflict finally reached her.

And then perhaps it was nothing but the leakage of the sorcerous energies that powered the Mid-World. She shrugged, turned from the north, and began her swift passage back to the inn. The steady pace of her loping run brought her a sense of comfort: it was not through soft living at the inns frequented by royalty, that she had maintained her training, her strength, and her endurance.

On returning, she glanced again into the taproom. Orantes remained, seated but alone, snoring, fast asleep with his head thrown back. As Sentauris approached, one very red eye popped open, slowly following her progress as she crossed the room. *A nice touch,* she thought. *Eleven portions of his mind lie overwhelmed by a heavy weight of wine, while the twelfth part performs a sentry's watch.*

Once again in her chamber, Sentauris slipped easily into slumber, with only the rushing sounds of the great river washing through her dreamless sleep.

Chapter Three

The Powers and Their War

IN THE LAST HOURS of darkness, the moon set over the Saugus, leaving only starshine to illuminate a time of dark quiet and of peace.

Warfare brewed far to the north in the Gangean Range, where a strange, completely unnatural weather system hung over its high mountains' peaks. Powerful winds were pushing storm clouds south, although layers of threatening weather seemed to snag on high mountain spires, so that fog and glistening mists that groaned and crackled with the partial discharge of pent-up lightnings were forced down onto the smaller cliffs and valleys beneath the upper mountains.

On the broad Cloudland Plateau, a mountain lake lay buried beneath thick layers of winter ice, its surface broken only in two places by some incredibly strong beast creature. From one of these cracks, a sluggish fog rose slowly to the surface. Its substance was a darker grey than the mists around it, with sections almost as dark as soot, ribbed with black bands. Strangely, it seemed to ignore the gusts of wind that swirled mist and sleet all around it, hovering as though waiting for a signal.

Bellowing, shrieking sounds drifted over the ice from the lake's farthest mountainside, and the greyish black fog gathered itself, rolling purposefully toward the noise. At the edge of the plateau lay a great dead hulking thing:

a fallen Stone Giant, a powerful being with the bulk of a score of human beings. But now its eyes stared vacantly into nothingness, and its yellowish grey flesh was cooling rapidly on the iceshelf. It was impossible to tell which of the two predators fighting over the carcass was truly entitled to its prey.

One of the Creatures of the Darkness loomed as tall as the Stone Giant, its dark flesh ropy with tendons, limbs knitted to its torso with a webbing of rubbery cartilage. The second moved spiderlike on a score of limbs, scuttling from side to side as it sought an opening; its oval shape was a sickly white in color, as though trying to blend with the mountain's ice. Sorcerous energies flared, radiating deep red, pale, and yellow lights as each creature raised a force of magic against the other. Then the two began to struggle, bellowing, shrieking, each striving with bites and stings, and surges of wild magic to drive the other off.

The two pulled free, stalked one another, then closed again. More cries of pain and rage followed. Deeper breaths, panting, sobbing sounds came as the two backed away. Then the two Creatures Indomitable studied each other cautiously for a long moment as though realizing at last that they were too evenly matched. The scuttling creature finally broke the stalemate: it began ripping with pincers from its mouth at the dead Giant's boots, then started to feed on rough flesh of yellow and grey. Warily, the taller creature knelt, then began ripping flesh from the Giant's upper shoulder, gobbling down great chunks of pale yellow and red meat, with streams of blood gushing out.

Perhaps the two would feed until they met in the middle, and then the greater would consume the lesser. The greyish black fog seemed to turn from the mountain, searching the lake's frozen surface and the rocky shelf beyond. Darkness would end soon, though mists still swirled through the night air, laced with sleet. Electrical discharges outlined dark mountain spires beyond the plateau's edge. Nothing came, no sign emerged. The fog seemed to shrug — perhaps its night watch at the edge of darkness had been wasted, with the brief duel of monsters providing only minor entertainment.

Ah.... Now, on the far side of the lake, a similar foggy substance vented from a cleft in the crags, as though making its way through devious means up from the mountain's heart. Throbbing with dark energies, the greyish black fog scuttled across the ice to meet its counterpart.

Two mounds of smoke approached each other warily: one was greyish black, pulsing with dark energies, while the second was lighter grey, linked by matrices of blue, and it bulked somewhat larger, pulsing with greater force. As the two forms touched, lightning flashed in the mountains' upper reaches. Daybreak was only an hour away, although the air remained heavy and dark, threatening stormy weather.

A strange meeting place, the greyish black mass whispered into the mind of the other. *You must have mighty foes, and strange fears yourself, to be so constrained.*

I fear only the Truce, the mass of blue and grey whispered back.

And I fear nothing.

Let me say this, my darker but lesser ally, the blue and grey mass hissed. *If the Truce were called against you, I myself would rise in might, and then you would know the reality of fear.*

Both cloudy figures seemed to pulse with dark radiances...then they subsided.

And this instruction in fear, the greyish black fog whispered in more restrained tones, *is this the real reason I was invited to so perversely transform myself then journey over shielded paths to a place of such obscure desolation?*

It is not. I therefore declare myself: I am Set, Greater God of Alantéa, Mid-World Power, and adversary of all Maker Servants, Truce or no Truce.

And I am Mordred, Renegade Dark God of the Mid-World, a Power blocked by Truce Terms I did not help to form, nor do I understand. I also greatly desire the destruction of the Wizards and their League.

Yes, whispered the mind of Set, *this League of latterday servants must be ground down, and all its adherents destroyed. Behold! See how the maggots dance, oblivious to the will of Gods and Powers.*

As the last hours of night faded, and a bleak sunrise rose over the Gangean Range, the two Powers shared images: of Thorian casually trapping a force of magic; of Balardi, exploding with sorcerous energies in a spasm of anger; of Merlin standing before *The Game of the Masters,* smiling softly as one of his pieces moved through the enchanted mists that hovered over his great gaming board; of many Servants kneeling in homage to the long departed Maker; and lastly of Sentauris and Orantes and Wylar swimming free of care in an enchanted pool within the massive Saugus river.

· X ·

In the dreams of Sentauris, she sat across a table from her Uncle Vlasoff, speaking quietly with him about the Wizards and their League. Vlasoff's face was at peace and every word that he spoke was filled with intelligence instead of madness. His eyes were gentle, without a hint of tears. She was nodding and smiling as she reached out to touch his hand.

They were silent for a moment, as a sense of peace passed between them, but then Vlasoff leaned forward and whispered, "You must wake, child. Much remains to be done. Do not be too angry with Ghorm."

Sentauris came awake suddenly, sensing that Ghorm was outside her bedroom, pacing and muttering to himself. She took a deep breath and sat up in bed.

"Come in, Ghorm," she called out. "It's morning and I'm awake."

Ghorm came in warily, staring around suspiciously.

"I'm alone," she said, "but you know that I'm no fairytale princess — I'm a fighter, and only occasionally a lover." She took a slender though sheathed dagger from beneath her pillow and set it carefully on her nightstand. "So how was your evening with Squint and Whisper?"

"It was good to be with them," Ghorm said, and he slumped down on a stool. "I have some questions. You say that this 'Wild Time' is coming. What sort of war is this going to be?"

"That's not yet known," Sentauris said. She rose and began pulling clothing over short cotton pants and a top that reached the level of her belt. "Might be skirmishes spilling back and forth along the border, or it might be Sorcerers leading ten thousand mailed knights across the border, or it could be something much different."

"Wouldn't this be a wonderful time," Ghorm said, studying her face, "to have those so called 'Lost Adepts' return to lead the League? What were their names again?"

"Hektor served Balardi while Antéus was led by Thorian. Both are gone about five years now, completely vanished." She glanced at a mirror, muttering as she pulled her hair back.

"But wouldn't it be useful," Ghorm continued, still watching Sentauris closely, "to have powerful, trained Adepts return to lead the League? You know what they call their 'Replacements,' Wylar and Orantes, both outside and inside the borders of the League? They call them 'The Inepts,' rather than 'The Adepts.'"

"And have you passed these comments on to Squint and Whisper?"

Ghorm shook his head. "No, those two are my friends, no matter how foolish the masters that they serve."

"I was a youngling," Sentauris said, "when the beloved Antéus and Hektor served the League. Though for what it's worth, Uncle Vlasoff was deeply suspicious of the two."

"Vlasoff liked almost no one," Ghorm muttered.

"Ghorm, do you recall that saying — 'When your Heart's Desires come true, then the Dark Gods dance with glee?' Do you wish the Replacements gone, with Antéus and Hektor to return? By all accounts they were bold, they were handsome, and they were powerful. How much more jealous would you be of them? And then what would become of Squint and Whisper?"

Ghorm shook his head and looked away. "I don't know what I really want. But you and I would be more likely to survive if we had stronger allies."

Sentauris hesitated. "Jealousy or not, that's a fair comment. So, here's what we're going to do. First I'm going to use my Farsight to look for these two 'Lost Adepts' — again — and then I'm going to use exactly the same search for Wylar and Orantes. You and I, both of us, will then accept the outcome."

Ghorm nodded grudgingly. Still seated, he studied the face of Sentauris intently. At first, her face grew slowly paler, whiter, as blood drained from her features. Then suddenly, she grew agitated, shaking, and her hands slipped to her waist as though seeking weapons. Then she stopped shaking and her eyes slipped open.

"Those 'Lost Adepts' are gone forever," Sentauris murmured. "I found nothing but grey shadows and darkness when I sought them — either they are dead, or they've been transformed into things unliving with no life left within them. Not even one of thousands of different futures showed even the slightest hint of them."

"And the Adepts," Ghorm prompted, "I mean the current ones?"

"Their futures are surrounded by lightning, thunder, stormy washes of water, and surges of dark magic," she said softly. "For better or for worse, war is coming, and our two Replacement Adepts will be in the middle of it."

·)(·

A little later in the morning, Sentauris found Wylar at the same table that had held their feast of the night before, though now it supported far lighter fare: broths of spiced, strong tea, accompanied by slender oatcakes. It was dark in the inn with a pale sunlight just beginning to peer through its upper windows. Serving staff carefully avoided them, though small fires had been set in two fireplace alcoves, to offset the morning chill.

Sentauris tried to relax, to enjoy a last moment of peace before skirmishes and battles swept over them. Periodically. Wylar's eyes flickered with amusement as he thought about the evening's swim, while Sentauris only smiled gently. After a time, they were joined by a grumbling Orantes, whose flowing cloak might have obscured a nagging Shade named Whisper.

"This was truly intended as a meal?" Orantes muttered, pushing aside the oatcakes. "Crumbling insect wings with pressed fingernail clippings, not fit for starving peasants. Poof! Bring me real food!" A nervous mind brought slices of bread and cured ham to Orantes. In spite of his large words, he was able to eat only a few small bites. If Orantes' red eyes were dulled by excess, still they gleamed with mischief from time to time as they glanced at Sentauris. She stared around the inn: alcove fires were burning higher, though the chill of early spring still hung in the air. She took a deep breath; it was time to speak, not of dreams but of warfare.

"So, your need is for military counsel," Sentauris began as Wylar sipped tisane and Orantes picked at his food. "You have militias; that's to the good, but these have no experience in dealing with any force of properly armed men, nor with incursions bringing a force of magic against your League. My first effort will be to send down mercenary captains to train your people. You must deal with these people with great caution: engage them for a fixed time, then release them with full payment; search their minds periodically for treachery; and do not show them any strong point you may later wish to defend. Remember that while some will be drawn to your cause, others might well seek your foes and sell their knowledge."

As she paused, Wylar again called down shielding spells, guarding them against outside intrusion.

"Yes, that will work," she continued, searching down future paths, "and while your tier-groups form, send to me the scouts, and swift riders, the wary hunters. These will form bands of raiders, and forest rangers, roaming across the border when needed so that no incursion will be staged just at the League's edge, without fear of a counter thrust...yes, that *may* work...a little, at least, but the rest...."

· ⟩⟨ ·

Plots, counterplots, stratagems, duplicities! the mind of Mordred raged. *Why do we not simply march at the forefront of countless legions and hurl those vermin serving the League into the sea!*

You must write in letters of fire across your mind, the greatest of the Truce Terms: that no two Powers may join against a third.

But these Wizards do not constitute this 'Third Power'! They did not exist at the birth of the Mid-World, and so stand outside of the Truce!

The transformed essence of Set seemed to sigh, his mound of fog rising and falling, then it turned to stare into the mountain reaches that lay beyond the plateau's edge. Daybreak was upon them, though only the faintest light was passing into the storm pattern that he had imprisoned over this region. He would need to release the weather in a brief time before other Gods came to investigate its unnatural quality.

Un-Maurag, Set said suddenly, *like you, a Renegade Dark God of the Mid-World. Does he still war incessantly against the Elf Lords and the Kindreds?*

So, it has been said. Mordred was suddenly guarded.

And has he never invited you or Haeglin, or one of the lesser Dark Gods to join him in this struggle? Come now, the truth, if we are to be allies.

Yes. And we were not unwilling, though the auguries were terrible, and we knew not why.

The Truce embraces not just the Gods, but new powers, even the Elf Lords, even the Wizards. Had you three Renegades joined together, the Mid-World of the Truce would have smashed down upon your evil but overly impetuous intellects. And there is a second reason for great caution.

Mordred, though prompted, remained silent.

Here is the second reason. Let us say that you and I together march against the League, and the Mid-World ignores us, believing that the League is outside of the Truce. Have you no enemies? Say that Amon-Ra, or Zôs, or Dagda, or Tel-Alantir, or Heimdall or Wotan chooses that moment of exposure to strike at you. As a third party, the Truce forbids me to help you, and you would be forced to retreat.

No more, Mordred said quietly. *Left so long to my own darkness, I have not troubled myself to master these strange policies. Return to your plots, counterplots, stratagems, and devices, and I will add more than a few of my own.*

·)(·

"There is a dark quality to the future that lies before us," Sentauris said softly, staring into the distance, "like a storm system ready to burst over us. Yet until it breaks, I can see little more of our fates." They had halted a short way from *The Weasel's Feast,* standing on a horse track that would lead Sentauris north, while the two Adepts sought ferry passage back to the League. Not far away, their horses browsed on slender grasses and wildflowers, enjoying the rising warmth of midmorning sunlight.

"The Wizards have never been generous when they evaluated our efforts," Orantes said seriously, "so words of undiluted praise do not come naturally to my lips. But there was a feeling of truth to your speaking, as though each word carried its own weight."

Sentauris embraced each of them; Ghorm looked pained, then stared up at Squint's form as the Owl-being returned from scouting the river's far side. Of Whisper, there was no sign.

"I share in my colleague's wise words," Wylar said, "and to them, I add a small gift." He brought from a pouch a slight device that was shaped like a flower and formed from tin or tarnished silver. Unpolished, almost crude in its simplicity, the flower's shape held only three petals.

"Alas, I am no Tanu craftsman," Wylar continued, "but should you need to speak to me from a distance, only break off one of these petals and breathe my name onto it. After, we will enjoy a few moments of hurried conversation, even though we are separated by a score of leagues."

"I thank you both," she said, clasping the talisman, "I —"

— *!* — Again, from the north, but stronger now, came an echo of some vast power, filled with menace.

·)(·

The Great God Set stared up into the upper reaches of the Gangean Range, where his storm cover was faltering. It was time to launch their war and be gone. *We are well shielded.* His unspoken thoughts reached into the inner reaches of the mind of Mordred. *Tendrils, invisible, untraceable linkages to our kingdoms have been set in place. You need only call upon a force of arms, and then our war will begin.*

The mind of Mordred pulsed with dark energies. *First, a plague of Vorrs, beings long ago crafted by Haeglin to assail both humans and other predators of Alantéa. Fleet of foot, strong and cunning, with twice the mass of large wolves, let them now feed on human flesh...there, they are unleashed.*

Set signaled; a tendril of almost transparent smoke reached down into the mountain's heart, and beyond. *I have committed* masses *of armed humans to battle; these will bear an emblem of the section of Mount Evergrey as it becomes obscured by the Cloudland Plateau; thus, it will seem that these represent the force of Alantéa and the Truce. Do not let your creatures with four feet open war on my peoples.*

I will warn them. Again, Mordred pulsed with dark energies. *Uraks are the creation of my Brother in Darkness, Un-Maurag. They have the strength of lesser Trolls, so human warriors cannot withstand them. They are now discharged in warbands to roam the length and breadth of the League.... As I speak, they are crossing over into the Wizards' League.*

Chaos and destruction are coming to this 'League', whispered the mind of Set. *Over the last five cycles of the sun, I have harvested many Creatures of the Darkness. These now lie stunned and dormant, awaiting my will. One is dispatched against an obscure Tanu smith who stands astride an intersection of power. The others are released to forage in the south of Alantéa. Let them feast!*

These are more fell than any monstrosity I can bring forth, and the Creatures Indomitable are not likely to respect either badge or insignia. I will warn my followers. Again, Mordred pulsed with dark power. *In my last cast, I call down score upon score of my own creations: Carags, shapeshifters and fierce assassins. With Carags on the battlefield, none will know if he stands beside a faithful friend or hidden foe.*

As we agreed, we will withhold our last and most powerful force until the Wizards are smoked from the warrens of their fortresses. Only then will we unleash the Enchanters.

The dark essence that was Mordred grew swollen with laughter. *Now I embrace all these sinister devices! From the greatest distance, with only the slightest use of our own powers, we have ruined this once formidable thing, this 'League'!*

That is what it is like, to be a God.

Sentauris recoiled several times as though struck by invisible hands. Wylar and Orantes turned in every direction, calling down spells to shield them against a force that they could neither see nor sense. Ghorm darted around Sentauris, dagger in hand, crying out in fear and defiance. Then came silence, as Sentauris stared frozen faced to the south, beyond the Saugus, where the borders of the League lay.

In her vision a vast figure was forming, like huge Wraith, hunched, utterly dark and grim, ten times the height of the surrounding hills. It was Death the Winnower, Death the Gleaner, Death the Dark Harvester. As it strode south, one gigantic hand held a sickle, the other dragged an enormous black sack. With one step, this figure crossed the Saugus, sweeping all before it, lashing at the peoples of the League, sweeping away all their dreams, all their hopes — and their lives.

"Enough!" cried Sentauris. She swept the vision from her mind, then turned to Wylar and Orantes. "Call your peoples forth to battle, for Vorrs and Uraks and well-armed human tiers are flowing into your lands. War is upon you! And it will not be the partial war I once saw: The strength of powerful Gods is at work, with the might to change all future visions." She turned from them and raced to her gelding. As she mounted, Ghorm caught up with her and scrambled to his place just in front of her.

"Sentauris, wait," Orantes said, struggling for words that would halt the Seeress.

"If this 'Wild Time' is upon us," Wylar called to her, "then join us. Help us fight this war!"

Sentauris faced north: Tallus was in mortal danger; if he died, her link to the mercenary captains would be broken. "I will return to your League, bringing aid, or so I hope. We will meet again at — at Tuvan." *If we three survive,* her mind added. "But you are both in great danger! Guard each other's backs, and do not let your lack of battle magic lead you into folly! Avoid your foes and do not fight them in open battle! Tuvan calls for you! Farewell!" She turned and rode north in a fury.

·)(·

Wolves, as always, spilled back and forth across the border, ignoring the lines the League had set for itself. Tonight, they howled like mad things, almost as though they themselves were being hunted by some greater predator. The farmer sat in dim light, shaking his head: it was becoming worse than the village carnival out there, with wolves baying and the poor old milk cows battering at their paddock walls, mooing like creatures maddened by disease.

With great reluctance, the farmer shielded a lantern against the night wind, strapped on a notched and rusty short sword to his belt, and prepared to investigate.

"Da, Da, can I come too? I'll get the knife." The boy, with thirteen springs behind him, was nearing man's height, but he remained spindly, gawky, with bursts of energy followed swiftly by exhaustion.

"Take the dagger, boy, but keep it sheathed — last time you tripped and nearly stuck your poor old Da with it." Both now were weaponed. They pushed open the farmhouse door, the flame of the lantern flickering in spite of its shielding. The night's chill transformed the boy's scampering into a hunched, frozen scamper with teeth that chattered.

Again, the farmer shook his head. Wolf sounds were fading as though they had been driven into the hills, but the poor old cows were still in a panic. What could have driven them so wild? Walking over shadowy ground, he stumbled over something warmish dead and furry. He held the lantern closer: the wolf was dead, partly eaten, as though something had feasted on its stomach and lungs.

Time to draw weapons, lad, he wanted to call out.

But then Vorrs, destroyers of both wolves and humans, took each of them by their throats, and in a single heartbeat, they were left forever silent.

· ⦀ ·

"Ten score, twelve score, may all the Powers curse them, fifteen score. Let them all be laid in shallow graves, that makes a full tier." Sentauris alternately cursed and counted as the columns moved south beneath her. She stood, hidden, in deep woods, with all but her dark eyes shielded, watching as more than two well-armed tiers marched south: more than a thousand trained fighters. All the militias in the League might withstand the forces that passed before her — on a good day — if the militias were gathered in one place — and if properly led — and not too many fearful, untrained peasants broke ranks and fled.

The last riders passed. She hurled curses at their backs then began picking her way down to the horse track. Pity she had not the time to hunt down a few stragglers to find out which deity they served; they bore an emblem of a mountain's upper slopes, likely those of Mount Evergrey, but she could sense the presence of some jealous Dark God, looming in the recesses of their minds. More than likely, however, that Power had taken steps to shield itself from discovery — magic might bar them from speaking, or they might not even know their remote God's true name.

Let's see just which Power they pray to before they breathe the Dark Wind. In the meantime, they've held me back from Tallus. Tanu renegade, I am coming! Guard yourself carefully until I reach your side!

Sentauris reached the bottom of the slope and turned suddenly: she was being watched. Over on the far hillside, a tall figure stood watching her, with a faint smile on its face. It stood nearly twice her height, powerfully muscled, features perfect, almost sculpted, and on its feet were slight wings. As she watched, the figure turned from her, rose over the hillside on feet that fluttered, and vanished into a seam in the sky.

"Now what exactly was that?" Ghorm muttered, roused from his nausea.

"An Emissary of the Gods," she muttered thoughtfully. "Most of the Powers keep one great servant as a herald, messenger, or powerful envoy. The Wizards have discouraged their presence in the League. The fact that this one appears so fearlessly on League soil, tells me that the strongholds of the Wizards are washing away like sandcastles at high tide."

She turned and rode north again, struggling to recover lost time.

· ⅀ ·

Warfare had spilled over the League borders, but none of the roving bands had yet mounted an attack on Amalric, though it was one of the League's northernmost cities. Amalric had also attempted to become more formidable, raising stone walls on three sides, and a more temporary barrier of beams and earth constructed on the fourth. At night, the gate watch had been doubled to twelve armed sentries, sealing the city from the tides of prowlers and stalkers that roamed the countryside.

On this night, the gate watch was having more than usual difficulty with its screening tasks: seven well dressed, softly spoken young men stood outside the gates, claiming to be emissaries from Gravengate, part of a new order of Heralds.

"Come down, come down!" one called up to the watchers on the walls. "We have papers signed by the Wizards." Those forming the watch exchanged glances. Something seemed wrong, but it was a thing so vague that it was almost impossible to explain. Was it that the seven seemed so alike that they might be brothers to one another? Was it that none showed blemish, scar, or trace of imperfection? Or was it that the hairs on the guards' necks seemed to rise when staring down at the seven "Heralds?" In the end, because of their own confusion, and because of the lateness of the night, the gates creaked open, and the seven passed within.

In a nightmare flurry of fangs and talons, the Carags reduced the night watch to a pulpy dead mass. Moments later more than two score Carag Assassins, forty-five shapeshifters in total, passed into the sleeping city, whose residents then began to dream so fitfully.

·)((·

The Halls of Merlin at Sea's Edge were nestled against a shoulder of cliff that was solid rock and overlooked a curl of the estuary that led to the broad ocean. On quiet clear days, the ocean could be heard, pounding away at the sandy beaches that lay beyond the estuary, less than a half hour's walk from Merlin's dwelling place.

Sea's Edge was unlike Gravengate or Stone Mountain; at its core, it was a dwelling, and not a fortress, lacking the strong points that would form any natural defense. The Halls of Merlin were designed for study and for thought, defended almost casually by the force of magic that surrounded the dwelling of the great Wizard.

On this morning, Merlin stared out into a misty, grey shoreline that dripped moisture over the barnacles, mussels, and crabs that dwelt in places of damp quiet along the beaches of Sea's Edge. Part of Merlin's mind remained in a dream state, while a second portion activated a minor spell, one that caused a great sealed book in his tower study to fall open and arrange itself for the day's entry.

In this great leatherbound volume, Merlin continued to inscribe his history of the League. Some early entries in this volume had reflected the green of spring, or the yellow of summer, showing hope. Current entries were in the brown of fall, touched by the red blood of conflict:

> *In the one hundred and twenty-first year of the League, the Powers of the Mid-World finally moved openly against our peoples, voiding, or circumventing that portion of the Truce that once prevented them from joining together. Two Powers, at least, have planned their war against our League; the presence of Vorrs and Uraks and Carags shows that one of them is a Renegade Dark God of the Mid-World, a rebellious Power. Whether this being is Un-Maurag, or Haeglin, or Mordred is a question that I will one day answer. The second Greater*

God seems more subtle, and powerful, likely a powerful God of Alantéa, whose name may never be known, and whose main thrust has yet to be made.

It is not truly productive to speculate about the nature of these two adversaries, and yet my mind seems unable to restrain itself. Of the Renegades, Un-Maurag has the strongest sense of personal destiny and therefore seems unlikely to cooperate with any but other Renegades. Of the Great Dark Gods, Arioch seems so consistently distracted that it would be difficult for that Power to focus on a long, complex struggle. Quarezokziil seems content to soar on gigantic wings over the Gangean Range, hunting Stone Giants and Greater Trolls. None of the other Great Dark Gods can be ruled out.

Great grief it is for our peoples to learn war, but they must rise and defend themselves. I fear for them, particularly for our Adepts, who have not been weaponed or trained for the war that will be waged against them. However, it is also true that neither of our Adepts has shown a large degree of talent as they developed their own forces of magic.

In fairness, I must add that we, the Wizards, have treated our Adepts poorly, as though two unfavored progeny followed the departure of two beloved children. What has happened to Hektor and Antéus? We have searched and searched and found nothing. The role of the Seeress remains an unsolved mystery.

Still, against armed tiers and Vorrs and Uraks and Carags, the resistance of our peoples might have some chance of success, while against the Creatures of the Darkness, only here at Sea's Edge, and at Gravengate and Stone Mountain is there sufficient strength to counter these monstrosities. I will not name all the Creatures that have entered our League and now wreak such havoc on our peoples, but I will offer a count: two score less one were released to the south of Alantéa, and I must seek devices that will cause thirty-nine deaths among the otherwise immortal Creatures Indomitable.

·)(·

Brown shapes, all muscled fur, pounded through woodlands in the last light of day. Darkness was coming and the Adepts were far from shelter. In the heights above them, Squint called out a warning, but Wylar had taken note of the Vorrs in the forest behind them, as Orantes did seconds later. Bolts of force leaped from outstretched staffs, and two Vorrs tumbled, then lay still. Eight others vanished into the treeline but moved in parallel with the two riders, still hunting the Adepts.

Both their horses were panicking with the scent and sounds of Vorrs all around them. Hooves thundered down the muddy track, yet they were still unable to match the Vorrs' speed. As they rounded a slight curve, huge bestial shapes leaped out at them. Orantes was thrown heavily, but Wylar slipped from his saddle, calling down fire against the Vorrs. One creature leaped over the wall of flame, lunging for the throat of the fallen Orantes. But Whisper coiled his shadowy shape around the creature's eyes, and as the Vorr stumbled in sudden blindness, Wylar sent streams of force-bolts through its brown, powerfully muscled form, until it lay dead.

Their horses raced far from them, galloping south into the last red light of sunset. The remaining Vorrs regarded the two Adepts through walls of fire; then they turned cunning eyes that were streaked with red from the humans and began to lope after the doomed horses of the Adepts.

Orantes groaned and sat up, clutching his right ankle. "Broken, curse the stinking thing." Wylar called down his wall of flame and knelt beside the groaning Adept, examining the cracked bones of his right foot.

"My only good fortune," Orantes muttered between clenched teeth, "was that Sentauris was not with us, watching as I flopped from the saddle like a sack of dry and useless dung. Now, Wylar, listen to me: those things will return after dark — I read that in their eyes. You should take yourself to a place of safety. If those creatures come for me, I will kill many. But you should be far from here."

"Nonsense," Wylar said softly, then he turned and called up to Squint, "we need to be behind strong walls this night. Are there any nearby?" The Owl-being had been staring mournfully at the darkening roadway that had swallowed up both Vorrs and their prey; now Squint flapped wings with soft feathers skyward in search of shelter.

"As for your foot," Wylar continued, "first a healer's work...." Words came to his lips, and Orantes could feel in the middle of his pain how the bones began to knit and tighten. Then Wylar tore strips of cloth from his own cloak and used them to bind tighter the leather boot enclosing the ankle; and lastly, the Adept caused the mass of cloth and leather to stiffen into a solid, stronger mass.

Standing cautiously, Orantes was able to hobble, though he grimaced in pain.

"Certainly, I'm not fit to chase scantily clad Nymphs through enchanted glades." Orantes took more painful steps, leaning on his staff. "Though perhaps now I may escape becoming an enormous feast for a pack of Vorrs. Lead on! On to the next debacle! Disgrace, here we come!"

"Less noise, my wounded but unquenchable master," Whisper said softly, then added chilling words: "Vorrs may be gorging on horseflesh, but they are staring with interest in your direction. Other beings — creatures with two, not four feet — are also approaching from the north. Although I cannot name them, they seem of roughly equal charm to the Vorrs."

"Off the road, then," Wylar muttered, then hissed, "Squint!"

Guided by the Owl-being they passed through a stand of oaks that seemed late in budding, then over a newly sown field of oats. Darkness lay deep over the ground, though the sky still held some of the glow of dusk. Orantes alternately grumbled and joked about his hobbling journey, though he was careful to make all his comments in a hushed, difficult to hear voice.

The farmhouse Squint had found for them was constructed of strong beams sealed with mortar, yet it was somewhat forbidding, looming dark and lightless in the twilight. Its owners had sealed it well, no doubt hoping to come back one day should the Wizards prevail and peace return. If its former occupants had good fortune, likely they now sat beside bright campfires, somewhere within sight of Gravengate or Stone Mountain.

It took several of Orantes' spells of opening and revealing before the dwelling's door could be persuaded to yield. Once inside, Orantes slumped in a rocking chair, while his fellow Adept worked to seal the farmhouse, using both magic and planks of rough wood to block the door and shuttered windows. It was only after Wylar had completely sealed all points of entry that Orantes was allowed to call down soft lights. They rested then, but briefly, before exploring their refuge.

Late in the day, marauding packs of Vorrs again forced Sentauris from the open road and onto forest trails that wound and humped over broken ground. Exhaustion gripped her as she plodded beside her weary gelding, while Ghorm, one of the land's least hardy travelers, hovered at the edge of nausea. As fatigue deepened, the powerful Farsight of Sentauris guided her into a zone of safe quiet, and at the last light of day, she slept deeply, intending to rise again when a clear moonlight was destined to guide their path.

An hour later, she woke suddenly to a sense of mortal danger...she stumbled to her feet, then stared quickly in all directions.... *She herself was safe for the moment...but to the north, Tallus...the Tanu warleader was in the gravest peril — his mercenaries had fled, and Tallus was gathering greater powers to his side.... No, Tallus, flee! Do not confront this thing!*

And to the south lay her Adept friends...death was coming for them too... as they stumbled around in a folly of ignorance.... At least set a watch, you fools! Why else would you keep invisible or winged servants, except to warn you of danger!

· ⱊ ·

Wylar explored methodically, while Orantes rested with his broken foot raised. Even using only soft lighting, it was clear that the farmhouse had been abandoned in some haste: a table had been set for six and never cleared, while above them, bed sheets trailed from sleeping lofts. After examining the outside walls and the loft, Wylar stepped pace by pace across the breadth of the main room, tapping gently at a solid flooring with his staff.

"Ahh..." he murmured, reaching down, lifting an iron ring that opened the cellar's hatch. "Most unusual — one wonders about the previous inhabitants of this place." A stronger light flared from his staff: he peered down into an empty cellar formed of stout beams and poured stone. "What might they wish to conceal or keep safe? Were they an advance party of our foes? Or simply smugglers? Anyway, here's a bolt hole for us if we become hard pressed."

Squint shuddered: always ill at ease in close quarters, the thought of retreating into a damp and dark cellar filled him with dread. The Owl-being hopped over to the fireplace. Yes, its chimney was large enough: from its center, he could peer up into an overcast night sky where a somber moonglow struggled with darkish clouds. If he had to, he could escape, though the oily soot from the chimney might take months to clear from his feathers.

"So, we can crawl down when they come for us," Orantes murmured. "I suppose that's to the good. But what is to be done until they come? No food lies nearby to slake our hunger, nor wine to ease the soul's dark pains. But instead, we have a taletelling Shade named Whisper! Come, Familiar and companion, one of your fine tales, and no gloomy nonsense about some obscure and mournful Kingdom of Death. Something light, perhaps, say with Nymphs in an enchanted glade."

"Orantes the Obese lurched through an enchanted glade, seeking Nymphs," Whisper muttered in a monotone. "Of course, with the Gross One's bulk and lack of agility, and other failings too numerous to mention, the Nymphs skipped easily away from him."

"Come now," Orantes prompted, "a happy ending."

"Skipped easily away from him along an embankment where the Obese One's bulk caused a minor landslide. Down tumbled both Nymph and Madcap Magician; though at the bottom, the Addled Adept was able to turn and whisper sweet and completely useless nothings into the many ears of the Nymphs. The End."

Orantes chuckled deep in his throat. "And after, they all loved me forever because of my discreet charm. Beautifully told, with so much amazing detail. Whisper, I could almost smell the flowers in the glade, and hear the stones rattling down the cliff. You —"

Pounding, thudding sounds hammered at the door. Orantes stumbled to his feet, the Gift within him showing images of Vorrs racing, leaping, then battering at the door's wood. Makeshift panels were falling back from the entrance so that the strength of their magic alone held against the hurtling Vorrs.

Suddenly the assault on the door was broken off. Then to the door's left, the dark shape of a Vorr smashed against a shuttered and barred window. Both the window and its frame shattered in violence. With a second lunge, the Vorr was inside, attacking them. Again, bolts of force struck it down, while other bolts drove away Vorrs approaching the open window.

The Vorr pack seemed to retreat, conferring in a language formed from snarls. Then came silence followed by low guttural voices and snarling Vorrs. Wylar edged toward the broken window's frame with some caution; Orantes hobbled just a step behind him. Warily, the two peered out. Dark night was offset only by a dull moonglow, reducing all outside shapes to humps of shifting shadows.

More Vorrs had gathered outside, but they were joined by, almost overshadowed by, massive mailed dark creatures, beings that stood impassively, speaking in low guttural voices with snarling Vorrs.

"So here are the Uraks," Orantes whispered. "Truly those images shown to us by the Wizards did little justice to their size or their menace." Wylar shook his head, struggling to clear it. *Why are we, two trained Adepts, having such difficulty dealing with these powerful, but not highly intelligent foes? In truth, we were so very poorly prepared for this struggle... and now an open and brutal war is upon us.*

Uraks, each massing more than twice the bulk of a well-armed man, strode toward the shattered window. Each bore a spiked mace; their intention to do violence was clear. Force bolts from the Adepts' staffs leaped out at them. Uraks recoiled as though stung, but their armor turned aside the bolts' killing force.

"I've had just about enough," Orantes rumbled in a deep voice, "of these dimwitted dung lickers." His hand darted, reaching into dark shadows; with a *twist*, the hand gathered a black and jagged thing from the other side of darkness.

Orantes stumbled clubfooted to the opening and hurled his jagged weapon at the oncoming Uraks. Instant thunder blasted the air outside, flashing lightning that was streaked with black, and the walls of the farmhouse trembled. Three Uraks fell back dead, while a fourth stared mournfully at a stump that had once held its arm. Others pulled the dead and wounded away from the window and then they vanished into the night.

"Now, exactly where did you learn that?" Wylar asked.

"You have spent too much time with Merlin," Orantes muttered. "Balardi and Thorian are less disinclined to violent magic. Come, for what it's worth, I prefer to have this place sealed." Orantes called down more light, and the two began to brace all entrances with chairs, frames of bed, and one broad table with wood thick enough to turn aside at least the Vorrs. At every weak spot, they called down words of magic so that the air around their outer walls tingled to the touch, glistening with power.

Outside a conference of Vorrs and Uraks began again in low, dark mutterings, with each speaking a distinct language, though it was one that each of the other creatures seemed to understand. If Vorrs and Uraks had real intellects, they were discussing whether less dangerous prey could be found. *Leave us!* Wylar's mind shouted out. *Dinner at this inn will cost you your lives!* As Wylar listened, Orantes foraged in upper cupboards seeking remnants of food for his constant hunger. Only moldy oats and dry lentils, hard as rocks, had been left.

"Piffle," Orantes complained, "not even a starving rodent would touch this fare. Can't we find—" Pounding noises came from the wall behind him and Orantes danced, hobbling away from the sounds. More smashing sounds came from other walls: Uraks had surrounded the farmhouse and were battering through its beam and mortar with maces made with spiked iron.

Thud! Squint hunched down, trying to stop up his ears. Chunks of mortar began to fall free. *Bam!* Dust began to slip in folds through the air. *Smash!* Again, Vorrs were hurling themselves against wooden doors and window frames. Wylar looked pale, his lean features with his emerging beard filled with doubt.

"Should we go below?" he asked softly. "Or is that indeed, as I fear, a deathtrap?"

"In twenty minutes, nothing will be left but splinters and dust and trails of blood up here," Orantes grunted, stumbling to the cellar's hatch. "Come." Hammering sounds grew louder as though the thickness of the walls was gradually wearing down.

"Wait," Whisper said. "Release Squint. He should be our outside sentinel."

Wylar coughed dust. "Yes, of course. Squint, you will be much more useful to us outside rather than trapped here in some dark pit. Out you go." Relief followed by hesitation and doubt swept over the Owl-being. Was he deserting his companions in their time of need? Along with Ghorm, they were his only real friends. On the other hand, there was little he could do in this crumbling farmhouse. Reluctantly he hopped over layers of dust and splinters, seeking escape before the oval chimney itself collapsed.

A wild, unnatural shriek burst through the night air, a noise that echoed down the chimney's vault. Squint recoiled: that sound came from neither Vorr nor Urak — it was louder, deeper, and wilder. The pounding on the walls lessened then stopped completely. Seconds later, Vorrs cried aloud in an even greater frenzy. Uraks bellowed: guttural chants of war. Some larger being shrieked in a frenzy of rage — and hunger.

Squint fluttered, scrabbled with his talons over bricks that were covered in ash, gasping through clouds of soot, and then with a last effort, squeezed past the chimney's cinder-trap. He was out into the night, eyes still clouded by soot, though his ears were assaulted by wild cries of rage, torment, and the turmoil of death in battle.

Fifteen or more Vorrs were leaping at some huge creature — a monstrosity. More than a dozen Uraks battered the thing with spiked iron maces. Vorrs and Uraks surrounded the Creature, ripping, pounding, tearing at it, but strangely enough, they were being beaten back. Squint blinked and blinked, struggling to clear his eyes, trying to see more.

A Creature of the Darkness towered over both Vorrs and Uraks like a giant ghoul. Its massive head loomed over a hunched back, and its skeleton head showed mostly white bone, luminous under a pale moonglow, skin falling away from eye sockets and hollow cheeks, as though it was transforming itself beyond flesh. On its back clustered a mass of writhing things that formed a dark hump, while elongated arms with brown fur batted away Vorrs and Uraks with the backs of huge hands...except...now it clutched an Urak with both hands and tore the powerful creature in half. And it defended itself too with a force of magic: coils radiating a dull yellow reached from its humped back...a Vorr snarled, snapping at nothingness, then it choked, gasped, and stiffened in death, strangled by yellow coils.

Moment by moment Vorrs and Uraks were being forced to retreat; they backed in slow confusion, as though astonished to discover a creature with greater malice than their own. Vorrs pulled back ten paces, then twenty. Mailed Uraks backed, then backed again, Vorrs forming on their flanks as they retreated.

The Creature of the Darkness feinted, stepped forward once, then back, with its coils of dark yellow magic probing at the Urak's mail. Then, as Vorrs and Uraks slipped deeper into the overcast night, the Creature sat ponderously, rattling even the rooftop that held Squint. Perhaps a dozen Vorr and Urak carcasses lay strewn around the Creature; almost idly the monstrosity gathered a Vorr, ripped aside its brownish furry skin, and nibbled at the muscle of its foe.

Pah! It spat out the bitter flesh of the Vorr and began with greater urgency to tear the mail from a blackish skinned, powerful form. The Urak was hairless, with a dark skin, but hard with muscle, bone, and tendon. Again, the Creature bit, even more tentatively. Then it rose in anger, spitting out bitter flesh for a second time, and it hurled the Urak into a darkened field.

Turning back to the farmhouse, the Creature regarded the dwelling thoughtfully. It began to sniff, but ponderously, as though the remaining flesh of its nostrils could catch only the slightest trace of Wylar and Orantes. *Maker's Touch!* Squint thought. *It hungers for human flesh, and now only the Adepts are close by!* Squint perched frozen just behind the chimney's oval cone, wanting to call down a warning, but afraid to even flutter or to speak.

As the Creature approached, sniffing, the Owl-being recoiled from the rotting flesh peeling from the thing's death mask skull and neck. Huge, yellowed teeth were supported only by fragments of grey gums. In a few places new flesh seemed to be forming, but casually, as though an afterthought. And what was that thing on its back, that writhing, rippling dark mass?

Get away! Hide! Squint's mind called down to the Adepts.

Inside, Wylar and Orantes stood frozen, aware of the Creature's soft, sniffing approach, listening as huge hands probed clumsily at the door. Then with their full Adept's strength, they launched a torrent of magic at the Creature Indomitable, struggling to grip it with magic then bind it.

The Creature recoiled: its dinner was armed with power! Its own magic rose in might against the Adepts. The three swayed, locked in battle as

Wylar and Orantes called out spell words from clenched teeth, while on the Creature's hump, writhing things whispered dark words.

And if the Adepts could not completely restrain and bind the Creature, still the two combined were greater in power than the lone monstrosity, so that the thing was forced to break free. It pulled away, then shambled back, until it stood twenty human paces from the sealed entrance, breathing heavily, and staring balefully at the dwelling that housed its dinner.

Squint stood frozen, hiding behind the chimney. To watch the Creature was almost to see its thoughts forming: *Magic is one test, let us see you match my physical power — and my hunger!* As the thing took one swift step toward the Adepts, Squint called out a warning down the oval chimney, then took flight. Crashing, splintering sounds shook the night.

Wylar and Orantes hurled themselves away from the fragments of the shattered door, then scurried on hands and knees toward the cellar hatchway. Through the shattered front portal, one huge hand groped for them. Bolts of force were nothing more than insect bites to a Creature Indomitable, and so the two Adepts and Whisper spilled down the hatchway, pulled shut the cellar door, then called out sealing spells with lips that struggled to form words.

The Creature alternately groped, peered, groped, and roared with frustration. After a time, it cleared more of the wall around the door's frame so it could watch as its hands shoved aside the building's wreckage in search of the strangely vanished mammals. *They were gone!* It pounded down more walls. *Wait, though wait...it sniffed through clumsy, eroded, death's head nostrils, and sought them with its force of magic.... They were still nearby...down at another level, sealed by barriers that did not limit its sorcerous reach.... Tendrils, yellow, coiled and glowing reached down through the floor's stony surface.*

In the dark quiet beneath, yellow, glowing coils extended through the storeroom's ceiling. Whisper's shade body recoiled — those tentacles had the power to harm him! Wylar and Orantes backed, then chanted the words of a spell. Whips of flame sprouted from the ends of their staffs. Wylar leaped forward, lashing with fire at dark yellow tendrils. Orantes skipped forward with surprising agility, trying to slash the coils from their source.

Again, the Creature Indomitable pulled back, howling. Its pain was great, but its anger and its hunger were greater. It thrust aside more of the walls and pounded down on the floor with giant fists. The basement roof began crumbling; its hatchway portal came ajar then sprang open.

Through the open hatch, the monster thrust one huge hand. Orantes *reached* again for a fragment of power, but this time his hand faltered. Wylar dropped his staff and drew a lean, slightly curled blade. With both hands, he hewed at the monster's enormous, groping hand.

To Orantes' everlasting astonishment, the blade bit — and bit deeply. The Creature's hand jerked back, ripping the hatchway from its foundations. Outside the Creature danced a ground-shaking dance of pain and frustration, howling into the night.

Orantes raised his voice over the uproar outside. "That was most unmagicianlike," he said, pointing to Wylar's blade.

"Ah, but it is an enchanted blade," Wylar said, wiping the sweat of fear from his forehead. "Though only partially enchanted — I still have much to learn when transferring sorcerous energy to things unliving."

"Partially enchanted is enough." Orantes stood for a moment, listening as the Creature's tormented sounds diminished somewhat. "Now, seriously, what are we going to do? If this perverse and obsessive Creature lacks brilliance, it has more than enough power to crush us, and enjoy our dead bodies for a late dinner."

"We have never seen it fully, nor studied it," Wylar said taking a deep breath, "while Squint may have seen of this thing more than he ever wished. Perhaps Whisper can bring back Squint's observations or make his own judgments."

"I was created for such a task," Whisper said in his soft Shade's voice, and his shadowy form passed in dark ripples through the stone of the ceiling and into the night. Wylar and Orantes listened in silence as the Creature Indomitable stomped around the farm dwelling's perimeter, alternately battering walls, or pulling down remaining walls and roofs. Every few moments, a fragment of beam or a tide of rubble would tumble down the open hatchway. *It's only a matter of time,* Wylar thought, *before this thing discovers a weapon and uses it to club down this ceiling and transform two theoretically powerful Adepts into its red, pulpy dinner.*

But Whisper was gone only a few short moments, returning with something resembling excitement.

"Here is what your two Familiars think," Whisper said with unusual intensity. "All the Creatures of the Darkness are perverse monstrosities, with elements of several forms all jumbled together. This being is like a giant ghoul, with a head that is slowly disintegrating, losing flesh, becoming more of a skeleton. But on its back and shoulders, a new intelligence is forming, with dark, twisted things guiding much of the Creature's actions. Squint says, too, that not only is its skull flesh falling away, but there are pitted gaps where brain matter once told this monster what to do. Also, a stench of decay surrounds it, with matted, tangled fur of dark brown that may never have been washed."

Orantes made gagging noises. "I suppose that it's a privilege of monsters, that they need not be tidy or neat."

"Wait, now wait," Wylar muttered, gnawing on his upper lip. "We are saying that this thing has had two centers of control, its decaying brain, and a growing hump on its spine, and it seems as though power is migrating to this hump portion."

"And in this process," Orantes said, suddenly focused, "all its senses might be dulled, their abilities become less."

"It sees only a portion of what transpires," Whisper added. "It can only smell those things that are close, and its reach of magic would become most restricted."

"Ordinarily, an illusion would be easily turned aside," Orantes said thoughtfully, "it would be perceived and broken casually by the power of this being."

Wylar took a deep breath. "But in this case, a finely crafted illusion, one with many layers, might just save our weak and vulnerable hides."

The Creature of the Darkness stared out into the darkened field: what was that sound, the movements of more creatures bearing bitter flesh? Its tentacles lifted the tree it had toppled and planned to use to break apart the stone surface shielding its prey. The sound came again, tinkly, elusive, and distant.

Bleating sounds came louder — of warm, soft, tasty creatures, trapped or threatened. Smells swept toward it from surrounding fields, urgent, delightful smells of wet wool, and the warm droppings of delicious, defenseless beings. And now too, in a blur across the far fields, a herd of small white puffy things was moving so slowly. The Creature's stomach gave a great groan of expectation, and it cast aside its club: those tasty but magical humans could wait.

And so, the Creature Indomitable began an epic quest for a herd of insubstantial sheep that looked and smelled so tantalizing, but ultimately faded into white mists.

For the remaining hours of the night, Wylar and Orantes sealed their shelter with broken beams and reinforced them with magic. Some hours later, Vorrs investigated the ruined farmhouse, but briefly and fitfully, as though fearing the monster's return. At daybreak, the two Adepts and their

Familiars made their way back to the horse track that led to Tuvan. Their pace was slow, and they showed a caution worthy of mice passing through an alley filled with slumbering cats.

"Our adventures have not been as I expected," Orantes grumbled quietly. "I imagined that we would ride to the League's defense in chariots of fire." No one in their party had ever heard Orantes quite so subdued.

"My hopes and visions were not nearly as extravagant," Wylar replied, "though I never expected to partake in the buffoonery of last night. If you and I are to survive, my good friend, we must become much, much more dangerous."

· X ·

In the last hours before dawn, Sentauris felt the pulse of Tallus' life throb and wane, struggle, and falter, like some powerful but wounded creature, dying of thirst with a distant body of water barely visible in the distance. If she was exhausted, Ghorm was comatose. Her gelding stumbled along beside her, kept moving more by the distant, rank odors of Vorrs and Uraks than by loyalty or training.

A half hour before daybreak, she felt Tallus slip over life's edge into the darkness. His spirit seemed to rise, to regard Alantéa and the Mid-World of the Truce with only remote interest, then he was gone. *Tallus!* She called, but only a brief rush of wind answered, heralding the dawn.

They plodded on, with the sun rising bright and fearless in front of their weary eyes. Sentauris glanced right, staring into the surrounding hills. *Something, someone is standing beside Tallus, waiting for me. It is shielded from my Sight, and I can perceive nothing of its nature or intent, though it does not seem to seek my death.*

They passed from the roadway and began to climb. Wreaths of mist were slipping from the shoulders of surrounding hills. Bits and pieces of the fate of Tallus were slipping into her mind, but she set them aside: all that she ever wished to know of the Tanu's passing lay before her.

She began to recognize outcrops of rock that she had seen in her vision: reddish sandstone layers were blended with seams of false ore. Thirty paces further she found the first of the fallen Sidhe: skin brown, tinged by grey, hair with a yellow touched by sunlight, this Sidhe had taken an enormous wound to his head, and after, he had staggered, toppled then died. Beyond was a clump of three other, powerful Sidhe warriors, and then another dozen lay in solemn patterns of death around the monster's feet.

Death and disfigurement from the violence of battle obscured the Creature Indomitable's strange shape, but its size remained intact: Sentauris measured twenty-five half paces from its feet to its head. And just beside the monster's head, Tallus lay dead against a wall of rock. Had they the strength to turn the Creature, Sentauris knew they would discover the gleaming weapon forged by the Tanu smith buried in its chest.

As she wept, the air just to her right seemed to shimmer; from a pocket of nothingness, an Elf-Mage slipped through. His hair was albino white, and with ageless features, he seemed less grim and distant than many of the Kindreds.

"Forgive me for shielding myself," said the Elf-Mage. "I feared the approach of Carags with Adept powers who can transform themselves almost completely into beings I would never wish to meet. Though after I saw your sorrow, I judged that no Carag-Mage would ever be able to weep real tears.

"I am Mír, author of this night's disaster. Tallus sought me in the aftermath of your foretelling, and I said 'Ah, but we will waylay this night stalker — you with your Tanu strength newly weaponed, together with my force of sorcery, together with a force of dauntless Sidhe knights, we would stand against any power short of a God!' Behold my folly! All are dead except for me, though I did not hide, I sought to die. I alone was spared, but to what end, to what purpose?"

"I did not foresee he force that Tallus and I envisioned," Sentauris said softly, "and you planned well against the force Tallus, as I envisioned. The power of a Great God is at work with the strength to transform all the visions of my Farsight. What am I to do now? My sight brought me images of a journey south, guiding mercenary captains to the defense of my peoples, and now I must journey to besieged Tuvan alone, with all my Seer's Sight blinded by dark mists."

"Perhaps this is the sole reason I was spared," Mír said, his Elf-Mage eyes staring without blinking into the bright sun of early morning. "Have I been touched by the distant hand of the Maker? No one on this side of life will ever know. On your behalf seven of the mercenary captains most trusted by Tallus have been summoned to a place just outside the borders of your League. You must speak to them there. All the wealth secured by Tallus is bequeathed to you. As well, my hidden allies among the Kindreds will supply you with any additional gold or weapons you might require.

"As for myself, many consider me nothing more than a hotheaded stripling, yet the Elf-Lord Voll is among my forebears, and for that reason, more than a few will heed me. I cannot become an open ally to your League. Yet the Kindreds — Elves, Tanu and Sidhe — have been attacked and waylaid by Dark Powers and their servants over thousands of years. We have chosen not to respond, not to defend ourselves only. Now I declare a merciless and relentless war on all those who have conspired against the Kindreds. Let Uraks and Vorrs and Carags and Creatures of the Darkness beware: death is coming for them from Elves, from Tanu, and from Sidhe!"

Sentauris knelt down and touched the fallen Tanu smith. *Tallus, harken to me from the other side of life. Tallus, they will never make of your grave a shrine, nor commit your features forever within statues formed of white marble. But Tallus, on the day that you stand before the Maker, He will tell all his servants how you delivered his people.*

Was that the slightest of smiles forming on the face of Tallus, or was it only his dark Tanu features tightening in death?

Chapter Four

The League and its Defenders

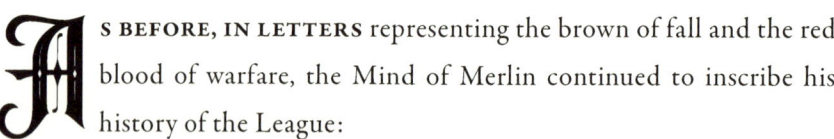S BEFORE, IN LETTERS representing the brown of fall and the red blood of warfare, the Mind of Merlin continued to inscribe his history of the League:

I must amend my previous count concerning the Creatures of the Darkness: an even two score monstrosities were unleashed upon us, confirming that the hidden Power governing this assault retains a powerful, well-organized mind with considerable attention to detail. I therefore restate my previous conclusion that the major thrust of his assault is yet to come.

Nevertheless, of the forty Creatures of the Darkness launched against us, one of the most powerful of these Creatures has been destroyed, though at considerable cost: Tallus, a self-styled "Tanu Renegade" perished in battle with this Creature Indomitable, and also swept into the darkness was a cadre of Sidhe warriors, who are among the most powerful and deadly military forces in Alantéa the Forerunner. This Creature was deliberately focused upon the Tanu, to sever his connection both with the Seeress Sentauris and with mercenary captains who served him and with the Kindreds. I know not at this time whether those potential alliances have been destroyed, for the Seeress moves beyond my Sight, proving, as always, a force incalculable.

To make this record complete, I must also note that our Adepts have responded to their challenges with more resourcefulness than I anticipated, though their ultimate survival remains considerably less than likely.

Here I must pause, for as I inscribe this record, distant events occur that must later pass into this journal. Balardi marshals his strength, preparing to assail by sorcery a Creature of the Darkness, one that has lingered just beyond that Wizard's reach.

· ҈ ·

In the five days and nights since the opening of war against the Wizards' League, Balardi had neither slept nor eaten, having summoned reserves of magic to maintain his awareness. He continued to pace and murmur, back and forth before his viewing screen, calling upon distant events to reveal themselves.

He watched as Amalric endured an unrelenting nightmare: murderous shapeshifting Carags slew dozens each night, with none of the townspeople knowing whether they lay with a loved one or a deadly hidden Carag monstrosity. Tuvan was held only because of the Uraks' lack of siege breaking ability, but the well-armed human tiers of their foes were gathering to the city and Tuvan seemed doomed. And, as always, images flickered through his viewing screen of the mighty and perversely formed Creatures of the Darkness, destroying towns and villages, pursuing, and consuming his people and their flocks.

Frustration surged over him; in response, the images from his viewing screen blurred into a grey nothingness. *Calm now calm.* Balardi closed his eyes, forcing a soft quiet into his mind, imagining still waters bathed in bright moonlight. From a distance he could hear distant sounds as work on Gravengate progressed: faint tapping sounds as though miners in some remote cavern probed at seams of soft metal.

As his mind cleared, the images on his viewing screen reformed. One of the Creatures of the Darkness had sauntered closer, less than a score of leagues from Gravengate — almost within his reach. Balardi summoned the image of the Creature Indomitable, watching as the thing pursued and devoured livestock, returning always to a village depot where grain had been stored in silos, and animals remained penned in broad fields, awaiting the green surges of spring. All the surviving humans had long since fled, but bullocks, cows, calves, horses, and sheep were consumed one by one in an epic of animal terror that had endured now for more than four days.

All this Balardi watched as though from a remote height, in which silos and barns seemed no larger than toys. At a whisper, his image lowered, bringing slowly into focus the Creature Indomitable that had terrorized his people.

This monstrosity was as huge as an ancient Dragon, and ugly beyond demented and fearful dreams: its form seemed mostly that of a dark black spider with spikes of even darker hair jutting from its many legs. All three of its heads were busy consuming a bound and dying bullock: one head sucked greedily at the beast's blood, while a second consumed flesh, and a third, dripping poison from pulsing jaws, used its magic to draw the life force from the dying beast.

And the misshapen Creature was swollen, bloated from its orgy of consumption.

Balardi could feel his own hot breath rise and fall, with the tension of sorcerous energies building all around him, prepared to act on the Wizard's anger.

Once more I must focus, to attempt again the use of a force of magic that reaches over great distances. Maker! Lend me the skill of Nablus the Binder of Creatures Indomitable!

Energies surged to the Wizard, gathering to him from the heights and depths, and from the many dimensional corridors surrounding Alantéa the Forerunner. With a *Shout of Sorcerous Energies*, he projected all his power across many leagues, eyes locked on the figure of the monster shown on his viewing screen.

As the succulent soft and warm bullock yielded the last of its life force, it stiffened, though it was bound so tightly that it could only quiver. The Creature Indomitable pulled back, exhaling satisfaction. And there were so many more beings, some bleating piteously, while others foraged stupidly in the farthest corners of their pen: a vast feast!

Faint warning signals reached its mind, and the Creature became suddenly alert. Portions of its many eyes scanned the horizon: a shadowy, fluttering turbulence was surging downward. A strength of sorcery had been launched against it, and the Creature's own magic was aroused for battle.

Whirlwinds of thickened air smashed at its spider's shape, and the Creature was hurled back. Coils of unseen magic embraced its dark spider tentacles, while the air seemed filled with flails of metal that lashed at its own force of magic. The air grew bitter with the stench of unbreathable, harsh vapors. A storm tide of sorcerous energy assailed it, creating tightness...pain...death....

With a great soundless cry of rage, the Creature Indomitable burst its bonds, then snarled defiance at its unseen foe.

In Gravengate, the violence of Balardi's anger shattered his viewing screen into ten thousand fragments.

· ☽ ·

As always, entering an abandoned temple involved a measure of risk. Any Power of the Mid-World might suddenly return to its former dwelling and decide to inflict vengeance on the temple's intruders. Sentauris entered first, calling out her devotion to that absent deity. Her calls were met by silence. Neither altars nor ornaments remained; only stone walls and the remnants of a vaulted roof were left, ancient, crumbling things that now sprouted scraggly ferns and the nests of emerald jays.

The seven Captains who followed Sentauris inside were all mercenary leaders summoned by Tallus. Silently, Sentauris identified them as they passed within the mostly ruined temple: Kura, broad shouldered and strong in the full power of his late youth, but with a certain remoteness to his eyes; Farad, just short of two score years, thoughtful, dark, tall and spare; Jabir, with fair hair, but several scars on this face, a seafarer, with a long stint at piracy; Gallandus, with grey hair, somewhat wide of girth, with age just beginning to slow his capability with a sword; Ptylos, the youngest, who seemed bland, but he was a master in dealing with sieges; Carlan, the oldest, almost an elder statesman whose trimmed hair was white as fresh snow; and lastly, Sardonicus, whom Sentauris trusted least because of his youth, his sharp wit, and his darting, wary eyes.

All seven found seats on blocks of stone or grey, weathered wood. Sentauris alone stood in front of them, struggling to brush aside the weariness of several days and nights of long travel. Above her, swallows and emerald jays swooped through the temple's upper reaches, while soft winds stirred the new springtime growth of emerging ferns. She *reached* for

Ghorm and found him, as before, safely hidden while sleeping a healing sleep, recovering from their rough passage to the grave of the Tanu smith.

"Tallus has called us to this place," she began, speaking quietly. "I know not whether our Tanu leader has been drawn into the Long Sleep, or to the Temple of Waiting, or whether he dreams in some distant place, waiting for the Maker's Return. I do know that Tallus was a friend for each of us, and he would not summon us here if it would cause our brief lives to end early, or if our venture would not weigh down your treasure chests with gold."

"Seeress," Kura said quietly, "of wealth I have no doubt, but of your people's chances in this war, to me, they come to nothing."

"They are far greater than 'nothing'," Sentauris replied. "If the chances of our League do not look promising, still the League has hidden resources; and some of you may be among those assets."

Sardonicus shrugged. "Win or lose, lose or win, all that is never critical. How many of us have fought for lost causes and still gained gold? The trick, of course, is to survive the last battle to dine and dice and sip wine, then play at war again. So, survival, not victory is the object, and therein lies my difficulty. Seeress, say that we muster two tiers, a full thousand, then march south. We would be met in open battle: Uraks would smash our front ranks, Vorrs would consume our flanks, while humans armed with longbows would destroy any reserves that remained. We would be crushed like a mass of drunken doodlebugs."

"I do not wish your people to fight," Sentauris said evenly, "but rather to train. We will march with a half of a tier. We *will* do battle at Tuvan, I see that, but after, your people will be organizing, drilling — and devising. A new form of war will now be created, and all your resourceful talents will be employed."

Gallandus had been staring into the far reaches of the vaulted ceiling, watching as patterns of sunlight spilled over slender ferns sprouting in the broken roof. "You speak with a sense of foretelling, that some of us at least will travel at your side." He turned to stare at Sentauris face to face. "It is said that you foretold the death of Tallus, or at least his time of danger. What do you see, Seeress, if you peer into the futures of the seven captains that sit before you?"

Sentauris drew a deep breath. "You would truly ask this of me, to know of your own fates beforehand?" Some hesitated, but in the end, all nodded in agreement. Sentauris then sat, clearing her mind. Her eyes peered into an infinite distance, struggling to capture ten thousand chances in the future into one likely frame of destiny. All sights and sounds around her seemed to fade, and her mind began to merge with the broad banks of sunlight that brought warmth and radiance to Alantéa the Forerunner.

After a time, she heard herself saying, in a small, remote voice, "Only three captains will join me as we journey to Tuvan the Besieged. Of these, three may die, or two may die, or one may die, or none may die...." The remote and distant voice grew suddenly more urgent. "Kura! Death stalks Kura! Let him beware!" Sentauris blinked, then shuddered, as her vision blurred then passed.

Kura was on his feet, glancing warily about him. "If Tallus was unable to listen," he muttered, "I am wise enough to fear death. Seeress, I confess my affection for this enterprise was faint before, and now it has completely vanished. I will leave you to plan with those joining you. Farewell."

"Nor am I one of the three bound for Tuvan," Jabir added, rising. "May all the benign Powers favor your enterprise, Seeress. I believe that all of those here will agree never to take up arms against you, in this war or others."

"That is the least I can do," Ptylos said, also rising, "for I cannot commit my people to this unequal struggle. Maker's Grace to you, Seeress." Sentauris struggled to hide her unhappiness, for the siege craft of Ptylos was badly needed for the defense of Tuvan. Despite her disappointment, the abrupt decisions made by the three captains came as no surprise to her: as mercenaries exposed to constant warfare, where life and death danced so closely, so intimately, they were forced to choose swiftly.

"Do not leave, not just yet," Sentauris said, and she drew from her traveling cloak a pouch made from soft cloth. Within were seven small pieces fashioned by the Tanu smith: lockets, rings, armbands, each graced with delicate gemstones, or one larger jewel. "You must choose among yourselves, for Tallus is not here to assign to you your gifts." The seven captains picked among the Tanu's possession with the caution of small children somewhat anxious not to appear too greedy. Kura chose quickly and was gone. Others selected a piece, and if it was not the one each most desired, still it was something to be set aside and contemplated when thinking of Tallus.

Jabir departed as did Ptylos a moment later, each with some reluctance, as though realizing that they were passing from the legacy of Tallus and the further adventures of Sentauris.

Four were left: Carlan, Farad, Gallandus, and Sardonicus. They sat in the ruined temple, speaking in soft tones about the marshaling of their forces and payments for their service. From time to time, each of the four glanced cautiously at one another, as though speculating which of them would next depart, leaving only the three foreseen by Sentauris.

Carlan took a deep breath, then cleared his throat. "Seeress, there is one, uncomfortable matter, that I, as eldest here, will raise on behalf of the Captains —"

"You wished," Sentauris interrupted, "to ask about my uncle Vlasoff, who has completely retired. His wounds remain great, and even if he healed slowly, he will never return to the field. Even if he were younger and untouched by magic, he would be the wrong person to lead this enterprise — we need an alliance of captains, not a warlord. I will lead, because of my Farsight, including the fact that I knew that you would ask about Vlasoff."

Gallandus laughed softly, then said, "Tell us more of your vision, Seeress. You mention a half of a tier, say less than three hundred men-at-arms. They will be mounted to move swiftly toward Tuvan, but do they carry weapons fit for a siege? What are their strengths of bow and spear?"

"You and others must determine some of these things; my Sight seldom sees enough detail that I can foretell the color of your garb...." Was there an itch, a touch of distant danger? She reached for Ghorm, but her Familiar still slept. "It is wise to understand the limits of my Seer's Sight. I foresaw danger for Tallus; an entity, hidden but strong, was sent against the Tanu; he responded by marshaling a force that would overwhelm that first Sending. But the Power that would destroy my people...."

She trailed off — hints of danger were growing stronger. "That Power unleashed a Creature of the Darkness, a thing more powerful than my original vision, and Tallus was destroyed, though...."

"Arm yourselves!" She leaped up, sword in hand. Shadows shifted beside the temple's gates, and through the entrance Kura staggered, both hands clutching a chest that streamed blood.

"The Gods..." Kura croaked and stumbled toward them. "The Gods have forsaken you, they —"

"No!" Sentauris cried. "This is not Kura! It —" With a shapeshifter's blurring speed, Kura's figure hurled a dagger at Sentauris then leaped after it.

Sentauris let the dagger shatter against her metal corselet, then slipped forward, slashing at the Carag's body. Her blade bit deeply as did three others, and the thing fell twitching and writhing until Gallandus hewed its head from its neck, and finally, it stilled. The strange gift of the corselet to Sentauris had finally proved its worth.

In death, the Carag grew pale, translucent, its skull shaped like some ancient beast's, with a blunt, hyena-like snout. Gallandus, always fastidious, looked for a cloth on which to wipe his blade. Carlan stood, his own sword only partly drawn, with a puzzled expression frozen on his face.

"So, this is the end," Carlan muttered, shaking. He turned away from them and sheathed his sword. "It's time for me to retire. Even five years ago I'd have nicked the thing, at least. Ten years ago, my blade would have been among the first. Now I must bid you farewell, and your numbers are reduced to the three captains foretold in the vision of the Seeress."

"Ah, these 'visions,'" Sardonicus murmured, turning the translucent body over with a booted foot. "Each of us assumed that Kura was endangered should he join us on our journey south — 'Death stalks Kura!' you cried, or something like that. In truth, this thing was on Kura's trail from the beginning, then it slew him and, after, came seeking the life of Sentauris. How interesting, Seeress, what you are able to see, and what remains hidden from you."

· ☽ ·

It wasn't just the bright light of noon, or his empty stomach, or the fact that his wings ached that made Squint so annoyed with the Adepts. *I'm a night flyer, a forest creature,* he wanted to call down to them. *If you wanted some farsighted being to soar over broad fields, you should have hired a hawk to be your familiar!*

Grumbling wasn't working, it just made him more tired. And anyway, the Uraks seemed to have scurried off. Squint circled one last time over the roadway leading to Tuvan, then floated slowly downward, back to the Adepts.

"Your road is clear for the moment," the Owl-being said, staring unhappily at the two Adepts, who lay slumped against tree trunks, carelessly, like two hungover vagrants. "The Uraks are probably at Tuvan as we speak — they were traveling in that direction, moving at about three times your speed."

"Faster than this swift Magician?" Orantes scoffed. "They must have winged feet." Orantes healed hour by hour and could now move at three-quarters speed, but his normal pace was slow, punctuated by frequent rest stops and other digressions. Still, at their present speed, they might reach Tuvan by nightfall.

"Come, another stretch along the road," Wylar said, pulling Orantes to his feet, "or as you so eloquently phrased it before, 'another light footed gambol over the enchanted passageways of the League.'"

Orantes put weight on his foot, gingerly. "Fornicating gambol, I just —" A chill struck all four of them as a broad shadow passed overhead. Each Adept whispered similar sorcerous words in hushed tones; their forms then seemed to blend with the tree trunks, and with the ground, while their new shapes exuded the earthly scents of springtime in Alantéa. By these methods, they had survived the last three days — by concealing themselves rather than confronting their foes.

Only Whisper was free to turn and watch as high above them a misshapen Creature Indomitable adjusted its huge, dark wings and then began to glide effortlessly south and east, heading toward the fortress of Thorian at Stone Mountain. After its passage, Orantes and Wylar brushed aside the illusions that shielded them and stood staring at the Creature's dark wings as it passed into the distance.

"Sooner or later," Whisper said in his soft Shade's voice, "the Wizards must confront these monstrosities. Who can guess at the outcome of those battles?"

·)X(·

Balardi had slept his first deep sleep in many days; he woke refreshed and lay listening to the muffled sounds of distant stonework as both inner and outer walls inched slowly higher with every passing day. *Tap, tap, clump, clump, tap, tap,* came the sounds of work on the inner keep. Many years ago, he had sworn a vow to Merlin that he would not be drawn from Gravengate, but now he longed to complete the great fortress, then leave it. If he were freed, he might confront the monstrosity that that spread ruin at the borders of his power and complete its destruction....

"Stop!" he called out — and the enchanted portion of his mind that governed such speculation brought his reverie to a halt. Another portion of his mind signaled, and kitchen staff were stirred from their torpor into a frenzy of preparation. The resulting overly elaborate meal was also overdone, but Balardi barely noticed. The Wizard ate standing beside a parapet watching as the morning shift toiled on the southernmost walls. Balardi's mouth worked mechanically, while his powerfully enchanted intellect reviewed his own mastery of magic.

The Gods — Powers of the Mid-World — in all respects dwarfed the Wizards and their League. They had lived from the beginning of Earth's Magic. They were born into the sorcerous energies that powered both the Ancient Wars and the Mid-World of the Truce that followed. But in every respect, the three Wizards, working together, had begun to replicate portions of the Gods' work. In so many instances, it was worth asking: if I were a God, how might this problem be approached?

Balardi turned to face the rising sun. The people of Gravengate remained untouched by war, and throughout the great Plain, banks of mist were rising over fields and vineyards as the sun's rays dissolved the morning dew.

The Gods and their powers. First, any God could project itself through an enchanted Portal and be transported to wherever that Power wished. Forming a tunnel like an oval cone through shrouds of nothingness, Portal Magic transcended space and distance. The Wizards had acquired a partial understanding of this magic, but their progress remained hidden from the Gods. Also, a Portal with low strength could be shattered by a greater force. And so: no Portal.

Secondly, the Gods could create or invoke a Sending. These Sendings might be formed from a lesser Power, some mightily armed Emissary of the Gods — or a construct of magic. A steady tide of these creations had been launched against his own domain and against Stone Mountain and Sea's Edge. He was not patient enough to consider the nature of these constructs for more than a few seconds, but Thorian had examined the Gods' Sendings in some detail, as had Merlin; and they had transferred this knowledge to him. So, he would attempt a new thing, he would create his own great Sending, a creation of magic that would go forth to do battle with the Creature Indomitable that was ravaging his people.

Balardi left the sunlit outer walls of Gravengate. As he passed through the inner portions of his fortress, workers fell silent or slipped into the shadows, wary of the Wizard in his time of strife. Guards and sub-tier leaders saluted; Balardi paid attention neither to the wary or to the alert.

He swept into his place of power, dark cloak fluttering, outer doors slamming shut behind him; then he stood for a moment, marshaling his thoughts. This chamber was among the largest in his combined fortress and castle of Gravengate; this room was circular, fashioned all of stone, with a ceiling shaped like a dome. At its highest point, the Wizard might grow ten times his own height and still stand freely.

With a *whisper*, Balardi caused the upper windows to cloud, and his chamber darkened. Other murmured words sealed his work from the many prying eyes of the Mid-World. The air was beginning to flutter as lesser dominions, spirits, and other partial intelligences began to gather to the Wizard. Some he called upon to depart, while others were instructed to hold themselves ready just beyond the dome's outer walls. He took a deep breath, senses heightening: somehow, as with all his strongest forces of sorcery, the air was filling slowly with the essence of almonds, and just at the edge of his hearing remote laughter echoed, as though the Gods mocked his presumption.

In low, rumbling tones, the Wizard began to chant a summoning spell that reached deeply into the forces surrounding the Mid-World of the Truce. Elementals of Air were called forth; ripples of sky blue shimmered through the chamber, accompanied by sounds of rushing wind. Elementals of Earth were summoned next, slow moving, deep brown, with low, groaning sounds; then Elementals of Fire brought red pillars of flame that crackled and shot sparks through the chamber's interior. Lastly, Elementals of Water appeared, grey, like the sea before dawn, moving through the chamber with the motions of waves, accompanied by the remote crashing sounds of a distant shoreline.

Balardi raised his voice over the ensuing tumult. Five each of the mightiest Elementals of Air, Fire, Earth, and Water were chosen; others were set free from the chamber with a sweep of his hand. More words of power flowed from the Wizard's lips. Twenty Elementals were bound together, woven once, then interlaced again, until they whirled before the Wizard, spinning in a whirlwind with many hues. The chamber became silent, except for low humming sounds created by constrained, but still restless creatures.

Balardi wiped his forehead with a fold of his cloak and paused to regard his creation. The force he had summoned was several times stronger than any bestial creature of Alantéa, but at present the vortex held only wild power with Elemental beings that would either unbind themselves or swiftly lose purpose.

He began chanting once again in even deeper tones, calling forth lesser Dominions, beings of a more transparent substance, but with greater intellects than the Elementals. Strands of subtle magic began to weave themselves into the rainbow whirlwind and its spinning motions slowed.

For a second time, the Wizard paused to wipe his brow. The Sending now had power and some purpose, yet it still lacked a solid shape. From that portion of his mind that dealt each day with enchanted dreams, Balardi called forth images attended by a *Shape*. A blue wisp formed on his brow like an enchanted butterfly. As it lifted from his forehead, the Wizard sent it fluttering toward the vortex with a single puff of breath.

A turmoil of contending magics shuddered over the spinning whirlwind and its shape blurred, shook, became whirling blue cloud matter, then changed one last time.

Before the Wizard stood an enormous, winged Griffin, a creature radiating blue light. Its head was shaped like an eagle's, while its powerfully winged body seemed mostly like that of a lion, though as a construct of magic it was several times larger than those beings. And it was wild, ungovernable. The construct cried aloud, then its beaked head darted down, pecking at the Wizard's form.

Balardi stepped back on feet of quicksilver; in the same motion, he drew dust from a pouch in his cloak and cast it before the construct's eyes. The Griffin drew back, blinking, bemused.

Again, the Wizard began to chant, now in softer tones, completing the last elements of his enchantment. For all the Familiars and spies of the Mid-World, spells had been crafted that bestowed beast creatures with intellect, so that they might speak and reason as humans. Three times Balardi called upon this sorcery: the first for wisdom, the second for strength of will, and the third to endow his creation with a force of magic.

And after, as the Blue Griffin stared down at Balardi, its eyes were filled with intelligence and purpose; though still, it did not speak.

"Behold your foe," Balardi called up to his creation, and he caused an illusion of the Creature Indomitable to appear before the Griffin; the spiderlike shape of the monstrosity was dark black, bloated from its prolonged feasting, and each of its three jaws dripped with venom.

"Other servants wait beyond these walls," Balardi continued. "They will guide you to your foe. Only destroy this one Creature of the Darkness and the being you have become will be released to find its natural place and pleasure in the Mid-World." The winged Griffin stared about as though committing to memory the hall of its birth, then it launched itself upward, bursting through the ceiling's stonework and out into the broad light of day.

As it rose into the upper air, ethereal beings gathered around the Griffin and began to guide it north, some singing praises for the construct's power and beauty, while others whispered entreaties for the Griffin to join them in forging new places of power in the Mid-World of the Truce. Balardi's Sending said nothing; but as it sensed the direction of its foe, its enchanted wings beat more swiftly, so that its entourage was left trailing in its wake as the Griffin hurtled through bright, cloudless skies.

· X ·

The Creature Indomitable stared at the ram's remains with diminishing satisfaction. All that remained of this warm-blooded creature was bone, a skull with horns, and wool seeped in drying blood. Lately, the monster had begun to yearn again for the warm bloods that walked on two feet: the force within them was so much stronger, their shrieks so much louder, their anguish so much greater as they struggled, then were slowly consumed. In pursuit of the two foots, though, it would need to become agile once again, reduce its bulk. A short sleep of hibernation was called for, and so the Creature Indomitable shifted ponderously toward the largest of the adjoining storage buildings where it could rest easily amidst mounds of stored vegetation.

But wait. Its many eye facets were warning of movement in the upper air. Its own magic was roused by the approach of some force of power. More swiftly now it scuttled into the sloping roof of the building then turned to peer out.

Down came a flying creature, radiating blue, both eyes staring fearlessly into the Creature's own multiple vision centers. The Griffin's form was larger than its own spidery shape, and it was symmetrical, perfect in every degree, and it seemed to glitter. But this being was a false creation and no Child of Dragons!

With anger that proved uncontrollable, the spider shaped Creature surged out at the Griffin, each of its three heads dripping venom. Griffin wings rose, and it descended on the monster, talons ripping at the swollen form, beak pecking at clusters of eyes. Spider mouths bit, passing venom.

Creature and Construct backed from each other. Elementals of Fire rose within the Griffin, and the venom burned away. The spider shaped Creature grimaced; and fluids seeping from its pulsing body became dry, sealing its wounds.

Torrents of enchanted webbing spewed from the Creature, coiling about the Griffin; Elementals of Earth rose in might, bursting the bonds. An Arctic chill was cast over the Creature by Elementals of Air; the Creature Indomitable shrugged, and the frost surrounding it boiled away.

Magic was raised against magic, force against force, will against rage, scuttling speed against darting talons. And so, the two beings fought through the long afternoon. Twice the Creature backed from the Griffin, inviting each to withdraw, but the Sending would not give quarter.

Three times the two beings closed with one another, the Creature seeking with venom and webbing to destroy its adversary, and three times the Griffin rose with heavy beating wings to batter the Creature against surrounding buildings or to rake the dark clutching shape against a nearby stand of trees.

Little by little, the sights and sounds of conflict drew humans from the adjoining farms and villages. Bells tolled, balefires blazed, heralds who had appointed themselves brought word that some power had at last risen in defense of the League. Slowly, in clusters of five and ten, the villagers gathered to the conflict, calling out in triumph as the Griffin struck some blow, or cried out in fear as the Creature Indomitable cast an enchantment, or in awe as the blue of the Griffin and the black of the Creature rose above them in flight, battling against a horizon that was beginning to be touched by red.

At sunset, many of the villagers scurried back toward their homes, while others built small watchfires against the chill of darkness, then listened to the sounds of struggle that rose and fell during the long night. Groaning sounds rumbled through the still air, while lights from sorcerous energies seared the night. Still later came an interlude of dark quiet, when the villagers huddled together, whispering in fear and wonder.

At daybreak, the villagers moved slowly closer: only muffled rasping sounds had been heard during the last hours of darkness, and curiosity was slowly overcoming their fears. Amid the wreckage of farm buildings, they found Creature and Construct locked in a deathly embrace, each with no more remaining strength than to clutch at the other with silent desperation. Both of the Griffin's wings had been shattered. Three of the Elementals of Earth had been consumed by venom, while two of the Elementals of Water had passed their poisoned substances into the ground and were no more. With their passage, the Griffin had become a translucent, sky-blue.

As for the Creature of the Darkness, several of its legs had been severed, one of its heads was smashed to pulp, while a second head seemed battered into stupefaction. And still, each being fought through the sunrise, unable to think, unable to plan, able only to clutch one with all their remaining strength, gasping for breath, unaware that so many smaller beings had gathered only a few hundred paces from their contest.

In the end, the Creature of the Darkness had the mastery, for it was a Child of Dragons, greater than any Wizard's artifice, and if it was not among the most powerful of the Creatures Indomitable, neither was it among the lesser.

In its passing, the Griffin stilled, grew ever more transparent, as slowly its component spirits slipped from its Construct's doomed form. It spoke then, one last gift of speech: "I regret only that I was not greater." The Griffin spoke in tones that were completely soft, and then as all else faded into nothingness, the butterfly thought that had come from the Wizard's mind flapped blue wings and rose skyward into a red and gold sunrise.

The Creature of the Darkness that bore the likeness of a spider toppled onto its side, completely spent. Barely alive, no longer indomitable, it could only force shallow breaths into its body; but already its enchanted portions were beginning to heal. The Creature sought only the relief of a few days healing, then it would reconstitute itself to feed and bring more terror to this land of warm bloods that walked on two feet and had such strong life forces.

Villagers moaned at the passing of the Griffin, some calling aloud for the Maker, while others invoked the benevolence of Wotan or Tel-Alantir or Pallas Athena. Many began a slow trek home, some weeping softly.

One woman alone stood unmoved; a grandmother with a grandson only three years old, she remained erect, still strong. From her wagon, she drew a grubbing hoe that was tipped with iron, then gravely embraced both her daughter and grandson, bidding them farewell.

"I have lived too long to endure such evil," she said quietly, then she walked in slow determined steps toward the monster. Her daughter's husband tried to block her path, but she rapped him sharply in the kneecaps with the mattock's handle, then advanced through the wreckage into the clearing where the monster lay. All eyes were upon her, and all the weeping sounds slowly subsided.

Both hands held her mattock as she chopped down at an outstretched appendage that bristled with dark spikes. Nothing. Again, she chopped; this time the leg twitched, and she was cast from her feet. Undaunted, she rose and hacked again. A cluster of boys slipped from their parents and began pelting the monster with small stones, then larger rocks. Emboldened, a few men drew longbows and began firing shafts into the Creature's swollen, bleeding torso.

A time of great creativity followed. Woodcutters were summoned and began reducing outstretched appendages with long saws. Caustic materials and fiery substances were applied to various extremities, each studied and noted as to its effectiveness. Catapults were constructed and blocks of stone and beams of wood were hurled into the Creature's pulpy mass. Jagged harpoons secured to ropes were hurled at the monster, withdrawn then cast again. Bonfires were built from the wreckage so that experiments might continue through the chilled spring night. Only once was the Creature able to rouse itself: it stood in the darkness, bewildered, wobbling on its remaining legs; but then a torrent of projectiles cast it down for one last time.

When at last the Creature perished late the next afternoon, the villagers felt a sense, not of triumph, but of vague disappointment. Were there no other wounded monsters upon which they could experiment?

And so passed the second of the Creatures of the Darkness that had been unleashed against the League.

· ⅺ ·

Powerful midnight winds sent the bat winged Creature of the Darkness careening through the skies. Fields and farms, lakes and meadows flashed beneath it in only a few, heavy beats of its own strong wings. Broad lakes, firelit villages, coils of winding rivers, all passed in brief blinks of the bright stars that seemed to hover motionless above it.

The great misshapen Flyer had been sent southeast to probe and to peck at the outer ring of the villages surrounding Stone Mountain, to bring grief to the Wizard Thorian and lure him from his citadel. But why had Set, among the most powerful of Gods, shown so much caution over a mere feeble human, a thing to be consumed and not treated with such wariness?

The Flyer adjusted its wings and a range of low hills passed beneath it. Smells of sea and shore were reaching up to it, and after came the sounds of surf pounding in the distance. Moments later, Stone Mountain loomed in the darkness, its lights shining brightly, fearlessly, like a beacon. With the slightest shift, the Flyer wheeled in the sky, passing the fortress in a wide circle, coasting far from the Wizard's reach.

But why, after all, should this mortal magician be feared? He was nothing but a warmblooded human and no Child of Dragons! If this Wizard proved too strong, then the Flyer would withdraw; otherwise, the Flyer would feast upon the flesh of Wizard and boast forever about its victory!

The Flyer was drawn to the lights of the tower like a moth.

As Set and all Dark Gods knew, to expect obedience from a Creature Indomitable was to place trust in the wind or commit sacred writings to inscriptions carved upon flowing sands. The Flyer arced closer, probing. Lesser powers like ghostly spirits swirled about the Wizard's domain — of little interest to the Flyer, though it could no longer expect to surprise the Wizard.

Strange unblinking lights poured forth from every opening of the topmost tower, where the Wizard seemed to be laired. Closer...from out of nothingness, a curl, a tendril of power caressed the Flyer gently, and the Creature recoiled, dropping a hundred feet. Nothing, no harm had been done to it. With a sweep of its enormous wings, the Flyer arced higher and closer. A second tendril embraced it. **Magic — and strange!**

Within his tower, Thorian smiled grimly then turned to other matters. This flying Creature of the Darkness was unaware of its doom — it had power, a powerful force of magic, but it was not clever enough to deal with a Wizard's spells.

As the Creature arced through the night sky, a strength of sorcery rose from within its own essence and the Wizard's tendril boiled away. Once again, the Flyer found no damage to its form. Still, it was wise to reconsider, to pause while feeding and quenching its thirst. When had it last taken water? It seemed an age ago. The Flyer wheeled toward the ocean and arced down in circles that always diminished until it settled upon the darkened shore. Wading fearlessly into the powerful surf, it leaned over and sucked greedily at a torrent of white, foamy seawater. The Flyer drank deeply then drank again, its thirst growing with every gulp.

For more than an hour the Creature Indomitable attempted to drink dry the ocean until its internal organs burst, and it collapsed into the boiling surf. Only months later was there sufficient decay of its enchanted flesh that the crabs could make of the Flyer their strangest and most bitter of meals.

And so passed the third of the Creatures of the Darkness that had been sent to destroy the League.

· Ж ·

At Amalric, murder ruled. Carags slew more than a score each night, while survivors fled from the city only to provide feasts for packs of Vorrs that scoured the surrounding countryside. The town council met, repeatedly, its members deadlocked by their own ambition, confusion, envy, and general stupidity. At last, one of their chief members, Nestor, rose and stalked from the chamber. Others were glad to see him depart, for he suffered fools poorly.

Nestor returned to his home to find his own wife newly slain, killed while he argued with the scheming merchants and dimwitted guardsmen who sat on the town council. With a grim face and shaken by grief, he armed himself then summoned his three strong sons. He spoke separately and quietly to each son, for he believed that a Carag might absorb a shape, but not the mind behind that shape. After a time of weeping and mounting anger, his sons were found to be his own grieving family and provided with weapons. Nestor then called upon his closest friends among the guardsmen. When these spoke with clear recollections of their time as guards, he called upon his sons' friends and listened while each was questioned and sanctioned. Some of those summoned refused to come, and these Nestor warned others to watch with caution.

Now numbering more than a score, Nestor's party strode into the town square. With an outer calmness, he stepped into the council chamber, surrounded by well-armed men.

"Your time has come to an end," he said in a voice that grated even to his own ears. "Your first task was to protect our peoples, and in this, you have failed utterly. Go. Be gone. We will surrender our authority to the Wizards, but until that time, we will take power in Amalric. Out, *now!*" A few counselors rose, drawing weapons; they were swiftly overpowered and disarmed. Nestor herded them from the chamber, and followed them out into the town square, where bells were rung, trumpets blown, and the townspeople summoned.

As the fearful citizens of Amalric slowly assembled, younger children were called toward Nestor's group so that they were shielded behind his war party. It had long been Nestor's thought that the shapeshifters would find it difficult to reduce their mass in order to pass as children.

When several hundred of the fearful villagers had assembled, Nestor addressed them with harsh, blunt words: "We have taken power. Shapeshifters are among us in disguise. They can take human form and replace those they have killed — but they lack the knowledge of those they have murdered. We are going to discover these shapeshifting assassins and destroy each one of them. For a time, you will lose your freedom and your privacy, but perhaps gain your lives." An unhappy rumble built among the crowd and slowly grew louder. Nestor signaled: arrows were loosed into the ground, striking just short of the mass of humans. The crowd quieted.

"One warning only," Nestor called to them. "Now, we are going to bring over in twos and threes those that we know by face, then question each to discover whether a human or a monstrosity lurks behind their features. Once cleared, these will call others that they know by sight. At days end we will have citizens on one side of this square and dead shapeshifters on the other."

"Whose death left you king?" one onlooker called out, and another, "Let us rid ourselves of this man!" Arrows flew, this time to each heart. One that fell dead was a Carag, becoming pale, translucent flesh with a snout nose, and blunt hyena features. The second — *alas!* — was simply another difficult, contrary human.

Nestor strode over and severed the Carag's head with a sweep of his sword arm. Then he lifted the Carag's head by the fur on its skull. "Here is one of our foes. No longer will our enemies be permitted to dwell among us and slay us one by one." As he stared again with hard eyes at the peoples of Amalric, a half dozen forms that had lingered at the crowd's outskirts cast aside human guise and raced away on four feet. Arrows took only two, and the others fled to distant portions of the city, either to hide or escape beyond the city's gates.

One by one, human by human, street by street, Nestor began the slow, bitter work of clearing Amalric of its fell Carag Assassins.

·)(·

The Elf-Mage Mír stood before a gathering, with more than ten score of the Kindreds listening closely to him. Many Elves were present, bearing longbows, together with clusters of Sidhe warriors clad in gleaming armor, joined by a dozen dark Tanu, bearing assorted weapons and shieldings of their own manufacture.

"The rule of the Wizards in the South of Alantéa is fading," Mír called to them, his voice rising in passion. "The borders of the League are now broken. In these wild, unclaimed lands, Uraks and Vorrs and Carags prowl, none of them acknowledged by Renegade Dark Gods or other Gods. We go, not to war, for instead, I declare a Great Hunt, called against the monstrosities that have plagued us through the ages. Others of our Kindreds will follow, and not by the Straight Paths alone. Behold!" Mír's hands gestured, fingers weaving swift and intricate patterns: a Portal formed before the Elf-Mage, a shadowy thing, a darkened corridor fit for ghosts. Mír's eyes seemed to flash with red fire as he turned and sped through. With a shout and a clash of weapons, the Kindreds followed, plunging through the dark, enchanted passageway toward the League.

· X ·

A force of magic lingered over Sea's Edge, and so beings of magic found themselves drawn toward the Halls of Merlin. Over time, and partly guided by Merlin, a cluster of several of the more powerful entities began to grow together, and one day they fused.

And so, the Sentinel was born.

Gradually, as the Sentinel became more aware of its tasks at Seas Edge, it developed its own initiatives and ingenuity, while cultivating a humor that focused initially on the Wizard whom the Sentinel had chosen to serve. Merlin's tools were hidden, his devices disguised by illusions, his spells thwarted by devious enchantments.

Merlin said nothing, allowing only a faint smile to flicker over eyes that had seen so many things. But after a time, the Sentinel found itself separating into its components at inopportune moments, while its own spells rebounded upon itself, and its memories proved strangely treacherous. With sudden understanding, the Sentinel raced to unmake the mischief it had crafted against its master. After this new understanding, all was well, with the Sentinel carefully watching the hills and the shoreline that surrounded Sea's Edge, restricting its humor to the rogue bears, ravens, seagulls, and scuttling crabs that populated its outposts.

The Sentinel also discretely studied his Wizard master, discovering that Merlin was more than passing strange — the Wizard seemed to have two distinct moods, one exceedingly remote, the other far more human.

When the Sentinel first felt the approach through the hills of a Creature of the Darkness, it drew back in alarm: this monster was enormous, with a snake's body, and a head belonging to some misshapen gargoyle creature. It was powerful enough to consume all the rogue bears that had populated the hills surrounding Sea's Edge, and it had a goodly strength of sorcery at its own command.

Agitated, the Sentinel waited for the Wizard to note and deal with the intruder, but as the Sentinel hesitated, a second Creature of the Darkness approached Sea's Edge, this time from the ocean. This being was also immense, strongly armored with a shielding formed of dense chitin, like that of a massive insect. It scuttled with legs that seemed like those of a crab, with a coiled sting much like that of a scorpion, though its grotesque monster head was like that of a ghoul, similar neither to insect or arachnid. At night, the creature lingered upon the beaches staring up at the Halls of Merlin with eyes filled with hatred. During the day it hid in deep waters, preying upon the huge, though unwary sharks that were drawn to the Creature Indomitable by enchanted lures.

Two monstrosities and still the Wizard would not act! The Sentinel had been allowed to hear conversations between Merlin and his fellow Wizards so that it was known that other Creatures Indomitable had been destroyed by Balardi and Thorian. Why would Merlin, the most powerful of the three Wizards, allow monstrosities to linger at the borders of Sea's Edge?

A voice came to the Sentinel then, counsel that came not from the Wizard but from some remote place inside itself. *Are you nothing but an observer, a watcher? Or are you also a defender? It feels as though the Wizard is waiting for you to act against these intruders.*

This inner voice spoke words that stuck the Sentinel like a blow, and the enchanted being recoiled. A time of contemplation followed, and the Sentinel decided to test its own powers against the intruders before seeking counsel from Merlin. After all, the Sentinel was more powerful than some partly aware Elemental that could only shriek warnings when challenged!

Dusk was coming to Sea's Edge, with a damp gloom settling over its jagged shoreline. Only the air fluttered as the invisible Sentinel took itself in brief flurries of motion down to the long beaches, watching as the Creature of the Darkness emerged from the depths.

What was the monstrosity thinking to be so unconcerned about the Wizard's power? Only a trace of light remained in the upper skies as the Sentinel approached the enormous Scuttler. It had dragged up a shark's huge carcass and was ripping at tough cartilage with the jagged teeth that protruded from its massive ghoul's head. Foam reached up to the carcass, though the tide lacked enough strength to drag the dead thing back into the depths.

Yet now the Scuttler looked up, aware of the Sentinel; and its coiled scorpion sting bobbed erect, dripping poison.

The Sentinel cast an illusion before the Scuttler, showing the body of a Creature Indomitable shaped like a giant snake looming in the darkness; the scorpion tail of the Scuttler pulsed with dark magic and the apparition vanished. The Sentinel raised a more complex spell, a deception for the Scuttler's eyes and ears. The Scuttler raced forward, forcing the Sentinel to flutter skyward. From a height, Merlin's servant employed even greater, more subtle magic, while the Scuttler hurled fire and frost against its adversary.

As the two beings danced and swirled through the overcast night, the sand of the beach became torn, boulders crushed by the Creature's bulk. A muted, pastel lightning flared over the beach as the two beings clashed, and the noise of wild magic reached up into the Halls of Merlin, but still, the Wizard did not stir. One part of Merlin's enchanted mind regarded an ancient book of spells, while the other slept, journeying to distant places through Gates of Dreams.

Gradually the Sentinel's wisdom came to match the Scuttler's raw power. Dead zones were found in the Creature's vision centers, and obscure enchantments were employed that the Scuttler could not counter. Sheets of grey mist loomed, then lowered over shore, cliff, and water. Dimensions seemed to twist and constrict themselves; as the Scuttler sought water, it found itself charging instead into sandy cliffs. When it found salt water, the incline seemed to turn back on itself, leading again to the beach.

The Scuttler found itself trapped in an enchanted maze, a series of twisting tunnels that coiled back and forth upon themselves. Racing back and forth, going nowhere, the monster's mounting rage only added to its blindness.

The Sentinel withdrew, its invisible substance quivering somewhat as though it panted for breath. With an unspoken summons, it called lesser Elementals to sustain its sorcerous powers, then it took itself in staggered flurries of motion to the far hills overlooking the Halls of Merlin.

The Creature with a snake's body stood on a ridge, staring down at the Wizard's lair, wondering again whether to cast aside its oath to the Great God Set and seek to feast on the Wizard's flesh. All the bulky bears with warm blood that sheltered in the forested hillsides had been consumed, and now it was growing hungry.

Still, there was reason for caution: flickers of light, sounds of strife, emanations of power had come from somewhere beyond the Wizard's lair. Might it have been the Wizard dueling with one of its brethren...and the mortal had won? It seemed — motion flickered to its right and its gargoyle head turned. A bulky warm blood, a luscious thing of fur and gristle! But no...it had no substance...and now it did! Again, some magic flared, and now the furred thing possessed scent and sound. The warm blood began squealing in fright as it scampered down the hillside, rockslides bounding around it in its haste to escape.

Food! The Creature spilled its snake's body down the hillside in pursuit of the bear shape. This warm blood was larger and more fleet than the others: it circled wide beyond the Wizard's lair then raced up the far hill that led to the ocean. The Creature Indomitable sped after it, beginning to close the gap.

But beyond the peak of the next hill, both predator and prey faltered then stopped. The bear paused halfway down the sandy cliff, while the misshapen Creature hesitated at the top. Both stared down at a ghostly matrix of grey mists that lay over the shoreline of the still bay; from within the mists came sounds of great power and uncontrollable rage. The bear glanced back and forth between maze and monster, but after what seemed an agony of indecision, the bear's shape stumbled down the cliff, and after one last second of seeming hesitation, vanished into the maze of mists that lay over the long beaches at Sea's Edge.

With a shriek of anger and hunger, the Creature Indomitable spilled down the sandy cliff, passed into the grey foggy substance, and so became ensnared. Moments later when the bear emerged, there were two areas where the maze of mist struggled and groaned, straining to contain both monstrosities.

Shaking with fatigue, the Sentinel cast aside its transformed bear shape then struggled with staggered flurries back to the Halls of Merlin. Here, the Sentinel halted uneasily. Which of the Wizard's moods would the Sentinel encounter? Sometimes it seemed as though two masters alternated in the Wizard's form. Hoping for the more human Wizard, the Sentinel finally spoke.

"Master..." the Sentinel panted aloud, rousing the Wizard, and these were the first words the servant had spoken to his master.

Merlin became fully awake and turned to smile gently at the Sentinel and its work. "Well done," said the Wizard, and this was also his first open communication with his servant. In lower tones and in a tongue not recognized by the Sentinel, Merlin spoke other words, and the Sentinel felt a flood of new strength surging into its invisible substance.

"Return to your design," the Wizard said, rising. "I will join you in moments." The Sentinel fluttered back to the sand cliffs to find his enchanted maze slowly giving way before the brute strength of two Creatures Indomitable: dark grey mists were becoming transparent so that the monsters could peer out into the overcast night sky. The two monstrosities had become aware of one another.

As the Sentinel struggled to reimpose the boundaries of its sorcerous maze, the Wizard trudged down the sandy cliff then halted beside the Sentinel. On either side of Merlin were a half dozen invisible torchbearers, while other beings carried bulky objects whose purpose was obscured by draperies of dark cloth.

Merlin carried nothing but his own staff, and as he stood on the sandy cliff overlooking the bay, the Wizard began to chant in hushed tones at first, then his voice was raised almost in song.

The maze beneath the bluff was made stronger and larger. Its outer surface became transparent so that those without could see the two monstrosities as they blundered through a series of confused, interlaced catacombs. In its central space, a larger dome began to grow, forming a small amphitheater. All the twisting, changing tunnels were altered so that they led back to the dome.

One monstrosity entered the amphitheater and stared about with mounting suspicion. Moments later, the second Creature blundered in. The two beings roared hatred and defiance at one another...then backed into tunnel's mouth, still growling. Each choosing a different path, they returned to the amphitheater only to face one another again, so that it seemed to each Creature Indomitable that the other was blocking its exit from the maze.

They fell to battle with all might and magic and venom that had powered their beings for so many thousands of years. The Scuttler had more bulk while the coils of the snake-bodied Creature seemed to possess a greater strength of magic. Gargoyle and Ghoul heads ripped at one another with savage teeth. Lights flared from dark energies. Bellowing, shrieking sounds echoed over the shoreline. Venoms were exchanged — then burned away. The substance of the maze shook and shuddered under their onslaught.

After a time, their energies began to flag and, their hatred diminished. Each monstrosity came to understand that it could not vanquish the other. As they hesitated, the Wizard on the bluff above them made a single pass with his staff, and after, each felt new strength, touched by a strange magic. They fell to battle again, with power fed to each being as its energies waned. As they struggled, it seemed to each monstrosity that the ground around them grew larger: sand grains became pebbles, stones boulders, and the small amphitheater around them seemed to grow into a vast coliseum.

With each pass of his staff, Merlin fed back to the Creatures energies drawn from their own substances, so that they consumed themselves. An hour before daybreak, the Wizard made one final pass with his staff, so that each Creature of the Darkness became frozen, transformed, while the enchanted maze and amphitheater vanished.

The Wizard then strolled casually down the bluff, humming under his breath, accompanied by invisible servants. Cloth draperies were removed from the attendants' burden, revealing a glass case hooded over a metal base that was covered only with a light coating of sand. Into this case were set the two Creatures Indomitable.

All their ferocity and power and malice were thus preserved, though they remained frozen in forms that had become no larger than those of kittens.

Chapter Five

A City Unmanned

"**N**OTHING I MIGHT SAY or show them," Whisper said in his softest tones, "will make them open the gates for you. Some may recognize you both, though, if you present yourselves before the guard."

"Yes, and by the time they take note of us," Orantes muttered, "Vorrs will be chewing on our intestines." Their slow passage had taken them to the outskirts of Tuvan's walls, but daylight had passed and roaming packs of Vorrs had forced them to hide in the burned shell of an outlying farm dwelling. Tuvan lay before them but so did a small camp of Uraks, and beyond the Uraks lay a separate, larger, fortified camp of human tiers, who were still preparing siege weapons by firelight. Within Tuvan's walls, nothing seemed to stir, fires smoldered as though untended, and only muted sounds could be heard.

Wylar peered out, measuring the space that lay between themselves and the gates: it was no more than a few brisk shuffling minutes even for Orantes, but Vorrs were prowling, and Uraks loomed large in the distance, framed by firelight against a grey glow of dusk. He glanced back to Orantes. At least his fellow Adept had held up so far — all of Orantes' bluster and bravado masked layers of uncertainties and fears, and so there was always a chance that Orantes would simply break down under the pressure of well-armed foes. But if they could only secure themselves behind strong walls....

"Orantes and I will disguise ourselves as broken, bedraggled Uraks," Wylar said quietly. "We've seen that they treat their wounded with disgust and don't bother to assist them. After we stumble closer to the gates, we'll be passing by their camps. Then we'll need disturbance to distract them while we scramble toward the city walls. When we reach the gates, we must speak words that are both swift and strong."

Orantes scowled, muttering something under his breath, then he began to chant spell words in muted tones. His form began to change, to become larger at the shoulder, and taller, and his skin darkened. Wylar spoke similar words, and the forms of each loomed larger and darker, to become those of Uraks, filled with menace — but wounded. To match Orantes' lameness, Wylar altered his Urak's shape so that his right arm lacked a hand, revealing only a stump bound in dark cloth. More words were spoken, and the smells given off by their bodies changed so that even Squint was hard pressed to distinguish the Adepts from their foes.

Disguised as Uraks, the two rose from their hiding places, leaving behind the jagged, burned-out walls that were no stronger than wafer-thin charcoal. With their cloaks pulled tight against the night chill of early spring, they began a winding passage to a point midway between the gates of Tuvan and the watchfires of Urak tribes. Prowling Vorrs took note of them, as did the Uraks standing watch on the outskirts of their camp, but their crippled, beaten appearance was quickly noted, and so, the transformed Adepts were pointedly ignored.

"I suppose it's unlikely," Orantes whispered, "that old or maimed Vorrs and Uraks retire to pleasant rest homes. I wonder what becomes of them?" Wylar failed to respond. Instead, he concentrated on weaving his way forward; but under his breath, the Adept murmured charmed words of magic.

"Maybe they just chop up poor old chaps like us," Orantes continued serenely, "and toss our remains into their pots of stew. There are certainly some savings in such a simple retirement plan." Wylar continued to chant, and devices as small as walnuts began gathering in his palm.

"Or maybe the maimed and infirm become hosts for new broods of Vorr grubs," Orantes said thoughtfully. "Must be a trifle difficult, lying there paralyzed, listening to a batch of little monsters chew on your innards." Wylar let the slight devices pass into the waiting hands of Whisper. His shadowy form sped through the darkness, creating only the slightest shift of shadows. Squint kept himself hidden within a fold of Wylar's cloak, waiting for their planned "distraction."

Orantes trailed off, having run short of gallows humor. Vorrs began to give more attention to the two stumbling and crippled Uraks as they veered closer to the city gates, and farther from the watchfires of the Uraks.

Suddenly the dark quiet was filled with explosions of light and sound: Wylar's devices had been slipped by Whisper into the Uraks' watchfires, and thousands of wood fragments and embers were bursting out into the night. Uraks bellowed, stumbling about, brushing hot ashes from themselves. Vorrs howled and rolled, trying to blot out the fires that sprouted over their matted fur. Outlying patrols turned toward the disturbances.

Wylar and Orantes cast aside their disguises as Uraks and raced for the city walls. Orantes panted, shuffling at top speed, as Wylar dragged him forward. Squint took flight, rising to watch as the Adepts struggled toward the gates. Three nearby Vorrs became aware of the Adepts and began speeding toward the gates at about five times Orantes' speed. The gap narrowed as the Adepts began to lose their race for the gates.

Squint called down a warning. The Adepts stumbled to a halt, then turned, not fifty paces from their goal. Orantes snarled, drawing deep breaths as Vorrs, with their rippling, muscled brown fur, sped toward them. Staffs were raised; jagged bolts of force left their attackers twitching and dying on the ground.

But other Vorrs approached, now more cautiously, and behind them, clusters of Uraks began jogging toward Tuvan. Wylar and Orantes finished the last fifty paces of their race and pounded on the outer gates with their staffs. No answer came. Watchtowers rose on each side of the gates, but no one seemed to be manning them. Orantes cursed and smashed again at the gates with his staff. At last, one lone face with grey whiskers appeared above them, staring down at them with fearful, wide eyes.

"Open the gates!" Orantes cried. "We are your allies, sent by the Wizards!" Another face with a dark beard joined the grey one; not only were the second man's eyes wide, but his mouth also hung open, with drool slipping down his cheek. Packs of Vorrs stalked Wylar and Orantes on three sides and the Adepts were forced to turn and call down a wall of fire against their foes. Snarling, muttering, Orantes kicked back at the gates as he faced the oncoming Vorrs.

Their wall of flame burned bright, searing the nearby Vorrs, but one great mailed Urak pushed his way through and strode toward the Adepts, his dark flesh still boiling with blisters from the fire. Wylar drew his sword; Orantes *groped* for his destructive device but could not reach it.

At that moment, with exquisitely bad timing, Wylar's petal-like communication link with Sentauris was activated. As he dodged the Urak's mace, he could hear the distant voice of Sentauris calling, "Wylar, Orantes, speak to me!"

"Sentauris! I —" Wylar called, then he was forced to leap aside again. Orantes stumbled back, lashing at the Urak with bolts of force — only a distraction. Squint swept down, raking at a gap in the Urak's armor, just as Whisper struggled to blind its sight — only another slight distraction. The Urak pursued them like horror in a dream.

"We are at the gates!" Wylar called, then he lashed at the arm holding the Urak's mace. His enchanted sword slashed through metal and sinew as though they were nothing but rotten meat. Wylar spun; a second slash took off the Urak's head, and it fell dead. But now their wall of flame, untended, had dimmed. Clusters of Vorrs and Uraks were slipping easily through gaps.

"Too many!" Wylar cried and readied for death. Orantes *groped* again and this time his hand emerged with dark, jagged lightning. He hurled it at their foes, blasting them back. Then he turned and looked up, his wild, red eyes full of menace, into a row of faces on the twin watchtowers astride the gates.

"Let us in, you sexless toads," he snarled, "or we'll blast down your dung stained, rotting walls ourselves!"

"It's the Adept who replaced Hektor," one small voice was heard to say, "the fat lover of wine. No magic could ever duplicate that performance. Let them in." The gates creaked open; the Adepts backed in, still watching their foes warily.

They were within Tuvan at last. Bands of iron and reinforcements of metal beams secured the gates. Uraks began hammering at the outer walls with maces of steel. A half dozen guards on the twin watchtowers dropped stones down on them halfheartedly then withdrew.

"Sentauris?" Wylar whispered into his oracular device, but the Seeress was no longer trying to reach them. The Adepts looked up into the faces of a dozen dispirited guardsmen who stared down from the walkway on the upper walls; the gate watch stared at the bedraggled Adepts with a complete lack of confidence. A broad cobblestone plaza surrounded the gates, but it had been mined for stones, left pitted, and scored. Beyond the plaza, Tuvan's streets seemed lightless and still, except for scrawny dogs that foraged furtively in darkened alleys. Tuvan the Besieged might still be standing, but it seemed almost completely defeated.

· 𝕏 ·

"The Adepts have entered Tuvan," Sentauris said quietly to Ghorm. "They were forced to fight their way to the gates and they succeeded — but barely. I do not think they will like what they find within the walls of Tuvan the Besieged."

"Why didn't you use your Farsight before you reached for the Adepts?" Ghorm asked, his sharp eyes filled with suspicion. Sentauris sighed and Ghorm continued, his tones becoming more intense, "It's because of the strong feelings that you have for the two of them, that everything has to be encountered as new, not be known beforehand — isn't that it?"

"Ghorm, when a Seeress sees everything beforehand, the newness of that experience is gone. Anyway, I am as I am, you are as you are, and only the Maker can alter these things at *The End of Time*. I will agree, however, to use my Farsight in the future. Now, what of our captains, whom you have studied so carefully in the last few days? Is there a weak link among them?"

"None. Each of them is better than good," Ghorm said grudgingly. "I still don't know why you mistrust Sardonicus. He may be the most capable of the lot."

"Ah, Ghorm, he is also the best looking. Are you beginning a new role as matchmaker?" Sentauris raised a hand to forestall a fresh outburst from her Familiar. "That is only banter, Ghorm, of the kind that you enjoy with

Sardonicus. I am glad that you favor our captains, though, for much will be required of them when we reach Tuvan...Tuvan the Besieged in three days, journeying by stealth. The Adepts must hold the city until that time."

·)(·

Such was the hammering of the Uraks and the howling of the Vorrs that more of Tuvan's guardsmen grudgingly roused themselves from sleep and made their way to the gates. They milled uncertainly, none willing to mount the twin watchtowers and drive their foes from the city walls. At last, a youth of fourteen years appeared, leading an older man across the cobblestone plaza to the twin towers. Then the youth returned to his own dwelling.

The elder, standing in a cloak that was lined with soft white fur, yawned twice then clapped his hands, murmuring, "The drill, my hearties." With poor grace, teams of men began mounting the twin watchtowers. Sputtering volleys of arrows began to slice into Vorrs. Stones, then larger boulders smashed at mailed Uraks so that even they were forced away from the walls. The elder yawned once again, then turned back toward his dwelling. Walking swiftly to the plaza's edge, Wylar moved to intercept him.

"Sir, are you captain of these men?" Wylar asked as Orantes limped to his side. "Head of Tuvan's council, perhaps?"

The elder smiled wanly. "I'm only the last of the Council left with even a trace of authority. My name is Breughal, a merchant by choice, and one day in the future a prince of merchants if the Gods favor me. And you two are...." His face woke in recognition, and he smiled broadly. "The Replacement Adepts! Servants and allies of the Wizards — and so I am released! You now rule Tuvan, and I will pass from this place. There's gold to be earned south or north of here, but nothing in Tuvan but glory and, or death, neither of them to my fancy." He turned to go, but Orantes reached out casually and with one meaty, but strong hand gripped the merchant firmly by his furry cloak.

"Not just yet," Wylar said softly. "I think that you will remain here for a time, assisting us in our defense of Tuvan."

"With your resources and cunning," Orantes added, "you might easily slip away. But think: if we have not the powers of the Wizards or the Gods, still our own dark magic might follow you to your restless grave."

Breughal studied the Adepts with a sour face, then carefully disengaged himself from the hold of Orantes on his cloak. "I deal each day with people who are far more difficult and stronger than you two; but in the end, all must bargain. Here is my offer: my best efforts for Tuvan until further help arrives. Is this agreed?" The two Adepts glanced together, then nodded slowly.

The merchant tightened his robe and moved slowly away from the Adepts. "By the way," he said in passing, "that lad you let return to his bed is the true leader of this town's defense. His name is Druss. I am only the mouth, while the orders are his." Breughal left them standing some distance from the gates, where a dozen or so guardsmen staffed the watchtowers, while another two score listless defenders attended to all the other fortifications and walls.

"The defense of Tuvan," Wylar muttered, "is not a pretty sight."

"Some time ago, the leaders of Tuvan lied to me," Orantes said quietly. "I drank their wine and smiled and let their silly lies go unchallenged."

"Other centers of the League have lied to me, too," Wylar added, "and even though I made them uncomfortable with their untruths, I should have challenged them further, and forced them to deal with their problems. Now, all that is in the past. Tell me what we're looking at. Are these Main Gates the key to the defense of Tuvan?"

Orantes searched his memory. "Both Towers face north, though the tower on the right facing the rising sun is called the East Tower, while that facing the setting sun is called the West Tower, and neither tower has a single hero in it. May the Maker curse us both as fools!"

"Enough!" Orantes took a deep breath, and called out, "Whisper!" As the shadowy being shimmered into view, Squint also descended to alight on Wylar's shoulder.

"Whisper, have I not been a lovely lad," Orantes continued, "a true, if minor hero?" Whisper seemed to nod grudgingly, and Orantes pulled from his cloak three small silver coins then passed them to his Familiar.

"Then secure for me at this considerable cost," Orantes said, sinking back against the wall of a dark, abandoned building, "two bottles of some obscure vintage. You need not rouse their owners to provide change." After only a moment's hesitation, Whisper's form slipped into the shadows and vanished.

Five minutes later the shadowy being was back, bearing not just two bottles, but three, together with two goblets and the leg of some scrawny game bird, brought for Squint.

"Brilliantly done, O faithful Familiar!" Orantes exclaimed as he poured a dark red wine into his goblet then drank with some satisfaction. "Now if you could only provide us with a few of the lovely nymphs that garnish your delightful stories."

"One vice is sufficient for this evening," Wylar said, settling down beside his fellow Magician and reaching for the wine bottle. "A modest amount of wine tonight, then we must go about the business of building on our meager store of battle magic."

"If you are allowed that much of a breathing space," Whisper added, watching as the Adepts drank wine and Squint's beak ripped at ragged, gamy flesh.

·)(·

In the night visions of Sentauris, she was staring down from a high place to the hills overlooking North Haven. Even though the days of spring were growing warmer, the chill of night lay heavily over the upper slopes, with a pale moon looming to the south. Morning would bring a deep frost over the region, a crust of ice searing all the new spring growth.

Muted fires were sprinkled over the hillsides — were these the sheltering places for refugees from the invasion, and was this the reason her night visions had taken her to this forbidding place? As bidden, her dreamsight brought her lower, closer to the flames.

No, they were Uraks, roasting a dead, headless human over a firepit. Sentauris recoiled in disgust; most nights the Gates of Dreams were opened to her so that matters of interest or things of beauty were brought into her sleep. Dreams of horror were brushed aside. She struggled to leave, but the night vision held her fast.

As she struggled to break free, she discovered that she was not alone, that other beings were traveling the Dreamways. Emissaries of the Gods, three of them, turning to watch her struggle with her night visions; two regarded her with detached amusement, while a third turned away from her in discomfort.

Suddenly, the hillside beneath the watchers burst into violence. A Portal flared, with Sidhe Knights emerging and slaughtering nearly a dozen Uraks before they could even draw weapons. Elves also surged through the portal, bearing longbows, so that as Vorr sentries hurtled through the night, arrows killed them silently, almost effortlessly.

An Elf-Mage paced among them: Mír. At his command, the carcasses of Vorrs and Uraks were heaped into the firepit. Mír spoke words; the firepit burst into towering flames, throwing wild lights over the hills of North Haven.

Mír! She tried to call out to him. *Mír! Our real battle is at Tuvan! Mír, come to Tuvan!*

The Elf-Mage looked up, as though hearing nothing but a distant echo, then shaking his head, led Sidhe and Elves back through his Portal, and far from the night visions of Sentauris.

· ✗ ·

Orantes' dreams were filled with the usual mixture of elusive nymphs, nagging Familiars, critical Wizards, and enchanted feasts that vanished as he approached them. But toward morning, he imagined himself completing a splendid performance as a taleteller standing in an enormous tavern where hundreds recognized his talents by bashing their mugs in unison on broad oak tables: *Thump...thump...thump....*

In his night vision, Orantes bowed deeply then waved to the crowd, in a gesture that was almost shy. Adoring hands were clutching at him; and still, his audience applauded with thumping sounds.

Though now, in an eerie transition, these clutching fingers were becoming more insistent, thumping sounds more threatening. A half dozen hands pulled him from dreamland to his feet. And still, the thumping sounds continued, both inside and outside of his head.

Orantes found himself standing in some darkened chamber, his hands gingerly holding his own pounding head. "By all the Demons, and Dragons, and Creatures of the Darkness, Whisper," he muttered, "I asked for an obscure vintage, not the last cask left over from the Goblin Market in Far Avalon."

"It's the gates," came a voice out of the darkness. "The gates are under siege. You must come." Orantes was pulled blinking out into the light of an overcast, grey morning. Though his head pulsed with pain, hands dragged him into a shuffling run across the plaza toward the city's twin gates. Pounding sounds grew louder. Around the gates, men milled uncertainly, some praying openly to remote, utterly indifferent Gods. Even now the wood beams of the gates were beginning to crack, and the gates metal supports were bulging under pressure.

Cries came from the East Tower, and a torrent of projectiles smashed at the tower's frame, some passing to either side. Orantes stared up, sensing Wylar's presence above. He freed himself from his attendants and began climbing to the tower's top, breathing heavily, moving with uncertain feet because the battering at the gates was shaking the tower down to its foundations.

At the top stood Wylar, together with a cluster of frightened men who held makeshift wicker shields before the Adept. As Orantes reached them, arrows and heavy stones were battering at their shields. More crashing sounds came from the gates, and tremors rocked the tower.

"I have called down a firewall against them," Wylar said evenly, "but I could not maintain it because their weapons are too many. See if you can shield me." Wylar's voice was calm, though his eyes were flashing with anger. His cheek and forehead were bruised, where stones had burst through the wicker shields mounted by the few guardians struggling to protect him.

Orantes cleared his head, then began to chant; columns of pale light began coiling around the two Adepts. More lights followed — sky blue in luster and shimmering. Wylar added a third tinge of grey and black so that they were enclosed within an enchanted barrier. Then the two spoke simultaneous words, and their barrier became transparent, completely clear to their eyes and to those around them.

The Adepts brushed away the makeshift wicker shielding and stepped to the watchtower's edge. Arrows and sling casts lashed at them but fell back from their barrier. Beneath them, a massive ram was wielded by two score men, smashing repeatedly at the sagging gates of Tuvan. Those bearing the ram seemed unopposed, untroubled, shifting their battering ram forward and backward with the sloppy motions of bored laborers.

The Adepts called down fire; walls of flame sent the siege party scurrying back. Then the stream of arrows and sling casts assailing the two defenders built to a storm. Uraks edged closer, hurling heavy spears at the Adepts. Under the onslaught of stone and metal, even their enchanted barrier began to falter, and the Adepts were forced back. Orantes turned to the half dozen men around them: the most steadfast of the gate watch and not even one of them was made from the stuff of hot-blooded warriors.

"You are excused for the moment, my lovely heroes," Orantes said gently. "Ask Breughal and Druss to join us if they can. Also," his look hardened, "tell those responsible for manning the West Tower that if they do not return to their posts, we will send them outside the gates to provide food for Vorrs and Uraks."

Again, the ram hammered at the gates; as before, fire forced the attackers back. In turn, the Adepts and their weapon of fires were pushed back from the tower's edge, and then the cycle began again. During the third cycle, however, archers began to mount the West Tower in defense of Tuvan, and shortly after, a few others joined Breughal and Druss in the East Tower with the Adepts. Arrows began piercing ram-bearers and Vorrs, while heavy stones smashed down at the Uraks, driving them back.

With their task now made far more complicated, the ram-bearers withdrew fifty paces, conferred for a time, then the assault on the gate slowly lessened until it was finally abandoned. The men of the gate watch allowed themselves a ragged cheer, but their cries soon slipped back into an unhappy silence.

"Well done," Breughal began, but Wylar interrupted him.

"A moment if you will. Squint! Whisper!" he called out, turning back to the streets of Tuvan. No answer came.

"When our servants are otherwise occupied," Orantes explained, "the devices of our enemies are the probable cause."

"Squint is chasing some creature," Wylar said, staring into the distance. As he spoke, the gates creaked open, and furtive guardsmen crept out to retrieve spent arrows and loose stones.

"While we wait," Orantes turned to Druss, "tell us more of Tuvan, why there are so few defenders among so many townspeople, and why...." The Adept trailed off, wondering how hard he should press the fourteen year old accompanying Breughal.

"Why so few, and why do they fight without much spirit," Druss finished in a young but surprisingly firm voice. "Not all blame can be fixed to the Town Council, but the story begins with them."

"Yes, the Council, the almost brainless Council of Tuvan," Breughal grunted. "So jealous were they of the watch captains, particularly this lad's grandsire, that they separated the guard into three: the Gate Watch, the West Watch, and the East Watch. Of course, when real trouble came, Tuvan's Council fled, seeking refuge in the hill country."

Orantes bowed and shook his head. "I was also at fault — I knew there was trouble even three years ago. But not a single Wizard told me that this war might be coming."

"It was left to my grandfather, Thelm," Druss said, "to deal with the other two captains appointed by council, yet he was unable to make common cause with either Murat of the West Watch or Fiüre of the East Watch."

"And worse, much worse," Breughal added somberly, "one of these two treacherous watch captains daggered this lad's grandsire and so Tuvan was left all but undefended."

"If there's a lull in the siege," Orantes said, "perhaps we should take time to pay a call on those twin legends of Tuvan: Murat of the West Watch and Fiüre of the East Watch."

"Squint is coming for us," Wylar murmured, "and also, I think, Whisper seeks his master." From the western portion of the city, rock doves began rising, swirling in panic. Seconds later, Squint rose above them; his owl-wings sent rock doves fleeing in all directions. As Squint neared the Adepts, his flight settled into a long, floating glide.

"Whisper is not far behind," Orantes muttered as Squint settled on the tower walls. "I can feel his nagging presence reaching out to me." The Owl-being studied the ground outside the gates for a moment, watching as men retrieved stones and shafts. One lone Urak woke from the stupor brought on by stonecasts from the towers; as he rose, men scurried away from him, letting the Urak stumble back unmolested to his brethren.

"Not all your foes lie outside of these portals," Squint said quietly staring at the Urak's lurching passage.

"We've been hearing lovely tales," Orantes said, "of the legendary East Watch and the heroic West Watch."

"Of these, I know nothing," Squint said, "but while the fight over the gates kept the watch occupied, ropes were let down over the southwest walls. Six figures climbed over the walls and slipped inside the city. Whisper pursued them, but they mingled with crowds of others so that not even the shadowy Familiar was able to tell residents from intruders. They seemed..." Squint hesitated. "They seemed without mage-power, yet they were able to use magic to disguise themselves. How can this be?"

Wylar and Orantes glanced at one another. "Shapeshifters," Wylar said quietly. "Thorian warned me that one of the Renegade Dark Gods had fashioned a race of beings called Carags, to join Vorrs and Uraks in their war against the Kindreds."

Orantes muttered under his breath, shaking his head as though to clear it. "Some devices must be found.... Ah, Whisper!" Orantes' eyes twinkled as his Familiar rippled into view. "Now, my charming advisor, may

I suggest an agenda before you begin your usual cycle of discrete urgings and promptings? I am intrigued by the bold champions of the East and West Watches. Let us pay them a brief visit, and while we meander down Tuvan's joyous boulevards, perhaps some method of tracking these 'Carag' creatures will occur to us."

"Talking to the other watches is a complete waste of time," Breughal grunted. "When last we tried, our conference with the West Watch ended with crossbows casting bolts at us."

"We now speak with the authority of the Wizards," Wylar replied. "The watches must heed us despite old feuds. Come." They descended cautiously — the violence of the assault had left the watchtower stairs splintered and wobbly. More stones had been uprooted from the plaza, further scarring it. Wylar shook his head: under true siege conditions, scores of women, elders, and younglings would have supported their fighters with food, water, and makeshift repairs.

Daybreak had come to Tuvan, though only a few of its citizens emerged to perform their morning tasks. Other wary residents had risen and were wandering down nearly abandoned streets as though searching for leftover food or weapons.

Wylar muttered a curse under his breath: Tuvan's citizens had begun foraging early in the siege; theft and looting would follow all too quickly.

"Hunger comes to Tuvan," Breughal commented. "As a merchant my supplies included stores of grain, and so the Gate Watch came to be allied with me. Both the West and East Watches have secured their own hoards of food. As for the citizens of Tuvan, ten days into the siege, their own stores grow thin and soon they will either weaken from hunger or flee from the city."

"The Gods know that I am no admirer of famine," Orantes muttered. His head was beginning to hurt once more, and he recited again charmed spell-words as they wove their way west, passing through winding, cobblestone streets. Not only did its streets wind, but Tuvan's thoroughfares alternately compressed and expanded, as buildings encroaching on the roadway had been brushed back by stronger ordinances. Overhead, Squint's owl shape forced more rock doves into panicky flight, their gaunt forms fluttering over rooftops and chimney stones so that the sounds of flapping wings broke the silence of a city that had become far too quiet.

Only once was there any hint of loyalty to the Gate Watch: an old woman moving at her best speed with the use of a cane, intercepted Druss, bowed, and pressed upon him a heel of bread.

At the far western end of the city, the ground rose, forming a small hillock. On its crest lay a series of buildings formed from stone and mortar and strong beams, creating a fortress complex. As they climbed toward the front entrance of the complex, faces began slipping away from narrow, darkened windows, though Orantes sensed a more than a few sets of eyes peering at them from peepholes above and to each side.

Wylar hammered at the entrance with his staff. "Many of you will know us by sight," he called, hammering again. "Still, for the sake of others, we declare ourselves: the Adepts Wylar and Orantes stand before you. You must hear us in the League's name, for we speak with the authority of the Wizards." From within came the shuffling sounds of booted feet clumping over wooden floors, but no one answered.

"Murat, come out!" Wylar called. Again, no answer came, except soft clicking sounds as crossbows were drawn.

"Launch but one bolt," Orantes snarled, "and I will visit a slow, weeping death on every stinking one of you." Again, Wylar hammered, and as before no answer came; except to Orantes it seemed that each of the two or three dozen men inside was holding his breath. Frustrated by silence, they moved from the gates, saying nothing until they were far from hearing.

When they had passed into a side street and had become obscured from view, Orantes murmured, "Whisper, what have you found?" The shadowy being seemed to rise in rippled dark clouds from the ground.

"Inside, they have built fortresses within fortresses," Whisper said in his dry voice, "yet their current efforts seem strange, almost irrational. Their workshops are laden, not with weapons, but with handcrafts — not charms but emblems — of the Gods, as though they prepared for some religious festival. Can this be?"

"Murat the deceiver," Wylar muttered, "Murat the fool. He believes that when the city falls, all his religious ornaments will save him from the besiegers. If the emblems of the Greater Powers caused any fighters from their human tiers to hesitate, they would simply stand aside and let Vorrs and Uraks feast on the still living bodies of the West Watch." Orantes was cursing under his breath, and in a seamless transition, he began murmuring spell-words.

"None of that, now," Wylar cautioned, pulling at Orantes' cloak. "Not only are such curses bad policy, but they are also expressly forbidden by the Wizards." Orantes muttered a few more dark phrases, but then fell silent, saving his breath for the journey over Tuvan's cobbled thoroughfares.

Throughout the morning the day grew brighter, with sunlight radiating through banks of upper clouds. More of Tuvan's residents emerged, showing somewhat greater energy, though most avoided the Adepts and their small party. Only one figure failed to avert his eyes as they passed: a tall man with a strong face watched them from a left-hand intersection, staring at them openly with cool, clear eyes. As they passed him, Orantes felt the hairs on his neck rise, with a ripple of fear spreading down his neck and spine. He turned.

"You, sir," he called. "Can you help us for a mo —" Before Orantes could finish, the figure had slipped behind a building, vanishing from sight.

"A strange interlude," Breughal commented. "I know most of Tuvan's people by their features, but that face was strange."

"A Carag," Wylar said softly. "I too felt its presence, though not as strongly as my fellow Adept." They pressed on, slowing as Orantes' limp grew more pronounced, with the pain of his partly healed ankle radiating up into a head that still throbbed. The passage of Squint overhead continued to send flurries of rock doves into the air, while feral cats prowled on rooftops, scowling and hissing as the Owl-being flew overhead.

If the West Watch was based upon a hill, the East Watch had constructed its headquarters on lower ground in a depression that deepened into a small valley. Its structures, too, were different — squat, low and flat, but still the barracks of the East Watch formed an unmistakable fortress. As before, Wylar was the first to the front portal, pounding on it with his staff.

"Fiüre, come out!" he called. "We are emissaries of the Wizards, Adepts in our own right. In the League's name, we call upon you to join in the defense of Tuvan!" No response came, a stillness as though the barracks had been abandoned. Again, Wylar hammered, at last bringing a response.

"Get away from here," said a voice, low, gruff, seeming to emerge from beneath the ground.

"Fiüre, you are summoned to Gravengate!" Wylar called out. "Come and explain yourself before the Wizard Balardi, the Master of Gravengate and ruler of this land!"

"The time of the Wizards has passed," said the voice, remote as before. "Depart and leave us to our own devices." With a stony face, Wylar and the others strode uphill and turned into an alley where they were shielded from the East Watch. As before, Whisper's dark and smoky form shimmered up from the ground.

"The strategy of the East Watch is more obvious," Whisper said in his soft Shade's voice. "They have dug down and deep, so they can retreat into a second or third level, and even, if needed, slip outside, beyond the city walls."

"Fiüre is certainly brighter than Murat," Wylar said, shaking his head, "though they are equal in their betrayal of Tuvan. I only hope that their stupidity is not repeated throughout our League. If all our people behave as they have in Tuvan, the Wizards' League is doomed." Orantes shrugged his shoulders as though determined to consider more cheerful matters. He strolled a little distance apart from his fellow Adept, humming in hushed tones, eyes studying rooflines and cornices.

When Orantes stood again in full view of the East Watch, and enough distance from Wylar, he drew his staff, clenching it in both hands. Rising in anger, he called down brutal, sharp words against the East Watch. Turning west, he intoned other words of power against the West Watch. Then, smiling and suddenly benign, he returned to his companions.

"There," he said brightly. "I have visited upon the East Watch a plague of the stinking itch, and for the West Watch, seizures of shaking feverish fits — measured discomfort for each that will last only six hours. Let them feel our unhappiness."

"Did we not say that the Wizards expressly forbid such actions?" Wylar asked. "I will argue, plead in your defense, but still...."

"All those restrictions were meant for a time of peace," Orantes said cheerfully, "not for a time of war." He waved one hand airily. "Besides, let the Wizards fine me a year's pay or even reduce some future pension that was never more than a vague promise. Anyway, my conscience is clear, and at last my head has lost its ponderous weight. Now, Whisper, where did you acquire the exquisite vintage that so ennobled our celebration last evening?"

·){ ·

Sentauris straightened and laughed softly. "Orantes has put aside some of the restrictions laid upon him by the Wizards," she whispered to Ghorm. "Both Adepts will need to act more forcefully if they are to survive the next few days."

It was midday, and overcast, though some of the chill of early spring was leaving the south of Alantéa. Their force of mercenaries — closer to three hundred than the original estimate of two hundred and fifty — was well concealed in deeply forested woodlands. Although stray Vorrs were always seeking for the forest's wild pigs, Sentauris had been able to anticipate and slay each one of those foragers. Now, less than two days from Tuvan, it was time for yet another swift, forced march. Their journey had become easier as the siege tightened around Tuvan, as it drew all the Vorrs and Uraks and human warriors sent by the enemies of the League away from the surrounding countryside. Even several of the uncontrollable Creatures of the Darkness were being drawn to Tuvan, a matter of some strangeness, though there were many other dangers to watch for.

"Ghorm," Sentauris murmured, "using all your sublime diplomacy, please ask Farad to meet me beside our provision wagons, in about ten minutes." Ghorm departed without his usual banter, dark eyes filled with speculation. Sentauris strolled through their hidden rest area as though passing time. While she glanced at many faces, she was seeking only one. When she found the man she sought, she called him aside with studied casualness.

"Soldier, good soldier," she said softly, "you know how it is said that I see the future and all its troubles?" The man nodded, face showing the first signs of alarm: was his own death upon him? Sentauris touched his arm gently. "No, fear not, I cannot see all our destinies. But through my Farsight we have avoided so many interceptions and ambushes, traveling through lands infested with our adversaries.

"Good soldier, a twist of fate lies over you and your sword: in scores of futures, your blade falls from its sheath or is drawn at the wrong time and so our presence is betrayed, and many die. All these chances come not from any flaw within yourself nor from the nature of your blade; these mishaps are only the subtle tripwires lain through lines of fate by a Death that hungers for our lives. Here." She unwrapped from about her neck a cotton scarf of woodland green. "Only bind your blade to its sheath and do not draw it until you are told to do so by your captains. Will you do this for me?" Slowly, gravely, the man nodded. Sentauris released him, and her eyes relaxed.

"See, it is over," she said softly. "Death must now find other lives to feast on. I will tell your captain that you bear a spell guard against the ancient Creatures of the Darkness. Good soldier, we will draw weapons together before the gates of Tuvan." Sentauris left the man binding his sword with the reverence of an acolyte handling talismans passed to him by a Goddess.

She found Farad waiting for her by a cluster of wagons; the captain's eyes were studying distant cloud patterns, though he smiled as Sentauris approached.

"Tuvan in two days," Farad said, "if our foes or the fates do not intercede."

"Both are seeking us with some eagerness," Sentauris said, bringing out a map scroll. As she knelt, placing it on the ground, Farad crouched down beside her. "Here, at this road junction is one of our most dangerous intersections." Her fingers traced over a slight tangle of lines that lay to the north of Tuvan on the map.

"Our advance guard cannot avoid this place, for all other pathways lead to greater dangers," she spoke slowly, as though her mind travelled down the paths outlined on the map. "But these crossroads are well guarded by five Carags. In a hundred futures that lie before us, in ninety of them, the Carags slay our advance party, or they escape and bring down violence and death upon our people, far short of Tuvan. You are going to trap these Carags and kill them all. Think about this, Farad, think about how that might be done." Both Seeress and Captain stood; Sentauris touched Farad lightly, her eyes staring south.

"Yes," she said softly, almost a whisper, "now only in fifty of those hundred chances in the future do any Carags survive, and yet these are still poor odds. Consider, Farad, that in all encounters those you meet at the crossroads are Carags, though they bear the images of brethren or allies, or even the Adepts, so you must choose hard men, while also counselling your party strongly. Ah, now we are down to twenty chances of a hundred. Farad, they ride swift steeds...now you adjust by bringing skilled archers... and the Carags are as close to doom as can be managed from this distance." She released Farad, glanced deeply into his eyes for a moment, then turned to other tasks.

Farad stood staring after her departing form for a moment, his dark spare features forming a strange expression. *What is happening to me? In my mind, the gold no longer gleams, and all my pride in power diminishes. I am becoming as one with her cause.*

In late afternoon they made another swift, forced march. The misfortuned blade of the forewarned soldier remained bound, and all five Carag assassins were destroyed before they could raise an alarm. But harsh weather, unexpectedly, swept over them. Rain, strong winds, followed by the violence of a thunderstorm forced them to slow, then halt. With his men made safe, Gallandus sought Sentauris, finding her sheltered with Ghorm under a slip of canvas held overhead by a cluster of branches. Above them, lightning forked, and thunder rolled heavily over them, and cracking sounds rippled through the forest as trees far and near shattered under the storm's fury.

Sentauris waved him over, and Gallandus joined the Seeress and her Familiar under their slip of canvas. "I suppose," Gallandus noted dryly, "that this must be the safest place in this stormy forest."

"So it is," Sentauris said, "though you came not for safety, but to ask me — ever so gently — why I did not foresee this event." She paused for a moment while lightning flashed, then thunder boomed over them.

"I do not know what it is like to be a God," she continued, "or whether the Gods truly sleep. But one God, rising with the dawn, looked down upon us and decided to bring down harsh weather on our heads — or upon Vorrs and Uraks and Carags — the effect is the same. Perhaps even...." More thunder rumbled over them.

"Perhaps some God being rose late in the day," Sentauris murmured, yawning, "and said, 'Ah, but my shrine in Piranus is honored on this day, and that city surely deserves better weather. Therefore, I will push these dark clouds south.' So, I can see something of what the Gods ordain, but not all."

"What you see is more than enough," Gallandus said quietly, not willing to hear sharp words from Ghorm. "Had we marched blind, we would have faced a running battle, with every league diminishing our numbers and our strength." Gallandus grunted as he rose, then he leaned forward against the force of the wind, raising his arm to keep sheets of rain from blinding his sight.

"Well done, Ghorm," Sentauris said lightly, moving her right foot from over that of her Familiar. "You were going to comment — again — about our captain's girth and greyness, and yet you held your tongue."

"Only because otherwise, you would have squashed me like a bug," Ghorm muttered.

In late afternoon, the storm shifted south to the shoreline of Alantéa, so that their war party was able to make a portion of its planned journey, though they remained well short of their goal. As always, Ghorm's system was shaken by their rude, jostling travel, and he readied for sleep at dusk, wrapped in cloth and canvas under a provision wagon. When the last light of day passed, Ghorm fell into a fitful, dreaming sleep.

He woke in stages. A hand was shaking him gently; he turned on his side, growling. His name was being called. As the shaking became more insistent, his eyes blinked open: Sentauris was kneeling beside him.

"Ghorm," she whispered, "we need you and your magic." It was deep night and quiet. The skies had cleared, and moonlight was passing through pale green and white flowers that were opening on the upper branches of the forest. Ghorm struggled to his feet, grumbling.

"You told me we had passed the last obstacles," he muttered, "that the path to Tuvan was cleared."

"The storm changed all that," Sentauris murmured. "It moved us into a zone of uncertainty. A Creature Indomitable blunders toward us unwittingly. Either we divert it now, or we fight it two hours before daybreak, and our numbers become sharply reduced. Come." Ghorm yawned and followed, scrambling to keep pace with Sentauris as she moved swiftly to the camp's eastern edge.

When they had passed beyond the outer sentries, Sentauris whispered, "I know how little you like this sort of travel, but we must make our best speed." Ghorm nodded grudgingly; with one arm, Sentauris lifted her Familiar and ran forward for a hundred paces, then set him down, and jogged beside him. Alternately carrying then running beside Ghorm, Sentauris made three quarters her normal speed; but still, they made a swift passage over moonlit forest trails.

They came to a halt at the edge of a deep and wide gorge. The land rose and fell all around them, with tall trees leaving only patches of moonlight to illuminate their paths. Swift running water could be heard in the depths beneath, as mists rose to sparkle in shafts of moonlight. Both Ghorm and

Sentauris felt magic and menace coming from the far edge of the gorge. The two moved in almost complete silence around the rim until Sentauris found a large stone hovering upright just at the edge of the ravine.

"This is what I've been looking for," she whispered in tones that rose just above the sounds of rushing waters. "Another storm or one swift push will send this stone over the cliffs, down to the stream below. The monster will be distracted from its hunt; then you must raise the noises of beasts from the bottom of the ravine, and so lure this Creature from our path. Are you ready?" Ghorm took a deep breath and nodded, preparing his small magic. Sentauris put her shoulder to the stone: it shifted, toppled, then smashed its way down the rocky slope. Ghorm's lips whispered words; from below came snuffling and snorting sounds.

Across from Seeress and Familiar loomed an enormous, dark, and lumpy shape. It seemed to sniff, hesitating at the ravine's edge; but it would not move. Cursing beneath his breath, Ghorm put forth his full strength: from below came wild snarling and growling sounds — wolves cornering some large, defiant beast. At the gorge's edge, the Creature Indomitable gave a great cry of desire and hunger, then it spilled over, scrambling, and slithering down the steep incline, and so it passed from their journey.

Ghorm sagged back, clutching a sapling: he was spent. As they returned to camp, only a few images reached his consciousness: Sentauris was carrying him, then he had struggled from Sentauris' hold and was stumbling over moonlit paths, and then Sentauris was carrying him again. At last, he was placed in a dark, quiet, motionless corner, and Ghorm retreated into a valley of fatigue where even his dreams seemed tired, helpless things.

The fog surrounding Ghorm lifted for a moment: they were moving again, building speed. Bright lights flashed into his eyes. He lay in a provision cart, surrounded by soft sacks of grain that were meant to cushion him against the violence of their travel. Even with the sacks for support, nausea swept over him, and the fog in his mind rolled back over him in dense waves.

Then it was nighttime: dark and still. He took a deep breath and became aware that Sentauris stood beside him, her soft fingers clearing matted tangles from his forehead.

"Ghorm," she said softly, "Ghorm, had we fought that monstrosity, we would have lost more than two score of our fighting force. You saved their lives, Ghorm. Rest now, preserve your strength so you can boast to your comrades, Whisper and Squint." Ghorm let the soothing touch of Sentauris' hands sweep over him: if this was not his heart's desire, still it was good, it was enough. He slipped back into a healing sleep.

More jostling motions came. His wagon passed through a sunlit glade so that he was forced to shield his eyes. *Come now, Goblin with the heart of a toad,* a portion of his mind argued, *it's time to rise. Not yet, not yet,* whispered the greater portion. *Sleep, Ghorm, sleep.*

He woke again in sunlight, this time to the sounds of voices arguing in low, intense tones.

"Never come to battle in a state of exhaustion," Gallandus was saying, "and that's our condition after a long march."

"You cite one of the greatest rules of generalship," Farad spoke in support of Gallandus.

"But if we arrive too late," Sentauris said, struggling to keep her voice low, "Tuvan will no longer stand. Our foes have built a siege-tower and in a short time, the Main Gates of Tuvan will be overwhelmed."

"Hold for a moment," Sardonicus said evenly. "Let's see if we can't find a third path between these two views." Ghorm heard their voices lower, then trail off as the four wandered from his provision cart, moving toward their war party's vanguard. Moments later, their jostling, bumpy pace renewed, and Ghorm retreated again into sleep, although more than half of his slight store of magic had now been restored by rest.

When Ghorm woke again, the air all about him seemed completely clear and still, though from a distance he could hear strange cries like muted bird calls. He slipped down from the provision wagon. Men all around him were frozen to the ground, eyes staring ahead. Farther back, their horses were held silent, groomed while being fed by hand. Behind them, the afternoon sun had begun settling down to its place of rest beyond the horizon.

Ghorm made his way forward, his feet still wobbly. They faced east, setting sun at their backs, so it seemed that they had passed west of the siege and now approached Tuvan from a side that remained unguarded. Ghorm pressed forward; again, came strange, remote cries as though distant seagulls were being felled by crossbolts. He reached Sentauris: she was armored in light chain mail, crouched beside her captains, staring toward Tuvan the Besieged, where war had been carried to the City's gates.

"...I wasted no time warning the Adepts," Sentauris was saying. "They alone hold the city. Look before you." In the distance, Ghorm saw that a siege-tower had been rolled into place and it loomed high over the twin watchtowers guarding Tuvan's gates. As Ghorm watched, magic flames swept over the siege-tower; it smoldered with dark smoke through its green wood and the dampened cloths wielded by their foes kept it from flaming into destruction.

"Wylar has taken a shaft..." Sentauris said slowly. "He fights on, though his wound saps his strength. We must ride now or forsake the Adepts."

"It is time now to earn our pay," Gallandus said. Farad and Sardonicus nodded, then the three mercenary captains clasped hands, murmuring together, "One blood, at day's end, one blood." Then they sped to their appointed positions. Ghorm unsheathed his dagger, checking the sharpness of its blade.

"Ghorm, Ghorm," Sentauris murmured, "you know this is not your fight...." She paused, peering into frames of future chances, then sighed. "Come with me now, Ghorm, but do not be overly brave." Hunched over, they made their way back toward the horse riders.

They assembled with some speed. At Tuvan the defense was shaken: fires on the siege-tower had been dampened, and now the East Tower smoldered, and the gates between the two towers were beginning to buckle.

Farad formed the leading phalanx of spearmen. Sentauris drew a spear and rode beside him. As their first horse riders passed from hiding into open space, she drew from her pouch the petal device given her by Wylar. She broke off its second petal and spoke into it.

"Hold fast, for we are at the gates of Tuvan," she called aloud, then cast the spent petal aside. Slowly their armored horse built to a faster pace. Vorrs stirred by thoughts of horseflesh came prowling at their flanks, but archers on horseback shot them down. Farad rode foremost, with Sentauris at his right. As their pace built, other hard, strong riders pushed their way to the fore. Bands of Uraks crowded in bunches in front of them, and then spears and a thunder of horses' hooves left them stricken on the ground.

A great cry of exultation slipped from the lips of Sentauris, and Ghorm felt a chill race through the core of his being and all his nausea fled. Vorrs and Uraks lay dying. Human warriors guarding the siege tower faltered, then fell back. Armored horses swept over them, then turned for a second charge, preparing to sweep the gates of Tuvan free of their foes. Though as they slowed, Vorrs tracked them, wary now of archers, but watching for the slightest openings.

Sardonicus rode up, leading a second group of men, who dismounted at the siege-tower's base. A band of Uraks drew closer, wielding maces; they were met and held by the bristling pikes and spears of hardened mercenaries.

Sardonicus led ax men to the Uraks' flanks, and the mace wielding Uraks began to collapse, bellowing, legs hewn from beneath them.

Gallandus had led the rearguard that escorted their provisions; now with their foes in confusion and retreat, his party took up grappling ropes. Scores of hooks and ropes began snaring the upper floors of the siege tower of their foes. Ropes tightened and were pulled tight. Vorrs watched from a distance, snarling in confusion as more men pulled, while other men harnessed the strength of their horses. The siege tower slid from Tuvan's gates then began toppling, with men falling and shrieking from its upper battlements.

The siege tower, still smoldering, crashed downwards, shaking the ground, and shattering into fragments. Farad and Sentauris made a second brief sweep of the area before the gates. Human legions were scrambling from the battle, while Uraks vented their fury into the air with bellowing cries, and Vorrs skulked, howling, from the siege.

Men watched from Tuvan's walls, mouths open in astonishment: warfare to them was confusion and chaos, but all the sharp, brutal violence beyond the gates had been choreographed like an elaborate dance.

As Ghorm stared up into their astonished faces, he felt his small heart lift, threatening to burst from his chest, for with the diminishing light of sunset casting a blood-red glow around them, Sentauris and her war party passed beyond the ruined tower and the tangles of corpses surrounding it, then rode through the gates of Tuvan and into the besieged city.

Chapter Six

Tuvan the Besieged

THE GATES THE GATES THE GATES THE GATES

Whispering voices reached Sentauris like echoes from a distant chamber. Her eyes slipped open: daylight was seeping through the window above her head, and the slight breezes of morning were flapping the windows' dark curtains. It was early, and the voices were not yet demanding. She pulled bedclothes over her face and slipped once again into a confusion of shimmering dreams.

The Gates The Gates The Gates The Gates The Gates The Gates The Gates The Gates

She sat up: morning had become much brighter, the voices more insistent. With a yawn, she rose and armed herself. She and Ghorm were housed in the servants' quarters of an abandoned manor house; this part of the manor was sparsely furnished but chosen because it was well secured against nightstalkers. She unbarred the door gently — Ghorm was sleeping just down the hall, and to rouse him too early might leave him grouchy for the rest of the day.

The Gates The Gates The — "Yes, yes," Sentauris whispered, making her way outside. Morning had slipped over Tuvan, bringing broad hints of the warmth and the lush smells of flowering trees that would follow later in the spring. She stood for a moment, studying sky patterns: blue radiated from above, as though calling on all flying creatures to take wing. After one last deep breath, she made her way down the side street leading to the main thoroughfare, and from there she passed swiftly over the cobblestone plaza to the Main Gates that faced north.

The Watchtower Guards gave hesitant little nodding bows as she passed, then backed from Sentauris as she climbed the wobbly stairs that led to the East Tower. The rising sun loomed low on her right, shining a bright light over a battlefield that was still littered with bodies, siege-tower wreckage, and shattered weapons. Their enemies had retreated, except for stray Vorrs whose heads lifted and stared at her with red eyes filled with hatred.

Outside the walls of Tuvan, fields of grain and orchards had flourished not too many days ago. Now, farm buildings had been abandoned, some burned, some battered to the ground. At night, rodents still spilled out of the woodlands to feast on ruined crops. The Saugus, the great river that passed north and west of Tuvan, was too far away to see. Beyond the nearby fields lay forests, and beyond those....

As distance caused her eyes to lose their focus, the Seer's Sight within her stirred.

The field before her began to darken and lose all hints of color. Images slipped through her mind, of spectral armies passing over darkened plains, ebbing, then flooding back with always greater numbers. Their foes had withdrawn for the moment, but they had not abandoned Tuvan. Instead, more human tiers, and bands of Uraks, and packs of Vorrs were being drawn to the siege. Creatures of the Darkness hovered at the edges of the forests, though they seemed drawn, not by Tuvan, but by their foes: a mystery. Yet still, the siege was tightening, bringing a force to bear that was far greater than any strength that Tuvan could muster.

As Sentauris let the vision pass, sunlight streamed back into her eyes. She stepped cautiously down the creaking staircase to find Ghorm waiting for her, rubbing his dark face with small, squat hands.

"It's so early," he said, yawning. "Haven't we broken this siege? Isn't Tuvan relieved, and can't we at least get one morning's rest?"

"To answer your questions: no, no, and no. Our enemies are gathering around Tuvan, as this city becomes the great focus of our struggle. Can't you feel the pressure?"

"If I could, I would be Ghorm the Sage, not Ghorm the Mutterer," Ghorm muttered, "not Ghorm the Grumbling Goblin." The little Familiar took a deep breath and squared his shoulders. "All right now. Which comes first — are we going to talk to Tuvan's Council or to the Adepts?"

"I know how little you love the Adepts, but —" Sentauris broke off, her eyes drawn to the south. All three of her mercenary Captains were walking away from the East Tower where Sentauris stood, passing farther from the Main Gates. They walked slowly along the West Walls, studying the fortifications as they walked. Each of the three Captains was guarded by two trusted aides, so there were six bodyguards in total. The three Captains were intent on their discussions, while their guards searched all the faces of Tuvan's residents with such intense focus that onlookers were stepping away from the mercenaries and their inspection of the city.

Ghorm's eyes gleamed with dark humor. "I have to guess that your Captains are discussing the defenses of Tuvan the Besieged."

Sentauris shook her head grimly. "It does not take a Seeress to foresee that they will be unhappy with what they find."

"Wouldn't it be interesting to hear exactly what they were saying?" Ghorm asked.

· ☾ ·

"So, the Main Gates face north," Gallandus said, "and from the north come intruders, raiders and more serious invasions. Thus, the relative strength of the Main Gates makes at least a little sense."

"Tiny sense," Sardonicus muttered, "for tiny minds." The three Captains were walking south, discussing the defense of Tuvan; Gallandus frowned as they passed a section of wall where the mortar had failed, and stones were beginning to slide free. Overhead were battlements — stone platforms where the West Wall could be defended by many hundreds of guards and citizens — but it was obvious that no one had repaired them in years.

"The city of Tuvan was built with a breakwater concept," Farad said evenly. "It has an oval, egglike shape, with its sharpest curve facing north and a less sharp curve facing south, while the wide curves of its shape are exposed to the west and east. Like a granite point facing the ocean, the Main Gates would absorb the powerful thrust of an invasion, turn that power aside, and send it south so that the Wizards might deal with it."

"I suppose that the southern gates," Gallandus said doubtfully, "the so-called South-West and South-East Gates, were intended to receive reinforcements from Gravengate or Stone Mountain, should those ever arrive."

"Ha!" Sardonicus laughed openly. "Tuvan the 'Breakwater!' Designed by some silly poet who had no real grasp of warfare. I must ask the most basic question: where is the citadel? Where do Tuvan's warriors and citizens retreat after the outer walls are breached?"

Farad nodded bleakly. "My heart sank like a dying thing after the first night that I walked through Tuvan and understood the city's flaws."

"Yet now *we* are here in Tuvan," Gallandus said. "We are strong, we are determined, and we are resourceful. Although not a substitute for a true citadel, Tuvan has hills, with thoroughfares at the top of those hills. Roadblocks might be set at those heights, and temporary strong points built to create a second line of defense should Tuvan's walls be breached."

"I also saw that possibility," Farad said, "though it gave me nothing like joy."

They were silent for a moment as they walked slowly toward the South-West Gate, each of them noting the disrepair of the battlements on the West Walls. In some places, battlements provided platforms that would allow a force six deep to resist invaders, but everywhere the stone was crumbling. In the worst sections, sections of the stone platforms had completely failed, and only wooden walkways linked the West Walls. Even the six bodyguards, focused on protecting their leaders, were shaking their heads in disgust.

One of the bodyguards even wandered over, pinching, and holding up a clump of sawdust.

"That makes for even less joy," Gallandus muttered. "They have fire ants or termites."

"Speaking of little joy," Sardonicus said, "this might be a suitable time to discuss the Adepts."

Farad glanced back to the Main Gates; Sentauris and Ghorm were out of sight. "Yes, we can speak openly about the Adepts now that the Seeress and her Familiar can no longer overhear us."

Sardonicus laughed. "It is interesting that Ghorm has no affection either for Orantes or for Wylar."

"Alliances are often clumsy, emotional, and temporary," Farad said. "We need to state matters in terms of warcraft. I have always considered that an Adept, a Magician fully weaponed and trained, is worth a full tier — five hundred armed men. In those terms, Wylar and Orantes would count as two tiers, a full thousand fighters. From what you've seen — and heard — what battle strength would you give for each one of them?"

"They might each account for a score of fighting men," Sardonicus said.

"Two dozen, each," Gallandus added.

Farad nodded. "Sadly, I agree, and now I ask, why so few? Why are they so weak?"

Gallandus paused before speaking. "Both outside and within the League, they are known as the 'Replacement Adepts,' because their powerful and highly regarded predecessors vanished so suddenly, without any explanation, and without a succession plan."

"Yet all that happened several years ago," Farad said, "so they have had more than enough time to grow to full power."

"Those who are kind call them 'Replacements,'" Sardonicus added, "while others who are less kind refer to them as 'The Inepts' rather than 'The Adepts.'"

"On the other hand," Farad said, "Sentauris seems to regard them more favorably, so perhaps they do have some potential."

Sardonicus barked out a laugh. "What we really need is her Crazy Uncle Vlasoff here in Tuvan, forcing both Inepts to sacrifice themselves in battle."

"The Seeress remains a force to be reckoned with," Gallandus said softly, ignoring Sardonicus. "As for the Adepts, if they are going to become stronger, they need to do so quickly."

·))(·

Sentauris had watched the three mercenary leaders and their bodyguards until they passed beyond a section of Tuvan's buildings that blocked her sight.

As she turned away with a sigh, Ghorm asked sardonically, "So our Captains were pleased with Tuvan's fortifications, am I right?"

"You knew that they would become unhappy," Sentauris said, "and you will be glad to know that they don't care much for the Adepts, but we need to speak with them anyway."

With the shouting and the clamor and the crowds, there had not been time last evening to exchange more than a few murmured words with Wylar and Orantes, so Sentauris had no idea where to find them. She let her Farsight guide her, and the two Magicians were eventually located in a dingy guardhouse that lay less than fifteen hundred paces from Tuvan's watchtowers.

Within that guardhouse, a haggard Orantes was rebinding Wylar's shoulder. Both Adepts wore grey cloaks that were stained with blood and grime.

Despite the grime and ignoring Ghorm's dark looks, each of the Adepts embraced Sentauris; the Seeress felt her heart stir, though she checked her response both for Ghorm's sake, and to keep her focus on Tuvan the Besieged.

"When last we spoke," Wylar said softly, "your parting words spoke of a meeting at Tuvan, yet I never thought we would see you again."

"I was just bidding farewell," Orantes added, "to this life and all its pleasures, when you came speeding out from the sunset, surging across the fields like some being of myth. Sentauris, I am glad to be beside a true hero — or heroine — for I confess myself to be made of comic, not dramatic, proportions."

"So you say," Sentauris murmured, examining Wylar's shoulder wound — just a few hours after being treated, the flesh was closing over it. "However, you are overly modest, Adept. Your strength as a healer has grown unless I am mistaken."

"As healers, we've shown reasonable growth," Wylar said. "We can also cast cunning illusions; while as Adepts in battles, we've shown only tiny improvements. But as politicians, we are nothing: of the thousands inhabiting Tuvan, only a few hundred rallied to us in the struggle for their own city."

"In some areas, the Wizards have given you neither reasonable direction nor training," Sentauris said, releasing Wylar and his wound. She glanced beyond the guardhouse door, where onlookers had begun to gather and peer within. "Now is a suitable time to meet with Tuvan's wayward leaders, while our foes still lick their wounds. Come, if you are able."

"Ah, time to deal with the twin heroes of Tuvan," Orantes said cheerfully. "Murat, Fiüre, the League is coming again to tippy tap upon your chamber doors!" Wylar, grimacing, pulled folds of cloak down over his wounded upper arm, then the two Adepts followed Sentauris out into the bright morning. The air was clear and fresh with only distant puff clouds hovering over the south of Alantéa. As they walked slowly through sunlit streets, moving toward the Main Gates, Sentauris asked about Tuvan's Council.

"I'm afraid that the rule of the Wizards has been too remote, too passive," Wylar said. "It seems that Tuvan was guided by self-serving, bickerings dimwits who fought among themselves over Tuvan's future, and then vanished when the League was attacked."

"Ah, but in spite of their failure, we have discovered local leaders," Orantes added, walking with just the trace of a limp. "These number four: Druss and Breughal whom you met last night, and Murat and Fiüre respectively of the West and East Watches. Druss is a good lad, though a youngling, while Breughal wishes mostly to escape Tuvan and seek his fortune elsewhere. The other two Watch captains are something short of being complete traitors — at least they did not stab us in our backs when we fought to save the city." Wylar then proceeded to relate their unhappy experiences at the strongholds of the two wayward Watches. As he spoke, Wylar saw the face of Sentauris become steadily grimmer.

"Tuvan must be reorganized to reflect its siege conditions," she said quietly, and then she stopped. A gaggle of onlookers had been trailing behind them; Sentauris turned and addressed them. "Good citizens, your town Council must have an appointed meeting place — can one or two of you guide us there? And others, might they seek for Druss and Breughal and bid them join us in that place?" Heads nodded.

"Ask your captains to come, Seeress," Wylar said quietly. As Sentauris hesitated, the Adept turned to the onlookers. "We have been too passive. As Adepts, we speak with the authority of the Wizards. Tuvan's Council and its Watch Commanders are summoned to join with us to discuss the defense of Tuvan. To this gathering, I call Sentauris and other defenders of the League. The Wizards are mighty, but the peoples of the League must rise in their own defense. Go, and speak these words." All but two of the townsfolk hurried away. Ten paces from the Adepts, Wylar's message was already garbled; and no one was willing to carry even the gentlest of summons to the West or East Watches.

"And I," Orantes said cheerfully, "I exercise my authority by inviting the Familiars Squint and Whisper to our gathering. In such a way, we will reserve the magical powers of Ghorm, who will no longer need to slip telltales upon our sensitive persons." Ghorm glanced sharply at Orantes, surprised that the Adept had discovered the Familiar's spying device back at *The Weasel's Feast*.

Tuvan's Council Chambers had been built some years ago, with a vaulting roof of wooden beams rising over walls formed from rough stone and mortar. Inside it was dark, though muffled light seeped through a few small, dingy windows. At one end, a large oval table had been set, with vat-candles hanging from beams above it, as though the old Council had gathered mostly in the dark of the night. The dust from several untended weeks had gathered on tables, chairs, and floors.

"Were I a Wizard," Sentauris said softly, as she peered inside the chamber, "my rule would also be light, though I would maintain a core of emissaries to report on conditions such as these."

"No doubt," Orantes said, somewhat subdued, "and you would probably choose as emissary an Adept who lacked a fondness for the grape, someone who would not so easily be lured into late night telling tales in some warm, dark tavern. Sentauris the Sorceress would surely choose an emissary who would deal directly with the obvious incompetence and open manipulation encountered three years ago, and again just fourteen months before the opening of this war."

So that's how it went, Sentauris thought. *A wayward Orantes represented the Wizards in Tuvan. I wonder which cities Wylar was assigned, and if those fared any better than Tuvan.*

"I will say this once and once only," Wylar added. "Hektor and Antéus — the Adepts who came before us — were far more effective than we have been in these last few years. The two of us, Orantes and Wylar, known as the 'Replacement Adepts,' need to improve both dramatically and rapidly."

The three captains arrived first, none of them touched by the sharp, hard battle of the afternoon before, except that their tour of Tuvan had left them with long faces. Druss followed, drifting toward the mercenaries with a combination of shyness and eagerness. Squint and Whisper made separate entrances and sought Ghorm, whose spirits rose noticeably when they arrived.

Only Breughal remained outside, and Sentauris could feel him approach, but he was moving slowly and reluctantly. Sentauris could feel his heavy heart as she walked casually to the chamber door and out into the bright morning. The old merchant was no more than thirty paces from the council chamber

— he was forcing his feet to move forward but came to a complete halt as Sentauris approached him.

"I am not eager to meet with you and your vision, Seeress," Breughal muttered turning his face into the morning sky so that his eyes would not meet those of Sentauris.

"I bring no curses, only clear sight," she said softly, reaching out to touch him gently by the arm.

"You bring pain."

"Yes, old and bitter pain," she said, reading his thoughts and visions, "but also strength, and a quiet honor.... You loved the grandmother of this child with the wisdom of a man, Druss, yet she chose Thelm...this lad's grandsire and Captain of the Gate Watch, the real leader of Tuvan. Throughout this city's strife and bickering and even when the parents of Druss were forced from the city, you supported the family of Thelm, your old rival."

"Both friend and rival," Breughal replied in a soft voice, face still turned away from the Seeress.

"And you see in Druss," she continued, "the features of your first love, and the grandchild you might have enjoyed, had matters turned otherwise. Honor remains strong within you, though disguised. The Maker will say as much to you, at Time's End."

"Will He then release me from this pain? A pain that comes late at night, and pierces beyond all my layers of wealth and power? Will He do this?"

"That and more," Sentauris replied. "Yet if you speak of pain, I must tell you that the pain for you that lies outside Tuvan's walls — even should you successfully escape — that pain is greater for you than the pain that lies within Tuvan the Besieged."

"I understand that I must stand with Tuvan," Breughal said softly, taking a deep breath. "So much of what you call 'honor' is merely the choice of lesser pain. Come, Seeress, enough — you have a war to fight." They passed into the chamber to find its occupants clustered into three groups: two Adepts sitting in silence; captains nodding as they responded quietly to questions from an eager Druss; and the Familiars speaking in hushed, excited tones in their own corner.

As Sentauris and Breughal entered, Wylar rose to his feet and spoke: "In this emergency, we must reconstitute Tuvan's Council. Breughal and Druss are the core of this new Council and are joined by myself and my fellow Adept, representing the Wizards and their League. Other citizens of Tuvan will be added as they emerge during the coming struggle — and they need not be war leaders, but men and women of good will and strength of mind. Can we agree on this?" Druss and Breughal nodded solemnly, Orantes with a wry, half mocking expression.

"Events move swiftly," Wylar continued. "In normal times this small Council would discuss matters at length, but more of our enemies' power is being drawn toward Tuvan, and our city may not hold unless we move with speed. I ask that Sentauris be appointed Siege Captain, defender of Tuvan. Subject to the guidance of our Council, her word will become law." Again, all nodded, Orantes more thoughtfully. Only Ghorm allowed humor to flash over his dark features: how the Wizards would love this moment!

Wylar turned to Sentauris. "What is to be done?"

"First, we are under siege conditions," Sentauris said evenly, as though assuming the rule of a city was an everyday occurrence. "All stores and weapons will be placed under the central authority of this Council and its Captains. Second, all citizens of Tuvan must participate in the defense of their city — if they wish to be released from this obligation, they must leave Tuvan." Breughal stirred but said nothing.

"Third," she continued, "the West Watch and the East Watch led by Murat and Fiüre are disbanded. We go now to advise them of this fact." Here Orantes raised a discreet palm.

"In my new role as grey eminence of Tuvan's Council," he said, speaking with unusual seriousness, "I must ask your intentions about these Watches and their commanders. The Wizards favor exile and not execution — and in this regard, I have to agree with them."

"It would be folly to cause the deaths of many, for we need every able-bodied human," Sentauris said, hesitating while she peered into the distance. "We will make an effort to avoid any deaths."

"Adept," Farad spoke for the first time, "make no mistake: those resisting by force must be put down by force."

"Fair enough," Orantes muttered, pulling himself to his feet. Then he sang to himself in a little nursery-rhyme voice, *Murat, come out. Fiüre, come out. To play, to play — until the ending of the day.*

Tuvan's new Council and its Captains emerged again, blinking, into the bright light of late morning. Several hundred of Tuvan's citizens had gathered around the chamber; from them came a mixture of muted applause and shallow, embarrassed laughter. Many followed them as Tuvan's Council and Captains moved to deal first with the wayward West Watch.

After a brief conversation with Sentauris, Farad and Gallandus turned back, leaving only Sardonicus to answer Druss' questions. The sun burned down overhead, though light breezes from the west cooled Tuvan's Council and the entourage that followed in its wake. As Squint passed above them, the Owl-being again sent gaunt rock doves fluttering and swirling. Casually, Sentauris drew her bow, notched it, eyes scanning the swirling flocks as though searching for a plump specimen.

With one motion, Sentauris wheeled and loosed her arrow into the crowd; onlookers fell back, crying aloud. One tall, grim faced man stood with one hand clutching the shaft embedded in his chest, while his other hand pulled a dagger from a scabbard within his cloak. A second shaft pinned the hand holding the dagger to his chest. The man stood, growling deep in his throat, radiating hatred at Sentauris; but then the mist of death rising before the assassin's eyes became too great, and the figure toppled, flesh slowly transforming, features becoming beast-like with a snout resembling that of a hyena.

The Carag convulsed one last time, then it stiffened, while its dagger slipped from lifeless, no longer human hands. Sentauris and others looked down on it with cautious, uncertain eyes.

"Other Carags remain hidden in this city," Sentauris said flatly.

"We were working on devices intended to seek them out," Wylar said, frowning down at the stilled, translucent form. "Certain lenses transformed by magic will show a blurred and shivering form whenever a Carag looking like a human comes into view."

"Save your magic for the battles to come," Sardonicus said, kneeling over the Carag's corpse. "Are there no hunting dogs inside this quaint village? I cannot believe that these shapeshifters can completely disguise their smell. Find me a few trackers and we will drive these creatures into Tuvan's darkest corners, and then beyond its walls."

"Good," Sentauris said. "Sardonicus, you will fight to make Tuvan secure from within. Call upon the Familiars as you need them. Farad is freed to assist Breughal with the organization of Tuvan's weapons and supplies. Gallandus, I think, will begin the training of the Gate Watch."

"Tuvan will be utterly transformed," Orantes said, nodding solemnly, then muttering under his breath, "As for this member of Tuvan's Council, he wishes only to be consulted after the wine stores are properly inventoried."

As the stronghold of the West Watch came into view, Gallandus and Farad also returned from side streets, leading a picked force of three score mercenaries. Behind them were horse drawn carts, holding long beams slung with thick rope, devices that might serve as makeshift battering rams. At a word, the carts were left standing, while the men arranged themselves in twin arcs, just seventy paces from the stronghold of the West Watch. Passing between these two sections, Sentauris and her Council and Captains approached the portals of the West Watch — but cautiously, as though the Seeress tested each step and its consequences.

"Murat, we come, we come, we come," Orantes sang cheerfully in muted tones. Behind him, men serving Sardonicus kindled a fire to provide warmth for themselves, and beyond them, onlookers grew in number, some showing the high spirits once found in village fairs of the past.

"This will do no good," Sentauris muttered, "except to maintain appearances." She drew a dagger from its sheath and hammered at the front portal with its shaft.

"Murat, come out!" she called aloud so that all might hear. "Tuvan's Council has disbanded your Watch! Set all your weapons aside, and we will deal with you fairly!" No answer came, not even the notching of crossbolts. Sentauris and those around her withdrew first twenty, then fifty paces from the stronghold.

"Now comes the bloodletting and loss of lives," Sentauris said, keeping her voice low. Then she turned to Breughal and Druss. "Death, needless death attends us unless you can persuade the Adepts to lay sleep or some other disarming enchantment over this wayward Watch."

Wylar smiled: a grimace that lacked humor. But Druss turned to him and said, "Save them. Save my people. Some of those belonging to this Watch have made themselves the enemies of my family, but not all, and who can tell who is enemy and who is friend, when the dying begins." Breughal nodded gravely, though he glanced at Druss with eyes that reflected the deep ache of old wounds.

"Ah," Orantes chuckled, turning to Wylar. "Ah, but this will make for a lovely and remarkable chat with the Wizards. Consider the nature of that discussion:

"Thorian: 'Did we not expressly forbid the use of magic against our own peoples?'

"Orantes: 'Of course, O wise and kind master, but we acted at the behest of the Council of Tuvan.'

"Balardi: 'And were not you yourself, Master Slack-Wit, a member of this so-called Council, along with your fellow Adept, Sir Addle-Pate?'

"Orantes: 'We were, your benevolence, and even though we abstained from this vote because of your instructions, we still felt an obligation to carry out the Council's desires.'

"Merlin: 'And was this violation not requested by someone outside this makeshift Council?'

"Orantes: 'Of course! Who might obscure events from you, greatest of the Mortal Magic Wielders? The lovely Sentauris, whom you admire so greatly, brought these events about....'

"And at this point," Orantes continued, "civilized discourse breaks down, and we can only hope that the Wizards transform us into newts or salamanders rather than crippled doodlebugs."

"What of the Stinking Itch, and the Shaking Ague?" Wylar asked. "What of the appointment of Sentauris as Siege Captain? Come, we have swallowed whole the hedgehog; now we are complaining about the parsnips surrounding its carcass."

"Yes, there is that logic," Orantes murmured, pursing his lips. "Perhaps when speaking to the Wizards, we should concentrate on the fierceness of the overwhelming numbers of the tiers of our foes, and the howling of their Vorrs."

"How the Uraks bellowed!" Wylar said, finally smiling. "How perversely shaped yet mighty were the dreadful Creatures of the Darkness!" Orantes glanced at the barracks of the West Watch and half sang, half whispered a remote and distant phrase. Wylar's voice brought forth another, equally hesitant note, though deeper in the tones of his voice, and with greater volume. More words came from Orantes, with a deeper chant flowing from Wylar, as the two voices joined, mingling together, then diverging, finally dwindling down until they became an echo of whispers emerging from an ancient crypt.

A cloud of yellow smoke formed in front of Orantes: glistening in the sunlight, it stood half a head taller than the Adept, but three times his bulk; as whispered words slipped from Orantes' lips, the yellow cluster took the shape of an enormous hand. Wylar nodded, his own whispered spell changing in midstream, and before him a column of green smoke began to squirm, turning and twisting until it gathered into the shape of a green hand, but taller and leaner, rising more than two heads above Wylar's height.

Ghorm watched on with a mixture of excitement and envy: here was genuine magic, a great part of his heart's desire. If only, if only, if only.... Crowd noises alternated between gasps and excited murmurs; and the sounds grew louder as the two hands turned to regard one another, bowed deeply, then slithered on huge fingers toward the barracks of the West Watch. The yellow hand powered by Orantes probed at windows and doors; then with a little hop, its fingers began to climb, using ledges and cornices and tiles to propel itself like a fat, clumsy spider to the building's upper reaches.

Wylar's device, that of the green hand, probed at the base of the building as though seeking a seam in its foundations. Ghorm's eyes darted from the enchanted hands back to the Adepts, and then to their lips, lips that whispered words of such power. *Orantes shapes the game, and Wylar joins in to indulge him, but my greatest wish is to just have the power to play!*

Suddenly the yellow hand halted — was that upper window ever so slightly ajar? And the green hand, too, hesitated before a seam in the mortar.

Separately, and soundlessly, each hand pushed, squirming, and slithering at its opening until it vanished inside.

A pause followed as hands formed of sorcerous smoke probed dark corridors. Then came muffled, clumping noises and shouts from darkened rooms, sounds of booted feet running over wooden floors — movements that began with swift steps and ended with soft, collapsing noises. After no more than a few hundred heartbeats a hushed quiet slipped over the building, as the Adepts ceased their whispering and the crowd behind them held its breath.

Orantes turned and bowed to Sentauris, just as Gallandus stepped to her side, his eyes watching the Adepts with little pleasure.

"All very pretty," Gallandus murmured, "though, at this stage, a demonstration of real power would be sound statecraft."

"My thoughts entirely," Sentauris said in an undertone. "Warn your men that some bearing useless talismans are awake and still weaponed, though these will be disarmed easily. Also, if they display the emblems of the Gods, those insignias must be stripped from them, though with some quiet reverence — we have sufficient complications without a rash of cranky Gods becoming aroused against us."

"We will work discretely, but we need to clear out this pesthole," Gallandus said, then he called out instructions. One cart bearing a makeshift battering ram was brought forward. A score of men pulled the ram from its cart and hauled it before the portals. As they readied their weapons, Gallandus walked among other veterans, choosing a few here and there until he had found another twenty who would listen to him carefully.

Boom! With smashing, rending sounds, the ram hammered at the gates, leveling them with a third thrust. Gallandus and others surged inside; moments later members of the West Watch were carried out like sacks of grain and were left in rows along the street, where they lay breathing heavily, twitching with troubled dreams.

Only three were awake as they were drawn from the stronghold: two came out limply, heads hung down in remorse or defeat; but the third fought like a mad thing, with wild eyes, haggard, raging. Finally, one hardened mercenary smashed a mailed fist against the wild man's head so that his struggles stopped; but even then, wild curses spewed from his mouth, calling on Dark Gods to bring pain and death to all his foes.

"Murat," Sentauris whispered, stepping toward him. "Let him be," she said to the men holding the wayward captain. Grudgingly, hard faced soldiers released Murat, just as Sentauris reached out to touch him.

"Murat," she whispered again, but Murat only redoubled his venom, calling on Dark Gods to come themselves and defile the Seeress before multitudes of onlookers. Suddenly, Sentauris wheeled and struck Murat: a smashing elbow to his throat that felled Murat like a toppling tree trunk.

"Traitor! Murderer!" she cried, then turned to Tuvan's people. "That blow was struck for Tuvan. Do any of you know what this man has done? He held Thelm tight while Fiüre stabbed the Captain of the Gate Watch, repeatedly. And all the while Thelm begged — not for his own life, but for Tuvan's, urging that one of the two become a leader who would defend his city.

"How did this happen, people of Tuvan? How did you let these venomous toads rise to power? How many heads were turned aside, how many thoughts were stilled, to let this happen?"

The crowd, pressing forward, swollen in numbers, began to murmur — some calling for the old Council to be put on trial, others for the death of Murat. "Kill him.... Kill him.... Kill him." The murmurs of the crowd built into a low chant.

"It would be justice," Sentauris raised her voice, "to slay Murat — but only rough justice that would lessen each of us. I say to you, people of Tuvan: if you wish to survive, all this murder of old friends and neighbors must end. Murat and Fiüre will need to pass from this city. Yet, as I will stand one day before the Maker, I stand here and say this: I will not deliver these venomous creatures to our foes. At the right time, we will release them, letting them pass to a place of safety or to their own ruin if they wish, but we will let them go.

"As for your own lives, people of Tuvan, how will you change them? It has been so many years since the founding of our League: a hundred years separate us from the jealous haunting of the Gods. Yet you have been content to go about your tasks in silence and let men with dark, pinched minds fill in the voids created by the absence of the Powers.

"Where are the songs, the celebrations of minstrels, the towering spires, the handcrafts slowly transformed into ornaments of great beauty? Where are the gardens that stir the souls of humans? Where are the tales that lift men's hearts? Where stands our daily quest for the Maker? All things flow to the Maker at the End of Time, yet your own passage will be greatly aided if you take the first steps toward Him in this life.

"Come, people of Tuvan, first you must struggle to endure this onslaught of Adversaries and after you must try harder to transform your own lives."

In a far more subdued mood, the crowd followed Tuvan's Council and Captains as they made their way to the East Watch. This time when the Adepts called down a charmed sleep over the East Watch, it was without the flourish of the yellow and green hands of Giants. At their spell's end, the Adepts only nodded to Gallandus, who again led the assault on the stronghold.

As before, the men of this wayward Watch were dragged out and hauled onto higher ground. But in the East Watch's warren of tunnels and deep passages, more than a few escaped. Some were tracked through underground mazes by Whisper and were later captured. Five others passed beyond Tuvan's walls and began to scurry in shuffling steps toward the deep woods that lay half a league's distance from Tuvan's eastern border. Squint reported that all these men were overtaken and consumed by Vorrs less than halfway to their goal.

Fiüre was among the last brought out. Unlike Murat, he was silent, though his eyes radiated an infinite menace. Sentauris spoke no words to him but had Fiüre, Murat, and several of their lieutenants secured in strong, well defended places. The balance of the day passed without confrontation, with foodstuffs being slowly moved to secured warehouses, while night watches were set, both within the city and at its outer posts. Men of the East and West Watches woke slowly, stumbling back to their old dwellings, and to those that would have them.

But at nightfall Sentauris was again stirred by distant noises, though no clear signals reached her mind. Again, she ascended a watchtower, this time the right-hand East Tower. Its guards withdrew, leaving her alone to stare out into moonless, dark, and shadowy fields, or up into the air, where the clear night sky left many thousands of stars glistening, radiating tiny pulses of pure light from enormous distances.

There, at the edge of her hearing: deep growling noises...one or two to the north...another to the east...and perhaps three others from the west, as though Creatures of the Darkness were being drawn toward the siege. But why would they come here? A Creature Indomitable was a greater threat to their exposed foes than to those enclosed within Tuvan's high walls. Unless.... Unless....

· 𝕏 ·

In the following days, Tuvan was completely reorganized. The Gate Watch was expanded to encompass the entire city, while kitchens and fire brigades were formed to support the city walls. Blacksmiths and woodworkers were assigned to the crafting of weapons, while stone masons worked to repair Tuvan's walls. A mixed force of young and old built devices to catch rainwater, to supplement the output of Tuvan's deep wells.

Under the sharp eyes of professional soldiers, the Guard began to train in earnest, undertaking drills that led them to all points of Tuvan's hilly streets, both in dark and daylight hours. Those who could not, or would not, meet standards set by the mercenaries were shunted into lesser tasks. Day by day, men of the former East and West Watches were slowly drawn back into Tuvan's Guard. It became a dark, secret jest among those of the Wayward Watches to whisper, "Ah, but Murat would have done this so much differently," or "Fiüre, now there was a man among men."

From their prisons, Fiüre glowered out in silence, hoping that Death would come to feast on Tuvan; while Murat's ravings became steadily less lucid so that it was no longer possible to understand which Dark Gods were being summoned, or which groups of humans were assigned to everlasting torment. And daily, the people they had led toward disaster grew steadily stronger in defense of their city.

With the tide of events shifting, Wylar and Orantes found themselves on dryer and more remote grounds: they were consulted less frequently, and the symbols of their authority and their magic needed less often. Only Sentauris sought them out each day, often late in the evening when her day's tasks were complete. Their own mornings and afternoons were left empty. Orantes might easily have amused himself for a time, but a few days after Tuvan's relief, Wylar called him aside.

"Come, old friend. The soldiers march, the blacksmiths hammer, while stronger and younger women train as female archers to support their brothers and husbands. It's time for the Adepts to practice magic."

"So?" Orantes' eyebrows rose a full inch. "The Guard is trained by Gallandus. Where are the Wizards who should have taught us battle magic?"

Wylar nodded thoughtfully. "We will have to discover that magic ourselves — or invent it." Orantes agreed only grudgingly, and his full enthusiasm was only completely engaged after the two Adepts had claimed for themselves the top two floors of the tallest spire of Tuvan: it was only seven stories high, but it was enough of a "Conjuror's Tower" to capture Orantes' imagination. Thereafter, the citizens of Tuvan gave the building a wide berth, for strange odors, lights and sounds seemed to emerge unexpectedly from its upper chambers, often followed by hoarse cries of frustration, shattering sounds, and muffled explosions.

·)(·

On the seventh evening of her time in Tuvan, Sentauris returned to her chamber to find Ghorm still awake, waiting for her while seated behind a low table on which a single candle flickered. She had shared wine with the Adepts, interrupting Orantes' wanderings and Wylar's contemplations for a few moments of relaxation.

Her eyes were soft, her mood was light, but then her heart sank as she saw that Ghorm's squat features were filled with accusations. *It's worse than returning from some escapade to find some spinster, maidenly aunt waiting awake for me. Ghorm!*

"It must be a lovely feeling," Ghorm said evenly, "to have not one suitor, but two. And if Orantes the Pig fails to delight you, then perhaps Wylar the Stoat can enchant you for an evening."

"Ghorm, we have been over this ragged ground before — you are as you are, and I am as I am. You know that I was never intended to live as a virgin princess sealed away in some lonely tower."

Ghorm's voice dropped. "There is a limit to what I can endure."

She sighed, sitting, and pulling off her boots. "For what it's worth, I do not see myself becoming deeply involved with either Adept, here at Tuvan. And if you take comfort in reassurances, know that I will not steal away to become Wylar's bride, nor will I seek shelter with Orantes and raise his children on some enchanted isle. But Ghorm, I do not see all or know every element of my future; in reality, a haze of mystery lies over it."

How convenient for you that you accept this 'fate' so easily, thought Ghorm, *that you take so little responsibility for your own actions.* Biting his tongue, Ghorm left her alone in the flickering candlelight.

Late the following night, rain swept over Tuvan, though in droplets so tiny they seemed no more than particles of mist. As on so many recent nights, Orantes prowled the streets, strolling up and down dark, winding alleys, humming softly to himself, nodding casually to a lone guard, with the reddish brown beard of the Adept glistening with a mist of rain.

He passed down an incline, through another darkened alley and came to a halt. The old inn's sign had been removed, though the sign's upper frame remained, extending out into the alley like the arm of a wraith.

It was here, his mind whispered, *some three years ago, that the head of Tuvan's Council entertained me so royally, almost until daybreak. What was his name? I cannot remember, though he had the eyes of a weasel. I understand now that he welcomed me because I was so much easier to manage than my predecessor, the greatly admired Hektor, an Adept who vanished years ago under mysterious circumstances.*

So, let us go back, Orantes, back three years. After securing a small cask of red wine from the inn's stores, you should rise with some heavy object in hand, then pound Weasel-Eyes repeatedly for past and future crimes.

The Adept stopped his humming and began whispering low, intense spell words. The air around him trembled with power and the inn's sealed door began to gleam with the force of his magic.

Despite the trembling and glowing and whispers of dark winds, his spells had come to nothing. Orantes shrugged: it was simply a daydream — or nightdream — thinking to dance back and forth through the years without any knowledge of the machineries of time. Humming once more, he passed by the sealed and desolate inn, strolling through the alley, out into one of Tuvan's meandering side streets. Behind him, the sealed door continued to glow and tremble.

Perhaps it was just as well to bypass the wine and ale of three years ago: reduced to one forlorn mug of ale each day, and with rationed food, the weight had begun to slip from his body. And Sentauris had noticed! Eyeing his slightly diminished girth, she had winked openly at him, causing him to draw his stomach in even further.

Sentauris: utterly delicious and delightful, she remained a woman worth changing one's life for. He paused, eyeing the hill warily, then he began to climb, beginning to show just the traces of his old limp. The Seeress and Wylar seemed made for one another, and who could blame either for such a choice? Yet Sentauris seemed to favor both ample and spare Adepts equally: a pleasant mystery, though one that called into question his proper place in this universe, a role Orantes believed to be that of a buffoon, a provider of comic relief for real heroes.

He reached the hill's peak, and stood bareheaded, with mist droplets slipping over his grey cloaked form. Usually, on clear nights, he could see beyond the high walls that faced west, out to a point where the watchfires of their foes blazed insolently into the night. But on this night, all was obscured, buried under fog and....

He turned. Sounds had been troubling him, just outside of his hearing. Now they were coming closer: dogs were barking, no doubt tracking the last of the Carags. A lone remaining shapeshifter had turned out to be extremely resourceful, imaginative, and unafraid. Once, after it had escaped, he and Wylar had helped Sardonicus reconstruct the creature's movements. They discovered that the Carag had transformed itself into what looked like a stone cornice — and no wonder the dogs had howled at the abandoned building!

Sounds were coming closer. Lights and a sense of motion passed through the fog beneath him. Orantes drew his staff and peered down the hill. Dogs were racing through the avenue, heads lifted, barking like maddened creatures. But what could they be pursuing? He could see nothing, but then the air shifted overhead: that motion was so completely unexpected that Orantes spun away from it and ducked down. Over his head passed the strangest creation he had ever seen or imagined: pale, translucent, headless, nothing but a set of awkward, flapping wings, with eyes peering out of its front wings nearly six feet in wingspan, flying with awkward, desperate motions.

Maker's Touch! The Carag had become a flyer! Rousing himself, Orantes took aim at the receding creature and lashed at it with bolts of force. Ungainly wings shuddered, dropped down ten feet, then righted themselves, still laboring steadily toward the west wall.

Laughing aloud, Orantes jogged down the hill. Packs of dogs swept past him. Sardonicus raced ahead, moving at twice Orantes' pace. Then

Sentauris, loping with easy grace sped past him, and a moment later Wylar jogged by, all heading for the West Wall. None bothered to call out to Orantes. What was this, a Carag hunting festival? Some new and bizarre ritual? Squint hurtled overhead, and Whisper's form fluttered through patches of fog. Panting, Orantes redoubled his efforts. A Carag hunting party and no one had bothered to invite him!

Like waves of nausea, a sense of strange magic swept over him. Others had reached the West Walls and were climbing stairs to the parapet's top. Breathing heavily, limp more pronounced, Orantes came to a halt at the wall's base. Again, some dark and twisted sorcery stirred all around him, so that his stomach threatened to lose its meager dinner. On the parapet above, Wylar was countering dark magic with sharp, harsh spell words. Orantes forced himself to climb, as quickly as he could, to the parapet's top.

The Carag had nearly vanished into the mist surrounding Tuvan; its pale wings had become no more than a tattered sail in a sea of mist. Then in the darkness another, much larger shape stirred, like a pillar of granite come to life. Lights flared as dark, jagged bolts rippled through the mists. The fleeing Carag cried aloud once, then its winged form flopped dead to the ground.

"By all the Nine Billion Gods," Orantes whispered. "What...." Raging, shrieking sounds came from a second shape, then jagged lines of force radiated dark reddish magic — power cast from the second being toward the first. Both Creatures Indomitable cried aloud: a challenge. Outside of Tuvan, from all the surrounding camps, horns began sounding, the drums of Uraks pounded, Vorrs howled as alarms spread from camps to the west and south, then to the east and north.

Listen to them, Orantes thought. *We knew large numbers of our enemies were gathering to Tuvan, but there must be thousands upon thousands of them! But now they've been discovered by two Creatures of the Darkness. So, go on, go ahead! Kill each other! Murder one another down to the last tier, or band, or pack, or monstrosity until every last stinking one of you is dead!*

Then once again, waves of nausea swept over both Adepts. Wylar began calling down spell shields, and seconds later the force of his spells was supported by Orantes; bands of white light began curling around their hunting party, and the sense of sickness eased. Out in the foggy night, two Creatures Indomitable groaned aloud, then shrieked for a time, raging into the mists as though both were being tortured. After a time, sounds of pain became muffled, and farther in the distance came two brief flashes of light, followed by even more distant concussions. Then silence and thick fog reclaimed the night.

Orantes drew a deep breath, muttering, "Curse me for a blithering idiot, but if all the Demons and Dragons and Creatures of the Darkness tried to torture the truth from me, I couldn't tell them a single thing about what just happened."

"I was only looking for the last Carag," Sardonicus said in a low voice, staring into the mists, as though realizing for the first time that he was trapped on a small island, surrounded by a sea of angry, powerful foes.

"Dark magic drew me," Wylar said in equally quiet tones. "This sort of sorcery is usually the trademark of jealous Dark Gods, though none, it would seem, has yet made his appearance."

Sentauris turned south, then east, then north. "Three, four, five," she murmured, counting, "though one is slipping its restraints." She turned to the others. "Come, this struggle is building to a climax, and we need to speak together. I had promised to meet alone with Breughal tonight, but all of us should gather, as we did just ten days earlier, and not in that dreary Council Chamber, a place that reeks still of old men's endless infighting, and the plots of idiots that would never work. Join me — Breughal will find room for us."

Breughal's home was several times larger than Tuvan's Council Chamber, and more imposing, though it avoided the elaborate display of a house built for a merchant prince. The sight of so many wet figures on his doorstep failed to surprise Breughal; he only smiled his half smile and led them down to a broad cellar, rather than to his ornate dining area.

Orantes looked doubtful, expecting mold, and damp mildew, but the cellar was well aired, free of dust, with broad beams supporting the weight of many rooms above. Breughal lit vat-candles and led them beyond a pantry space into a corner where tables and chairs had been set casually in random patterns, as though deliberately unstructured. Orantes sat, one finger discretely testing for dust on the table before him: there was none.

With a pretense of surprise, Breughal then discovered a stray cask of ale, one that stood openly on a low table against a far wall. The cask had already been opened, its tap dripping one slow droplet every fifty seconds onto a damp cloth beneath.

"Aha," Orantes murmured, brightening, "contraband ale! Now confiscated on the authority of Tuvan's council! Of course, this delightfully cool and foamy material must be sampled, to make certain it is not tainted." With a faint smile, Breughal drew tankards for each of the Adepts, for Sentauris and her three Captains, and just the slightest cup for Druss. He then turned and bowed gravely to the Familiars.

"And for you, our Magical Allies, what may I offer you?"

"Eye of newt," Whisper said in his soft Shade's voice.

"Wing of bat," Squint added.

"Heart of Cockatrice," Ghorm said, not to be outdone.

Breughal smiled a bit more deeply than he had before then waved to his pantry section and to the broad cellar beyond. "Those may not be among my sharply reduced stores but take whatever you wish." The merchant poured a small portion of ale for himself, then turned back to his guests. "You know,

I have nothing approaching the Sight of Sentauris, and yet I have foreseen this event many times in dreams, how we come together to discuss our foes and the nature of the Creatures Indomitable."

"Yet to deal properly with these monstrosities," Sentauris added, "we must first discuss the Ancient Powers and the way the Creatures of the Darkness came into being." Wylar and Orantes stood abruptly, and began intoning low, intense, spell words. Cautiously and carefully, they roamed through the cellar, murmuring spell words intended to seal themselves from the prying eyes and ears of the Mid-World.

Orantes returned and sat heavily, then downed half his tankard in one deep draft. "Now," he murmured, sitting back, "before we call upon Wylar the Lore Master to explore these ancient mysteries, will someone tell me — however briefly — exactly what happened on this night beyond the West Wall?"

Sentauris nodded somberly. "One of the Powers has provided our foes with devices to control the Creatures Indomitable, to forge them into weapons that would break the siege. A trial of these devices was interrupted by the flight of the last Carag. Our enemies will succeed in turning at least three or four of the Creatures of the Darkness — against the walls of Tuvan. We need to focus on these beings and their origins, but it's worth noting that other forces were present — those two soft concussions were made by Emissaries departing the outskirts of Tuvan. The Gods are sending their greatest servants to observe our struggles with these monstrosities."

As Orantes sank further back, staring thoughtfully into his tankard, Sentauris turned to Wylar. "Is this a new title, Adept, that of 'Lore Master'?"

"Only by chance, and with very little help from the Wizards," Wylar stared back at Sentauris with brooding, dark eyes. "No one asks Thorian or Balardi about the Ancient Powers, for they will say that such discussions might well raise the anger of the Gods. But Merlin occasionally will nod vaguely at a scroll containing an oblique reference to the time before the Gods, or at some dark, sealed volume that tells truths that the Wizards are unwilling to speak aloud. From those references, I discovered that in the beginning, Seraphs and Demons arose, two powers equal in the Dominion of Earth. The Seraphs brought forth the Spirit Lords, while the Demons produced the Dragons. These four sets of beings constitute the Ancient Powers, beings of enormous might, precursors, I believe, of the Gods. Later, the Spirit Lords brought forth humankind, something of an afterthought and a general disappointment. Then the Dragons begat the Creatures of the Darkness, producing Horror."

"Yes, note well," Sentauris added. "The Creatures of the Darkness are children of Dragons, though whether they are accidents of confusion and misunderstanding or weapons of war, has never been made clear."

"After the Creatures were born, the Ancient Wars began," Wylar continued. "Those standing for the Maker were called Servants of the Maker — our own heritage — while those opposing Him were known as the Adversaries. Not all the Demons and the Dragons served the Adversaries, while a few of the corrupted Spirit Lords and Seraphs stood with the Adversaries. Humans struggled on behalf of the Servants — though they were weak and ineffective, while the Creatures Indomitable fought openly and powerfully for the Adversaries. In the end, however, a stalemate prevailed, and from this stalemate was born the Mid-World of the Truce and the Gods of Alantéa."

"We will not discuss further the Origins of the Gods," Sentauris interjected, "only to say this: no Power — Ancient or New — has ever come forward to defend a Creature Indomitable from its foes. Whatever became of their ancient ancestors, none of the Dragons is likely to step forward and defend its offspring."

"All of this talk is great heresy," Farad said, glancing at his fellow mercenaries. "Most Gods do not acknowledge a time before their own creation, and so comes the friction between the Gods and those serving the Maker. Yet it is known to those of us capable of independent thought that the Gods are most evasive concerning the distant past and that their different histories are in conflict, with no clear patterns pointing paths to the truth."

"It has been told to me," Sardonicus said in an undertone, "that the Creatures of the Darkness were fashioned by the Ancient Lords of Dragons as weapons of war, then later abandoned, though all such information is exchanged in muffled tones in dark taverns long after midnight. Whether true or not, how do these tales affect us?"

"First, the matter of hierarchies," Wylar said, studying the eyes of Sentauris. "You would think that a Seraph would in all ways be greater than a Spirit Lord, and a Demon forever greater than a Dragon, and a Dragon always mightier than a Creature of the Darkness. Yet it was never so; amazing overlaps in power were discovered in the Ancient Wars: Demons were felled by Spirit Lords, Greater Seraphs destroyed by Dragons, and...." Wylar's eyes sought guidance from Sentauris.

"And Creatures of the Darkness," she said, glancing into the eyes of each, "mighty in sinew and sorcery, destroyed Seraphs and Demons, Spirit Lords and Dragons."

"What!?!" Now Gallandus stood suddenly, ale spilling from his tankard. "A Creature of the Darkness greater than a God, greater than an Ancient Power? What dark nightmare tale of horror is this?"

"Sit," Sentauris said evenly. "Reassurance follows. First of all, many of the most powerful of these Creatures Indomitable were struck down during the Ancient Wars, leaving more than five score greater monstrosities who retained such power of magic and sinew that no force of humans could stand before them. For an age, Creatures Indomitable roamed over Alantéa devastating all those human settlements they encountered, except for those cities that the fickle Gods chose to defend, so that many humans in Alantéa lived in fear, on coastal fringes, or in swamplands, or on remote hills.

"Yet the Mid-World of the Truce is a strange collective entity, capable of action independent of the Powers. With Creatures Indomitable roaming free, the Mid-World gave birth to the Elf-Kindreds, and to Trolls and Stone Giants: beings capable of resistance to the monstrosities plaguing Alantéa the Forerunner. Separately, benign Gods raised Gift Born humans to Adept level, and a few of these attained the rank of Sorcerer. A new balance was forming, when into the Mid-World slipped Nablus the Binder, the Stalker of Monsters.

"An image comes to my mind, a true image I believe, of Nablus with his lizard's face, and scaly skin, though his grey eyes are filled with wisdom. A force of magic was wielded by Nablus, but more importantly, he was utterly swift and cunning, able to place himself outside the reach of Dark Gods and the most powerful of the Creatures Indomitable.

"Over scores of years, Nablus sought out and bound many of those Greater Monstrosities, after baiting their lairs, studying the patterns of their migrations, noting various strengths and weaknesses. As required, Nablus arranged alliances with the Kindreds, or Sorcerers, or other forces within the Mid-World. In the end, many of the mightiest Creatures Indomitable were trapped and bound and hidden in deep places within Alantéa or the many continents of the Far Lands."

"So," Sardonicus said softly, "most of the mightiest of the Creatures have departed — those that might, say, destroy a Wizard in close combat, or fight a lesser God to a draw. And those that remain, such as those stalking about our walls, what of them?"

Sentauris began to speak, but the remote force that governed her life again tugged at her vocal cords. *Three of the Creatures Indomitable will come tomorrow,"* she heard herself say in a distant, faraway voice. *"Unless we stop them, Tuvan and our peoples will be destroyed."*

"And this is our 'reassurance'?" Gallandus asked.

"Such as it is," Sentauris said in hushed tones, her power of Farsight no longer in command. "That is our reassurance."

Chapter Seven

Tuvan the Battleground

THE FOG BEGAN TO lift two hours after midnight, though a slight drizzle made the overcast night even damper. Sentauris managed only a few hours sleep before the turmoil in her mind drove her to the East Tower of the Main Gates. At its pinnacle she paced, staring north and west into the dreary nightscape surrounding Tuvan. Out beyond the dark, ruined fields, patrols of their human foes and packs of Vorrs were gathering to their camps, preparing for battle. Daybreak would bring warfare and an end to Tuvan — if the Adepts failed, or if her own plans were overwhelmed by the strength of their foes.

She turned back to the sleeping city. Perhaps it was her own pride, but she had promised justice and one last task remained before dawn and the next day's battle. Farad was captain of the night watch, and he stayed within sight of the Seeress, in case he was needed. She hailed him silently, waving one lone hand slowly, back, and forth, until Farad was drawn to her side.

"All the Vorr-packs have been called north," she told him, "gathering to the war-camps of the Uraks. The way is clear for Murat and Fiüre, and so they must leave Tuvan." Farad's face remained impassive, but his eyes flickered with surprise.

"Yes, I know," Sentauris said quietly, trying hard not to yawn. "The two Defilers may become the lone survivors of Tuvan, but I did swear that I would release them, and only now has a passage been cleared. Also bring a few of their old guardsmen to witness this event."

So, just a few hours before daybreak, Murat and Fiüre were brought before Sentauris. They stood bareheaded in the drizzle, their encounter lit by only one lone flickering torch, but witnessed by a score of guardsmen drawn from their old watches. Fiüre radiated an unspoken malice, while Murat had woken spewing harsh words, and had again been hammered into silence, so that blood spilled slowly like two thin, red tides from his nostrils.

"The way is clear," she spoke calmly to them, though neither would meet her eyes. "Seek to pass first through the woodlands to the east of Tuvan, then north to the League's border. Although nothing is certain, your chances are good — if you are careful, and if you do not delay, or become diverted. But you must leave this land, because after the waning of the next moon if we find you on League soil, you will be killed outright. Go. I cannot bring myself to wish Maker's Grace to both of you, but pass from the League, and try to live new lives, better lives."

Each of the two renegade captains was given a small pack filled with rations, together with a small pouch of silver coins. Murat was lowered first from the eastern walls, and he jogged quickly and quietly into the darkness, without a single backward glance. A half an hour later, Fiüre was released, and he paused only to spew saliva on Tuvan's outer walls, then he, too, became only a damp, dreary shadow, finally vanishing into the overcast night.

Witnesses called by Farad returned to their resting places, though only a few managed a restless sleep. Sentauris paced again on the East Tower of the Main Gates, struggling to keep her enchanted sight from following the journey into exile of Tuvan's former leaders, as they scrambled east, away from Tuvan and its enemies. A short time later the watch changed, with Gallandus leading a fresh sub-tier of seventy-five. And still, Sentauris alternately paced and stared out into a darkness that would soon give way to dawn.

They are gone, but still, some part of my mind struggles to follow them — why should this be? She turned then, sensing the emerging presence of an Adept. A tall, cloaked shape slipped from damp, shadowy side streets and walked toward her over the scarred plaza: Wylar was coming to her side. In the last few days, she had spoken rarely with the Adepts, understanding only that they were working in a frenzy on their devices. How were they planning to counter their foes? As Wylar reached the base of the outer wall and began to climb its wobbly wood stairs, Sentauris peered into his mind: scores of interlocking possibilities presented themselves — the Adept was disguising his thoughts. She laughed out loud.

"Adept, you are trying to hide from me!" she called to him, then more softly, as Wylar came to stand before her, "This is a game you cannot win."

"I admit to curiosity," Wylar said, eyes twinkling, reaching out to touch her hand. "Look more deeply."

"Yes. In your mind jumbles of false constructs are surrounded by a maze of chambers, with corridors leading to darkened alcoves."

"Take care," Wylar said softly. "You might discover an image of yourself hidden within one of those most remote and dark alcoves."

"Performing acts of strange, passionate acts no doubt," she murmured, "though I suspect you offer yet another deception...." She fell silent then: beyond Tuvan's walls many shapes were moving quickly through the darkness, with the noise of creaking wheels accompanied by the muffled sounds of metal armor.

"Almost an hour before daylight," Wylar said, staring to the north and to the west over the dampened landscape, where strands of mist hung suspended over wet grasslands. "Give me just an overview of the battle that is to come, and then I'll wake Orantes."

She released his hand and stared out into the night. "My Sight has been blocked by stronger magic, so glimpses of what will come are all I can offer." She paused as her eyes followed the movement of their foes over the ruined fields outside Tuvan's walls. "I sense that the West Walls and the Main Gates will be the focus of our foes. As for our battle plan, Gallandus leads the defense of the gates and walls, while Sardonicus leads the interior defense. For now, Farad has maintained our mounted forces intact to prepare for a counterstrike. That's your 'overview' — and yet even now the Vorr-packs share muffled growling sounds, preparing for battle."

Sentauris turned from Wylar and called down to Gallandus. "Rouse the next watch! Send Sardonicus to me!" Beyond the walls, only hazy forms could be seen, masses sensed mostly by sound — except now, Vorrs were slipping out of the darkness, approaching the stone foundations of Tuvan's walls.

"Pity they didn't come an hour earlier," Sentauris muttered, considering that Murat and Fiüre had by now passed beyond the Vorrs' reach.

"It's a pity they come at all," Wylar said. He stared down at the Vorrs while their red, hungry eyes stared up at the Adept. "We must arm ourselves. I will rouse Orantes and send Squint and Whisper to you. Seeress...Maker's Grace to you on this day." Wylar turned and descended swiftly.

Vorrs were beginning to crowd more thickly at the base of Tuvan's walls, some stretching their muscles, and sinews by racing to the walls, running a few swift steps upward against the sides, then falling back. The exercise became a game, with each Vorr seeking to outdo the others, increasing their speed and leaping, until one sleek creature raised itself to three fourths the wall's height.

Sentauris then shot it neatly through one of its fierce red eyes, and it flopped downward, thrashing on the ground until it stiffened and died.

Other Vorrs stared upwards, growling deep, low noises of menace, while backing away from the Seeress and her bow.

Sounds of soft clapping came from her left and Sentauris turned to find Sardonicus offering halfhearted applause.

"I would have done as much," he said, "had I your bow or your eyesight. Now, what's to come?"

"Fire comes with the dawn," Sentauris said evenly. "Flame arrows will seek to burn as much of Tuvan as can be set ablaze."

"Fire?" Sardonicus lifted a hand into the seeping drizzle. "We are prepared, but in this weather...." He trailed off under the unyielding gaze of the Seeress. After a mock salute, the mercenary captain scrambled down from the upper walls and sent men to rouse the fire watches.

With Tuvan facing a grey dawn, the forces of their adversaries emerged: Uraks formed north; tiers of armored humans massed west and northwest, while packs of Vorrs circled around the city's walls. To the north and northwest, two devices shielded by wicker were moving slowly through the receding darkness, but their purpose was hidden from Sentauris by the power of their adversary's sorcery.

As the Seeress peered down from the East Tower of the Main Gates that faced north, Squint came to rest on her shoulder, while Whisper fluttered up to the walls to take shape beside her. Behind them, Ghorm mounted the shaky stairs on stubby feet, with all his sharp, bad-tempered words silenced by the mass and the power of the forces arrayed against Tuvan. In the space behind Tuvan's main gates, Druss arrived, a young, slight figure armored in light mail, and moments later Farad joined him, rubbing sleep from weary eyes.

A grumbling fire-watch began to slip throughout the city in groups of four and five, their unhappy faces dampened by the drizzle. Sentauris *reached* for the Adepts; Orantes was up, and warned by Wylar, was arming himself — but with what? Daybreak and shifting clouds brought light to Tuvan, and all her concerns about the Adepts were pushed to the edges of her mind.

Now, as the first full light of day slipped over the besieged city, their foes kindled flames from scores of clay pots filled with pine resins strengthened by magic. Hundreds of flame arrows were launched high over Tuvan's walls, and small points of fire burned throughout Tuvan, accompanied by the smell of burning wood and pitch. A second cast hurled more fire and was followed by a third. Men and women carrying buckets and damp brooms raced through the smoldering city, calling to one another, slopping water on the flames, and sweeping fire from wooden surfaces with the wet straw of damp brooms. Deep pounding sounds of muffled drumbeats roused all its remaining sleepers, as Tuvan the Besieged began to gather itself for battle.

A fourth volley of flame arrows lifted high over the walls. As fire descended, Sentauris peered beyond the fall of flame arrows and its aftermath — though made of fire that had been reinforced by magic, the city was too damp, and its fire-watch too well prepared and too numerous. She patted the right claw of the Owl-being perched on her shoulder.

"Squint, beyond our walls are two constructs shielded by wicker and by magic." She pointed to the northernmost construct: it seemed to be moving — slowly, foot by foot — toward the Main Gates and the West Wall. "Each construct is shielded by a talisman that blocks my sight. But the northern one is an enormous source of menace. Find out what lurks beyond its shielding. Go." After a second of hesitation, Squint took wing, arcing lower, just a few feet above the snapping jaws of leaping Vorrs, then the Owl-being curled east, slipping through a bank of low-lying mist, circling behind the construct's wicker shielding.

Throughout the city, teams of guards marshaled, rising swiftly, then jogging down broad streets to their posts. Beyond the gates, drumbeats pounded, low muffled sounds, as their foes shifted slowly, like a sluggish monster, toward the city walls. Fires smoldered, then were beaten down. A short time later Sardonicus returned, leaving the fire-watch to put an end to the last few fires. He sprinted up wooden steps by twos, to stand again before Sentauris.

"Whoever leads our enemies," he said, taking a deep breath, "was given detailed instructions, and was not allowed to change them. With the dampness, a seasoned commander would have abandoned fire as a weapon. We —" he broke off, as Squint swept to the left of the Watchtowers and came again to rest on the shoulder of Sentauris.

"Human warriors and old oxen," Squint panted, "are dragging a throwing weapon. What is that hurler of stones called, a cata, cat—"

"Catapult," Ghorm finished.

"But what size?" Sardonicus asked impatiently. "How thick a beam, and how many lengths of a man's height?"

"Just a little less thick than yourself," Squint replied, though only Ghorm appreciated the wordplay. "And about four times a man's height."

"Then it's a feast of dung," Sardonicus snarled. "Tuvan's walls will never stand up to weapons of that size." He glanced to the northwest, where horseriders — many scores of them — were cantering slowly toward the walls of Tuvan. Shaking his head, the mercenary captain turned to go.

"Wait," Sentauris said, touching him, reading a portion of his thoughts. "Your people have been working in secret on different casting devices. What of those?"

"Ballistae," Sardonicus said shortly, glancing again at the riders. "They are like huge crossbows that hurl large javelins — but they have nothing like the range of that stone caster."

"Still, at the edge of your mind," Sentauris said, tightening her grip on him, "you have another thought. Stop for a moment and finish that thought." Riders were picking up speed, bows in hand, and as they neared Tuvan, they swung wide and launched flights of arrows.

"Thoughts," muttered Sardonicus. An arrow flashed by twenty paces to his right; the mercenary captain ducked down, as did Sentauris, still reading his thoughts. "As you might suspect," he said dryly, "my first reflection is that Tuvan is a place where only greedy fools and dimwits gather. Secondly...while working with the shadowy Whisper, to secure Tuvan, I was impressed with his use as spy or agent. Understand this: catapults are sensitive devices, strung with webs of heavy cords. Even if a few strands are severed, the weapon's usefulness will end, at least for this day's battle."

"Such a wonderful plan," Whisper said, its ghostly voice suddenly more intense. "Sawing for ten minutes on a rope might sever one strand, but I would last fewer than ten seconds. You should realize that Shades can be wounded, mutilated, or even destroyed."

Sentauris placed her hand gently on what might have been the Shade's shoulder. "No human or servant of Dark Gods or Creature Indomitable close to that casting device now has the power to harm you. And do not seek to 'sever' the tension cables: fire will serve even better; out on the fields, they have left clay pots with fires still burning. Use those potions to burn the catapult's webbing — go!" Whisper paused as though considering its last moments in the sunlit lands, then the Shade slipped down through the stone of the outer walls and passed from view.

Ghorm peered out behind ridges of stone and mortar, watching as riders and guardsmen on the West Wall exchanged fire: skirmishes only, resulting in few casualties. With a sigh of regret, the little Familiar drew his long knife and began to climb the tower wall, as though ready to slip down its far side and give battle to prowling Vorrs.

"Stop it, Ghorm!" Sentauris reached out and pulled her squat Familiar back. "What in the names of all the Nine Billion Gods were you trying to do?"

"Squint is a spy, Whisper a secret agent. Others have their tasks. I thought I would just slip down and slice a few Vorrs before I take my last breath."

"Fine thinking, Ghorm," Sentauris snarled. "Next —" But then the Seer's Sight again seized her speech: "Captains...Captains...one will die unless Ghorm reaches him in time." The Familiar pulled free and glanced at Sardonicus with raised eyebrows.

"I don't find that very reassuring," Sardonicus muttered darkly, "and should you wish more encouragement, your Adepts, widely known as the 'Replacement Adepts' are now coming to join you in battle." With a snarl of disgust, Sardonicus skipped swiftly down the stairs and began jogging toward the sub-tiers assigned to the inner defense of Tuvan.

In fact, the Adepts as they moved toward Sentauris were at their least inspiring: Wylar was already damp, face haggard as he withdrew into his own thoughts, while Orantes was full of the false bravado he used to conceal his inner fears. Each of them seemed only lightly 'armed,' without mail, with only a staff and slender blade lashed to belts on the outside of their cloaks. The eyes of Orantes were touched by red, showing that somehow, during the previous evening, he had obtained too many tankards of ale. *At least,* Sentauris thought, *that small white worm of fear that lies coiled within the heart of Orantes remains sleeping, or it's only been dulled by drink.*

"Well met, Seeress!" Orantes called from the base of the stairs, and he bowed as though he was dealing with royalty.

"Our Divinations were blocked," Wylar added, more directly, "and so your Farsight must also have been obscured."

"Come up," she said. "Even if our farseeing devices are checked, matters are beginning to reveal themselves. See for yourselves." At the top of the West Tower of the Main Gates, the three peered warily over the walls: unchallenged by outriders or siege weapons, the two devices shielded by wicker were now being pulled by more oxen and more humans, moving at several times their previous pace. As they drew closer, it became obvious that the shielded catapult to the right had only a fraction of the mass of the second device: the second was broader, far heavier, drawn by teams of struggling oxen and horseriders. Their passage left a trail of torn, muddied ground on its way to the West Walls.

Humans guided teams of oxen and horseriders as they pulled south and west, while Vorrs and Uraks gathered to the north of them, having been told that even their scent would panic the draft animals led by their human allies.

"I suppose," Orantes muttered to Sentauris, "that escaping with you to a sunlit bay is no longer a realistic option."

"To our right," Sentauris said, pointing to the construct headed northwest, "is a catapult, intended for the Main Gates and the West Walls. The device to the left remains shielded from me, though harsh weather seems to be slowing it. Stay beside me until —" The horseriders of their foes began drawing closer, launching arrows with greater volume and focus. Sentauris and the Adepts hunched down. From behind the wicker barriers that shielded each construct, other horsemen spilled out, hauling long devices made from rough boards. Plank bridges were dragged, jostling, and bouncing, over rough ground toward the city.

"Vorrs will soon breach Tuvan's walls!" Sentauris called out. She rose and shot down two of the oncoming riders, dancing right then left as countering arrows surged past her. "Squint, you should have told me about the plank bridges."

"They were stacks of wood, something like firewood!" Squint called back with some heat. "They meant nothing to me!"

Sentauris paced, then ducked down, as an arrow flashed above. "Druss! Sardonicus!" she called down. "Vorrs will break through! They will be inside Tuvan!" Guards raised uncertain spears, staring about them, as though Vorrs might materialize in the middle of the air. More calmly, mercenaries notched longbows.

Then bridges made from planks were set against the walls in almost a dozen sections of the West Walls. Vorrs — snarling, howling powerful beings with muscled brown fur — raced over the walls and sprang down into the city, teeth tearing, ripping, raging, leaving trails of red blood as they ripped at Tuvan's defenders. A second set of plank bridges followed, and more Vorrs poured into Tuvan.

"Farad!" she called down. "Look to the horses, shield the horses. Be ready to mount! Gallandus, hold the upper walls, let Sardonicus deal with the Vorrs!"

Wylar drew his staff in his right hand, slender blade in his left. "This is also our fight."

"No. Hold," Sentauris muttered. "Leave the Vorrs to Sardonicus and Druss. Our fight for Tuvan has only just begun." Shrieks and screams of terror could be heard throughout the city, mixed with calls to the guard. The voice of Gallandus could be heard above the din, bellowing for those on the walls to hurl down the plank bridges. The first bridge crashed down, as did others; but still more Vorrs were leaping down from the walls, raging through city streets, with only a few knots of men beginning to cluster together to wield weapons against the intruders.

Then Sardonicus emerged from a broad avenue, with one of his bodyguards on his left, another on his right. Those three led two score mercenaries with longbows; and Druss fought to their left side, supported by many men of the Gate Watch.

"Whisper has failed," Sentauris said in a soft voice, "they are ranging the catapult. Tighter...tighter...almost.... You, down below!" She called to a cluster of twenty guardsmen, who stood before the Main Gates, facing a pack of Vorrs. "Come toward me, away from the Gates! But watch!"

Warily, they edged toward the Seeress, pikes, and swords facing their foes. But a Vorr took one of them, though pike and sword thrusts from nearby Guards severed the creature's left leg. As the Vorr squirmed and writhed, the sky seemed to darken over it: a huge stone flew over the Main Gates. As it dropped down, both the Vorr and its human adversary were smashed to pulp, and then the boulder bounced and slid over the plaza, finally demolishing a makeshift guardhouse.

"They missed the Main Gates," whispered Sentauris. "But the next cast, the next cast. Ah, dark fortune, it comes to this place — for the three of us! Come!" Sentauris and the two Adepts scrambled, hunched low, moving swiftly along the upper West Walls away from the Main Gates. Squint fluttered, hooting, before them. A crash shook the walls, and only the swift reach of Sentauris kept Orantes from slipping and toppling from battlements made slick by rain.

"I see now," Sentauris murmured. "Now I see — they will use a battering ram against the Main Gates — and spies have told them where the fortifications are failing along the West Wall."

A broad stretch of the West Wall had been reduced to rubble so that only half of its previous height remained. From the other side, Vorrs were scrambling over broken stone, while mailed Uraks began climbing more awkwardly to the fortification's top.

"Breach!" Sentauris called, but now with the noise and confusion, she could not be heard. "Squint! Tell Sardonicus we have a breach that must be sealed. Go!" She peered out, then began sliding along the battlements back toward the twin watchtowers. "Next cast, next cast," she whispered, reaching for the feel of the future.

"I may be faint of heart," Orantes muttered, "but I think it's time to boot some of these jackals in their groins." Sentauris whispered again, *reaching, reaching.* Below them, Sardonicus and his bodyguards led a mixed force of mercenaries and guardsmen toward the breach. Arrows took down Vorrs, while Uraks were pushed back by spears, then their legs were hewn from them by the axes of other warriors. The breach was hemmed, almost sealed.

"No, no," Sentauris whispered. "The next cast marks the end of Tuvan the Battleground. Wait, now wait. A huge stone flies, and then it falters."

They watched as a boulder rose in the air — but it wobbled, drifting far to the south, striking a glancing blow to the southern edge of the West Wall.

"Their casts are hobbled!" Sentauris leaped to her feet. "Whisper, well done!" Above the catapult, a curl of vapor lifted, followed by billows of black smoke, then fire blossomed.

"Whisper!" she cried once again, then glanced to the breach, where men ordered by Sardonicus were mounding stones higher. But Vorrs surrounded the fighters sealing the breach, while other Vorrs raced free: brown whirlwinds of wild slaughter. The swirling battle had carried Druss and his guardsmen into side streets, and he passed from sight.

And now to the west, the second device was closing upon Tuvan. Its wicker shielding had been cast aside to reveal a broad battle platform, surrounded by several ranks of human tiers and smaller bands of Uraks. Fighting from such a platform, their foes would easily overwhelm the West Walls and burst into the city.

"Come, Seeress," Wylar murmured. "Do not save us for the Creatures Indomitable. Put us into play."

"Soon." Sentauris tried to read the wild melee as Vorrs spread throughout the city. A number lay pierced with arrows, sprawled beside the corpses of humans who lay clutching torn throats. "Druss, Sardonicus, clear these vermin from Tuvan!" Sardonicus heard her cry; he stared up at her with eyes filled with sullen thoughts but began rallying the guard against the ring of Vorrs surrounding them. Again, Squint carried messages: first to Druss, the second to Gallandus and third to Farad.

"Where is this Sight of yours?" Ghorm grumbled. "You're going blind, and I'm as useless as these Magicians." Just behind Ghorm, a dark shape began to emerge; as Ghorm spun back, knife ready, the shadowy essence of Whisper poured upwards from the stone.

"They saw me but once," Whisper laughed aloud, "and then...what's this — Vorrs inside Tuvan?"

"Yes," Sentauris murmured, using her Sight to stare into the heart of Tuvan the Battleground.

Chaos ruled all around them; the main struggle against the packs of Vorrs had shifted from the Gate into the broad streets beyond and from her view. Druss had formed a strong point, with guardsmen all around him, with a grim faced Breughal guarding his back. Sardonicus and his bodyguards were fighting toward Druss, leading a mixed force of mercenaries and guardsmen. Vorrs were falling by twos and threes every few seconds. Men and women were spilling from houses, bearing makeshift spears and long knives, slowly picking up a chant: "Druss, Heir of Thelm! Druss, Heir of Thelm!"

"Druss, Heir of Thelm," Sentauris whispered, but other images were crowding into her mind, with the greatest hazard on the battlements of the West Wall. "Come," she called, and raced, hunched over, another six score paces toward the Main Gates. Adepts and Familiars followed more cautiously. Last came Ghorm, who was watching the siege platform to their left with some fascination: torrents of missiles were spewing back and forth between walls and platform as they closed. Gallandus had called upon the main force of Guard; fighting off Vorrs, they struggled toward the West Wall.

As Ghorm reached the Gates, Guardsmen manning the twin watch-towers were calling to one another, pounding on their shields, struggling to reassure one another with cries that were strangely unconvincing. Sentauris and the Adepts were peering over the edge of the fortification, almost timidly, like children spying on their elders.

While Tuvan's defenders were occupied by siege weapons, marauding Vorrs and Uraks had gathered at Tuvan's Main Gates. Now they were wielding a massive battering ram, one with the many arms of a centipede, so that two score Uraks could grasp it. Struggling to lift the massive ram, they moved toward the gates behind tall shields made of dampened hide. Outlying Vorrs guarded the flanks of the Uraks.

"They fear our fire," Wylar muttered, watching as the Uraks picked up their pace. "We will show them something greater than mage fire."

Sentauris shook her head as though struck. "No, beware: Creatures of the Darkness are held for a final assault, but powerful magic will cause them to come early to battle."

"Then I'll shower them with piss pots," Orantes muttered, "filled with stale urine. Is that magic 'small' enough? If not...." He sputtered into silence: Uraks were stumbling, sliding into a shuffling run not thirty paces from the gates; only the dampness and slickness of the ground kept their thrust from its full power.

SMASH! The gates held though the northern walls were shaken, and men were toppling, shrieking from the Watchtowers.

"Find Farad," Sentauris called to Squint. "We need three score horsemen to the Main Gates in full armor. Tell him to mount and ride!"

Uraks stumbled, slipping, and sliding, back ten paces, then another twenty, readying for a second rush at the gates. The Adepts rose, chanting.

Cocoons of white light enfolded them so that arrows fell back or veered away from the two. Uraks halted, faltering in uncertainty. A pause ensued, a strange interlude as Uraks glanced in confusion at one another, then began smashing, ripping at the metal and cloth shielding their bodies. Images of white adders slipped up from the ground about them, leaping at the dark black flesh that lay exposed above their heavy booted feet.

Uraks howled, danced, slipped in the muck, ripped at mail, smashed at their own shaking, itching flesh. The great battering ram held by so many warriors began slipping from their hands, then fell awkwardly to the ground.

Orantes turned to Sentauris. "We have supplied you with 'small' magics — discomforts and illusions. These will not, sadly, hold them for long."

"It was enough." Sentauris pointed left to the West Wall. "Behold your true challenge." At last, the siege platform had been pressed against Tuvan's broad walls. Rank upon rank of pikes and swords and spear pressed against the defense and bows sang from beneath and behind them.

Gallandus was rallying the Guard, stiffening them with knots of mercenaries, sending to Farad for aid. But the platform was too broad, its fighters too fresh. Guardsmen began dropping from the walls in clusters of four and five, back from the city's fortifications, onto the streets of Tuvan.

A great breach, forty paces wide was forming, as a section of the West Wall began falling to their foes, and the enemies of Tuvan spilled into the walled city.

The hand of Orantes left his blade and slipped into his cloak to retrieve a slender skin of wine. "My forebears were fighting men," he said in calm tones, washing the words down with a thin stream of red wine. "May I not disappoint them on this day. Come." The Adepts scrambled to the ground, jogged across the broad plaza, and passed into the press of men, vanishing from view.

"A strange anticlimax," Ghorm muttered, watching the passage of the Adepts. "The cockatrice eggs burst open; two downy and innocent baby chicks emerge. Where are their Chariots of Fire?"

Maker forgive me if I have misjudged the Adepts, thought Sentauris, *but here, at last, is Farad.* The mercenary captain rode to the gates leading three score spearmen, with both men and horse well armored. Farad stared bleakly at the fight at the west wall, as the defense of Tuvan faltered. He pulled up his visor and looked to Sentauris.

"This is not our best use," he called up, "but open a passage and we will kill many before we are dragged down."

"Others must deal with the West Wall," she called to Farad, then turned to the Gate Watch. "Open the gates. We must strike down those Uraks and their battering ram." Astonished, men manning the gates glanced back and forth to one another, then back to Sentauris, each waiting for the other to move first.

"The gates, you halfwits!" She roared at them, then called down more evenly to Farad: "We fight three battles — the West Wall, Vorrs within the city, and this assault upon the Main Gates. Your sortie may reduce these three battles to two. Watch for wet ground. Uraks dance in discomfort beside their massive beam. Do not break your horseriders against this ram — take them to either side."

Farad turned and called out instructions, then slipped his visor down. The gates opened. Farad circled his lancers through the plaza to help them gather speed. With a rumble of metal shod hooves passing over cobblestones, the lancers surged through the gates.

Sentauris raced along the West Walls back toward the Main Gates, then scrambled down creaking stairs. Drawing her bow, she raced behind the last lancer, calling for others to follow her: Ghorm with his fierce eyes, was first. Vorrs beyond the gates fell as her bow sang. Pikemen and others armed with swords or bows surged from the gates to attack the besiegers.

Uraks stood beside the fallen battering ram, smashing openhanded at one another, building a rage that would overcome their pain. They looked up, dumbfounded, as ranks of lances and iron hooves and metal armor surged toward them. Weapons. Why had they set their iron shod maces aside? Some tore wooden arms from the battering ram, others stood bellowing with both fists raised, then a great tide of horses and men and armor surged over them. Those not trampled howled and ran from the fray, seeking weapons.

Farad pulled up, lifting his visor. Dampness lingered over the battlefield, though both mist and darkness were yielding to daylight. Uraks armed with maces were beginning to cluster beside the fallen ram, and to the west, masses of archers and pikemen were pulling away from the platform on the West Wall, streaming toward Farad and his small force. Sentauris held the gates, but with fewer than three score guardsmen — and none of them were trained mercenaries.

Shaking free from his dreams of triumph, Farad led his force up a slight rise, then down again, building speed. The last Uraks broke and scattered, crying in fury up into overcast skies. The ram wielded by their foes was abandoned, but a full tier of five hundred men was marching toward Farad in a solid phalanx that could not be broken by his much smaller force of horseriders. Everything else was glory and death, and so Farad, who weighed all matters with precise balances, led his men back into Tuvan, where the small force holding the gates waved them through, then scurried to seal Tuvan from their foes.

Again, Farad raised his visor, though his call of triumph faltered as his eyes flickered over the fight at the West Wall. A great press of guardsmen and mercenaries were struggling mightily against the invaders, but the defenders were vastly outnumbered, and their city seemed doomed. Sentauris had returned to the battlements and was racing left along the parapet toward the West Wall, pausing every seven paces to send arrows into the foremost warriors or captains leading their foes.

"We must become lighter," Farad called to the nearby guardsmen. "Help us shed some of this mail."

Sentauris fired her last arrow and glanced back. Their Familiars were struggling to resupply her. Squint was floating toward her with a half of a dozen shafts in his talons. Back beside the gates, Farad and his heavily armed troop were refitting themselves — all her captains were incredibly smart — and swift. Sardonicus and Druss were killing dozens of Vorrs, while Gallandus was rallying the great mass of defenders committed to the West Wall.

But Tuvan's fate lay not with the captains but with the Adepts.

"Adepts!" she called out, taking an arrow from Squint. "For the League, Orantes! Wylar, one great stroke for the League!"

Now, as the Adepts passed their way to the forefront of the press, their weapons became fully engaged. Slender swords radiated silver light, slashing through armor like flesh, and through flesh and bone like parchment. Bodies and portions of bodies fell all around them, though some of their dead foes were held upright in the press of battle — sagging corpses spurting red fluids.

"Gallandus!" Sentauris cried, "the Adepts are your spear points!" With all the shouting and dying amid the clash of arms, her words could not be heard, but Gallandus could feel their battle shift — and moments later he could hear the impact of the Adepts. For as their foes backed from Wylar and Orantes, the Adepts drew their staffs, then pointed and blasted at their enemies. No longer were they using invisible bolts of force; instead, jagged shafts of dark lightning surged from their staffs. *Flash!* A knot of five pikemen was blasted back, bodies flopping dead to the ground. *Flash!* A phalanx of three Uraks toppled, their dark flesh smoking in ruin.

Arrows, javelins, and stones were hurled at the Adepts, but translucent cocoons of white light embraced the Adepts, catching each missile and spinning it, arcing, back toward their foes.

"Adepts," Sentauris whispered, and stepped up her own fire, shooting down all those among her foes who sought to lead or command others. Gallandus sought higher vantage from the walls and watched as the Adepts crushed all before them, bulging through the broad lines of Tuvan's invaders. Pikemen were sent to shore up the Adepts' flanks, while Gallandus himself led his veterans against soft points forming in the wavering lines of their enemies. On the upper ramparts of the West Wall, Tuvan's defenders massed four abreast, and began to pinch the breech, foot by foot, struggling to retake the city's battlements.

With the battle turning against them, the invaders countered: ranks upon the broad platform parted; a dozen Uraks sped through and dropped lightly to the soil of Tuvan. Armed with scimitars, leaner than their brethren and blindingly fast, they hurled themselves at the Adepts with the rage of berserkers.

The arrows of Sentauris failed even to slow them, but jagged lightning from the Adepts shattered all but a few. Pikemen pinned the others. Only one came close enough to strike Orantes; with dancing feet, the Adept slipped inside the stroke and swept the Urak from his feet with a single slash from his slender, enchanted blade. Pikemen pinned the dying Urak to the ground until it stilled.

"One stroke for the League!" Orantes panted, wiping sweat from his brow with a fold of cloak. "Come, let's put some steel into the guts of these dung lickers!"

Now, as the invaders fell back, a chant could be heard, dimly at first, then louder as the people of Tuvan joined the chant: "Druss, Heir of Thelm...Druss, Heir of Thelm." Tuvan's plague of Vorrs had been overcome, leaving many scores of Guardsmen and mercenaries and armed citizens to join the battle at the West Wall.

Sardonicus had secured horses for his own men, and they were dragging two siege weapons mounted on carts toward the West Wall — ballistae, like huge crossbows. Farad, too, rode toward the struggle, his heavy cavalry transformed into light horseriders. And Gallandus, feeling the tide turn, redoubled the Guard's struggle on the walls, seeking to block the invaders' retreat to their siege platform, and so make of Tuvan a slaughterhouse for the enemies of the League.

Sentauris edged forward, bow drawn back, seeking an opening. On the northern section of the West Wall, men were fighting four abreast, pushing back the invaders. With the thick wedge of her own people, a clear shot was almost impossible — except *Now!*

As her bow sang, her hands lost strength, barely able to hold both bow and her own body upright on the walls. Her vision dimmed, and the noise of battle diminished into remote, muffled sounds. As though to compensate, an echo reached out to her, a stray sound that had passed from a far chamber toward her after a journey of several days.

And it was a God's voice, some jealous dark being, a Power who greatly desired the destruction of the League. The voice was giving — had given — instructions to his leaders.

Only then, when all their strength is revealed, are you to release the Creatures Indomitable against Tuvan and its defenders.

And it was not Arioch! Somehow, she had suspected the hand of that Dark God. Messengers were calling to her from beneath the walls, but she ignored them, turning slowly as though in a trance to an area beyond Tuvan's walls.

My Sight, my vision that fails so seldom! How had they learned to block it? Though a God, a God might do almost anything.... Wait! Creatures of the Darkness are coming. Monsters inside the City!

Chapter Eight

"Monsters Inside the City!"

N TORN AND MUDDY ground, just to the north and west of Tuvan, three arcs of air seemed to shimmer, to blaze with dark fire, then billow into clouds of swirling mist.

Blurred images loomed in the mist: Creatures of the Darkness, three of them, standing in confusion as though they had just awakened from long sleeps that had lasted decades. Behind each monstrosity a small band of men clustered together like mice herding lions. As each of the Creatures perceived another of its brethren looming in the mist, that monstrosity howled first in rage, then with increasing torment, until its attention was forced back to the walls of Tuvan the Besieged.

As sounds of torment dwindled down into those of lingering pain, each monstrosity began its first staggering steps toward the walled city. As before, waves of nausea swept over both Tuvan's defenders and their foes. Though quickly, Sentauris could hear over the dwindling tumult of battle, how the voices of the Adepts were raised in counter spells.

As the Creatures Indomitable shuffled forward, moved by the power of some strange, compelling magic, layers of mist began to fall away from them so that their features were revealed.

To the right, at the northern arc, dragging itself forward on rows of stubby arms, came a powerful dark shape, with coils writhing behind it. The head of that monster had the Dragonish features of a Fire Drake, though twisted, disfigured ones, with muddied, squinting eyes that seemed almost completely blind. And on its massive snake's body, tiny dark batwings grew in clumps, flapping in a parody of all flying things.

Sentauris shook her head as her mind whispered, *Power — this blind Drake comes for the gates with a mass of pure power.* It took an effort of will, but she forced herself to turn and study the second Creature, the centermost, who was emerging from its foggy shroud more rapidly because of its great height, and because its pace was building as it stepped toward her.

Ah, the Grey Mantis comes for me! This being formed the pillar of granite that seemed so black in the darkness, but it is made from grey chitin, not black stone and it comes for me.... Standing two times the height of the other monstrosities, the Grey Mantis stepped forward with the staggered, jerky thumping sounds of an enormous insect. Huge legs like trunks supported its upper torso, though its upper arms were spindly, more like those of an insect, and some coiled tail or stinging apparatus bobbed behind it.

It comes for me, Sentauris thought, *and it is fierce and swift, and about ten thousand times my strength. But wait, Sentauris, wait and turn. What monstrosity might they have sent against the Adepts?* She turned left, mechanically, as though her head and neck were controlled by another being.

A shuffling, shambling Creature emerged from low mists. Humpbacked, bulky, a giant among trolls, with a great deformed head that was shedding skin and brain matter...with twisted black coils writhing on its hump.... This Giant Ghoul, a monstrosity that had nearly defeated and consumed the Adepts! Now it was lurching straight toward their positions near the West Wall!

She looked back to the Grey Mantis: it wobbled toward her, with eye plates the size of cupboard doors locked on her slender frame. *Maker! Why did you allow these strangely formed monstrosities to come to power? They do not belong even in the horror dreams of feverish and demented children!*

"Let's go." Ghorm sheathed his dagger and tugged at her sleeve. "We'll escape through the tunnels. These *things*, the Wizards will have to deal with them." Sentauris ignored him, her mind searching desperately for strategies or devices that might slow or stop these monstrosities. Panic and confusion scattered all her thoughts. Ghorm pulled harder, his squat feet beginning to dance in frustration.

Taking a deep breath, she cleared her mind, closing her eyes and using her Sight to peer through scores then hundreds of frames of future chances. A collage of visions fluttered through her thoughts, then suddenly her eyes flashed open. *Strange, so strange.* Only one frame offered even a chance of survival — if she led a force of archers to the gates, a wide range of possibilities opened. But how could a force of archers contend with so much power? How could such a trivial action lead to such consequences?

Act now or perish! A voice came into her mind, one that had nothing to do with her power as a Seeress. She snarled defiance, both at the voice, and to the oncoming monstrosities, then slipped from the walls back onto Tuvan's main plaza that now held more rubble than humans. Three Familiars followed, with Ghorm still trying to urge her to safety.

"Save your breath," Sentauris muttered to her Familiar. "Squint, tell Gallandus not to falter. Tell the Adepts that our foes must be forced from Tuvan." She jogged toward the main gates that lay between the twin watchtowers, calling upon those armed with bows to follow her. Sardonicus, his mind again seething with dark thoughts, led fighters and his own horse drawn casting devices toward the Gates, riding roughshod over fallen Vorrs and human adversaries.

At the Gates, Sentauris again scrambled over wobbling and splintered stairs up to the righthand watchtower. Ghorm followed, calling out in a high-pitched voice that was almost a shriek, "What are you thinking about? Are you crazy?"

"As the Maker is my God," she muttered, "I have no idea what is supposed to happen." She rose to the watchtower's upper floor, where men hunched down beyond its bulwarks, their eyes fixed on the clouds of mist that only dimly obscured the oncoming monstrosities. Sentauris stepped up onto the wallss, standing unsupported on the wooden palisades. Upright and alone, bow held aloft, dark hair flowing behind her, none could mistake her for any other of Tuvan's defenders.

"Tuvan!" she cried aloud. "Tuvan the battleground! Tuvan, the place of doom for our foes!"

As she spoke, the Grey Mantis changed direction, veering toward Sentauris and Tuvan's Main Gates. The human entourage of the Grey Mantis scrambled to keep pace with the Creature, some making little mewing sounds of alarm. For as its path neared that of the Blind Drake, that monstrosity bellowed in anger and picked up its own pace.

The Grey Mantis turned slowly, as though preparing to meet an ancient and deadly foe. Humans beside each monstrosity called out to each other, fumbling with unseen devices. Both Creatures Indomitable cried out in rage and defiance.

Then came moans of pain, followed by cries of everlasting torment. The Grey Mantis struck its own head with spindly insect arms, while the Blind Drake smashed its enormous, gnarled skull against the ground as though seeking oblivion in death.

A compulsion reinforced by pain forced the Grey Mantis first to turn, then to stumble back to its original path, where it wobbled with uncertain, jerky motions away from the Main Gates back to Tuvan's West Walls.

Sentauris stepped back from her high perch and dropped lightly down beside Ghorm.

"It should have been obvious," she muttered. "A Creature Indomitable is not so easily enslaved. Control over these monstrosities is ragged — at best." She looked up into the faces of confused guardsmen. "Come. Much remains to be done. Tuvan may not be lost, but the twin watchtowers and the Main Gates are doomed." She led them down cracked and splintered stairs, calling to those manning the East Tower to follow.

A motley, fearful group gathered around her in the plaza just before the gates. Sounds of battle magic rose in the distance as the Adepts lashed at their foes, but other sounds of warfare diminished as more eyes were drawn to the monstrosities approaching Tuvan. Even hardened mercenaries were skittish, though Farad was calm, and Sardonicus flared with anger.

"Hear me," Sentauris called to them. "This Creature, this Blind Drake, comes for the gates with a power we cannot match. In moments, it will enter Tuvan. But! Know this: we are *not* doomed. Strike down this Creature's followers, but not the monster itself. Again, do not cast arrows or javelins or choke spears at this thing, but only at its entourage. Now, acknowledge these words!"

Confused faces nodded, but Sardonicus called out loud, "By all the Nine Billion Gods, what stupidity is th —" Cries and movements along the walls interrupted him. Two hundred paces to the left of the Twin Watchtowers, men were crying out and dropping from the walls, scattering from the battle.

Again, the massive figure of the Grey Mantis loomed over the walls midway between the gates and the battle for the West Wall. Still wobbling with pain, the Creature took one, huge lurching step and passed over the crumbling walls, battering down more of the walls' stonework with its bobbing, coiled tail sting. Behind it, the monster's entourage cried out in alarm — they were trapped outside of Tuvan.

Pain lashed at the Creature of the Darkness. Again, the Grey Mantis shrieked, a cry so high pitched that those nearby were forced to stop up their ears. Once more, the Grey Mantis lashed at its own head, though as it stumbled further from the walls, its agony seemed to diminish, to fade and finally cease. As it passed further into Tuvan, the monstrosity was drawn to some of the largest of the city's buildings. Lurching down a broad avenue, the Grey Mantis began casually to rip at the upper floor of a five-story building, seeking food — children or the elderly hidden behind the upper walls.

"Farad," Sentauris called out, "on light horse seek only to distract this thing. Do not close with it!" Farad's mouth sought to form words, but a huge dark presence loomed over the gates as gnarled, twisted Drake features peered down at them with blind eyes. The Blind Drake drew back then lashed forward: the gates were unhinged and flattened with a single thrust. Men scattered from the ruin of the gates, but only a few abandoned the Seeress.

"Farad, go!" she called out. "The rest of you don't strike at this thing!" Again, the Blind Drake loomed high, thrashing first left then right, reducing the East and West Towers to splintered wreckage. Then it paused, lifting its head, seeming to sniff the air with thick blubbery nostrils. In thickness, the Blind Drake was nearly the height of a tall man. Ropy tendons supported the neck of its Drake's head, with dried muck caked about those tendons, as though the Creature had festered for years in some deep, lightless mire.

Sentauris motioned; those around her backed from the gates, forming a rough semicircle of men armed with javelins and bows and short spears. Farad slowly, cautiously, pulled his force of light horse from the press, leading them through side streets on a path to intercept the Grey Mantis.

Smashing, battering sounds, erupted to its right, and the Blind Drake spun, further devastating more fortress walls. Over at the West Wall, came the third of the Creatures of the Darkness: the Giant Ghoul, sensing the elusive Adepts, was ripping down wall sections with huge hands like those of a troll. Stepping over the wreckage, it became the third of the Creatures Indomitable to enter the walled city.

"Three are within," Ghorm muttered. "Time to depart now on a swift horse and live to fight another day." The Blind Drake inched forward as though held by an invisible leash. Behind it, a face partly hidden by chain mail peered from behind the rubble, eyes scanning the city's defenses. Sentauris shot him neatly through the gap in his armor, and he slumped, clutching his face.

"Stay with me," Sentauris murmured to Ghorm as she edged forward just to the Creature's right. The Blind Drake seemed to rise in confusion as though its constraints were stretched to their breaking point. From the Creature's entourage, three men leaped forward, pulling their fallen confederate back from the gates. In the distance, sounds of battle magic rose and fell as the Adepts confronted the third of the Creatures. Near the city's center, the Grey Mantis lashed back at harassing riders: one horse and rider fell stricken with poison, while a second rider was lifted from his saddle, drawn to the Creature's mouth, shrieking and squirming.

As the Blind Drake wavered, struggling to hear, staring about with confused and blind eyes, Sardonicus ranged his casting devices, seeking to strike at soft places where folds of dark flesh seemed less thick beneath the Blind Drake's neck and quivering tendons. The face of Sardonicus was a study in controlled fury, as the mercenary captain cursed himself for joining a doomed enterprise.

"Sardonicus!" Sentauris called to him. "All such casts lead to the death of Tuvan!" Sardonicus stared at her, then at the monster as it turned in uncertainty, with all its tiny grotesque batwings fluttering as though calling upon the bulky monstrosity to rise in flight.

With his face set hard as stone, the mercenary captain pulled back his horse drawn ballistae. "I will not," he muttered between clenched teeth, "pass into the everlasting darkness without a single cast at these monstrosities." He mounted, leading his horse drawn casting devices from the gates. "If not this monstrosity, then another. Farad, we come!" Picking up speed, Sardonicus and his bodyguards dragged their bouncing war machineries toward the heart of the walled city.

Again, the Blind Drake rose as though to follow, but as before it was snared by an invisible leash. As it sagged back, frames of future chance flashed before the eyes of Sentauris: all the power given them by Dark Gods that shielded their foes was beginning to slip.

"Squint! Whisper!" she hissed. "Get Ghorm to Farad and Sardonicus. If you fail, one of our great captains is doomed. Go, now!" As she spoke, the Blind Drake edged forward; just behind it, clusters of mailed figures passed into Tuvan, shielded by wicker shields. Behind them, Vorrs and Uraks gathered, preparing for the final ruin of Tuvan.

"Listen!" she called to those around her. "On seven wrists are talismanic devices of red and black, used to control this Creature. Kill the seven humans holding these devices and the Blind Drake might choose a different path." Saying this, she ducked down and shot at an exposed human limb, then drew a second arrow. Others followed her example, slipping to the left or right of the Blind Drake, hurling javelins, or stones at the humans behind their barely tamed Creature Indomitable.

One of its human controllers fell, then a second. The Blind Drake reared, tiny batwings fluttering, making desperate mewing sounds of pain and confusion. Stones and javelins battered the wicker shielding behind it. Racing like fire, Sentauris again sprinted to the top of the walls, approaching the ruin of the gates from the right, firing down at exposed human shapes.

A third human bearing a wrist talisman fell with an arrow in his throat. A fourth turned, scurried from the gates, and stumbled, wounded in the calf. Two of the remaining three began ripping talismans from their wrists, but the devices created by Set would not release them.

No longer constrained, the Blind Drake wheeled and turned on its tormentors. Spilling back through the gates, the monster crushed all the humans in its path. More of the walls shuddered and toppled from its passage: a huge gap was forming, an open passage for scores of Uraks and Vorrs beyond.

But the Blind Drake rolled and writhed, turning on the allies of its tormentors. Uraks and Vorrs were crushed beneath its massive coils. Vorrs leaped at its flanks and were battered back; other Vorrs escaped by speed of foot, howling as they fled. Knots of Uraks opposing the monster were hammered into masses of dark pulp as the Creature's head smashed down upon them. And during the onslaught, the ground shook and Tuvan's walls shuddered and crumbled.

At last, having reduced its tormentors to the dead, the dying or those who fled swiftly away, the Blind Drake spilled in swift coiling motions to the northwest, where its water senses discovered the serpentine river that fed Tuvan's aquifer. The monster slipped beneath the water's surface, seeking relief from its own pain, and so it passed from the battle.

The Sight within Sentauris was finally released: *This Blind Drake had no interest in feeding on warm blooded humans. It has been living on dead and decaying creatures of the marshes. As for the other two monstrosities, they are still seeking human flesh.*

Shaken by the Creature's fury, Sentauris turned slowly back to Tuvan's struggle. The city had been delivered from one monstrosity, though two remained. Which of the two should be fought next? Showing unusual hesitation, the Seeress felt her gaze drawn to the Adepts and their struggle to hold the West Wall.

·)(·

Sheets of perspiration ran down Orantes' chest. For some strange reason, his protective cocoon of light was holding moisture inside; as he fought toward the walls, his shuddering heart was dragging the weight of his soaked garments. Stepping forward, his staff rose again, leveled against clusters of humans.

Flash! They were using dead men as shields now, but it would save them only for seconds. *Flash!* He took a deep breath and glanced down at his long dark cloak: not only sweat dragged him down, but splotches of blood had been added, although only a trickle of it was his own.

Flash! Screens of dead flesh fell away from dark, jagged bolts. He glanced left: Wylar could only be dimly seen, but Gallandus was up on the walls with his veterans, leading a fierce battle to win back control of the left breach on the West Wall. On the right-hand side of the West Wall, Druss and his bodyguards were pinching down that perimeter. Some of the invaders were escaping back to their siege platform, while others were lowering weapons as though tempted to surrender. He let his own staff sag down and reached for the wineskin within his cloak. *Maker's Grace, but it's almost over!*

As the red wine spilled down his throat, a sense of nausea again assailed him, and he spewed most of his wine up. *A minor oversight, Orantes, but you have overlooked a few of the Creatures Indomitable.* Battering sounds came for the walls; stone crumbled and toppled. The Gift within him brought an image of the Creature of the Darkness, the

Giant Ghoul, with its decaying forehead and the writhing black tentacles on its back — the same nightmare that had sought so single mindedly to murder and consume both Adepts.

"We have become bitter meat," Orantes muttered. Then, turning to the pikemen guarding his flanks, "Get back." The wall crumbled, with segments of stone and mortar toppling into the city, and the Giant Ghoul stepped over the rubble into Tuvan the Battleground. Humans scattered, leaving Orantes to face the monstrosity alone.

I still want to run, Orantes thought, drawing a deep breath. *Just look at this thing!* More gaps could be seen in the Monster's skull, where its brain matter rotted and fell away; eyes and head rolled about in wild delirium, with drool slipping from a mouth that still held yellow, gapped teeth. Yet the hump on the Monster's back seemed to have grown, with its coils writhing and twisting, and the Creature's sense of power and purpose had become greater.

Maker's Touch! These Creatures of the Darkness were never "created" as weapons of war; they were the most tragic and evil misfortunes to befall Alantéa the Forerunner!

The Giant Ghoul stepped forward; Orantes' feet — unbidden — took two steps back. Tendrils, coils of power, black and red, swept from the Creature's writhing hump and lashed at the Adept. Orantes danced left, raising his staff: flails of white light sprouted, raking at black and red tendrils. More flails erupted from Orantes' right: Wylar was at his side. And if the Creature's reach had become greater, so had that of the Adepts.

The Giant Ghoul cried aloud in pain and rage. All the grief delivered by its controllers was forgotten, as it focused on the Adepts and their magic. Coils of power were withdrawn back to its writhing hump; the Adepts' flails also withdrew.

Arrows and stones were cast at the Creature. A few struck, but others were waved away as though encountering torrents of stormy air. The Monster stepped toward the Adepts: they drew enchanted swords with their right hands and raised staffs with their left hands. Bolts of dark, jagged power blasted at the monster, but as it staggered backward, vibrating sounds emerged from its writhing, dark hump: an invocation of magic. Masses of red and black vapor surrounded it, a cocoon of dark energy. The Adepts hurled power at the Creature, but now that power was turned aside. Very calmly, the Adepts sheathed both swords and staffs and stood weaponless, facing the oncoming monster.

Sentauris watched on from a distance, then she mounted and rode in a fury toward the Adepts. Were they surrendering, accepting death? They seemed so calm, but what—

Before Orantes flared a circle of radiance, sky blue, a coil of power with nothing but air at its center. Wylar was chanting: a second circle, lava red, formed behind the blue; then a third circle, yellow and gold behind the two, so that three circles pulsed in alignment before the Giant Ghoul.

Wylar stood behind the three pulsing rings, forcing his arm through them, pointing at the lumbering Creature Indomitable. From his fingers, dark flames sprouted. Focused by coils of power, a beam of black fire leaped at the Creature. Burning through the Ghoul's reddish black cocoon, then its massive frame, a dark fire raged through the hump of writhing tentacles. The Creature Indomitable stood statue still for a moment, as though unwilling to acknowledge its life's end. Then it toppled, stone dead, shaking the ground.

Some distance away, Gallandus blinked twice, trying to focus, then his mouth slipped open in shock. What in all of Alantéa had transformed those Replacement Adepts?!?

Staggered, Sentauris came to a halt. *Maker's Touch! The Adepts have devised a form of Dragonfire. But does this mean that I have approached the wrong monstrosity? Ghorm!*

·)(·

Again, Ghorm was lifted in flight, with the Owl-being above him gasping and straining. Beneath him, Whisper's insubstantial form struggled to provide a measure of lift. It was too stupid! Sending him with a man on horseback would have been so much faster! As he fussed and fumed, Ghorm was set down, feet racing as they touched the ground.

He ran until his breathing shuddered, then was lifted again. Sounds of battle grew louder, reaching his ears through a labyrinth of side streets — the hoarse cries of many men were mixed with deep groaning sounds from the Grey Mantis, but whether the Creature was groaning in ecstasy or pain could not be known. Ghorm was set down again and he raced forward, with Squint flapping overhead and Whisper at his side, the Shade fluttering through the air like a shadow blown by magic through a stormy night.

Sounds grew louder. The three Familiars passed through a long, curled alley; at its end, the lane was partially blocked by a heap of broken beams and torn, stretched leather thongs. *One of the casting devices made by Sardonicus,* Ghorm thought. *Dregs of dung!* At the alley's end, Ghorm leaped over the wreckage and into the battle.

The Grey Mantis stood in the middle of an intersection of broad streets, surrounded by dead men. Those killed by poison lay bloated and white with puss. Others had been decapitated or severed in two. All the casting devices in view had been broken and ruined; but in two places large javelins extended from the Grey Mantis like pins in an insect, though the Creature seemed undiminished by its wounds.

Not all the men surrounding the Grey Mantis were dead. Horse archers were launching arrows from a distance, while a score of Pikemen held one side street. As Ghorm raced closer, he saw three men bearing axes emerge from a darkened doorway, chop quickly at the monster's hind leg, then scurry back inside, as the Creature kicked them casually aside.

The Grey Mantis was leaning over, focusing on a lone swordsman it had trapped in a corner formed by a broad building adjoining a high wall: Sardonicus, shouting curses at the ungainly monstrosity, slashing, and parrying as the Grey Mantis extended its spindly insect arms toward him.

"Squint! Distract it!" Ghorm panted. The Owl-being rose to the height of the Grey Mantis, raking at its huge eyes, but was batted aside like a gnat. Whisper's dark shadowy substance reached the Creature's tail-sting, but Whisper recoiled in pain, forced back by a pulse of dark magic. Undistracted, the Grey Mantis struck aside the sword of Sardonicus and began lifting the mercenary captain toward its jaws.

Focusing all his strength of magic, Ghorm's mouth formed a *shout*, a noise of magic thrusting against the monster's head. The Grey Mantis dropped Sardonicus, clutching its painful ears with spindly arms. Sardonicus fell, then barked in pain. Totally spent, Ghorm toppled, easy prey for the least powerful of their foes.

As he faded, his eyes seemed to bring images of the Adepts, riding in a fury alongside Sentauris, hurling a deadly fire at the Creature Indomitable though coils of power that had many shades of different colors. Ghorm knew then that he must be sinking into his last dream because the Adepts had never shown anything resembling that amount of power. Anyway, those images were no more than wisps of fog, rising from the sea of delirium into which his squat form was sinking so rapidly.

· ℋ ·

Ghorm slipped from dark dreams into awareness, blinking in the shuttered light of late afternoon. The scene was dreamlike, wavering, though the light pained his eyes — an unlikely sensation in any passage through the Dreamways. He rolled over, lifting his head: low voices could be heard, speaking in an adjacent room. One of those voices belonged to Sardonicus.

"...foolish to believe that any man might pass without danger through such enormous events. For this, I ask your pardon." Another voice, that of Sentauris, spoke in such hushed tones that Ghorm could not make out the words.

"It was not professional," Sardonicus replied, "to deal with these events with so much emotion. Cool thoughts are clear thoughts. I must never again become trapped by my own feelings when battle rages. And do not ever let me again cast doubt on your Adept allies. They, together with your Familiar, saved our lives, including my own." Sentauris spoke more words in low tones. Ghorm smiled and turned on his side: the exact words spoken by Sentauris were not important; she and the captain were reconciling and that was good. He slipped back into a healing sleep, one that offered only gentle dreams that were filled with light.

· ℋ ·

When next Ghorm woke it was late at night. He lay beneath a canopy of bright stars, gleaming, glistening points of light that stretched from one end of the horizon to the other. He was on some high rooftop, with all the lantern lights and night sounds of the city made remote by distance.

"We are above the 'Conjurors' Tower' of the Adepts," Sentauris said softly just behind him. "When I foresaw your rising by starlight, the Adepts thought to honor you by transporting you undisturbed to the best stargazing tower in Tuvan."

"So, you could foresee the time of my awakening," Ghorm said. He found a nest of pillows just behind him and pulled himself up so he could sit. The days of late spring had grown warmer, but the nights were still chilled, so he drew his covers up. "It's always interesting which visions come to you, and which are barred."

"Strange, even to me," Sentauris said, and she pulled up her chair, to sit beside her Familiar. "Since we are stargazing together, I will tell you of one vision that comes so often to my mind, yet it makes not the slightest sense. I watch a child of nine or ten years as he plays with some winged creature that flies periodically over the high beams of an inner keep of the fortress. The castle resembles Gravengate somewhat, though it is older and different, and the face of the child seems hauntingly familiar, though I can never place him." She paused, watching as a cluster of sky stones slipped from the Cup of the Heavens, trailing fire as they flared toward the earth.

"Other visions are strange and wonderful," she continued, "and so hard to understand. You are in one of these visions, Ghorm, but do not take offense that you and I are not the only focus of this vision. We stand together, joined like fused statues in the night. You are there, as I am, with Wylar, Squint, Orantes, and Whisper. Great events take place in the distance, but we are not dismayed. We stand as a pillar of the League, and we radiate a green fire into the darkness.

"I believe that this vision is clear: we are indeed a pillar of the League, a force outside of the Wizards and their schemes, activated when the League is threatened. I understand this part of my vision, but then the images shown to me grow more complex. Across from us, perhaps at two hundred paces, and blurred by a shimmering haze, a second pillar forms. Is this haze a separation of time? Is this distance a separation of space within Alantéa, so that this pillar of strength is raised in Varaj perhaps, or Far Avalon? I cannot say.

"But in this second pillar, I see the image of a youth, an Apprentice, or Adept, whose Gift is as great as that of Wylar or Orantes. Beside him is a captain of great strength and wisdom, and another warrior bearing the most fell of Mid-World Weapons."

"Familiars?" Ghorm asked.

"Of course, there are Familiars, two of them, though why one lone magician would require two Familiars is a mystery. One of them is a slight, winged flyer with less range even than Squint. The second flickers in and out of my vision, like some secretive Mid-World Spy who can only be seen when he wishes. But this pillar constitutes a separate force, like our own. Was it present at the founding of the League? Or is it destined for some future time? Perhaps one day when the moment is right, I will ask Merlin."

Ghorm lay beside Sentauris, watching the glistening Cup of the Heavens shine over them, listening to tales of Sentauris as she continued speaking of heroes with Mid-World Weapons, of Sorcerers contending with Creatures of the Darkness, of Sidhe warriors on distant battlefields, and of Gods clashing in remote kingdoms of the Mid-World. Ghorm sighed — a long deep sigh, expressing both contentment and longing. If his inner soul found a voice, it would call out his desire to be much, much more to Sentauris than her aide and companion. Yet, if this moment did not hold the uttermost desires of his heart, at least it left Ghorm in a deep, healing peace. After a time, as the voice of Sentauris grew as remote as distant chimes, he turned and slept.

Later, Sentauris rose and paced around the rooftop, staring in all directions, extending her senses. To the south lay the fortresses of the Wizards, and she could feel the strength of those bastions steadily increasing, with more of their foes pushed each day from their fringes. In ones and twos, Creatures of the Darkness were perishing as they strayed too close to the Wizards' zones of power. But to the north, the borders of the League had been overrun, with tens of thousands of the League's people fleeing south or hiding in remote hills.

At Tuvan, they had fought the first great battle of this war, but at Amalric resistance burned bright, while at Khiva an assault by sea had been thrown back. Durian and North Haven were abandoned, but in hills, and swamps, and deep forests throughout the League, resistance was growing as fighters and hunters learned to counter Vorrs, Uraks, and Carag shapeshifters. Mír and his allies blazed destruction over their foes at every turn, emerging from nothingness to spring at their enemies, so that none of their foes' strong points could be relied upon.

As she paced about, she could feel not only the power and the terror of their foes but also the hidden and growing strength of the League. The League was mighty; the battle fought in Tuvan by two Adepts, three Captains, one lone Seeress, and many others had made it still stronger.

Their League would not be overcome so easily.

Chapter Nine

The Coming of the Enchanters

S BEFORE, THE MIND of Merlin continued to inscribe his history of the League, yet now those letters of darkened flame seemed to tremble as they raced across the pages of his journal:

Balardi recoils in astonishment, although after his shock I can almost hear the bark of his laughter echoing across the many leagues that separate Gravengate from Stone Mountain. Thorian's response is more restrained, and his satisfaction is lessened by worry: after all, if we completely misunderstood the Adepts and their ally, the Seeress, how many of our other understandings will turn out to be utterly false?

My own reaction is of a different order, for I have seen visions of the Seeress that my brethren have not.

We thought of our Adepts as pale shadows of their predecessors, a season of "replacements," as they were called, simply to be endured and outlived. In a moment of confusion, we simply exiled the Seeress because of her outspokenness.

Our understanding of human beings must now be reconsidered: we believed that a difficult childhood would produce a grown human with greatly reduced effectiveness. Wylar was abandoned by his parents and raised without affection by his grandparents. Orantes' father was an agent of some hidden Power, while his mother was lost in dreams, and the younger sister of Orantes devoted herself to making his life much more difficult. The parents of Sentauris were killed in battle when she was young, leaving her to be raised by her unstable, warlike, and now mentally exhausted uncle Vlasoff.

Yet now they have emerged as heroic figures beyond any of our remotest expectations.

Some force, some power is at work in this matter, an intelligence that we have completely overlooked. For in the aftermath of their astonishing triumph, I followed through Gates of Dreams, the vision of Sentauris, as she stood staring into the darkness.

In her vision, two pillars stood gleaming with a green light into the darkness. The forms in one pillar I recognized — Sentauris was present, together with Wylar and Orantes, and their three Familiars. The second pillar was completely strange to me, for there stood five figures I have never before encountered: some great Captain, a Warrior with his powerfully enchanted weapon, and an Apprentice with two Familiars.

From this vision, I must conclude that our Wizards' League when threatened by destruction, is supported by a second theme of heroic mortal servants. The first challenge has come now, as two Gods of the Mid-World assail us. This second challenge must come at a later time in the future, and yet how can any future struggle possibly be equal to the one we face today?

I cannot tell.... Wait, now wait. My vision screens have been following the Seeress. Now she stares north, and a look of foretelling is frozen on her face. Some momentous event, some gathering of forces beyond our understanding is taking place in the Mid-World of the Truce, and Sentauris reaches toward it, but she cannot quite reach it. What is happening?!?

· X ·

In the Vale of Whispers, ghosts murmured night and day, speaking in hushed voices of their ancient devices and desires. Apparitions drifted aimlessly, murmuring, always murmuring. The light all around them was subtly altered by the enchantments that had transformed the Vale of Whispers so many thousands of years ago: broad beams of sunlight had become more subtle and remote, yet the air seemed to glow with a muted, hidden radiance. And in the background, ghosts spoke endlessly of their ancient lives.

This recounting of dreams by ancient ghosts was a lonely process: all wished to tell their tales of woe, but none wished to listen, and so they droned on in dry voices, heedless of one another. Yet strangely, to one side, against the ruins of some great hall or temple, two ghostly figures were speaking quietly to one another — casually, lacking the sense of loss or desperation shown by other spirits.

One of these beings was Set, the other Mordred, and they spoke in soft voices in a place that no Mid-World Power truly wished to visit.

"We have been denied," Mordred said, speaking in the same hushed tones employed by other ghostly spirits in the Vale of Whispers.

"It is true that the League has proved stronger than we thought," Set replied in remote and judicious tones. "Hidden alliances appear, new defenders emerge each day, while those so-called 'Replacement Adepts' proved stronger than we once believed...and still, the Wizards will not be drawn from their lairs. What are your thoughts?"

Mordred would not respond; again, he was being baited, manipulated, invited to rash action or premature retreat. *Can you not sense, Great God Set, that I have transformed myself to become craftier and wiser, and thus able to match your guile? Of what use is it, being a God, if one cannot reincarnate oneself?*

Instead of replying, the Renegade watched the ghosts of the Ancient Powers as they murmured their tales of woe, unable to find listeners in the Vale of Whispers. Of the Ancient Powers, only the Demons and the Dragons showed the bulk of true Powers. The other two — Seraphs and Spirit Lords — were barely two heads higher than the pitiful humans.

From these four sets of beings — Seraphs and Demons, Spirit Lords and Dragons — the Mid-World of the Truce had produced the hybrid Powers of the Mid-World, the Gods of Mankind. No Power openly acknowledged its origins, and Mordred was filled with an uneasiness bordering on dread that his own ghostly antecedent as a Lord of Dragons would penetrate the Renegade Dark God's current disguise and speak its tale of abandonment and woe in a low, moaning voice.

Seeing his ally's discomfort, Set laughed aloud, then murmured, "No, it will never find you, for I have crafted your own disguise too well. But come now, my Dark Brother, what do you propose?"

"I have several proposals," Mordred said evenly, though he lowered his voice, "but first a question. We must deal with these 'Replacements,' but what of their predecessors? Is there a chance that the ones called Hektor and Antéus will suddenly reemerge to change the course of our struggle?"

Set laughed and laughed again. "Those two may or may not be completely and utterly dead, but they will never 'reemerge.' Also, I will reassure you about those 'Replacement Adepts.' The thin one may stand and die under pressure, but the fat one will break and run. I have seen that event clearly in the future. Now, what are your suggestions? I am most curious."

"I have much more than 'suggestions,'" Mordred said evenly, though he lowered his voice. "As you will hear, I have already taken action. First, the Seeress has taken no wounds, felt no pain, so I have dispatched a Death Squad to deal with her mad uncle. They will make his death a time of torment that the Seeress with her so-called 'Farsight' will feel from a distance.

"Secondly, since the numbers of Creatures Indomitable are diminishing, I also have 'harvested,' as you call it, a dozen, or so additional monstrosities of equal might, and directed these to the League. As a third measure, Un-Maurag, my Brother in Darkness, has agreed to reopen his war against the Elf Kindreds. In truth, he requires no prompting for such an effort and stands ready with mature broods of Vorrs and Uraks for this conflict.

"And last," Mordred continued, "I will direct to you two of my most powerful servants — Carag Mages — to swell the ranks of the Enchanters and join with the three mortal Sorcerers who have allied themselves with your cause."

"Yes, the Enchanters," Set murmured. "I saw them once as a final windstorm that would level a dying forest, but there is still a strength of green in the sheltering stand formed by the Wizards' League. So, I will make of these Enchanters a more powerful force: with the Carag Mages their numbers will be five, and with new weapons, they will have the power to bring fear, even terror to the Wizards. I will raise them to a new level, for I have discovered fragments of a fallen, undead, Ancient Power. I will bind these fragments to the Enchanters, and so they will become mightier, perhaps even immortal."

"You will not harm..." Mordred began, fearing for his own servants trapped in the malice of Set, but then he halted, realizing how much more he desired the destruction of the League than the success of his favored Carag Mages.

Set laughed quietly. "Thus, you are learning diplomacy and other virtues. Perhaps one day you can aspire to the form you now wear." In the fullness of his mockery and malice, Set had disguised each of them as the ghost of a Seraph, angelica once fashioned by the Maker, and a form far from those of their own beginnings as Demon or Dragon.

Mordred studied Set's face for a time, pondering the Great God's confidence in his new devices, the Enchanters. Mordred also wished to ask about the Emissaries of the Gods who flocked fitfully to the League, though he sensed that Set would offer only amused disinformation. In turn, Set considered Mordred, wondering if the Renegade realized that he was being manipulated. After a time, the two forms slowly lost their shapes, then dissolved into the glistening mists that floated endlessly around the Ruins of Dahlak.

Layers of aromatic incense wreathed the Halls of Set, but all the scented barks of Alantéa and tinctures of woodland herbs and tropical spices could not completely mask the smell of decay that rose from the crypts that lay beneath the upper palaces.

A remote music drifted through the palaces, a chorus of many voices, singing an endless chorus of praise for Set the Redeemer, Set the Lord of the Undying Realms, but the voices seemed so completely dry, distant, and soulless, that it sounded as though the Undying Realms were populated solely by the Unliving.

Five figures sat in silence in an upper antechamber, one or two staring at the others with furtive eyes, while others sniffed the air with wrinkled noses. One, a highborn woman of midyears would not so much as glance at the other Sorcerers and Mages but fixed her eyes into the distance as though regarding dreams of her own devising. To her left sat a hawk faced man with a dark beard, whose eyes darted constantly to his left and to his right, while his lips seemed poised to speak, but whether his mouth formed greetings or words of power could not be known.

To the right of the dreaming Sorceress sat an albino, with a seemingly ageless face, with tufts of white hair ranging over his scalp and jutting out from thick eyebrows. The albino's eyes were of light blue, so cold and clear that they might have been transplanted from an arctic skyline. The chilled blue eyes of this Sorcerer studied with interest two figures that sat across from the three mortal wielders of magic.

To the untrained eye, the two men seated on the far side of the room might have been brothers; a trained observer might have called them twins, though one bulked somewhat larger than the other, and the leaner form seemed more detached as though preoccupied with events of a higher order. Each was clothed as a courtier of some wealth and standing, smooth shaven, light brown hair cropped in fringes about their ears. Such was the strength of their disguises that neither the Sorcerers nor the Witch Queen could perceive the Carag Mages as other than human.

The five had sat quietly for the first two tremors. When the palace shook for the third time, they heard groaning noises, as though some great beast stirred at the heart of the world.

"How restless these 'fragments' have become," the hawk faced Sorcerer muttered, breaking the long silence.

"Yes, we must speak," added the albino, eyes remaining fixed on the Carag Mages. "In a brief time, we will be brothers and sisters, part of a new order of demigods — the Enchanters." Again, the building stirred, and this time even the Witch Queen was drawn from her trance by the sensation of distant torment, vibrations ending just at the edges of her hearing.

"Yes, the Enchanters," murmured the hawk faced Sorcerer chewing on his dark beard. "*If* the Great God Set masters these 'fragments.' *If* He succeeds in binding us with this Ancient Power. *If* the process does not destroy us."

"I can perceive no telltales in this place," the Witch Queen snapped at him. "But be certain that Set will know each word that you speak. Do not endanger the rest of us with loose talk. You there!" She called across to the Carag Mages as though addressing serfs. "How are you named? What do the other slinking creatures with their putty faces call you?"

"Names?" asked the larger of the two. "Names are devices of humans and none of our affair. We know each other at a much different and deeper level. Call us what you will."

"Call us Wrack and Ruin," suggested the second Carag Mage.

"Plague and Rapine," offered the first.

"Dimwit and Rotbrain are much more appropriate," snapped the Witch Queen. "If you b—"

"Stop for a moment," the albino Sorcerer interjected in surprisingly mild tones. "Consider how unwise it is for us to quarrel. We are to be allies, joint rulers of the South of Alantéa, Enchanters destined to replace the Wizards. We must work together toward this end. I am Pentarchus, a Sorcerer dwelling in remote kingdoms of the Mid-World. Known to me by reputation is her Majesty, Azüre, whose waspishness may be caused by the collapse of her kingdom in the Isles of the Sorcerers. Next to her Nairn fidgets, his swift, enchanted intellect always seeking an advantage. You, as Servants of Mordred, should also select names, then build minor personality traits about those names, for then we can deal as equals."

The two Carags glanced together, then nodded slowly.

"I will become Manassas," said the larger of the two.

"And I, Helcar," said the other, after a brief hesitation.

"Good, good," muttered the hawk faced Nairn, pulling his chair forward. "We must speak openly, staying within the designs of the Great God Set. He will overlook our candor, for we seek only to further His designs. Firstly, what are your thoughts regarding the aftermath of our victory? Will you two seek a portion of the League as spoils of war? Or will you wish to return to Mordred, your Dark God, and Master?"

Both Carags looked uncomfortable. "We have been given a choice," murmured the one called Helcar, glancing at his fellow Carag. "We may return to our Lord, or we may forge our own realms elsewhere. This choice has not yet been made." The Witch Queen laughed aloud — rough, jarring sounds.

Pentarchus nodded gravely. "We will not fault Nairn, for it is his nature to seek advantage during every waking moment of his existence. But a recurring theme is played out with some consistency in the Halls of the Powers: when servants gather too much strength, they tend to vanish suddenly, or if the God remains benign, they are merely exiled."

"You will become too strong," the Witch Queen added, watching the two with more than a touch of malice. "Mordred will no longer be comfortable with your powers."

"Then the choice has been made for us," Manassas said easily. "We will each claim a fifth portion of the League as spoils of War. I do not think the humans will savor our rule, for Carags and Vorrs and Uraks will be called upon to serve us."

Nairn sat back, gnawing on his upper lip, glancing at the Witch Queen and at Pentarchus with little pleasure.

"It may well be more than a fifth portion," Pentarchus said quietly. "These trappings of power have little attraction for me. Divide my portion among the four of you; only allow me an isle or a fragment of land on which to build a single, strong place. True power lies in the mastery of magic, not in land or weapons or slaves. In my own quest, I tremble at the edge of dark designs, yet I sense the life force beginning to ebb within me, no matter how many times each portion of my own body is enchanted and reconstructed. I *will* live. I *will* supplant the Wizards and their League. I *will* journey to the farthest shores of dark magic and discover the deepest, most powerful of mysteries. But the land, the land is nothing to me."

"So," the Witch Queen smiled with the first trace of real humor. "Lust for power is on display here, and malice, and a certain low cunning. But do we have any wisdom to share? We are to be bound to an Ancient Power, and so become ourselves immortal. Of these Ancient Powers, there were said to be four: Demons, and Seraphs, Spirit Lords, and Dragons. The Great God Set will not tell us which of these has furnished the 'fragments' that will be bound to our bodies. Come, I invite your speculation."

"The Spirit Lords were closest to humanity," Nairn said cautiously. "We might be most easily bound to such an entity."

"My gorge riseth," Manassas said, puffing out air.

"But beyond that," Helcar said reasonably, "consider us in battle with the Wizards. Suddenly, this Spirit Lord component urges us to stop and frolic among the wildflowers. No, the Carag tribes are products of the left-hand, side sinister of Creation: the true Ancient Powers, the Demons, and the Dragons. One of those will be our fate."

The Witch Queen tittered. Within the Halls of Set, one last tremor shook the foundations of the Great God's land, then it faded into stillness.

"No, one moment," Nairn muttered. "The misunderstanding of an adversary is an advantage, but not the confusion of an ally. Firstly, those four Ancient Powers fought to a draw, and thus the Mid-World of the Truce came into being, so we should not underestimate the might provided to

Spirit Lords and Seraphs. But you are right that the Great God Set would be more familiar with the substance of Demon or Dragon, and so that will be my fate, our fate. So be it; power, and strength of mind, and everlasting life: these things will make our 'bonding' no sacrifice, but a great leap forward."

"Wisdom —of a sort," said the Witch Queen, dryly. "But since we have opened a wider discussion, I must ask: why should we trust this process? For all the oaths and the promises of the Great God Set, he owes us nothing."

The eyebrows of Pentarchus rose briefly, as though he stirred from sleep. "In this respect, I can speak something of the hierarchies of power. At this moment, should I bring a force of magic against Balardi on neutral ground, the event would be in doubt. With Thorian, the scales would weigh against me, and with Merlin, disaster would follow. The Great God Set knows our relative strengths, that if we of our own cunning and might were to attack this League, we would fail. And so, if he wishes to destroy the Wizards, he must raise us to a higher level. Is this not completely evident?"

Unused to having her power questioned, the Witch Queen snarled, and blustering noises came from the Sorcerer, Nairn, but as each heard the other, both halted in mid speech, and the room fell suddenly quiet.

"How interesting," the Carag called Manassas murmured.

"I do like our new friends better with every passing moment," Helcar added, then he favored his human companions with a strange, soft smile. "You should know that we may take shapes that are pleasing to you, and so with sensuous arts reward your allegiance to the cause of the Enchanters."

"We will save those matters," said Nairn, "for the victory celebration." While his own essence offered confused messages of desire and revulsion, he noted the immediate interest of the Witch Queen, and the slight curl of disdain from the lips of the albino Sorcerer.

All of this might work, thought Nairn. *It may be that we complement each other in many ways, though the Carag Mages are in love only with themselves and appreciate only the malice shown by their human allies. I wish, I so wish....*

His thought patterns shifted abruptly then, for the air in the chamber's midst was beginning to swirl and glow. A column of dark radiance was forming in the center of the room; all five beings knelt quickly, then abased themselves, burying their faces in the thick carpeting of the antechamber. None dared to look up when the voice of Set was raised in speech.

You will now retire, each of you separately and alone, to the chamber set aside for you. There, you must yield gracefully to the enchanted sleep that beckons, for such slumber is the gateway to the transforming arts at My command. And when you wake, a new race of beings will have been brought forth: Powers, Dominions known as The Enchanters.

·))(·

None of the Wraiths serving Set was truly alive, though each mimicked the life patterns of one of the Great God's ancient foes or living adversaries: one Wraith, taller than most, resembled a Spirit Lord, with long flowing hair that tumbled over haggard features; a second Wraith might have been the shambling, twitching ghost of the long departed Elf-Lord Voll; while a third was formed in the image of Merlin, though a comical version, with bulging gnome eyes and twisted gargoyle features.

When sounds of torture began emerging from the crypts, scores of Wraiths drifted down toward the lower vaults, beginning to gloat: *Soon, soon, others will join us, beings to be mocked as we once were scorned! Meanwhile, hear the sounds that bring the Great God Set such pleasure!* Shrieks penetrated the deepest stone, groaning noises echoed through the farthest corridors. In two separate chambers, Carag Mages unwittingly transformed themselves into outlandish shapes, as their bodies were wracked so much pain that they struggled desperately to escape.

The Witch Queen screamed with increasing panic while the Sorcerer Nairn in delirium called upon the Maker to set him free. And as the sounds of torment grew ever louder, the Wraiths began huddling together, murmuring in fear. *What is happening in our dark kingdom? These beings are not even awake to endure such pain. What does the Great God Set wish with them?*

Again, the foundations of the crypts trembled, as though some sleeping giant stirred. Once more the Great God Set bellowed in rage, lifting His voice above the shrieking humans and sobbing Carags. Wraiths began stopping up their ears, then they fled in horror, seeking the most remote regions of the lower palace, where the dust fell slowly over abandoned and forgotten creatures that had been dead for centuries.

· X ·

Nairn woke slowly as though recovering from a century's hibernation. He coughed and turned ponderously, with pain radiating through every portion of his body. By all the Powers, he had become suddenly an old man! Alarmed, he struggled to his feet. Every motion was an effort, but with one hand he ripped the white gown from his body then stumbled across the room, where one wall held more than dozen mirrors.

His body was wasted and drawn, with his jet-black hair glistening with a sheen of white. His feet seemed heavier now, more leathery, and was that dark hair curling between his toes, or some other growth? *Nairn, you fool! Trapped so easily in the malice of Set! Wait, though, wait: if humiliation were his object, Set would be here in the fullness of his divine mockery; and if the Greater God's binding work had failed, then Set would not have permitted you to live.*

Moving somewhat more easily, Nairn walked to the alcove that held his old clothing. Holding it against his frame, he discovered that he was taller, larger, nearly a foot higher. Distracted, he reached for an urn of water that was set on a cabinet to his left. His hand crumpled the urn, then casually smashed the cabinet's thick hardwood surface into kindling.

Power!

· X ·

The Witch Queen lay on her bed, moaning quietly. Her body had been healed, but all its enchanted portions held memories of so much pain that they wished to cry aloud. With a twitch of irritation, she stifled her soft cries, then she began tracing her fingers carefully from her forehead down to her toes, searching for the seams of slight scars that might betray surgery.

Wait! Were those scales on her breasts? About her stomach? And her thighs!

She leaped to her feet, with all the joints in her body popping and cracking, then tore off her gown. *Scales!* The slight, silvery green scales of some sea creature extended from her shoulders down to her thighs.

Set! You will pay! She paced, raging, but struggled to control herself. *Calm, now calm. First escape — then revenge!* She called down spell words: interlocking illusions created the appearance of pale flesh over the scaled portions of her body.

It was better, but still, she paced. *I will become the first mortal to assassinate a Greater God, but first, where do I find my clothes? I have not had to dress myself for a century, and now I do not even know where they have placed my garments!*

Some remote portion of her mind surged into action; her mouth spoke whispered words that were completely unintelligible to her. A side door flew open. Garments, the regal cloths of a Witch Queen, surged through the air and began wrapping themselves about her, concealing both naked flesh and layers of illusions.

May all the Nine Billion Gods feast on dung! Control over the inanimate is nothing I ever thought to do before! I must rethink matters....

·))(·

The Carag Mage called Manassas lay bloated and limp, his body showing the soft putty colored image of four worm segments, though patches of hair and ridges of cartilage on its outer skin suggested a vaguely mammalian heritage.

As Manassas woke, groaning, his form shuddered in surprise on discovering it had lost its shape. *That human guise was a strong transformation, heavy with real and powerful magic! What torment have I endured that it has been stripped so completely from me?*

He struggled to resume his old form of Manassas, with his body shaking and squirming before again assuming its human disguise. *Set, what have you done to me?* The Carag Mage stood slowly, awkwardly, his head brushing the chamber's high ceiling.

Set! I am about six times my old mass! I can no longer hide as a human! But words whispered in a strange tongue slipped unbidden from his lips; his form became more fluid, lessening until he stood in his old indisputably human guise.

I have new power, to become much larger, perhaps even much stronger, but has this change also been visited upon my brother Mage, whom the humans have been told to call Helcar? Furtively, he slipped from his chamber out into a broad hall, and stood silently, searching with heightened senses for his fellow Carag Mage. A muted radiance cast shadows over marble floors. Broad pillars supported a high ceiling that was obscured by darkness. Wisps of ghostly matter seemed to pass just out of the corners of his eyes, while a strange magic ebbed and flowed all around him.

Manassas drew a deep breath. His brother — yes transformed, but still his brother. His own power of magic guided him across broad marble floors to a side chamber similar to his own. Silently, he slipped within, easing the door shut behind him.

The head, the head alone remained of the Carag Mage called Helcar; the rest of his body seemed completely transformed, becoming a growth like a furry carpet on the floor, though now as he watched, the growth was inching slowly up the left-hand wall. As Manassas peered forward, mouth open in horror, he saw that the head of Helcar had become smaller and that it whispered softly, intoning spell words in a strange tongue, working a magic that reached far into the distance, with an object and purpose known neither to Carag nor human.

Set! What have you done!

· ✗ ·

Pentarchus, too, felt both pain and strangeness, although so many times had his form been reconstructed through enchantments that he understood some great transformation had been visited upon his body. A graft — as Set had promised, a graft.

The Albino Sorcerer lay motionless, eyes still closed. A portion of his enchanted mind drifted through various sections of his body, testing them while bringing a strength of healing. The greater portion of his sorcerous intellect examined the nature of his graft.

Rough seams, O Great God Set, as though you have bound together unlike creatures, like a tiger and killer whale, each raging violently at such a joining. Though perhaps such resistance was inevitable.

He reached into the graft, touching it with his mind. So, fragment of an Ancient Power, what have you to say? Unintelligible words and thoughts spewed forth; only malice and anger and confusion could be deciphered.

I would feel much the same way, he thought to the fragment, *had our roles been reversed. It will take a season or two for us to become accustomed to one another. In the mean time, have you some selection of magic to show me, some power you once took pleasure in employing?*

A pause ensued. Outside his chamber, silence prevailed, though magic swirled though shadowed halls, forces released by the absence of the Great God Set. Then words, completely unrecognizable, spilled forth from his mouth. A force of dark sorcerous energy, also unknown, gathered about him. Furtive rustling sounds could be heard, passing through the halls and into his chamber, but still, he kept his eyes shut, letting the strange black magic work its will.

As the force of sorcery dwindled down, and the sounds within his chamber stilled, he let his arctic blue eyes slip open. And Pentarchus gasped.

A small army of rats and mice attended him, sitting up on their hind legs, awaiting his will. Interspersed with the rodents were larger, unnamed creatures that stood like withered and stunted gnomes. But all were dead, mummified creatures that had lost fluid life, then died in the walls or abandoned chambers of the Halls of Set.

He had become a Necromancer. A master of the dead.

Even Gods grow weary, though most simply refresh themselves at the deep wellsprings of power that flow so freely through the Mid-World of the Truce. Some Powers withdraw into a silent stillness, viewing events of their world as though from a pinnacle, and only return to their dwelling places after their fatigue passes. A few Gods, by far the least in number, retreat into dreams of their own devising; and such was Set's retreat.

In his dream, the Great God Set paced down a long corridor. On either side of the passageway hung enormous paintings done in meticulous oils, each showing images from Set's own memory: Demons battling Seraphs in the upper firmaments, amid turmoils of dark and light vapor; Dragons waging a midair war of wild magic against Spirit Lords; Creatures Indomitable raging through human settlements; and jealous Dark Gods surrounded by legions bearing banners, crushing lesser Powers and their hosts.

Such were the memories of Set. In the dreams of Set, the Great God reached the corridor's end, and the door before him sprang open. He emerged onto a broad dais, one that overlooked a temple filled with worshipers.

"Great God Set! Great God Set! Great God Set!" They cried, leaping to their feet; Set's "worshipers" stood less than halfling height, with bulging, knobby heads. They danced and frolicked, calling all the while, "Great God Set! Great God Set!"

"My little Trufflekins," Set murmured, "do not become so excited. You are all far too delicate."

The Great God beamed down on his servants and their clamor, as they cried again and again, "Great God Set!" Each of his puff headed Trufflekins held the features of an ancient adversary. The features of Adonai, mightiest of the ancient Seraphs, were shown by one, another was cast as Wotan, though this Trufflekin form would not have reached halfway to that Great God's knee. Present also were Zôs, and the ram-faced Tel-Alantir, and Pallas Athena, and the bird-faced Thoth, and the ancient Spirit Lord Llara, and Heimdall, and Dagda, and many others. Strangely, one Trufflekin held the features of an ancient Demon Prince, though how that being came to be counted among Set's enemies, only the Great God himself could say.

"My little Trufflekins," Set spoke again, raising his hands to quiet them; gradually the noise of their celebrations dwindled down into low murmurings.

"Now, my sweetings," the Great God smiled down on them, "as ever, on these occasions, I will entertain a few of your questions." A hubbub of uncertainty followed. Finally, the Trufflekin of Zôs raised his small hesitant hand and was recognized.

"Great God and Lord of Creation," said the Trufflekin, and tiny flickers of light swirled around this Trufflekin's knobby head in mockery of lighting, "will these Enchanters ever know to which of the Ancient Powers they have been bonded?" As though unbidden, the small creature's eyes glanced at the bulging Demon-like head of his fellow Trufflekin.

"At the end, they will know." Set smiled and acknowledged the timorous, tiny hand of Heimdall.

"Greatest of Gods, you have raised these Enchanters to a new level. Are they now equal to the Wizards?"

Set nodded judiciously. "Not at this very moment, for in the next while, they must integrate old and new powers. After, should the Wizards and their Adepts be raised against the Enchanters on a field of battle, the League would be crushed." With a touch of benign sorrow, Set acknowledged the three-fingered hand of the Trufflekin bearing the head of a Demon Prince. "Yes, Voritar the Diminished, my brother of old."

"Lord of Darkness," said the Trufflekin in a deep voiced parody of Demon tones. "Is there hope for the Wizards in their strongholds? Of old, it was said that they might withstand a great weight of foes behind strong walls."

"It is true," Set spoke in somber tones, "that the Wizards — one or two — may withstand the first thrust of the Enchanters. But understand this." Set brightened. "It is only necessary to smoke one Wizard from his warren and after, after, I have crafted a Great Spell, the Sending of all Sendings, to bring down that wretched creature. And then the League will topple, like an edifice resting tripartite upon three pillars that cannot be maintained by two."

As though spontaneously, all his Trufflekins burst into applause, calling again, "Great God Set! Great God Set!"

"Yes, Yes," Set murmured, again quieting them, "though none of you has asked as yet the most interesting question.... Llara, you may speak."

"Great God, and Master of All Dark Things," said the tiny, squeaking voice of the ancient Spirit Lord. "Great one, after you have supplanted the Wizards with the Enchanters, how will you deal with their greater power, should they not heed your will?"

Set beamed down upon her. "Excellent! Indeed, it would not be the first time that an Ogre has been sent to smoke out some Troll creature, thus leaving a greater cave dweller to fill the void. Behold! I have fashioned the Enchanters; I may unmake them by speaking ten words."

A gasp spilled from Set's Trufflekins, followed by torrents of wild applause.

"Ten words..." Set murmured. "Ten words alone..." Set clapped once, returning the applause of his dreaming slaves.

As Set's hands smote together, each of the heads of his "Trufflekins" exploded, showering temple walls with red blood and yellow and orange brain matter. Then Set threw back his own head and laughed aloud in the fullness of his divine mania.

· ҄ ·

At sunset, Sentauris stood watch beside the ruin of Tuvan's gates, staring into the oncoming night as the city's outside patrol rode back toward Tuvan and the blood red sun that shimmered over the city's western walls. Gallandus had led this afternoon's riding, with Orantes providing a shielding of sorcerous energies. As Sentauris glanced at the Adept's form, she noted again that he seemed slimmer, and he was considerably more dangerous and respected than at the beginning of the Wild Time, although his thirst for wine remained legendary and unquenchable.

Gallandus led his riders through the gap formed by the ruined gates and broken towers then waved them on to their homes or barracks. Only the Adept and two of Gallandus' bodyguards lingered. Orantes seemed unusually thoughtful, but seeing that Gallandus sought to speak with Sentauris, the Adept offered only a partial wave and turned away to pursue other matters. As Gallandus dismounted, his aides led his horse away.

"Ghorm would offer choice, barbed words," Gallandus said, moving stiffly, "if he knew how much these old bones of mine ached and groaned. But here is the essence of what we learned this day: all signs point to a withdrawal north — stray Vorrs still slink about, while maimed Uraks lurk like Ogres in dark places, while the fit and weaponed have been pulled north."

"It is far from over," Sentauris said. "My own belief is that the worst is yet to come, though you should tell your men only that our foes regroup, that they have not left the League."

Gallandus stretched. "This League of yours is, in essence, a fair thing, a worthy cause to fight, and a fine place to retire to — if it survives." He turned toward his barracks, passing Orantes in silence as the Adept walked cautiously over the plaza, where cobblestones and potholes alternated. His right hand held a slight goblet of wine for Sentauris, his left an enormous tankard of ale for himself.

"A parlay!" Sentauris exclaimed in mock delight. "Though we lack seating and from the size of your tankard, our discussions may well last all night."

"The work of minutes, not hours," Orantes said, passing wine to her. "When I rose this morning Wylar told me of your dreams that they were more than strange, conflicting with our Divinations. I have learned to trust this Seer's Sight of yours, but can you tell me more?"

Sentauris glanced west into a furnace-red, fading sun, and sipped wine. "It will make no sense to you either, but on each of the eight nights following the battle, my dream visions have drifted to Murat and Fiüre. Both sought refuge in the woodlands lying east of Tuvan. Becoming aware of the other's presence, each began to stalk the other, in a macabre little dance of death that lasted five days. At last Murat, a shade smarter, dealt a deathblow to Fiüre, though Fiüre was better armed and slew Murat in his last spasms.

"Both lie in deep woodlands, three nights dead, and still my dream vision returns to them. But why? Each seems to glow with a feral light, and none of the forest creatures has yet been able to pick at their carcasses."

Orantes set down his tankard in the slight hollow left by a vacant cobblestone. "A mystery to myself and to Wylar," he said, rubbing his face with both hands. "Our own Divinations are of a different order — distant tremors, as though the earth moves at the mountain's heart, telling us that the land will soon be torn apart."

"So, why should my vision," Sentauris murmured, "like some nagging aunt, return repeatedly to these fallen traitors?"

Once more in darkest night, the dream vision of Sentauris visited again the lifeless forms of Murat and Fiüre. Each glowed faintly with the phosphorescence of decaying organic matter. As she watched the forms seep and glow, a night raven swooped down beside the dead thing that had once been Murat, though as it probed at soft eyeball, some force bounced its beak away.

Why has my vision brought me to this place? Why do I not instead behold the mountain's heart, where the Adepts perceive such tremors?

All else is shielded from you. A voice, in the powerful tones of a Goddess, spoke words of crystal clarity into her mind.

But come, erstwhile daughter, let me show you something of the new forces raised against you and your League.

The fabric of Time seemed to accelerate as her dream vision raced from the woodlands. Sentauris felt herself rising high up into the night. Above her, the moon rose swiftly then dropped like an arcing stone. Beyond the circles of the moon, the stars above her wheeled in the sky, spinning like some Wizard's enchanted display of light, but then starlight yielded to a swift sunrise. In its transition from darkness to light, all things flew by as though the earth had been spun by the hand of a God and its long night hastened.

With the coming light, all the wheeling, spinning motions of the sky began to slow then return to normal. In her dream vision, Sentauris hovered over a distant point far to the northeast, where the river Asaram formed the border of the League. There, at daybreak, a dark oval cone formed at the southern bank of the river, a Portal that flared seven times the height of a man, and twelve times as wide. Five figures emerged, riding abreast, seated on dark stallions. Her vision had become a nightmare; Sentauris expected dark clouds to blot out bright sunlight, but all was still, clear, and quiet as if the land awaited some great act of destruction. Slowly, the five figures advanced over League soil.

One of these she knew of old: Nairn the Sorcerer, but subtly changed. To his right rode a richly dressed, haughty woman of midyears. To Nairn's left, centermost of the five, rode an Albino Sorcerer with arctic blue eyes.

The two figures to the Albino's left seemed to be brothers, with shortish brown hair and without beards.

Each of the five seemed strangely transformed: partly changed as though some complex spell had just begun but was not yet complete.

"Here is the League," Nairn said ponderously, "destined to be the foundation of our empire."

The haughty woman rolled her eyes. "So, you have said, perhaps half a dozen times since sunrise. Forget your empire. Today, we should focus on those fragments within us. What have we learned? I feel both old and new powers struggling within me — a jumble of different magics. How am I better off than before?"

"Time," said the Albino Sorcerer. "In days you will become stronger, and in weeks to come, mightier still."

"One caution," said the leaner of the two brown haired riders. "Do not seek close contact with one another, for these 'fragments' still yearn to join with one another."

"What?!?" Nairn muttered.

The larger of the brown-haired men laughed darkly. "Only reach out to touch our beloved Witch Queen, and you will understand my brother's words all too quickly."

"Enough," said the Albino Enchanter. "So, we cannot embrace one another — is this a true concern? Let us deal with matters at hand. A nodule of power has formed at Tuvan. We must destroy this City first, and in doing so, our own powers and devices will sharpen. Come."

"First," Nairn muttered, "we must put an end to the prying eyes and ears of the Mid-World." The Sorcerer's fingers danced in jagged, spider motions and the dream vision of Sentauris was swept away and replaced by a dark night. She took a deep breath, struggling to wake and consider her night vision with a clear mind.

She was unable to clear her mind. Instead, she found herself in a darkened temple; and on the temples' altar, a figure began to form, to glow, slowly shaping itself, then drawing upon its image a fullness of bright light.

Pallas Athena, brushing aside the Gates of Dreams, came to stand before Sentauris. As ever, the Goddess loomed tall and powerful, her head covered with an armored helm, some tiny owl perched upon her shoulder. Warily, Sentauris sank to one knee and bowed her head.

"Hail, Holy Mother," Sentauris whispered, struggling to mask the thoughts within her that Pallas Athena might so easily read.

"Hail, Wayward Daughter," the Goddess said in a remote voice. "When first you left my service some seven cycles of the sun gone by, I did wish for your return, though later I understood that you were forever lost to me. Now, Wayward Daughter, now that you are doomed by forces you cannot hope to withstand, you still have time to reconsider. Might you wish to return to my kingdom?"

Sentauris looked up at the glowing figure. "Holy Mother, if I am doomed, I must accept my fate, though I will struggle mightily to resist that fate with every force at my command. And, Holy Mother, I still love you; I never rejected you. Though my sight reaches far, it does not carry to Time's End, yet I understand that on Judgment Day you and I will stand together, bathed in a radiance of blessing."

"Time's End, Child," the Goddess said sharply, "what talk is this? My fear is that in less than two days you will sleep a forever sleep, and then I will feel sorrow that I cannot watch you struggle so powerfully against your foes. Is it not said, 'The Gods love a Hero'? To this end, and not because you were once subject to me, I tell you this: abandon Tuvan, flee south, so these Enchanters I have shown you will not slay you so quickly at the beginning of their war. Will you do this, child? Or do you wish for this Maker of yours so strongly that you hunger for death?"

"Holy Mother,in two days' time, we will move south with every pack horse, every —"

"You must flee before dawn," the Goddess interjected. "I have guided matters so that you will wake before midnight. Go and rouse your city."

"The Adepts...at times...."

"I will help to guide those softheaded toadies of the Wizards. Wayward Daughter, you remain precious to my eyes. Rise now and save your people."

Such was the force of Pallas Athena's message, that Sentauris found herself awake, standing beside her bed, beads of sweat slipping down her forehead, even in the cool, lightless dark.

"Ghorm!" she called out, fumbling for flint to light her bedside candle. "Ghorm, wake up! You can fornicate with your Goblin Dream Princess later!" She muttered curses, but with her third effort, the candle beside her was lit. One cloth garment was discarded, with another swiftly replacing it. Her corselet came next: even with its finely wrought metal, her armor seemed cumbersome. She was just pulling on her boots when Ghorm pushed her door open.

"You're a fine one to talk about 'fornication,'" he muttered, rubbing his eyes. "Think back fifteen months to that night in Varaj when —"

"Ghorm, I'm sorry. Listen: in a few hours time, we, and the entire population of Tuvan must be on the road. Rouse your friends the Familiars, then seek Druss, who captains the night watch. Tell him to call out all the other watches. Then raise the city. I will deal with the Adepts."

"What brought all this about?"

"Pallas Athena. The good news is that she seems to have forgiven us; the bad, that she watches us with great interest. Ghorm, speed is needed."

Sentauris hurried out into the night, eyes adjusting easily to starlight as she ran swiftly toward the Adepts and their conjurors' tower.

How best to persuade the two Magicians? Wylar had taken the third floor of the tower, Orantes the second. Should she bypass the second floor, wake Wylar, then enlist his aid in the formidable task of moving a sluggish Orantes? As she ran, the sky above her radiated a full strength of starshine — fixed light, so much unlike the wheeling, spinning motions of starlight racing through her night vision.

· X ·

She turned the corner that led to the tower of the Adepts and slowed in surprise: torchlights flickered from both their second and third floors. The Adepts were awake. Had Pallas Athena roused them? A burst of speed led her to the tower, up the stairs and into a second floor chamber that was lit by sputtering torches.

Orantes was moving — sluggish, like a zombie, but he was moving. Wylar had gathered their meager belongings — bits of clothing, vials of fluids, packets of healing powders — into a leather satchel. Both Adepts were clothed and weaponed.

"Did the Goddess..." Sentauris began, but Wylar held out a scrap of parchment. She took it from his hand and read:

Wylar and Orantes:

Gather all those that will follow, and fall back south, either to Stone Mountain or Gravengate, as events dictate. Do not deliberate, do not delay, for mighty and fell events have befallen our peoples.

Merlin counsels that the main thrust of our foes is upon us, that Dark Powers have created the Enchanters, to destroy the Wizards and their League. Doom is upon us, though we will fight mightily against it.

Maker's speed to you and to our peoples.

Thorian, for the League.

As she looked up at Wylar, drumbeats, uncertain at first, began to rouse the city, and seconds later, distant warning bells began to ring.

"Yes, the Goddess Pallas Athena also sought us out," Wylar said, "though she found us already awake. Portal Magic has long eluded the Wizards, though at this crisis, while they remain unable to master the opening of Portal Passages, they have found some hidden side corridors and used these to transmit warnings. Thorian is closest to us, so we received his message. Khiva and Amalric were probably warned by Balardi. Pallas Athena may have sought to rip us from dreamland, but she found us wide awake."

"Your Goddess did have some choice words for me," Orantes added with a lopsided grin. "My self-esteem may never fully recover." Outside of the tower, the city was stirring, making murmuring, and groaning sounds like some shambling beast that struggled to wake. Drumbeats were building, while shouts came from guards gathering by torchlight, and clattering sounds of iron shod horses passing over stone streets reached up into the chamber. Though now in the presence of Wylar and Orantes, Sentauris hesitated: was it wrong to flee? The Adepts had become far more dangerous in the last few weeks, and she herself — supported by armed tiers and strong captains — could not be treated lightly.

"Not this time," Wylar said, gauging her mood with a glance. "Sentauris, listen to me: you have long criticized the Wizards for withdrawing into their places of power. Now you will see how much stronger they are, wielding magic behind their fortress walls. Lead us in our flight south — the time to turn on our foes will come later."

"So be it." She took a deep breath. "Every living thing except ticks and fleas and rodents will move south before daybreak. Orantes, make haste: you will be at the forefront of this ragtag procession." She turned and was gone before the slow waking Adept could sputter a response.

Outside, the night was cool and clear but no longer calm. Guards were ranging about, calling everyone to emerge and follow them, bringing only warm clothing and food that might easily be transported. Small children were crying, while others dozed in their mothers' arms. Side streets swirled with clusters of uncertain families, some arguing with always louder voices.

"To the Gates!" Sentauris called to them, but few could see that she was the Seeress, their captain during the siege. She broke again into a run, dodging around the slow moving, confused people of Tuvan. All around her rose the cries of children, the noise of bad tempers, with alarm bells and drumbeats building. Dimly, she felt Squint's presence pass overhead, while Whisper's shadowy form fluttered along adjacent side streets, each of them returning in haste to his Adept Master.

At the Gates, bonfires had been lit, with the guard more than half marshaled. Her three captains stood waiting for her, with Druss and Breughal murmuring together just to their left.

She took a deep breath before speaking. "Tuvan must be abandoned. Some alliance of Dark Powers has unleashed a powerful new force called the Enchanters against us, intending to supplant the Wizards. One benign Power has urged us to flee, while the Adepts were instructed by the Wizards to escape south before daybreak. Do any of you question these words?" The three captains shook their heads somberly, though they studied her firelit features for any sign that her mind had been tampered with.

"The Sight is powerful within you, and we must heed your visions," Breughal said. "Druss agrees, for we both understand that without your counsel, we would all be festering dead meat in the intestines of Vorrs or Uraks. Where do we go? And who leads us?"

"Flee south, to Gravengate or Stone Mountain, for the Enchanters are coming at us from the northern border of the League," Sentauris said, looking to her mercenary captains. "Which of you three should be chosen to order such an evacuation?" Farad and Gallandus glanced to Sardonicus but said nothing.

"Who else of course?" Sardonicus muttered. "So, I have become master of the defeated, have I? Give me a moment then." As he pondered, more of Tuvan's citizenry gathered to its gates, some struggling with enormous burdens, while others made nervous, rustling sounds, like leaves fluttering at the beginning of a storm.

"It will not be pretty," Sardonicus said. Sentauris came to stand beside him, reaching out to touch his shoulder and so better read his thoughts. "Three waves," he continued, "with the first including the elderly yet fit, with younglings of ten years or more, and those newly healed or healing. Scouts ride before them, and their way is lighted and supported by a contingent of the Guard. The slowest move first, so if there are stragglers, a second or third wave gathers them."

"Breughal leads these on foot — at least until daybreak," Sentauris added. "Farad leads a vanguard of outriders. Squint and Whisper are advance scouts."

The eyes of Sardonicus flashed a mixture of irritation and amusement. "In our second group, all the able bodied depart on foot. Among them are the greatest contingent of guardsmen, a half tier of archers, a second half tier of men armed with pikes. These will aid either rearguard or vanguard should those groups falter."

"The rearguard is at risk only," Sentauris said. "You, Sardonicus, will captain this second group. Druss will aid you."

The mercenary captain nodded. "Last come those on horses: the wounded, the young and very old, together with our stores in carts and wagons, with a little space set aside for those who become lame, or stragglers. Horse archers and lancers form a rearguard — and you have left Gallandus to captain this group."

Sentauris stared into the distance. "If we delay, a crushing weight of dark magic will batter this rearguard into pulp; Orantes and Wylar will help to shield them. For myself, I will link all three groups as best I can, with some swift horseback riding. Keep a second fresh horse set aside for me. Now, for the love of the Almighty Maker, and for the safety of our peoples, make haste."

· X ·

Only seven people remained in Tuvan. Wylar had woven a deep sleep over three of the elders who lay so close to death that they could not be moved, and then he joined Sentauris as she searched for the last two children who were still hiding in fear.

"Child," Sentauris called out into the darkness, with her voice half soothing, half raised in anxiety. "Child, you must hide no longer. Our foes will be inside Tuvan at daybreak, and they will not be kind to you."

"Come," Wylar murmured beside her, "it must be now for this youngling — or never. Already we have stayed too long." Sentauris and Wylar rode slowly down darkened streets, the last of Tuvan's Council or citizenry within the city's walls. The third of three refugee contingents had departed more than an hour ago.

"I know this!" Sentauris hissed. "But a second feral child follows, listening intently. If I speak harsh words to this one, the second will most certainly hide in the darkest cellar." Their horses, made skittish by the strange dark quiet of the abandoned city, were eager to escape. To the north, a weight of power and terror loomed — death, if they were not swift or mighty enough.

"And yet now the Enchanters are upon us," Sentauris muttered, "and if sweet words will not lure this lamb, I must try harsh ones." She raised her voice: "Stupid boy! They will place you on a spit, and roast you — still alive, and shrieking, calling aloud! Run! Run, boy, run!"

A slight, feral boy of eight years let out a wild shriek and raced from them, crying out in fear. From Wylar came a coil of incandescent blue, embracing the child, and the boy collapsed, flopping with arms outstretched onto stone streets. The Adept rode swiftly to the fallen youngling and raised him to his saddle.

"Ride," Wylar said, "or we — and perhaps all our people — will perish."

Sentauris turned and called out into darkened side streets, "Child, we tried to save you! Die by your own hand, if need be, for the Maker will not judge you harshly!" Wylar pulled away, riding swiftly toward the gates. Daybreak was only a few hours away, bringing an end to Tuvan the Citadel. Sentauris followed the Adept, showing even at this late time one last moment of hesitation; and to her enormous relief, a second slender youngling came racing through the night, running, weeping wildly, and waving her arms.

With one arm Sentauris swept up a girl of eleven years — an orphan of the conflict, left ragged, crying, with hair matted like a fall pasture. Sentauris embraced her as their horse carried them through the gates, then they wheeled from the north facing portals, moving at a great pace to catch up with the rearguard.

Tuvan! Her mind called to the abandoned city. *Tuvan, a dark fire comes for you and so your stonework will be transformed into dust. But if the Maker permits, I will return with all my memories intact, and every point of beauty or majesty that once made you gleam will be restored. Tuvan, may all brave hearts speak your name!*

· X ·

In the deepest portion of the night, the people of Tuvan passed several leagues south of the abandoned city. Their leaders had begun to disperse them onto side roads, some leading south to Stone Mountain, others passing southwest to Gravengate. By separating themselves into smaller groups, they hoped to become lesser prey, offering little interest to the Enchanters.

Druss and Breughal were leading a contingent toward Khiva and the coast — mostly the young, the old, or wounded, supported by a powerful force of militia. Only a few hurried farewells had been possible, but Druss realized that he was leaving the main struggle of the League, and he glanced at Sentauris and her captains with haunted eyes before passing from their view.

Through the long jostling night, the Adepts had felt the Enchanters probing for them, reaching for the Magicians with a strange, dark sorcery: tangles of tree limbs or mounds of grass began to come alive, with eyes flaring from matted brush. To conceal themselves and Sentauris, the Adepts had constructed shielding illusions that were triply reinforced, so that any seeker was required to search long and hard before encountering Seeress or Adept.

With darkness lessening, Sentauris could feel the halfhearted probes of their adversaries weaken then fade, as the Enchanters lost interest in the separated clusters of humans fleeing south. As the long reach of the Enchanters passed from them, Sentauris felt a different weight replacing it: her Farsight was calling her to witness Tuvan's last moments. She looked up into a night sky where starlight was fading. Ghorm had retreated within himself as he always did when dealing with rough travel. Her senses reached for the Adepts: Orantes straggled behind her, while his fellow Adept moved on ahead to higher ground, lighting his way with shimmering werelight. She urged her horse toward Wylar, moving upslope from the bottom of the dark valley that shielded their passage from the Enchanters.

Then with Wylar at her side, she turned back to locate Orantes, finding him nearly asleep in his saddle, wobbling on a steed that had lost interest in travel by starlight. The three rode up a hillside, Sentauris leading them along a deer path then up to a ridgeline that led to the crest of a broad hill.

It was still dark, but two vastly different rims of light struggled at the edge of the horizon: to the east, the pale first new light of day; and to the north, the strange radiance of Tuvan's death, as it glowed purple and black, flaring with sickly pumpkin-colored lights. Sentauris and the Adepts dismounted, staring toward the North with strained faces.

"We have been summoned here to witness distant events," Sentauris said softly. "You two cannot call upon your Divination work without alerting the Enchanters to some faraway act of magic. But my Farsight cannot so easily be traced; and so, I must use words to describe the death of Tuvan. Hear me and help me to bear witness." She drew a deep breath, and when next she spoke, it was in that dry, remote voice that was used to utter words of farseeing.

"The five Enchanters come to stand before the gates of Tuvan, positioned in a semicircle, with so much distance between each of them, that they must call aloud to be heard. So much power is being released that they no longer bother to blind my Sight, and their names come to me. The Albino Sorcerer called Pentarchus is centermost. To his left stands the Sorcerer Nairn, while to the Albino's right is the Sorceress they refer to as the 'Witch Queen.' At each edge of the semicircle stands a powerful Mage — brothers to one another, brown haired, fair of feature. They have only recently chosen names, and so one is called Helcar, while the other is named Manassas. All five of the Enchanters are curiously distended, no longer completely human.

"Sorcerers and Mages and Witch Queen raise their hands together as though they are one being. From their palms and fingertips lifts a strange magic; it builds and coalesces, then surges toward the Gates, like some mighty Djinn or Elemental of the netherworlds. The stonework of Tuvan begins to burn, purple and black with dark flames. The Enchanters laugh aloud in the fullness of their malice, although some portion of their beings seems to twitch in frustration, like some beast within each of them stirred from sleep while not fully aroused.

"Dark flames leap from stone to stone, engulfing Tuvan the Citadel. Beyond the stonework, wood and mortar burst into flame, radiating a pumpkin-colored light, with dark magic, not air, feeding the fires. Tuvan becomes a Place of the Damned, with huge, thrashing forms lifting from its fiery cataclysm; though these forms struggle mightily to be free, they collapse always back into the flames, writhing in agony."

The Adepts stood transfixed, faces haggard as they stared north. Orantes felt his old fears stir; the panic that had slept in Tuvan came suddenly awake. For such was the strength of the vision showed by Sentauris that the images of her Farsight flared in their own minds as they stood, frozen, listening to the Seeress as she described Tuvan's nightmare in remote tones, like some lifeless oracle describing a fairytale for infants.

"As Tuvan lies smoldering, destroyed beyond recognition, the Enchanters release their hold over it. They glance to one another with eyes flashing an elation touched by horror; then they turn from Tuvan the Vanquished to the surrounding countryside. They stand as before, backs to the seething city, in a semicircle, though now their arc bends outwards. Again, their hands are raised, and as before, power flares from them, but this time it is dispersed, passing through the broken fields, and battered woodlands surrounding the city. For nearly a league around them, the ground stirs and...." Even the dry, remote voice of the Seeress seemed to catch.

"The ground stirs," she continued, voice rasping, "and the dead rise from their graves. The dead arise, not as living beings, but as slaves of the Enchanters. They rise not as they once were; their forms are rotted, maimed, and dismembered as they were when lying in a state of death. Though as I speak, new limbs seem to form as clumps of rotted flesh gather from the soil and join with the Undead; or the clay itself forms something harder than human tissue and takes the place of missing limbs; while in a few of those most strongly touched by the Necromancy of the Enchanters, strange growths of dark chitin emerge, where limbs or heads once formed.

"Now the earth groans and gives forth the enormous shapes of the Creatures of the Darkness, beings we believed utterly destroyed. These join a throng that mills together and sorts itself, then journeys south: an army of the newly risen dead. And at their forefront stand the two figures of Murat and Fiüre, glowing with a fey light, as they lead south an army of the undead, intent on destroying all living beings in its path."

Chapter Ten

The Undead and the Dying

NAIRN WOKE IN THE last hours of the night, hearing nothing but stillness. One hand idly rubbed his hawk faced features then drifted down to his dark, bristling beard. A sense of wrongness lay over him like a dark cloud. Nightmares lurked at the corners of his mind, and it was an effort to remember how a long evening had ended. Tuvan had been destroyed by dark forces he barely understood, and in the aftermath of victory, a celebration had been decreed by the Enchanters. Pentarchus had suggested this gathering both as a diplomatic function whereby the varied Enchanters might learn more about each other — including gifts of wine and spirits to their allied armies. So, their festival had continued deep into the night, and there, late in the night, lay the horror — or was his revulsion simply one final reaction to his long journey over dark roads?

He had brought his reluctant old lover, Sylvie, through the Portal Passages, almost always a mistake. She still loved him, but his long pursuit of dark power was a source of great sorrow to her, and late at night her tide of tears had threatened to drown them both. When Sylvie wept, his own feelings trembled at the edge of a terrible regret. He would leave her now, forever, to find another, someone with a lust for power and glory and a carnal delight in the perversions of evil that was equal to his own.

He leaned over to touch and wake her to send her back through enchanted Portal Passages.

"Sylvie..." he whispered. She was still there beside him; he touched an arm, a cold thing, in the darkness. Then his magic *reached* for her lifeforce and found: death.

Nairn leaped to his feet and his palms bathed his command tent in beams of werelight. Sylvie, his lover all these many years lay stiff in death, bloated, eyes bulging, flesh darkened by poison — the poison of his own transformed substance. His love had killed her! Set had killed her, destroyed his last link to humanity! Set would suffer! Set must die!

He burst from his command tent, ready to cry out his hatred for the Maker, for the Gods, for all Powers, Ancient or New, but what emerged from his throat was an ear piercing shriek of triumph in tones Nairn had never before spoken or heard.

·)(·

With the first light of day, smoke could be seen, rising from Tuvan's ruin, joining with low cloud masses that surged south toward Gravengate and Stone Mountain. The morning air was heavy with ash and cinder, while a stench of death rose from the valley below them as a long column of dead things shuffled south, moving on dead feet, guided by dead eyes that focused on nothing.

On a rise above the valley, Gallandus and Farad and a score of picked horsemen stood watching the stumbling army of the Undead as it passed below them. Some of those decaying bodies were recognized and the horsemen whispered their names until Gallandus waved them into silence. Finally, Farad found a man he once knew and signaled to five of his followers. Led by Farad, the five mounted their wild-eyed horses and spilled down the slope, each holding a strand of coiled rope.

As they surged downslope, horses neighed in fear, and ashen faced men felt their stomachs churn. When they reached the fringe of the Undead, five ropes were cast. Two missed but the other three looped over one dead form and were pulled tight. A writhing, twisting form was dragged up the hillside, while Farad and the two men who had missed their casts slashed at their undead pursuers with sharp swords.

Passing over the hill's crest they rode down into a shallow valley then up another rise, all the while dragging a struggling once human form behind them. Stones gouged flesh from the dead form, but no blood flowed from its grey, broken skin. When the riders halted, they watched with ashen faces as its dead flesh knit seamlessly in a few brief seconds.

The dead man rose, ripping at his bonds. From behind the dead figure, Gallandus reached out and neatly severed the ropes, leaving the dead form free. With considerable reluctance, one of Gallandus' veterans tossed a sword before the figure; the dead man stooped swiftly for the blade, then whirled to face Farad, who was similarly armed.

"What do you recall of your life, Sendor's son?" Farad asked softly, curiously, and without fear. Their blades clashed, and Farad backed from the dead man.

"Sword lessons," Farad said, "do you recall those, Alfar, son of Sendor?" Again, their blades clashed, and the dead man's eyes began to glow with a feral light. Farad no longer backed, but stood parrying, slashing, while others looked on.

"Nothing of Alfar's swordplay remains," Farad panted, "but this thing does not lack skill!" With a skipping step, Farad avoided the dead man's blade, then hewed at its sword arm; the severed arm, still clutching its blade, fell to the ground. From its wounds, no blood flowed, only a stream of milky fluid in which tiny particles of crystal seemed to catch the sun.

Casually, as though retrieving litter, the dead man's left arm reached down and reattached its sword arm. Again, Farad chopped at the dead thing, then wheeled and chopped again: arms, legs, head, all struggled to rejoin the dead form, as Farad panted and hewed.

"This is not a gentlemanly contest!" Farad called out. "See how finely minced this thing can be sliced!" Other swords were drawn; the dead man's enchanted flesh was butchered, but still, its quivering dead portions struggled to rejoin themselves. But then their time for testing the Undead suddenly ran out — on the ridgeline below them, scores of dead things had begun to climb toward their living opponents. Gallandus used his dagger to pry the sword from the dead man's severed hand, then mounted his horse.

"Enough!" Gallandus called down to Farad. "You can chop this thing into ten thousand pieces, and still its life force continues undiminished. Let's be gone!" As they rode from the advancing columns of dead men, their butchered foe had begun to thrash on the ground, rolling and twisting about as it reacquired its many extremities.

· X ·

A surge of wild emotions swept over the Witch Queen as she woke and discovered both her lovers blackened, dead, stiff with poison, pain, and horror forever engraved on their features.

I have become a monster! I am no longer human! Set, you have made of me a nightmare so that my lovers twist and writhe and die in the night! O Great Dark God, we will take power, then you will pay, for the blackened form of your own Godly essence will lie twisted and dead!

She turned one of the dead bodies over with her foot; with the new strength of her limbs, the heavy body flopped over easily and lay stiff as a statue, face to the ground. It was hard to remember their names, but with the victory celebration, she had drawn her usual complement of two. Fear had begun to infect her little remnant of exiles, for none of her intimates lasted long, and when they fell from favor, death was likely to come quickly. These two might have lasted no more than weeks; and even last night she had required magic to rekindle their lust and reduce their fears.

The two had been doomed; the poison transmitted from her new form had merely made that process even swifter. Again, she flopped the figure over with a nudge of her foot so that both forms lay face up. As poison bloated their bodies, their sexual organs had become stone stiff, each far more rigid than it had been the night before. Despite her anger, the Witch Queen found herself laughing.

· X ·

Ten strong hands grasped the struggling dead form and pitched it into the bonfire, where it writhed, twisting, and burning, releasing a stench of putrid, charred flesh.

"Back from it," Sardonicus murmured. "This is, after all, only a test of the Undead's strength."

"Die! Die!" Ghorm called out, standing just ten paces from the roaring flames. "In the Maker's Name, burn and die!" But the figure rose from the bonfire, and the fire on its body died down. Gathering itself, the dead man sprang from the fire and leaped at the horsemen. Riders cried out and pulled away: grey, dead flesh had become a black, still smoldering substance, and still the Undead sought to destroy the living.

Sardonicus leaned down and swept Ghorm up to the forefront of his saddle. "Interesting," their Captain said softly as they rode swiftly from the flames. "Note how much of the thing's substance was transformed by fire, and yet it still had power to do us harm." The voice of Sardonicus was remote, detached, but when Ghorm glanced back into his face, the captain's eyes seemed dull with horror.

·)(·

Pentarchus studied the motionless body with great interest, and with the force of his own strong magic, he explored her dead substance. It was astonishing just how powerfully his transformed essence had corrupted the human flesh of his bedmate! Fascinating, and so strange!

Not that her death mattered; she was nothing to him. The Witch Queen Azüre had chosen the woman from her gathering of exiles and assigned her to Pentarchus from some confusion of tangled motives. Punishment was one possible motive, a desire to blight the soul of the younger woman, who had lived nor more than thirty years. Also, no doubt, Azüre had desired to entangle Pentarchus in the Witch Queen's spiderwebs.

This poor creature, this dead thing, how relieved she had been to discover that Pentarchus was only moderately depraved, that she might survive the night without lasting damage. Now she was dead...touching her, Pentarchus read from her flesh the sequence of her final moments.

Fatigue had been softened by wine, followed by sleep...then came the first touch of and everlasting nightmare...she had tried to rise, but was frozen, tried to call out but was stilled. As horror festered in her system, her mind shrieked for a long time, retreating into insanity just a brief time before she died.

Pentarchus leaned back. Most intriguing! But how did this new factor affect their alliance and their war? It seemed more than likely that the other Enchanters were similarly affected, but had Set been aware of this conjugal poison? And how would these events affect his own quest for power?

You there, Pentarchus whispered to his inner soulmate, to the presence joined to his own inner being. *Did you mean to cause death, or is this transmission of poisonous fluids merely a byproduct of our union?*

Something within his body shuddered and twisted, struggling to break free.

You have nowhere to go, Pentarchus whispered. *The Great God Set has brought us together — and we may as well become accustomed to our union.*

From the throat of Pentarchus came a scream of unrelenting rage.

· ☫ ·

"Dragonfire, cold spells, transformations, transmutations," Orantes intoned wearily. "Spells of forgetting, of remembering, illusions singly, doubly and trebly wrought...have I omitted anything?"

"Nothing of substance," Wylar said, face bleak and haggard in the early light of dawn. "Not a single one of our spells seems to work." He watched on grimly as three of the Undead rose again, and advanced through the fresh green springtime forest, arms outstretched, reaching toward the Adepts. Grey with fatigue, Orantes raised his staff and blasted at their dead forms: tangles of limbs, heads, and torsos were hurled backward to the forest ground...but moments later, the Undead had renewed themselves, knit again by the strange plasma that ran through their veins, a substance that glowed white as milk, glistening with particles of tiny, white silica.

Orantes watched on grimly. That the dead rose again to attack the living seemed even more perverse because the forest of springtime was surging with new life. Sunlight should be radiating over green, growing things, not over dead things that belonged to darkness and decay.

"I am done," Wylar said, turning toward their horses, "unless you have some other device or Whisper has a suggestion."

Orantes shook his head; Whisper added in a murmur, "I have none — if I cannot harm the Undead, neither can they disturb my substance." The Adepts mounted and edged their horses through a narrow deer path, then down a shallow incline. As agreed earlier, they sought Farad and Gallandus, and after their final tests, both Adepts and Captains would return to Sentauris, reporting the failure of all their many devices.

Squint hovered overhead, staring down at the dead things that pursued his masters. *These things should flourish at night, in the dead of winter, but now in the height of spring, with daybreak at their backs, they only seem to be getting stronger.*

They found Farad and Gallandus at a junction of streams that formed a small river. Most magic was altered by the presence of running water, and The Adepts suggested that such a flow would hinder the ability of the Undead to renew themselves.

The reality was entirely different, and the test of water was touched by horror — and revulsion. As before, the Undead sought to destroy the living, but as they approached the picked veterans led by Gallandus and Farad, each dead man was butchered and cast into swiftly moving streams...though the Undead merely renewed themselves in the flowing water, then climbed a downstream bank to seize stones or branches and try again to draw the living into their ranks.

Some of the mercenaries had steeled themselves to the chopping and hacking, but others stood retching into the river or stared with wild eyes into the depths of the forest as though considering flight. Farad and Gallandus stood in the front rank, hewing and slashing, though their own faces were tense and grey. When Gallandus caught sight of the Adepts, he wiped his blade clean against green moss then sheathed it.

"Let's be gone," he called to Farad. "Acknowledge failure. This is a matter for magic, not the focus of soldiery." Others began sheathing weapons, booting oncoming dead forms into swift waters, then backing from the river toward their tethered horses.

As they backed, the face of Orantes lost its dreamy, distant expression. "Hold for a moment!" he called down to Gallandus, then dismounted and shuffled quickly down to the river. "Hew and hack and chop for just a moment more." The Adept extended his hands over the waters, chanting spell words, while puzzled soldiers again reduced dead forms to chunks of meat and pitched them into swiftly moving waters.

The Spell of Forgetting, Wylar recalled, *but it failed before.* All the bobbing portions of the Undead — that had so swiftly joined together before — seemed to lose focus, and after one vain effort to find a matching chunk of flesh and bone, began to sink, or drift into eddies, or pass swiftly downriver. In less than ten minutes nearly a dozen of the Undead had been released into their final deaths.

Wylar came downslope and dismounted, to stand beside the haggard faces of their mercenaries. "Orantes has always been our creative force. He has just employed a *Spell of Forgetting*, which failed when used alone, but when combined with dismemberment and the enchantments of swift waters, they caused the Necromancy of the Enchanters to falter — finally, thank the Maker."

"So," Farad murmured, "in five or ten years we might so deal with each of the Undead, and thus rid your League of this festering plague."

Wylar nodded somberly. "Yes, it seems clear that our magic is not a solution — in five years the numbers of the Undead may have easily increased a thousandfold. Come, let us seek the Seeress, and report our difficulties in dealing with the Necromancy of the Enchanters."

· 𝕏 ·

Deep in the darkest portion of the night, the Carag Enchanter named Helcar woke to find himself far from his command tent, far from his Carag companions, transformed into a distorted shape that held more than eight times his old body mass. Some dreaming, night walking portion of the grafted power within him had done this thing.

Helcar glanced downward: his hand had formed a gnarled, contorted talon; beneath the talon, on the moonlit ground, lay the fleshy husk of a dead Urak. His beaked head swept down, and he examined the Urak with steely raptor's eyes.

Something — likely his now transformed shape — had drawn all the fluid substances from the once massive Urak. As well, all the lifeforces had been absorbed from this onetime ally. Recoiling, Helcar could feel and taste the strength of the Urak's bile coursing through his frame.

Were other Enchanters nearby? Had he been seen? No, the "graft" within him had taken its prey into a deeply wooded portion of the forest. Even so, it was best to dispose and hide the remains of its prey. Shuddering, Helcar changed his form, to become the largest of Uraks. As though ridding the forest of rubbish, the Carag Enchanter dragged the carcass of its lesser brethren to the edge of a cliff, then pitched it over.

Again, Helcar's form shook as it changed, though in seconds he had become again what seemed to be human. As he returned to his pavilion through circuitous routes, the sun had risen, and the torpid camp of the Enchanters slowly began to stir itself. When he reached the bloated command tent, he shared with Manassas, he allowed himself one human gesture — a sigh of relief.

Though as Helcar entered the high ceiling cloth structure, he discovered more horror — greater horror. The forms of five Carags lay stretched, twisted, and blackened. They had tried to transform themselves from Death's final embrace, and now they lay frozen in their last desperate and final efforts. Here lay his old lovers, lesser Carags who had striven so mightily to match his moods, to take shape themselves into beings that were picaresque, or grotesque, or vile. Helcar touched each one to make certain that no life remained.

Only Manassas was alive, returned from the night's lovemaking to his human form, lying blissfully asleep under a weight of strange, narcotic enchantments. With the sun fully risen, Helcar shook Manassas awake, though not without a certain gentleness.

"Rouse thyself, my brother," Helcar whispered. "Thou must open thine eyes and behold how Mordred, our God King and Master, has betrayed us unto the malice of the Great God Set."

·)(·

At dawn, Sentauris paced the hills, glancing north, south, east, and west as her Seer's Sight brought images of failure and defeat. Tuvan's refugees were struggling to reach Gravengate and Stone Mountain, leaving all Tuvan's best trained soldiery to counter the shuffling masses of dead creatures who pursued Tuvan's survivors south. Yet, the Undead could not be reduced again to death, it was as simple — and as difficult — as that.

They could deflect the Undead but not unmake the Necromancy of the Enchanters.

She closed her eyes, reaching to the north, and west and east. The army of the Undead passed through valleys and narrow gorges, with Uraks and Vorrs following — with uncharacteristic caution — behind them. Shapeshifting Carags had tried to blend with the Undead but had been driven off, barely escaping with their lives. Other Carags had sought to infiltrate Tuvan's rearguard; two had been slain after bluffing with incorrect passwords, while others had fled.

She turned north again, taking a deep breath, and letting her Sight peer far beyond the hills, to the camp of the Enchanters, where it lay bathed in the early light of morning just two leagues south of Tuvan.

Great power lies in this place, a force of mortal magic unequaled in Alantéa the Forerunner, unless the Wizards were to gather themselves in one fortress to withstand some greater God of the Mid-World. Despite the power of the Enchanters, a sense of sluggishness and indecision lingers over their camp. And they have not bothered to shield themselves. Why?

Wait! Horror and revulsion were hidden beneath their billowing pavilions. What have they done? Are they beginning to destroy each other? But no, if some were dead, then their mass of magic would be lessened, and instead, it has grown. What lies within these halls of canvas, some larger than the antechambers of lesser Powers?

As she tried to peer into their pavilions, one of the Enchanters roused himself, and her vision was swept aside. She recoiled as though from a blow and stood shaking her head. *This may well be very interesting, but nothing has changed: we fall back under pressure, unable to decide for Gravengate or Stone Mountain. Thus....*

Sentauris spun and turned from the rising sun, sliding a little down the layer of small stones that covered her hill path. Not fifty feet from her a frame of air seemed to shudder in turmoil. *Portal magic — two Powers contest an entrance from the Mid-World to Alantéa the Forerunner. One of them is unknown, and the other is Pallas Athena.*

The midair turbulence suddenly halted. After one frozen moment, a column of dark smoke poured through, forming, thirty feet in height, the image of the Goddess Pallas Athena. Sentauris knelt before her former patroness, as the statue of smoke spoke in tones suitable to a remote, judgmental deity.

"Sentauris, my servant of old, I have deflected a lesser God who wished to aid your League in its struggle with the Enchanters. Know that it is not seemly for the Gods to support those who deny them and serve the long departed Maker. You might have given these matters more thought before you left my service." The statue of the Goddess then raised its arms and suddenly became a transparent breath of morning air, and so vanished.

As Sentauris rose warily to her feet, the voice of the Goddess spoke far more gently into her mind. *"Valiant but preoccupied daughter, you do not need the Powers of the Mid-World to deal with the Undead. Consider the Wizards and the Necromancy of the Enchanters — do you honestly believe that the masters of the League would struggle and falter as your people have failed? To this end, you should speak to your half trained, dimwitted Adepts."*

Sentauris stood for a moment, searching the hillside with her eyes and her Seer's Sight. Both Adepts and Captains were riding toward her, but what precisely was she to say to them? *Holy Mother, I love you most dearly, but I wish your messages were much less subtle.* She sped down the hillside toward a slight clearing where two outriders guarded her horse. As she rode toward the Adepts, Sardonicus and Ghorm could be seen, moving in a parallel course toward a conjunction of lesser streams that formed their agreed upon gathering place. *A full-fledged parlay! And meanwhile, our peoples flee not five hours march from a tide of zombies, while the Gods toy with us.*

She calmed herself then listened patiently to a recounting of stratagems, tests, trials of magic, devices of fire and water, hearing that only with extreme difficulty could the Undead be returned to the death that had once claimed them.

"It was a cumbersome process," Wylar added thoughtfully, "and only with a mixture of three factors did the Necromancy of the Enchanters falter...I — what have I said?" Wylar looked to Sentauris, who had been shaking her head ever so gently.

"You must seal us from the Mid-World," she said softly, "then I will share my understanding with you."

"Ah," Orantes murmured, struggling to shake off his fatigue, "if ever we needed the superior vision of the Seeress, that time is now. Come, Wylar the Dour, perhaps if we seal ourselves from the Enchanters and their Undead Servants, my flesh will stop crawling."

Others followed the Adepts until they stood thirty paces from the stream, in a slight clearing, while behind them sunlight beamed down over a green forest that was filled with the new leaves of spring. As the Adepts began their spellwork, Squint took wing, perching high above, watching the valley below where columns of dead beings stumbled and lurched South. Wylar and Orantes continued to whisper, all the while circling the others, until the air around them seemed to still and harden, taking on the opaque quality of clouded crystal.

When the Adepts were done, Sentauris took one deep breath, then spoke briefly: "The Farsight within me remains blocked, either by Dark Gods or by the Enchanters, yet another God — one who has been largely benign — suggested that I ask this question of the Adepts: how would the Wizards deal with the Necromancy of the Enchanters." Wylar and Orantes exchanged glances.

"Suggesting that the answer lies within our grasp," Wylar said, frowning. "As a first step, the Wizards would employ counter spells, to unmake the magic of the Enchanters."

"And if these failed?" Sentauris prompted, then shot a warning glance at Ghorm so that the scornful comments died on his lips.

"Counterforce," Orantes muttered, "they might raise their own army of unliving constructs."

"Powered by Elementals," Wylar added, looking up as though coming awake.

Orantes nodded. "Or Elementals employed as entities of pure power. Of course."

Wylar glanced at her Captains. "By way of explanation, the Elementals of Earth and Air, Fire and Water are most attuned to the natural order of Alantéa the Forerunner. Thus, the Wizards might easily arouse them against some evil creation, but of their own nature Elementals would move most reluctantly against a force of men — or even beastly creatures such as Vorrs and Uraks."

"These are matters of magic," Sardonicus said, "and thus outside my expertise. But since you two Adepts are revealing these things while looking to us with wondrous big eyes, I suggest this: rouse these Elementals and destroy the Undead."

"Easily spoken of, yet not so easily done," Orantes said, shaking his head.

"The Wizards have not yet trained us in these matters," Wylar added.

Sentauris snorted in disgust. "I must have a brief chat with your Wizards one fine sunny day. But some sense is emerging from this ragged parlay. Firstly, the Undead are most unnatural, and the Elementals as upholders of the earthly order might be more easily aroused against them. Secondly, how did you bring forth Dragonfire? You trained yourselves. Thus, it must be with the Elementals — you must learn how to employ those forces against the Undead.

"And thirdly, we must now choose — or guess — whether to defend Stone Mountain or Gravengate. One of these will soon be the focus of the Enchanters, their many legions, and their horde of Zombies. Come, I invite your speculation."

Gallandus glanced at Farad and Sardonicus, who nodded, imperceptibly. "Gravengate, purely for military reasons," Gallandus said. "Its reduction would divide the League in half, and the League lacks a mobile force to shift to its defense."

"Yes," Sentauris said, "the Wizards were most unhappy with me when I pointed out their need for mobile reserves."

"Had matters turned out differently," Orantes added, "Wylar and I — with far superior training — might have been the core of such a reserve. But I will also argue for Gravengate, because Balardi, my great though temperamental master, is accounted the weakest of the three Wizards."

Wylar raised his eyebrows. "Are the untested Enchanters prepared for such a decisive stroke? Were our roles reversed—"

"The weight of armed might will fall upon Gravengate," Sentauris interrupted in the strange, dry tones she used when her Seer's Sight took control of her mind and her speech. "Our Captains and their tiers must pass southwest to Gravengate. A great trial of magic builds around Stone Mountain where the Adepts and I must journey. Mír, the Elf-Mage, Mír awaits us at Stone Mountain."

· ✗ ·

One by one the Enchanters regained control over their emotions. Tentatively, without speech or messenger, the enchanted portions of their minds began reaching for one another so that just before the noon hour, they gathered, having dismissed all their servants, lackeys, and hollow eyed, grim faced followers. The five sat alone in the shadows of their largest pavilion, while outside, waves of brilliant sunlight cascaded down over Alantéa the Forerunner.

When they had sealed themselves against the Mid-World, Nairn glanced briefly at each, then said simply, "Set must die."

"And our former master Mordred," Helcar added, "must join him in the deep, dark pits where treacherous weak and dead Gods twist and writhe."

Pentarchus laughed softly. "It is an old dream of mortal conjurors, to bring down an immortal Deity. But I agree that Set's motives and actions are now far more than suspect. Did each of us reach the same pact with this dark souled Power?"

"He promised support for us in our war against the Wizards," Nairn said quietly. "In preparation for this war, we were to be strengthened by joining us with a greater Power. If we are stronger, we are also no longer human."

"Further, Set promised that we would inherit the Wizards' rule in the south of Alantéa," the Witch Queen added, "to hold it all our days, though whether our days would be long or short was not said, and now in the grim light of day, all his words seem most wonderfully weaselish."

"Set also swore that he would not seek to supplant us with servants of his own," Manassas said somberly. "And of course, our master, Mordred the Accursed, advised us that the promises of Set, though sparse and fragmented, were most worthy of trust. We were fools, Helcar my brother, with less wit even than the pitiful humans we have so often preyed upon."

"And yet," Pentarchus added, the white tufts of his eyebrows raised, "all the promises of Set may yet come to pass. We may master these 'fragments,' and eliminate all their complications. The Wizards may crumble even before we come to full power. We may achieve something close to immortality and rule forever as tyrants who are neither benevolent nor wise. *But....*"

"But we can feel from afar the laughter and malice of Set," the Witch-Queen murmured in surprisingly subdued tones. "Nairn, imagine yourself to be the essence of Dark-Souled Set. Say that you greatly desire the ruin of the League but would rather see the destruction of *both* the Wizards and the Enchanters. How would you go about achieving such a goal?"

Nairn stared out into sunlit meadows for a moment. "Firstly, I would raise the Enchanters to a new level of power to enable them to destroy the Wizards. Secondly, while I held their innermost substances under the scope of my power, I would plant destructive seeds — wild and incurable cancerous growths, ugly ones that would sprout only after the triumph of the Enchanters and the passing of the Wizards."

"Yes," Helcar breathed out. "That sounds much like the mind of Set."

"Let us begin by looking within ourselves for such seeds," Pentarchus said. "I do not believe that Set would be so unsubtle, but let us look, very, very closely." They were silent for a moment, with only the buzz of insects and the rustle of midday breezes intruding upon the silence of their prolonged review of their inner selves.

"Nothing, not even a hint," Nairn said after a time.

"Within me only is this being, Demon or Dragon," Manassas agreed, "I can feel nothing else but its strength and growing power."

Pentarchus nodded gravely. "We are, each of us, becoming stronger by the day — that part of Set's pact has surely come to pass."

"I am not relieved," the Witch Queen murmured. "I can feel from a distance the malice of Set. We will never be secure until we have spied out and countered all his devices, then finally destroyed this insane and treacherous God."

Nairn drew a deep breath. "My opening comments were, 'Set must die,' and I hold to those words, but first the Enchanters must ensure their own survival. To this end, I urge that the strongest of us — you, Pentarchus — and you know how unlikely I am to acknowledge this fact except under intense pressure — that you pull back from this struggle and focus on the malice of Set. It does not matter that the Wizards survive for a few more days, even weeks or months, because when we triumph, we must be prepared for Set and his devices."

The other four Enchanters stared at Nairn in quiet astonishment. "Here, unlooked for, is sober, superior wisdom," the Witch-Queen murmured.

"To satisfy our pact with Set," Pentarchus added, "our war must continue, though it may take us longer, and we may even suffer minor setbacks. Stone Mountain is next, and if the Wizard Thorian survives our onslaught, Set and Mordred must understand that we are still learning to assimilate the grafts within us — or so we will tell the Emissaries of our Godly Masters should they inquire about the continued existence of the master of Stone Mountain."

Helcar looked up with a strange expression, as though hearing far-distant voices. "Yet, should this Wizard falter, he will die."

Chapter Eleven

The Lightning Fight at Stone Mountain

THE SHADOWY BEING NAMED Whisper wrapped himself around the base of an overturned, darkened stump, and so vanished from view. Whisper's eyes became little more than hollow, dark knots that shifted slightly as they followed the zombie-like progress of the dead thing. This particular member of the Undead had journeyed far from its brethren, who had always chosen low pathways, like water running downhill. This one sought higher ground, and it also seemed more alert and watchful, even halting now in a patch of shadows. Then, rippling with the motion of swift waters, the Carag transformed itself, to become a wary human outrider of Tuvan — a ranger, making his way cautiously up the hillside into a sunlit meadow. Focusing, Whisper *reached* for Ghorm and signaled.

Ghorm, suddenly alert, glanced down to the meadow, where the ranger climbed uphill toward them over a ragged deer path. The Familiar caught the eye of Sardonicus, then made shifting motions with his hands and gestured to the figure. Sardonicus touched three archers then pointed to the oncoming outrider. All this communication took place without a single word being spoken.

With the archers in position, Sardonicus walked three paces out into the sunlight, then hailed the ranger: "Hold, good soldier. We require a password — I know how tiresome this process has become, but you must speak."

The soldier spat. "'Serpent Mage' it was, just a few hours earlier."

"Well spoken," Sardonicus said, turning and signaling. Three arrows leapt out of the shadowed woodlands, trisecting the Carag Assassin. It collapsed, writhing, then transformed by death it became again a snout nosed Carag.

"It would be interesting to learn," Sardonicus murmured, "how much pain you inflicted before forcing those words from one of our sentries. Yet I suppose we will never know."

Whisper unfolded himself from the trunk and stood amid knee high ferns, staring first at the dead Carag, then turning to Ghorm, watching the little Familiar with some concern. Part of Ghorm was drawn to the Adepts and their magic, but Ghorm's jealousy was an obstacle, and so the little Familiar preferred the company of the swift witted Sardonicus. Soon though, if the Adepts could check the Undead, their Captains would shift west to Gravengate. Then Ghorm would be forced back into the company of the Adepts as they journeyed east to Stone Mountain. Trouble would certainly follow. But first, the Adepts needed to counter the Necromancy of the Enchanters. Whisper's senses reached to the far hillside, to Wylar and Orantes, whose progress was not entirely reassuring.

"Watch, now, watch!" Wylar called out. A spout of fire burst in the air not three paces from the face of Orantes. Winds assailed them, accompanied by the sounds of rushing water. A half second later, an explosion rocked the hillside, and the Adepts were smashed to the ground. Each lay stunned, face up, staring at the sky of late afternoon, while birds scattered upwards from the forest canopy, then fled from the strange, owl shaped creature that circled overhead.

Squint was battered by gusts of wind that rose from the ground as Elementals of Fire and Air again rebuffed the Adepts. Even though he was pushed higher, Squint's eyes remained focused on the columns of dead creatures that shuffled through sunlit valleys, moving south. At least the dead things passed through valleys and low country so that live humans could retreat to higher ground. If the undead climbed higher, only the swiftest or those with wings could be safe against their relentless passage.

The Owl-being glanced back to the Adepts, who were now sitting up, dusting themselves off, and speaking together in low voices. Squint could make them out only vaguely and could hear nothing of their speech. Again, Wylar's Familiar wished that he had been born as a hawk.

From a greater distance, Sentauris heard the muffled explosion and watched Squint flutter higher and farther into blue skies. With her heightened senses, she felt the frustration of the Adepts and the movements of forces — both living and dead — toward the fortresses of Stone Mountain and Gravengate. From the beginning of this war, some powerful God had blocked her sight, though every now and again the block slipped, or lost its focus; then she was like a partly blind creature, suddenly dazzled by shafts of light.

Her sight was now heightened, and a bright light of revelation swept over her. The Adepts were nearing a solution to their problem; some device or stratagem might give them sufficient power to enlist the Elementals. Yet Wylar might lose focus, or Orantes concede defeat, and the Undead would sweep over her peoples. *Adepts, I cannot guide you, but do not weaken! No matter how much you lament your lack of preparation, you are one of the cornerstones of the League.*

"A goodly measure of wine would be most inspirational," Orantes muttered, sitting up and brushing himself off. "Say half a dozen bottles of sun ripened red or seven pale northern wines with grapes taken in the fall from the vineyard's upper slopes, wines now well aged and properly chilled. After such a delightful interlude, Elementals would flock to me, attend my every whim."

Wylar stood, staring north. "I do not believe that we will ever *command* these beings, not even if we discover the magic wine cellar of some enchanted Goddess to enhance your inspiration. We cannot even *invoke*; is it possible to *invite?*"

Orantes snorted. "These creatures of the base elements are not known for their brilliance, so it would be most difficult to bargain with them. And what would we offer them? Gold, of which we possess only trivial quantities? The substances of Alantéa, which they have long dominated? Objects endued with sorcerous powers, of which we have none?"

"Imagine, just for a moment," Wylar murmured, "that both you and I are Elementals. What would we wish for?"

"You would make a most dull Elemental, my friend, likely of Earth, and you might wish for...shelves of dark basalt looming over brown mesas, or mountain spires of grey granite. While I," Orantes continued, warming to his subject, "would most likely find myself among the Elementals of Air, a being who would delight in storms or sky patterns around Mount Evergrey, and the Cloudland Plateau beneath it."

"Then why not offer such things to these beings, our natural allies?"

"In images, visions?" Orantes was intrigued, though still dubious. "Would our illusions be enough to engage these beings?"

"Not just illusions, but *layers* of illusions," Wylar said. "Recall that as we lacked battle magic, we were forced to develop complex illusions. Also, even if those visions fail, the Elementals would be less likely to hurl us to the ground." Wylar walked over to stand beside Orantes, and in a display of his own lean strength pulled Orantes to his feet. "Phase one was the failed invocation of the Elementals. Phase two is the invitation, which begins now."

· ✗ ·

By sunset, the turmoil of sound and motion surrounding the Adepts had built to such a degree that it was impossible for other leaders to ignore. Led by Sentauris, captains and Familiars walked cautiously to the far hillside, where columns of smoke and dust and fire and whirling vapor had been jostling one another for the past few hours.

Wylar and Orantes stood in the center of a small clearing, surrounded by beings that whirled and spun in agitation. As Sentauris watched, the hands of Orantes seemed to glow and shimmer; then bright lights flowed from the Adept, surging through and around the clearing, forming a broad, high tapestry. Images formed in midair, showing fragments of scattered clouds hovering over mountain spires, while water spilled down in torrents over granite cliffs, forming the greatest waterfall seen or imagined in Alantéa the Forerunner.

From Wylar, images also flowed, but of a dark, grim, and menacing nature: images of the army of the Undead, reduced to the size of ant hordes, flowing toward brilliant lights, transforming everything beautiful and gleaming into grey and black death.

The waterfall was turned into slag and ash. Granite spires seemed to crumble into dark mounds, while above the mountains, clouds that were filled with sunlight sagged toward the Undead, then were transformed into a grey lifelessness. And as dark images consumed bright and spirited ones, the Elementals in the clearing spun and whirled, buzzing noises building like an agitated beehive. Many columns of whirling matter began to edge toward

Wylar, while a few perceived Orantes as the source of their discomfort and made menacing motions toward the red bearded Adept, and all the time the anger of the Elementals built to a dull whine.

Suddenly all the images vanished. Then, with Wylar and Orantes whispering in hushed voices, the cloudy, ringed spire reformed in the far end of the clearing, and hung in the air undiminished for a moment, then was assailed — as before — by grey, dead beings.

But now a third force was shown, gathering to the scene: tiny whirling columns of dust, turmoils of vapor, whirlwinds of fire — images of Elementals swept over the dead things, breaking, burning, destroying, hurling dead fragments into remote waters, or into the farthest reaches of Alantéa, where all their dark necromantic purposes were forgotten.

Moments later, as the tableau of sky, spire, and waterfall was restored, Wylar and Orantes bowed to the Elementals, then the images crafted by the Adepts vanished. All the Elementals began to grow quiet, as though lost in thought, then one by one, they disappeared from the clearing.

Wylar looked up into the assembled faces and said, in a quiet voice, "We have tried to incite the Elementals against the necromancy of the Enchanters. Now we must wait and see if our devices have worked." If the Adept's tones were restrained, Wylar's face could not completely hide a sense of deep satisfaction.

By all the Nine Billion Gods, Ghorm thought, *the feeble seeming Adepts have raised a force of great power against the Undead. First, they called Elementals to view images of beauty, then they showed the destructive nature of the Undead, and last, how Elementals might oppose those beings. And it seems to be working! No wonder that I envy the Adepts so much while part of me rejoices in their triumph! They are becoming what I would wish to be if I were human.*

Orantes rubbed his hands together with obvious satisfaction. "It might be useful," he said, looking to Wylar, "to view this collision of powers as it occurs. Something of the balance of these two forces might be clarified, with interesting developments should the Enchanters choose to defend their servants. What do you say?"

Wylar glanced to Sentauris. She *reached* north, finding a storm of low-level magic, while beyond lay the brooding, almost impenetrable power of the Enchanters. *And still, my Sight is blocked, but one day that blockage may fail, it **must** fail, but for now....* Imperceptibly, she nodded.

Orantes drew his staff. "If we are under equipped with battle magic," he said, "the Wizards have at least not stinted in teaching us of Farsight and Divination." As the red light of sunset faded into dusk, the two Adepts used their staffs to carve a pane of air — a rectangular Divination screen that stood seven feet in height and about twice as broad. With the fading light, the Divination's edge gave off a bright glow, as though the panel had captured bright sunlight to release at dusk.

With the panel's edge glowing brightly before them, the Adepts stood back and began intoning spell words in low voices. All light in the panel grew dark and black as though showing a starless night. Then slowly the light of dusk again filled the panel — but dusk in a different region, and from such a distance that the stumbling columns of dead things were reduced to the size of large insects.

Even as daylight within the Divination failed, the onlookers found new sources of light. Small whirlwinds of fire raged amid the dead beings, incinerating all flesh. Whirling columns of dust drew the ash into the heavens and spinning turmoils of vapor sucked ash fragments into deep rivers.

The ground began to give way from beneath the dead beings, as Elementals of Earth reached up to reclaim flesh that had been buried. Whirlwinds, columns, vortices, ripples of ground, all raged against the Undead, consuming them like a firestorm withering dark petals.

"The answer, at last," Farad said, though his tones were cautious. "Had we —"

"Watch now! Be wary!" Sentauris called out in her remote voice. As the onlookers stared, a knot of resistance seemed to form within the Divination: Elementals were hurled back, rebuffed, and even a few of the smaller whirlwinds of air faltered and failed, as though they themselves had been consumed.

"Two Creatures of the Darkness," Orantes breathed out.

"Even in death they have kept a strength of magic," Wylar murmured, eyes straining to follow events in the darkened panel. "And they are not alone."

"Murat and Fiüre," Sentauris said softly, "have also been endowed with power, a matter worth knowing, for — weapons, draw weapons!"

Events within the Divination panel seemed to blur and blot. The fabric of the Adepts' magic rippled and thrashed. An arm, huge as the waist of a strong man, burst through the panel and grasped the cloak of Orantes.

"Helcar!" Sentauris cried. Her first arrow recoiled from the Enchanter's flesh. Orantes was being drawn, thrashing and twisting, toward the panel. Sardonicus hewed at the arm, but his sword rebounded. Wylar slashed; his enchanted blade bit deeply, but after, its metal boiled away, consumed by dark fire.

"Strike at the wound!" Sentauris cried and drove an arrow deep in the gash. Farad stabbed at the seam, while Gallandus hewed across the cut.

From the other side of the Divination, Helcar bellowed like an angry God. Orantes was released, though smashed backhanded to the ground. Sentauris buried a second arrow in the wound. Muffled howling sounds passed through the Divination panel as the Enchanter withdrew his stricken arm. Then the Adepts' Divination began twisting in midair, consuming itself like dark fire pursued by smoke, while its onlookers were left standing, shaken, breathing hard in the shadows of twilight.

· X ·

Many leagues from the brief melee, Pentarchus laughed softly to himself, watching Helcar as the Carag slowly transformed damaged flesh into patterns that concealed his wounds. *The damage remains,* Pentarchus thought, *it is only internalized. But what Helcar has just encountered is no more than a sideshow — our real struggle is with the Wizards, then with the designs of the Great God Set, and these conflicts have barely begun. Mine begins now.*

His own powers of Divination had been developed over many years — perhaps three times the lifetime of a normal human, and it seemed unlikely that man or God would have the strength to halt or even interrupt him. Pentarchus remained cautious, however, and in spite of the isolating darkness of twilight, he sealed his billowing command tent a third time against any intrusions.

The Enchanter then rose and paced to the edge of his design, extending one hand out into the night. The invisible servant who attended him on these occasions had prepared for Pentarchus a broth of toadflax from the Vale of Whispers, and wolf's bane and hemp berries — a tisane that strongly reinforced his powers of concentration. He drained the mug in a single draft, then stood eyes closed, focusing, drawing all his strength inwards.

You there, Pentarchus thought toward the being within himself. *All this exploration might be made unnecessary should you step forward and identify yourself. What was your nature of old?* The Enchanter hoped for a murmur or a growl, but instead, the hidden Power within him seemed to retreat, farther down and deeper into the core of Pentarchus.

"Why am I not surprised?" Pentarchus said aloud. "Though if you look out from behind my eyes, I will show you many great mysteries. First...." The broth rushed to the farthest reaches of his mind, making him curiously lightheaded. "First, and at the beginning, is the Maker, the First Fashioner, and Great Enigma. If we are to explore the Ancient Powers, why not begin with the Maker?"

To reach so far back in time was pure whimsy, though unlikely to be dangerous: the Maker never came when called, nor did He wreak vengeance upon those who mocked Him. Many Sorcerers treated the Maker as a remote, almost comical figure, but Pentarchus had learned that both Greater and Lesser Gods became extremely wary whenever the Maker was mentioned. Therefore, he would be cautious, though not fearful.

The words that came to his mouth were half sung, half chanted, like the music of a tone-deaf old crone. Images formed in the midst of the tent, showing Earth in upheaval, shrouded by layers of storm clouds. As Pentarchus chanted, struggling to peer beyond the veils of time, the image of Earth's beginning slowly cleared. Then vague as a mirage shrouded by grey mists, the Enchanter watched as a small figure slowly formed: seated on a stone outcrop, hooded, bent, gaunt, with ropy, gnarled flesh a greyish brown, features like no other being born of Earth, the figure seemed to regard Pentarchus with an amusement mixed with sorrow.

And this, this is the Maker? The Enchanter recoiled from both the image and the thought.

As Pentarchus twitched, the image before him suddenly changed. A lone mountain of mountains formed, reaching above an Earth that had become suddenly lopsided, for all other ranges became in comparison tiny as ridges in the sand. Then with a rippling motion, the image changed again, with a single titanic tree replacing the mountain, showing greyish black bark and showers of green leaves where dark granite had prevailed.

A fourth change followed: Earth's tree became a gigantic Goddess, the greatest of Powers, a creature with blue hair cascading over sun-darkened skin, holding aloft a shield as though rising in defense of the small planet that seemed no more than a globe beneath her feet. *A Goddess, Pentarchus thought, was the Maker indeed the first female deity? How could —*

With blurring motions, the image changed one last time: metal seemed to shimmer over the Goddess, replacing tanned skin, until the colossus towering above earth stood like some vast machine, head turning slowly, mechanically, as it stared beyond the circles of the sun. Then all images vanished, leaving Pentarchus staring open mouthed at dull, empty space.

I have been shown a great mystery, but by all the Nine Billion Gods I have no idea what to make of it. He took a deep breath and stared beyond the fabric of his ornate pavilion, where darkness had fallen, and countless small night creatures were beginning another epic of exploration, predation, and death.

"Shall I gather from your silence," Pentarchus whispered to the being within himself, "that none of the images shown are ones you recognize? Or have you merely concealed yourself so deeply that you are not able to react?" Silence. Stillness...but a watching quiet.

"Then let us begin with those of the Right-Hand Path," Pentarchus continued. "It seems unlikely that Seraph or Spirit Lord would react as you have, but more than a few were corrupted by the many pleasures of evil, and so fought beside Demon and Dragon on behalf of the Adversaries. Behold a Seraph."

A tall, golden image formed, with noble features, godlike, radiating power, though the Seraph's eyes stared far into the distance with lost eyes. Standing three heads higher than the Enchanter, the image of the Seraph turned slowly, the light of a deep harvest gold seeping from its form.

"No, I do not think you are one of those," Pentarchus murmured. "Not even the most demented of renegades would show your desires. Though what of the Spirit Lords?" The Seraph's image vanished, to be replaced by that of an equally tall figure, with long silver hair flowing over shoulders that seemed less broad than those of the Seraph.

"So might Llara have seemed," Pentarchus whispered, "before the time of the Ancient Wars. With the Spirit Lords comes the first hint of female deities, and I do not sense any of those attributes within you, my charming guest. Now, on the Right-Hand Path, the humans are lesser beings but should also be shown." A youth appeared, with ringlets of dark hair curled over his brow, and a slight smile playing over features that were nearly perfect. The Enchanter felt a shock of recognition, though he had never before encountered this youth. And within Pentarchus came the faintest of movements.

A stirring at last. But what is this reaction? Revulsion? Hunger? Lust? I cannot say.

Pentarchus waved his hand and the youth's image vanished. "Those were indeed only included for the sake of completeness, for I do not believe you were borne of the Powers of the Right Hand of Creation. Now we must examine those of the Left Hand. Behold a Mighty Prince of Demons, a being unequaled in power."

Pentarchus stood back, for this image loomed larger than the others, taking much greater space. Tall as a Seraph, the Prince of Demons bulked three times a Seraph's mass, with a head larger than any bull's. And the figure was not entirely under the Enchanter's control; outside the tent, the night seemed to grow still, as with increasing self-awareness, the red-hued image of the Demon Prince stared around the tent, radiating menace. Sorcerous energies slipped toward the image as though distant, unknown forces were challenging the Enchanter's Divination.

Pentarchus stood erect, unshaken, albino hair gleaming white, while his arctic blue eyes remained serene. Muted spell words spilled from his lips as he gradually renewed his control over his Divination, until the image of the Demon Prince stared into the distance, with eyes both vacant and remote.

"Not even in my youth," Pentarchus said softly, "were my Divinations so wayward. My own strength grows daily, so I must judge that we tremble on the edge of profound knowledge."

He waved his hand and the reddish colored image vanished. Pentarchus then placed himself in the farthest corner of his canvas chamber. More words were spoken, and a far larger image began forming within the tent: greenish, winged and scaled, the Lord of Dragons seemed to stare out into the distance, wings poised to lift its enormous form into deep space.

Yet this form differed from the others: it was faint, almost incomplete, and when Pentarchus reached out to touch the Dragon's scaled wing, its form was colder than ice.

Casually, as though brushing aside cobwebs, the Enchanter motioned with one hand, and the form vanished. "Still no reaction from within, my most intimate and charming of friends? If we have learned little of your past history from this exercise, there are yet several most interesting conclusions to be drawn, though these are unlikely to have any impact on our struggles with the Wizards and the designs of The Great God Set.

"Firstly, though the Maker passed from Earth so many eons ago, there still seem to be mechanisms in Alantéa the Forerunner that support the Maker's Will.

"Secondly, we are told that all of the Ancient Powers — Seraphs and Demons, Spirit Lords and Dragons — were transformed into the Gods of Alantéa. I will guess that one of the Demon Princes, at least, remains outside of this Truce, with interesting consequences for the Mid-World.

"And thirdly, my fine friend, though it was not apparent from this exploration, I will one day discover your nature and smoke out the designs of the Great God Set. You must become accustomed to this fact."

· ☿ ·

Warmth gathered to the coast, as the last ice of winter slipped from the coast's lower hills, daily transforming itself into vapor. Sun on water, streams of higher air, moisture seeping from the ground — all these yielded layers of clouds that provided a dark overcast night. Swooping beneath low clouds, Squint watched as two patterns of werelight drifted toward one another. From the Adepts came beacons of green and yellow, while from the Elf-Mage Mír, pools of silver light surrounded his party. Sentauris guided the Adepts until the two parties joined, radiances mingling, producing a patch of strange moonlight in an otherwise overcast night.

"Well met," said Sentauris. "I know that this phrase is overused, but I have watched and waited for you these many days, and say I again, well met."

"All great words are worn down by overuse," Mír said, "though we are indeed well met." Solemnly, almost awkwardly, he embraced the Seeress. Mír stood nearly half a head taller than Sentauris, flesh a marble and white touched by grey, with features both sharp and smooth, as though carved by some cunning sculptor. Behind the Elf-Mage stood two massive Tanu warriors, their dark features contrasting with those of Mír, though they also seemed crafted rather than born of flesh. Great heavy, spiked maces were strapped to the backs of each.

Wylar and Orantes stepped forward to greet the Elf-Mage. If Wylar matched Mír's height, his unshaved, bristling face stood in sharp contrast with the gleaming white, hairless features of the Mage, and as for Orantes, no one could have believed that he and the Elf-Mage belonged to related species. Seeress, Elf-Mage, and Adepts then drifted away, speaking in hushed tones, carrying their moonlight with them, so that others were left alone in the darkness.

Ghorm groaned and sank to the ground; rough travel always made him weak and nauseous. Swift passage by horse toward Stone Mountain had left him feeble and useless. That Orantes had adjusted to such travel was even more galling to Ghorm; the Adept was even developing physical reserves while some of the weight slipped from his frame. Now Sentauris had left her Familiar in the darkness, to venture off with her two possible lovers and another wielder of magic with considerable power.

Maker, why was I abandoned in this place? To be as I am, to think such thoughts, have such feelings, and hopes as I have, and yet be at the end, nothing more than Ghorm the pitiful little goblin? No answer came, either from the Maker or from the two Tanu bodyguards who stood, still as granite, staring into the darkness. But Whisper's shadowy form came to stand with Ghorm in the overcast night, and Squint coasted toward him with silent, downy wings.

"Since we have not been introduced," Whisper said softly, "I do not think these great warriors will mind if we leave them to their own devices. Come, Ghorm." Guided by Squint and Whisper, Ghorm climbed with them to a high overlook, so that the three Familiars could stare down on the pools of converging moonlight crafted by their masters and by the Elf-Mage. All their captains and soldiers had passed east toward Gravengate, as had the lumbering legions of the remaining Undead. While a warfare of flesh and metal gathered to Gravengate, a storm of magic was drifting toward Stone Mountain.

"For the first time in months," Squint said, "I can smell the ocean, and the scent of death has just about vanished."

"Had the night been clear," Whisper added, "we would see the distant beacons of Stone Mountain. Even in the dark, I can sense Stone Mountain, for the might of Thorian reaches out toward me, though the oncoming power of the Enchanters will soon surround him."

Ghorm was silent; his small heart was hammering from the climb, while nausea assailed him as it always had, and he watched down upon pools of werelight with deep unhappiness.

"Let it be, Ghorm," Squint murmured. "If we are lesser forces, at least we are taking part in significant events."

"So, these are 'significant events?'" Ghorm muttered. "On one side we have a powerful Wizard — at least he is strong only by reputation — aided by an unknown Elf-Mage, a Seeress rendered partly blind by the power of her foes, with a stoat and a pig masquerading as Adepts. Against this feeble coalition are ranged, five Enchanters. Not three, or four — already too many for the defenders of Stone Mountain — but five...."

· Ж ·

"...so, there will not be five, but four Enchanters," Sentauris was saying. "For reasons unknown, the fifth Enchanter, the one called Pentarchus, and perhaps the most powerful of the five, lags more than a half a day behind."

"And their pace is measured, almost sluggish," Wylar added. "Instead of slipping through enchanted Portals, they are moving south by carriage, with a score of wagons drawn by beasts carrying stores just behind them."

"Are they attempting to develop their powers as they journey south?" Mír asked. "Or is there discord among them?"

Sentauris stared northeast where the Enchanters had made their camp less than five leagues from Stone Mountain. "All such bickering came to a halt several days ago," she said softly. "I reach, I probe, I dream troubled dreams, yet I cannot tell what new force has so united them."

"So, we must come to the aid of a lone Wizard," Mír said doubtfully, glancing at the two Adepts, "who confronts at least four Enchanters. Is this the task of martyrs, not heroes?"

"Mír, I understand you too well," the Seeress said. "You may indeed have prepared an escape hatch, but you will not flee until the outcome is no longer in doubt. Even if my Farsight is hindered, I can see clearly that the result of tomorrow's battle is far from certain. Here is what I foresee: the Enchanters surround Stone Mountain except on its seaward side; Thorian resists mightily. Does aid come from Merlin or Balardi? I cannot say, but a balance of forces is maintained, and at that time, we thrust at the Enchanters. Mír, you are the sword thrust, while the Adepts, who are less trained in battle magic but are strong with counter spells, are your shields. I will function as your added senses — increasing both your sight and your hearing."

"And so, by combining," Orantes added with false bravado, "we are saying that lesser forces might check a greater one, like weasels nipping at the ankle of a griffin, or enraged salamanders trying to swarm the talons of a dragon."

"We are much greater than your 'weasels' or 'salamanders,' Orantes," Sentauris said. "At least I hope we are."

They had left the middle portion of the night for sleep, hoping to capture a few hours rest before the Enchanters' onslaught against Stone Mountain began. Sentauris spent a precious hour consoling an unhappy Ghorm, then she passed into Dreamways that had become increasingly strange and troubled.

The architecture of night in her dream vision had become extremely complex, with scores of dark, jagged columns looming high in the night, while other buttresses gave off muted glows of pale yellow or deep purple. Both columns and buttresses seemed to pulse and flicker with a sense of movement, but little radiance. Only one light could be seen clearly, and even that radiance was dim, no more than the light yielded by a table filled with candles. Sentauris felt herself drawn to that light, and did not resist, for an ally was reaching out to her.

Merlin was leaning over his great gaming board, staring down at his many pieces as they moved ponderously over The Game of the Masters. In her night vision, Sentauris drifted closer, examining both the Wizard and his board. Merlin stood a hand's breadth shorter than she; he was mild seeming, with a white beard, and soft, grey eyes. She had encountered Merlin only a few times before, finding him cool, remote, and judgmental. Perhaps because the Wizard was now reaching for her though Gates of Dreams, he now seemed warmer and human.

She leaned over the great field that held The Game of the Masters. Pieces were moving, slowly, as though passing through thickened water: The Fortress stirred, while The Wizard and The Magician drifted forward, and The Great Spell trembled as though readying to add its own power.

Merlin looked up from his board into the eyes of Sentauris. "Hail, Seeress, and ally," he murmured. "Behold The Game of the Masters, a device that reveals much of the nature of the Mid-World. I cannot engage either of the two Powers ranged against us, so I have moved both sides of the Game to simulate play, and perhaps discover the authors of our ills. As I play, other Powers of the Mid-World watch me — those are the dark columns and glowing buttresses you perceive looming in the darkness. The lesser pillars are formed by the Emissaries of the Gods, beings who have haunted the League since the beginning of this war. Whether these Emissaries are forerunners of the Gods, or carrion crows, or some device of the Truce, I cannot say.

"Now, Seeress, through devices of the Game, and through other investigations, I am close to naming the Renegade Dark God who has waged a portion of this great war against us. From you, I seek nothing but confirmation. What names come to your mind when you consider the authors of our ills?"

Torrents of images, names, faces of powerful and weaker Gods, insignia, heraldic devices flooded through her mind. None brought flashes of insight or understanding. Then, as though outside her command, the lips of Sentauris formed words and spoke: "The second author of our misery is the Renegade Dark Lord, Mordred. His ally cannot yet be named."

"The Sight is mighty within you, Seeress," Merlin said softly. "I greatly regret that you and I ever quarreled." The Wizard looked beyond Sentauris, beyond his great gaming board, into the pillars of night with their many pulsing eyes, and into the floating buttresses of the Dreamways that glowed with such a strange incandescence.

"I now name one of the two Powers waging war against us," Merlin called out into those clustering in the Dreamways. "His name is Mordred, Renegade Dark God of the Mid-World, and his work is evil beyond dreams of malice and retribution. O ye Gods, mighty Powers of the Mid-World, send your Emissaries forth to discover this truth for yourselves, that the renegade Mordred seeks to destroy us, and we of the League never sought advantage from him, nor have we ever disturbed his peoples, unless they waylaid us and tried to slaughter our servants."

Merlin turned to Sentauris and spoke in much lower tones, almost in a whisper. "Go forth now, daughter and handmaiden of the League. You must rise and wake from your dreams with the coming of the light, for on this day much may be required of you."

As Sentauris struggled to pull herself from her troubled dream images, she woke to a gloomy, overcast daybreak. Layers of heavy grey clouds hovered overhead, completely blocking the sun. Her eyes found Mír, standing just a little to her left, staring into the distance. She scrambled to her feet,

reaching for the Enchanters and for their intended victim, the Wizard
Thorian.

*Three of the four were moving, with considerable purpose, while the
fourth gathered herself, bristling with rage at some unknown development.
Strangely, the Witch Queen's anger seemed directed not at the Wizards or at
her fellow Enchanters, but on some other being and his work. Yes...and the
name of that being was....*

*With a sudden shift, Sentauris found her link to the Enchanters broken.
She turned to Thorian, the Master of Stone Mountain, who seethed with a cold
anger. For unknown reasons, he seemed to sense her, to be seeking for her, and
this Wizard had always been the least sympathetic to her presence....*

*She pulled back and became aware that other, lesser powers were entering
the zone of conflict surrounding Stone Mountain. Creatures of the Darkness
were nearing the shore, drawn to the oncoming collision of magics like jackals
to a feast of death. She lifted herself free from her trance.*

·))(·

"The Enchanters move more swiftly," she said to Mír in soft tones. "Unlike
their cautious movements of recent days, they have risen with the dawn.
Our best approach lies to the south, where Stone Mountain meets the
shore. Come. We should rouse the Adepts."

Wylar was up in a flash, and Orantes barely grumbled as he stumbled
to his feet. Even Ghorm rose with few complaints, though his movements
were stiff, and his eyes watched the Adepts with little pleasure. Mír accepted
the use of a pack horse with good grace, while his Tanu bodyguards needed
no such transportation, as they set off in advance of the others, marching
tirelessly over misty, dampened hills and hollows. Whisper and Ghorm

remained with the Adepts, while Squint rose in flight, trying to keep both the Adepts and their Tanu guides in sight.

The forest canopy lessened as they passed south and east. The ground grew more level, with scrub pines and bush thriving in lighter, sandy soil. On other days, breaks in the forest canopy would have yielded greater light, but on this day, the gloom seemed to deepen as the hours progressed.

Mír's farsighted elven eyes were the first to perceive Stone Mountain as it rose from the shore; patches of mist were layered around it, and the shoreline sea that lay a half a league from the peak remained hidden from their view. Their war-band made steady progress so that others came to see the mountain a short while later, with its fortress dwelling nestled on its broad, rounded peak.

Stone Mountain seemed to rise majestically from the ground as though it been constructed by Gods, not by nature. Its sloop was steep, and it lacked foothills, with few ridges or lesser spires, it seemed that only skilled mountaineers could reach its peak. Mosses grew in slight crevices, while ferns and scrub struggled for footholds along its steep sides.

Perched on the crown of Stone Mountain stood the fortress of Thorian, its walls emerging seamlessly from the rock's surface. Those walls were high, with broad parapeted battlements forming strongpoints that were most difficult to reach. Turrets rose on the battlements at every turn of its walls, while inside the outer barriers, a second ring of fortifications shielded a broad keep. Sentauris sensed but could not see that the people of Stone Mountain had mined deep beneath the fortress, with honeycombs of tunnels providing shelter for the besieged. All such construction was made possible only by the forces wielded by powerful magic, for only lightly equipped and skilled mountaineers could scale Stone Mountain's peak.

"This is the work," Mír commented, "of an overlord who does not lack enemies. Why —" The Elf-Mage broke off, for a greyish black mist was beginning to hover to the north of the fortress; and by the devices and designs of the invaders, the mist was forming a vast, gnarled hand, reaching out as though to engulf Stone Mountain. From within the mists emerged sounds of the misshapen Creatures of the Darkness, snarling and growling as though they had scented prey.

"The Enchanters have come to Stone Mountain," Sentauris whispered. "We cannot go forward in our present forms." She looked to Wylar and Orantes, who glanced to Mír, then back to the massive dark hand that was gathering around one of the three pillars of the League.

Wylar began intoning spell words. Seconds later, the voice of Orantes rose over Wylar's, as though guiding their craft. Forty feet away, the forms of the two Tanu warriors began to change; they halted, standing stone still as their outer forms became those of maimed and hobbled Uraks, outcasts seeking spoils amid the ruin of war. One Urak dragged a sack attached by cords to an arm that lacked a hand, while the second Urak bore two weapons to compensate for hobbled, limping feet. The two Tanu stood and stared back at the Adepts with hard, unforgiving eyes.

"You must apologize for us, Mír," Orantes said, struggling not to chuckle. "See, we will become equally lovely." More spell words followed: Orantes became a lout with one good eye, and a head covered like a corsair's with a dark cloth. Mír's features showed a human disguise, grey whiskered and toothless, so that his gums met, his lips puffed out. Wylar retained his height, but his arms lengthened, he became hunched, and his features coarsened, as though, apelike, he might scamper away on four limbs. Even Sentauris was not spared: her form became waddle-plump, with the smile of a halfwit frozen on her face, though her squinting eyes were completely sharp and calculating.

The Adepts then sealed their spell with a second, then a third gathering of illusions, so that as they moved forward into the mists, none of those with the Gift could pierce the disguise of the others.

"Here is magic both grotesque and subtle," Mír said under his breath, glancing at Orantes.

"A fair description of that perverse pirate, Orantes," Sentauris said. "But recall that the Adepts are not weak, they merely lack battle magic, except for Dragonfire, a force that the Enchanters have prepared for. When called upon, they will shield us." *If we are to live,* she thought, carefully concealing her reservations.

As they grew closer, the darkness surrounding Stone Mountain deepened; an early dusk had gathered around the great fortress. As if to compensate for the gloom, Stone Mountain itself began to give off a glow of gleaming white, drawing them like a beacon toward the fortress; yet after a while, even that light was dimmed, and they were forced to dismount and lead their horses on foot. Clustering together, stumbling through dark mists, brigands and Uraks formed the strangest and most powerful mix of rabble ever to approach Stone Mountain.

Orantes led his horse forward, all the bravado inside him slowly fading. Stone Mountain was as obscure and remote as its master, Thorian. To the north, four powerful Enchanters approached the stronghold; he could feel the pressure of their dark magic like a huge dead weight. *Why can't we, even for just a few days, contend with lesser powers, like sylphs, or gnomes, or solve some slight puzz —*

Out of the darkness, an enormous creature loomed. Furred, thick bodied with the squat features of a goblin, it reached for the Tanu disguised as Uraks. Behind the Tanu, horses reared and bolted. Leaping away from her panicked steed, Sentauris buried an arrow in one bulging goblin-like eye. The foremost Tanu smashed at the creature's arm with its heavy, spiked mace, while the second slashed at its ankle with a dagger that pulsed with sorcerous power. Whisper's dark shadowy form embraced the Creature's remaining Goblin eye, blinding it.

With a great howl of pain and disappointment, the Creature Indomitable ripped the arrow from its eye, and staggered away, shrieking its anger into the darkness that had gathered around Stone Mountain.

A swirling motion of flashing light spun through the darkness.

"Down," Sentauris snarled. "Be as dead things." A split second after they slumped to the ground a gleaming lens device floated through the darkness, casting light over low scrub, fallen pillagers, and wounded Creature. As the Enchanters' lens peered closely at the Creature Indomitable, the monster lashed out, shattering the viewing device. Then the monstrosity drifted away, alternately growling and moaning, lamenting its misfortune.

They waited cautiously for a moment then rose, discovering that the air about them was changing — specks of orange and purple radiances were forming in midair, beginning to glow. Some particles were clustering together, while others investigated the scrub forest at the base of Stone Mountain. Mír began to chant: layers of white and silver luminescence began fending off the magic of the Enchanters.

"It cannot be helped," Sentauris murmured to Ghorm. "The Enchanters have launched their necromantic forces. We cannot become part of their kingdom of death." The air began to hum, while the purple and orange haze deepened. The scrub brush all around them began drooping then withered and died. A rumbling sound pulsed through the earth, while the air surrounding Stone Mountain began whimpering with the soft whispers of young, dying creatures. With increasing caution, they made their way forward on foot through a darkened, misty haze.

I may love those around me, thought Orantes, *but I have no real part in this, the work of heroes. I would rather be anywh* — A deep concussion rolled through the ground. The purple and orange haze flared briefly then vanished. Thorian had countered the Enchanters.

"'A Wizard is Master where he dwells,'" Wylar quoted in a whisper, moving forward warily. Was the darkness wavering just a bit, and was that Stone Mountain looming in front of them? The Tanu disguised as Uraks began to pick up their pace, forcing Orantes to follow, breathing heavily while Ghorm scrambled to keep up.

As they surged forward, the forest cover began to lessen, and even the scrub pines emerging from sandy loam grew sparser. Glimpses of Stone Mountain slipped into view as banks of dark mist drifted past the steep walls of the fortress. A fitful wind seemed to be gathering, accompanied by low, moaning sounds. Orantes could sense power all around him, like a riptide in stormy waters, as sorcery flowed both to the Wizard on his mountain peak and to the Enchanters approaching from the north. Thunder rumbled over the land, though it seemed to come from the ground rather than the sky.

With the ground trembling beneath their feet, Sentauris raced forward and called Mír's Tanu bodyguards to a halt.

"Hear me for just one moment." She turned to the others. "Battle begins soon, sorcery against dark magic, pure power against mighty force. Stray thrusts may destroy us, so be guided by my signals, and I will bring us safely to our goal. Should we become —"

Without further warning a sheet of bright lightning surged from Stone Mountain, hurtling toward the Enchanters. Flash blinded, Sentauris dropped lightly to the ground, while the others were thrown from their feet by the explosion. More bolts of lightning followed, white hot casts from the Wizard, racing through the darkness blazing with wrath.

The ground stirred as though come to life. Creatures of the Darkness shrieked like maddened things. Then from the Enchanters came forces to counter Thorian. Twisted, jagged pulses of dark power smashed into Stone

Mountain, shaking the stonework of the fortress to its foundations, sending shattered debris cascading down the mountain's side.

Again, Thorian exploded with power: bursts of gold and silver leaped through the darkness. One Enchanter cried aloud but halted only for a moment before returning more rippling, pulses of jagged power that hammered at the mountain's base.

Light exploded all around them, racing through darkened, gloomy air. Their ears were deafened. Lurching, scrambling through the murk, they followed Sentauris as she struggled forward. Stray discharges tore into the ground all around them. Scrub brush burst into flames, so they were forced to seek passage through patches of green safety, surrounded by the gloom of dark, red fire, moving through a darkness shaken by bursts of power, white-hot bolts of lightning, glares of light as sorcerous energies gathered to the Enchanters. Creatures of the Darkness stood stricken, crying out both in fear and rage; those possessing ears stopped them up.

Scrambling, panting, sweating as he ran, Orantes found his mind stirring in wild revolt. *By all the Nine Billion Gods! Look at Wylar: his gaunt face is grim, untouched by fear and his eyes seem made of metal. Sentauris is racing forward, mouth half snarling, intent on destroying our foes. Mir glides toward Stone Mountain like a hawk descending upon prey. And you, Orantes, a buffoon with only one life, are stumbling forward to your death....*

Suddenly Sentauris cried aloud and turned sharply to her left. The others followed her, racing down the channel of a stream then throwing themselves to the ground beside the Seeress. Less than a foot above them, jagged dark lightning bolts surged overhead as though seeking their moving forms.

"One of the Enchanters has taken note of us," Sentauris murmured, "though only briefly, for in this struggle we are no more than a diversion. Take ten deep breaths, then we are gone."

They crept forward to the edge of the stream channel and peered out. Lightning surged from Stone Mountain, jagged bolts of power that raced through the reddish black hazy gloom and blasted at the adversaries of the Wizard. From the Enchanters streaked black, rippling bolts of dark power smashing against Thorian and his fortress. Sounds burst all around them. Strange lights glimmered and flared in the gloom. Fire swept the land, and monstrosities wandered purposeless, crying aloud as though they were losing their minds.

"A place of the damned," whispered Orantes, glancing back and forth between Stone Mountain and its adversaries. The Enchanters seemed to swell in might, to delight in their open display of power, with new magic flaring in their minds, and cunning, destructive lightning flashing from their fingertips. Stone Mountain seemed to tremble with pain. *Time to disappear, Orantes,* his mind whispered*, but you have never mastered a proper vanishing spell.*

"We are again forgotten," Sentauris hissed, and she rose. As before, they sped through the gloom behind Sentauris, matching her sharp turning and twisting as she navigated a passage toward the Enchanters. Fire along the ground singed their feet, and scrub brush tore at their clothing. Dark smoke choked their throats and lungs. Twice a Creature Indomitable rose from its confusion and sought to attack their war-band, but each time their Tanu bodyguards smashed the monstrosity's feet with spiked maces, and it limped away, howling.

Storm sounds grew louder all around them. Stone Mountain loomed larger in the gloom. Lightning, both dark and light, surged overhead. The earth shook and trembled; three times they were hurled to the ground. Sentauris could sense the Enchanters, swollen with power, as they hurled blast after blast against Stone Mountain. The four Enchanters stood in an arc to the north of the fortress, with almost five hundred paces separating each from the other. Their forms were shielded by fallen trunks from the broken forest that lay smoldering in heaps and tangles and they scould be sensed only as mighty beings radiating power and menace.

The Enchanters...masters of strange forces...Sentauris let her mind probe each of them, carefully, so cautiously...the Enchanters were no longer human! Some powerful sorcery lay over them...or had they been more profoundly altered, joined to some other Powers?

She recoiled, then forced herself to renew her search. *We cannot transform them, we can only divert one, but, which one? Which of them is been made insane by his own newfound might? Helcar is closest, but is this only a trick of fate? Pentarchus is far away, consumed by strange explorations so that he views the battle almost as an afterthought. What subject could possibly draw him from —*

With an eerie cracking sound, the northern rock face of Stone Mountain gave way, dragging parapeted walls down the mountain's side. An avalanche of shattered stone and rubble cascaded down toward the Enchanters. Clouds of dust joined the murk and fog of battle. Sentauris and her war party threw themselves to the ground, shielding ears and eyes from the disaster.

"Doom comes to Stone Mountain," Mír called to Sentauris. "Is this battle now becoming an act of suicide?" Sentauris peered out: lightning and the werelight of wild sorcery were diminishing, though the menace of dark magic almost engulfed Stone Mountain. The Enchanters were waiting for the rockslide to end, but their minds radiated triumph, while from Thorian....

Abruptly, she rolled over, turning toward Orantes and Wylar. "Some new force is being called upon — Merlin showed me but did not explain. Tell me, and quickly, about *The Great Spell.*"

Wylar stared south, toward the ocean. "In the *Game of the Masters, The Great Spell* lies upon the third rank, with other mighty forces, perhaps not as great as *The Mid-World Power*, or *The Wizard*, though equal in might to *The Fortress* or *The Armed Host*.... So that is how the Wizards have chosen to project their power. I can sense it now. Merlin is reaching for us."

A stillness gathered about Stone Mountain. The air seemed to tremble with the hushed quiet of creation. Powerful winds rose from the south, ripping, tearing at the fog surrounding the fortress. Patches of murk began to give way, sliding north like streams of vapor drawn into a whirlwind.

Winds whipped at smoldering ground fires, sending sheets of flame leaping from scrub patches to the northern deeper forests. A great uncertainty held Sentauris frozen, though she could see that their remaining green enclave would soon be engulfed. She stared south: a vast disturbance was building beneath the ocean, as waves, twice her height smashed down on the shore, and contending rip tides tore at each another. Gusts of wind slashed great gaps in the fog. Shafts of light beamed down over Stone Mountain.

"Up now," Sentauris whispered. "The Wizards have brought forth powerful magic to counter the Enchanters. No matter that it is not very pretty." Orantes found himself transfixed, staring south with unbelieving eyes. Huge formations could be seen through gaps in clouds, rising from the ocean. Mounds of strange matter rose from raging waters, each holding the features of a Storm Giant. Strands of seaweed were plastered like tiny flecks over enormous foreheads. Shell fragments were embedded in dark, greyish, angry eyes. Five huge, knobby heads rose from the shoreline; necks seemed to form from beneath white waves.

Sentauris reached over and tugged Orantes from his trance. "They rise from the depths, the League's own version of Storm Giants — or whatever the Wizards found in their crazed dreams that were fueled by so many potions. Come." Led by Sentauris, they raced forward, dodging around waves of fire. Lightning flared again from Stone Mountain, but Ghorm's eyes were drawn to the Storm Giants rising chest high from the ocean: electrical discharges were flaring and pulsing through bodies formed of thickened, dark cloud matter. Now, as though responding to Ghorm, one figure raised an enormous hand and reached toward the Enchanter Nairn.

Lightning flared: huge, flat, and wide, the blast hurtled toward Nairn, smashing both the Enchanter and his spell shields back from the mountain. Sounds burst over Ghorm's hearing; he stopped up his ears but found himself deafened, staring south with wide eyes — other Giants were raising cloudy, dark hands, and lightning hurtled toward the Enchanters.

Sentauris called to them, but none could hear her. The Enchanters were being smashed back, battered northward, their spell shields shaken, hanging in the air like tufted, battered clouds. Signaling, Sentauris led them toward the Enchanters, circling further north to intercept the retreating Helcar.

Orantes held his deafened ears, not even able to shout out his objections: *Why, if the Enchanters are being forced from Stone Mountain, why must we confront them? Why are we endangering the fat and feeble Orantes, who should be preserved at least for light entertainment?* Sweating, fearful, deafened, the Adept struggled to keep pace, as they raced over a land where lightning, dark magic, and fire reigned.

Helcar came into view, battered back by the force of the Great Spell. The land all around him lay blackened, except for broken trees that still smoldered with grey smoke. The Enchanter had swollen to twice Wylar's height, his fair featured human guise mottled with grey blotches. Patches of brutish hair sprouted from his forehead. Words of rage sped from his mouth: jagged bolts of dark lightning leaped at Storm Giants, but those bolts were casually brushed aside.

Though now, as they slipped cautiously toward the Enchanter, one Storm Giant seemed to hesitate, to falter. Creatures of the Darkness had clustered about one huge leg and were ripping at its substance both with their strength and with the fire of sorcery within their own forms. Nairn took note of the struggle: beams of necromantic power lashed at the Giant's other leg, and it toppled, so slowly that it seemed to take forever to reach the earth. And as it fell, it lost substance, dissolving into mist.

The lightning fight surged anew: thick blasts from Storm Giants; white-hot casts from Thorian; and from the Enchanters, dark, writhing bolts that leaped toward Stone Mountain and its defenders. The Enchanters began holding their ground. Thorian redoubled his efforts, shielding the remaining portions of his Great Spell while lashing at the Creatures Indomitable.

After one final scramble, Sentauris called a halt, sinking down behind a tangle of fallen tree limbs that had not yet caught fire. She stared into pale sweat streaked faces: Orantes was trapped by his own inner fears, Wylar's determination was diluted by shock, while Mír's features showed a profound uncertainty. The Familiars — alas! — had been reduced by events to onlookers.

She reached out to touch Orantes with her left hand and spoke into his mind. *Adept, dissolve the illusions concealing us, for we must go now, openly into battle.* She touched Wylar with her right hand. *Protect us, Wylar the Resourceful. We will force this Enchanter to take note of us. Then he will tear at us with a rage of dark energies. Shield us while Mír counters — and then takes us far from this place with Portal Magic.* She held each of them until they nodded, faces streaked by ash and streams of sweat.

She turned and grasped the Elf-Mage with both hands. *Mír, the Adepts will help — they will shield you. But their force of Dragonfire has been too well noted by the Enchanters. Mír, you must distract the Enchanter, Helcar — force him to break off his assault on Stone Mountain. Then as the Adepts shield you, forge Portal Magic and free us to fight again another day. Mír, within a thousand future chances several hundred of these show us transforming this battle and then fighting free. Mír, Maker's Grace to you, for this is your moment.* Mír nodded and stared at the battlefield, where the Enchanter Helcar had grown swollen with dark necromantic energies.

Sentauris turned and touched Mír's Tanu bodyguards, who had regained their fair, powerful forms. *Great Warriors, stand ready, for this is Mír's transcendent moment.* Then, touching each of the Familiars, she whispered into their minds, *Pray for us, then prepare for flight.*

Mír rose from concealment, standing less than two hundred paces from his foe, the Enchanter. The Elf-Mage began whispering in hushed tones, so quietly that his words might not have been heard five paces away, though shouted words could not have been understood in the storm of battle, by deafened ears. Mír's Elf-Mage form had been returned to him, and as he chanted, he drew erect, with a white mist gathering about him, and his own substance seemed to brighten, as though a servant of the Maker put forth his strength in a pit festering with Demons.

Wylar shifted forward to stand behind Mír on his right, then Orantes shuffled to a place just behind Mír on his left. The Adepts, too, began chanting soft words: the air shimmered in front of them, as transparent curtains charged with sorcerous energies shifted into place.

Mír's form glowed silver and white. Sounds attended his gathering strength: mountain streams in spring, the forest at dusk. With ears deafened by thunder, Sentauris could only sense the music, though in spite of their muted tones, in spite of the Enchanter's great contest before Gravengate, Helcar was becoming aware of them.

The Enchanter stiffened, lifting his head like an enormous beast, sniffing an air filled with ash and ozone. His stream of dark flashes of lightning faltered, then failed. Slowly, as though discovering that Death lurked behind him, Helcar turned to face a gleaming Mír. Sentauris reached forward to touch both Orantes and Wylar.

"First cast!" She called into their minds. "First cast comes from the Enchanter! Stand ready!"

Helcar the Enchanter raised both hands: a torrent of necromantic energies leaped toward Mír and his Adept guardians. Wylar and Orantes cried aloud as their spell shields withered and died. But a second, greater shielding flowed from their outstretched hands: it held for a moment, then blackened, withering as dark energies tore at the Adepts' magic. Orantes sobbed and staggered. His own life force was being drawn into faltering shields and becoming consumed. Panting, chanting aloud, both Adepts fell back, then sank slowly to their knees.

Mír's voice rang out above the thunder of battle magic. Strands of brown mage power rose from the ground and wound themselves about Helcar's feet. Wisps of silver and white emerged from midair, striving to bind the Enchanter's arms.

With a snarl, Helcar burst free. Jagged, dark lightning surged from one outstretched hand. The shielding before Orantes was shattered and Orantes toppled to the ground.

Again, Mír's voice rang out: sky blue tendrils slipped over the Enchanter's arms and shoulders, while filaments of earthy brown and forest greenish wove themselves about his lower body. A stricken Orantes pulled himself to his knees and resumed his invocation of spell words from lips that dripped blood.

Writhing, twisting, Helcar began transforming his shape; he became three times human height, still growing larger as strands burst from his swelling form. At that moment, Sentauris *reached* with all the power of her Seer's inner voice and called out to Thorian.

Wizard, we hold one Enchanter. You must strike him down — and strike now!

A single bolt lashed out from Stone Mountain, white hot, pulsing with matrices of destructive power. Lightning smashed into Helcar's side, casting the unshielded Enchanter from his feet. Body smoking with burning flesh, the Enchanter began transforming himself into an instrument of rage: a monstrosity formed from dark cloudy material, with glittering eyes, jaws armed with pincers, and sharp mandibles.

Sentauris grasped Mír and turned him from the transforming Helcar. "Stone Mountain is preserved," she shouted at him. "Get us far from this place." Mír's mouth opened: soft but swift words followed. A Portal began forming before them, like a hazy midair tunnel. The two Tanu entered first and with powerful shoulders, they held the corners of the Portal firm, like twin pillars. Squint flew through, hooting aloud with his owl's voice. Whisper followed, but Ghorm would not leave the side of Sentauris.

Helcar lumbered toward them, bent on destruction. A second lightning cast smashed him aside, though he rose again on six feet, bellowing, flesh smoldering, stumbling toward the Elf-Mage and his Adept guardians.

From across a landscape of destruction, the Witch Queen raced toward them. Her own form had grown powerful, having become more than two heads taller than Wylar, flesh strong and supple, so that she leaped easily over fallen, smoldering tree trunks.

Dark lightning raced from her hands, smashing into Mír's Portal. The Tanu were shaken to their knees but did not fall. With Ghorm at her side, Sentauris pulled Wylar and Orantes through the Portal's opening. Mír then backed slowly through, eyes watching with fear and wonder as the form of Helcar stumbled toward them.

As their Portal dissolved, the Witch Queen arrived. Snarling, she shoved Helcar's monster shaped body aside. Pushing her hands into the

Portal's vacated air, she began chanting sharp words that were filled with doom. A second Portal opened, and the Witch Queen leaped through in pursuit of Mír and his band of interlopers.

With lightning still raging against them, Nairn and Manassas fought toward Helcar. In his transformed monster's rage, the Enchanter had destroyed the Goblin-headed Creature of the Darkness and was ripping at its warm flesh with sharp mandibles.

Helcar was mastered and dragged senseless from the battlefield. Fires raged over distant forests, while fallen trunks below Stone Mountain smoldered with dark flames. Thorian called swift rains down upon his place of power, and as the cloud cover passed rain downward, Storm Giants grew thin and frail, dissolving into a grey mist. At day's end, Thorian was left master of Stone Mountain — at least for the moment — ruling over his maimed fortress and the ruined lands surrounding it.

Chapter Twelve

Deadfall at Gravengate

AT DAYBREAK BALARDI PACED his upper battlements, watching as a gold sunrise rose from the east, shining first on Stone Mountain, then later, on Gravengate. Warfare had raged at Stone Mountain, far beyond the reach of his magic, except for the power of the Great Spell that the three Wizards had crafted for the League so many years before. Thorian had survived because of that spell, though the Enchanters remained only slightly damaged and completely unafraid.

The forces of the Enchanters were assembled just beyond the reach of his own power, but he understood that Gravengate was next. Had he the strength of Thorian? He might *aspire* to such power, just as Thorian wished to be the equal of Merlin, but he could not face four or five Enchanters, not even with a Great Spell in reserve, not even if aided by an Elf-Mage supported by two Adepts.

And the Seeress? Who could say what role she had played? Her part in the balance of forces at Tuvan could not have been that great, but it was wise to explore all chances to discover a rift, weakened strands in the Web of Fate that was gathering around him. One of the captains following Sentauris could be tolerated — what was his name? Farad? As for the others, Balardi found Gallandus somewhat ponderous, while Sardonicus seemed too cunning and self-assured. The Wizard sent a swift runner to find Farad.

· 𝕏 ·

Like a grey wolf, Balardi thought, as Farad neared the upper stone walls facing the rising sun. *If age has taken from him a fraction of his strength, he has gained a great deal of wisdom to replace that loss.*

"Recount to me again," the master of Gravengate said to Farad, "the course of battle at Tuvan. Specifically, I am interested in the role of Sentauris, how her strength of foretelling aided your cause."

Farad glanced at the morning sunrise then looked back to the Wizard. "Yes, the Seeress, our war-leader, and defender of the League. I know nothing of how such things are done, but it was as though she viewed a thousand future-chances, sifting, sorting, maneuvering until she found a few options that permitted our survival. Then she chose the best of those. In the first phase of Tuvan's defense, we fought the many legions of our foes, while in the second, we strove against the Creatures of the Darkness...." Farad drifted into silence because Balardi's eyes had wandered back to his golden sunrise.

So, I have stumbled quickly across a partial answer, early in this warrior's tale, thought Balardi. *The Seeress perceives a thousand future-chances and chooses only actions leading to her triumph. Thus, her vision must be put to use by the defenders of Gravengate. I greatly resented her brashness, her opposition to our policies, and even, if truth were told, to the way she treated the Wizards as asexual beings. But now I must make of this impetuous daughter of the League a fully recognized ally. It is astonishing that Merlin —*

Motion came just to the right of the sun's red rim. Patrols were waving through a lone, slumping rider — Orantes. Balardi recognized the disheveled Adept in the distance. Yet where were the others? All of them would be needed for the defense of Gravengate: two Adepts, an Elf-Mage and the Seeress. Murmuring brief words of apology to Farad, the Wizard left his sunlit perch and descended through shadowed passages to greet Orantes by the great rune-carved gates that gave the fortress its name.

From these open gates, Balardi watched the progress of Orantes, as the Adept made his way through the farms and vineyards that graced the inner Plain of Gravengate. If anything, Orantes seemed more distracted, less decisive than ever.

I had such high hopes for my Adept, Hektor, then after he vanished to be replaced by Orantes, my hopes sank like a sliver of stone into a dark marsh. Now Orantes and Wylar have unexpectedly prevailed, not only at Tuvan but also at Stone Mountain. But look at this confused, shambling creature! My heart sinks when dealing with this Adept, though perhaps I am misjudging him again. More must be learned.

Orantes' cloak was streaked with soot, and torn, while his beard was matted, his eyes heavy-lidded and his mouth drooped. As he reached the great rune-carved portals of Gravengate, swaying in his saddle, two of the guardsmen set aside spears and helped him down from his steed, and helped him through the gates toward the waiting Wizard, who found the slumping figure of the Adept somewhat discouraging.

Perhaps he has simply taken a measure of damage, thought Balardi. *Yet, whatever the case, you must restrain yourself, least mighty of three Wizards serving the League, for anger is your adversary and not your ally.*

"What tidings, Adept?" the Wizard asked quietly.

"Master," Orantes said in a strange, choked voice, "I come alone. Whether Stone Mountain survives, I cannot say, for we vanished in a turbulence of destruction. The others must be taken or destroyed by ruined Portal Magic. I fear I am the sole survivor."

"The others may yet win free," Balardi said, glancing at his guards. "Come within. You will see that Gravengate is as stoutly defended as Stone Mountain." *Why am I now called "Master" when before I was "Balardi or "Lord" when Orantes feared my anger? Much has happened to this Adept, and so I must remain patient until I understand these things.* Like a wisp of invisible smoke, the Gift within Balardi reached out and confirmed that Orantes indeed stood before him, and not some Carag shapeshifter sent by the Enchanters.

Balardi led Orantes from the gates, moving through the inner keep, where captains and sub-tier leaders were marshaling the day's watch. Orantes acknowledged their salutes with a distracted half wave, shuffling two paces behind Balardi, using his staff to support a left side that had become lame from warfare and rough travel. Twice the Adept paused when climbing the interior stairs — once to catch his breath and the second for a coughing spasm.

As they moved through the inner passageways, the Adept seemed to breathe more easily. Several times the Wizard used broad iron keys to open interior barriers, while the last portal was unsealed by an incantation.

"You must forgive us," the Wizard explained, "for failing to train you and Wylar in the devices of the League. We do not have open discussions with the Powers of the Mid-World, for they regard our alliance as something of a quiet rebellion. But the Gods have made it known to us that they are not willing to have the League expand its power — to include, for example, five Wizards, or even three Wizards and two powerful Adepts. Thus, your training was haphazard, performed in secret when the Gods were otherwise occupied." *And also, we had little confidence in the abilities of our two 'Replacement Adepts.'*

They passed through the great domed conjuring chamber in which Balardi had fused several Elementals into a Griffin. Not even a lone feather from its great wings remained. At the far end, the Wizard again intoned spell words; doors slid open, leading to a labyrinth of alcoves and recesses, where clusters of strange devices lay motionless and silent. Wall shelves held frayed grimoires and rolls of parchment. Muted lights cast a strange glow over corridors and alcoves so that most of the Wizard's constructs remained concealed by shadows.

Balardi took a deep breath before leading the Adept forward: Orantes was to become the first human permitted into his innermost places of power. "As a Wizard," Balardi said, concealing his discomfort, "in the noontime of my strength, sleep occupies but two hours of twenty-four. Another four to six hours are spent in matters of governance — decisions of state or dealing with the needs of my people. All remaining hours are spent in the craft of magic."

Orantes nodded solemnly. "And in such a place the Great Spell was crafted and used in defense of Stone Mountain. Has there been another such spell fashioned for Gravengate? I ask, Master, only because the Enchanters will soon be upon us."

Why does this make me so uncomfortable? The Wizard struggled with a sense of wrongness. "Merlin will have much to say about such matters," he said, leading Orantes to a curtained area that was somewhat more strongly lit, "and so we will ask him directly." At a motion of the Wizard's hand, the curtains were swept aside. Orantes drew in a slow, deep breath: inside a broad alcove lay a series of stone steps — marble, but tiny, terraced steps, each half a hand's breadth high, leading into the shadowed recesses of the ceiling.

Mingled on the steps were scores of hand-height figurines carved from nephrite, jade, or ivory, some inlaid with tiny gems. Not one of the figurines was recognizable as a Power of the Mid-Word, or beast-creature of Alantéa, or even an image from *The Game of the Masters*. Some were strange and remote, others stood lopsided or hollowed like primitive idols, while a few of the intricately carved figurines showed fangs and talons.

"Our Portal Magic is weak to the point of nonexistence," Balardi continued, "and so we do not leap from point to point to speak with other Wizards. When need arises, we invoke one of these small carved figures. Its counterpart is activated at Sea's Edge or Stone Mountain. No Power can know beforehand which of these small devices may serve for our communications, and no Power can successfully employ Divinations to explore these unfamiliar images."

As Balardi raised his hands in invocation, a warning rang through him like a trumpet sounding from a distant valley. In support of his wariness, devices in adjacent alcoves began rustling as though stirring in alarm.

"Something is wrong here," Balardi muttered, turning to Orantes. "Is it you, Adept? Are you carrying some talisman of the Enchanters? Have you betrayed us?"

Orantes stood ashen faced. "Master, I am as I was. But can you not sense the Portal Magic of the Enchanters? I can feel them, as though nearing the walls of Gravengate, ready to burst through."

"They will not force their way into Gravengate," Balardi said flatly, though there seemed a stirring of magic at the outskirts of Gravengate's broad plain, "not while I rule." *The eyes, Balardi, the Adept's eyes,* his mind whispered, *there's not a touch of red, no hint of wine upon his breath. Has this Adept then reformed? Or has he been transformed by sorcery?* The Wizard's mouth opened again to activate the magic that would reach to Merlin, but then another, far different voice reached into his mind.

A Carag! Sentauris burst through a distant Portal onto the Plain of Gravengate and cried out to Balardi with all the power of her far-reaching mind. *The Carag-Enchanter called Manassas stands beside you! Watch out for him!*

Balardi hurled himself to one side, but a full blast of necromantic energy struck his right arm and shoulder. The Wizard rolled and writhed: his arm, powerful with enchantments, was reaching for his own throat. He rose, scurried, and fell again, striking down talismans, devices.

Struggling to flee, the Wizard found himself slowing: the hand obeying the Enchanter had reached his throat and was beginning to crush it like a ripened fruit.

Manassas laughed and shed the form of Orantes with a single shrug. "Wizard, are you 'Master' where you dwell? I do not believe so." The Carag-Enchanter began to amass bulk, casually becoming twice the height of Orantes. As he pursued Balardi, the great arms of Manassas smashed and crushed all the talismanic devices in his path — the lifetime's work of a great Wizard.

Balardi lurched into a dark alcove and struggled to breathe. His mouth croaked out spell words, so that power flowed to his left hand, and it was able at last to tear its dark twin from its master's throat. As his arms grappled with each other, the Wizard scrambled through his labyrinth of workrooms. Behind him, the Enchanter casually smashed the work of decades.

"Old fool," the Carag called out to him, "you are far too weak! Our agenda called for a time of hesitation so that we might pursue greater matters, but we can no longer prop you up!" The Enchanter began smashing down walls, struggling to reach the Wizard and crush him forever. Balardi ran, calling out spell words and at last his right hand fell to his side, still and cold as stone.

"How did you gain your reputation, old man?" The Carag called Manassas boomed out. "At best you were nothing but a sickly sister to the other Wizards."

Balardi halted, panting. Only two walls lay between himself, and the Carag-Enchanter named Manassas, though now a hot wrath was blazing inside the Wizard.

"Weak I may be," Balardi snarled, "but I am the might and the power in my fortress!" Spell words leaped from his lips; a storm of Entities, Dominions, and Elementals rose in defense of Gravengate. Manassas was battered, but he held his ground, leaning as though against a mighty wind. Spell words also sped from the Enchanter's lips, though his magic became twisted, deflected, and blunted. A huge, night-black hand loomed in the darkness, reaching for Manassas, but he destroyed it, blasting the hand into nothingness with necromantic energies.

A strength of sorcery surged all around them, power summoned by Balardi. Manassas struggled to draw it to himself, but only a fraction could be diverted. Slowly at first, then more rapidly, the Enchanter was forced to retreat. More destruction followed as Manassas broke apart every instrument of magic in his path. The Enchanter burst through the labyrinth out into Balardi's great conjuring chamber, pursued by entities, as well as crippled sorcerous devices that lashed at the Enchanter with energies that he could not completely identify.

Again, transforming himself, Manassas first dissolved the stonework of the high ceiling, then launched himself like an enormous bat-creature though the gap. Balardi emerged from the labyrinth, hurling blasts of power at the floating Enchanter with the one good hand left to him.

Words of power flashed from the bat-shaped mouth of Manassas: a Portal formed in the morning sky, and through this seam in the air the Enchanter vanished.

· X ·

At the outskirts of the great Plain of Gravengate, Mír slipped to the ground, completely exhausted. Orantes collapsed, groaning, while Wylar stood beside his fellow Adept, bent like a tree battered by fierce winds. The

Familiars lay sprawled on the ground like discarded toys. Only Mír's Tanu bodyguards and Sentauris stood erect, and she panted as though she had just completed a great race.

She *reached* for the Witch Queen, the Enchanter who had pursued them with such ferocity through thrusting, pulsing tunnels in the air. The Witch Queen Azüre had finally lost their trail; once again Mír had saved them. Yet in the heaving, twisting passageways, one completely grim power had sought their doom, while a gentler and weaker one had attempted to preserve them. Sentauris thought she could name the second power but not the first.

The second, more feminine power, was calling to the Seeress in remote, discreet tones so that only Sentauris could hear, and in the quiet aftermath of their pursuit, she could easily recognize the tones of her old patroness, Pallas Athena. She turned to their war party; only Ghorm, always tuned closely to her moods, met her eyes.

"The Wizard waits for us at Gravengate," she said softly. "Go with the others to stand before him. Let the Adepts speak flowery, delicate words on my behalf, to say that I have been summoned elsewhere for a few hours, but after I will attach myself, in all humility and good will, to this Wizard's service."

She reached out and touched Ghorm gently, speaking into his mind, *An old patroness calls for me, Ghorm; it is possible that she has wise words to offer us. Go, and do not transform my words with subtle double meanings.*

At the outskirts of Gravengate's broad plain, where orchards and vineyards flourished, Ghorm watched as Sentauris jogged quietly and quickly through a white-blossomed apple-grove, then vanished into a stand of trees. He stared up into the clear skies of midmorning, then back toward Gravengate: wagons were being sent for their war party and Ghorm thought he could recognize the forms of Sardonicus and Gallandus. *They are better company than the Adepts, at least.*

When the wagons arrived, Orantes let strong arms lift him into the wagon, then he slumped to the wagon's base, though his mind twisted and turned inside his head. *I have stood against Vorrs, stood nearly weaponless against Uraks. Against Creatures Indomitable my legs called on me to flee, though I stood my ground. But these Enchanters...that they began as humans makes them an even greater horror. If I only had more strength...but I am like a fat lapdog ranged against a pride of lions, and I do not think I can stand again in battle against our foes.*

An exhausted Mír gathered enough strength to sit as a passenger beside a greying captain named Gallandus. Mír's mouth spoke polite words, barely understanding what his own voice was saying. Behind them, Orantes sprawled, face up with closed eyelids, while Wylar struggled to sit. Mír gathered his remaining strength and summoned his Tanu allies.

Turning to speak with them as they trudged alongside his wagon, Mír murmured, "We knew that this moment would come. I must become a lone renegade; otherwise, the Gods will choose to see this war as an alliance of the Tanu, the Sidhe and the Elf-Lords with the Wizards and their League. Our peoples would suffer greatly." The two Tanu warriors shook their heads gravely: no, they would not depart.

"All three of us know that you must be gone," Mír continued in a soft voice, "and you must advise all who will listen about this struggle. Our brethren have places in the courts of the Powers of the Mid-World. Let the Gods know what is truly happening in this unequal struggle. Go, before you become known as allies of the Wizards. Go with the Maker's blessing."

The Tanu halted with heads bowed. A seam in the air rose from behind them, swallowed them up, and they vanished.

Mír also bowed his head but would not permit himself to weep. As Gravengate came closer, more fully into view, the Elf-Mage roused himself to study the fortress-dwelling of Balardi.

Gravengate the Unfinished it was called by the sharp-tongued servant of the Seeress, though only the western walls are less than full height, and much of the inner keep seems complete. I can feel its strength, as I could the fabric of Stone Mountain. Turrets form strong points along battlemented parapets. To the west, a tall tower rises, looming over two inner strong points. One fortress is hidden, but the other, known as the Citadel of the Keep, is massive, housing the Wizard and his devices.

Balardi, by reputation, is the least powerful of the three Wizards, though his real strength reverberates through the Plain of Gravengate. Of my people, the Elf-Lords are mightiest in arts magical, though I do not believe any one of them is the equal of even Balardi, the least of three Wizards; and such an outcome is more than passing strange. Yet the Wizards' open display of power has angered one or more of the Greater Gods, and so the Enchanters have been loosed upon the Wizards and their League. I do not believe the Wizards' alliance will prevail when the Enchanters fully focus their might against the League. And so, Mír the Elf-Mage, when does the vow sworn over your Tanu ally, Tallus, expire? When do those powerful but vain words lose their force?

· X ·

Gravengate greeted its new arrivals with a fanfare of trumpets. Wylar stood as their carriage passed through the gates, though Orantes could only manage to sit up and extend one weary hand in a half salute. Balardi met them with an enthusiasm that seemed intended to reassure his own people as well as making the newcomers feel welcome.

Mír, you are tired, the mage-power within him prompted. *Rouse yourself and regard this Wizard and his still-as-stone right arm. Mír, this Wizard has taken a great wound, caused by the powerful necromantic magic of our enemies. Mír, this struggle for Gravengate may be over, even before we added our strength to the great fortress.*

Sensing their exhaustion, Balardi had quiet, dark inner chambers set aside for each of them. Wylar fell instantly into a deep sleep, dreaming of Sentauris as she swam naked beside him in warm river-pools. Orantes faded after a single goblet of wine, while Mír, utterly drained, slept for once as mortals did. The three Familiars struggled to wait for Sentauris, but Ghorm and Squint found themselves floating adrift on the backwaters of old, tired dreams.

Only Whisper remained awake, and so he left the darkened chamber, exploring again the vast, unfinished fortress. In former times, he had been forced to care for a wayward Orantes, but now he was left to his own devices in the fabled Gravengate the Unfinished. The smell of strange magics seemed stronger to his Shade's senses, and he passed deeper into the keep with growing interest: like a bloodhound discovering an ancient bog, he found scores of essences he could not identify, but a number of them excited his senses.

Many passages were blocked, some more thoroughly than others; but they were barred to creatures of flesh and blood, not to a Shade. Blocks of stone were sealed carefully by mortar, but everywhere lay open cracks, gaps through which denser creatures than himself might easily pass. Slipping past barriers, he became gradually aware that he was following Balardi's footsteps as the Wizard passed deeper into his hive of magic, moving slowly toward his great conjuring chamber.

Perversely, Whisper followed the Wizard, not to spy out his devices, but to test all the spell words and sealing devices employed by the Master of Gravengate. The Familiar slipped through one sealed door, then passed through an adjacent wall to bypass a second. At a third, he halted; some entity regarded Whisper with a sense of confusion, not knowing whether to give the alarm.

Whisper backed away, slipped beneath the floor, and easily avoided the guardian. Pleased with himself, the Familiar continued on the Wizard's trail. As he traveled, Whisper sensed ghosts, echoes of the Wizard's many previous passages. Only one lone scent accompanied that of the Wizard's, a recent addition that had the smell of Orantes, but it was a subtly changed Orantes, somehow mixed with a completely non-human scent

The Wizard took out a circlet of great iron keys and unlocked the door to his labyrinth of workrooms. After entering, Balardi sealed it behind him. Whisper was unable to proceed: beneath and above, to the left and right, this last passage was secured even against himself.

Whisper drifted away, intent, and excited, tracing the scents left by the false Orantes. If his suspicions were correct, that same being — a Carag joining the Enchanters — had masqueraded as Orantes; so perhaps Whisper had learned to smell out the Enchanters.

Balardi allowed himself a half smile as he felt Whisper withdraw. The Guardian of the Third Gate would need to be retrained or replaced, but the exercise had been useful. He passed through his many alcoves of ruined devices; unseen servants had struggled to reorder his places of magic, though few of his devices could be restored or reconstructed.

No matter: what mattered was his imminent defeat and the forthcoming destruction of Gravengate. With his good left hand, he threw back the curtains of the alcove containing his many communication devices. Choosing one at random — a bulbous creature crowned with a jumble of ears and tentacles — Balardi leaned forward and spoke into it.

"Merlin, it is I, Balardi, your fellow Wizard and the sorely beset master of Gravengate. I come to you for counsel." As always, there came a pause, as Merlin left his labors and sought his own communication devices.

At last, from a smaller distended shape on an upper shelf, came the voice of Merlin: "I am here; I will listen and respond."

Balardi drew a deep breath. As always, to speak with Merlin was to deal with the unknown: at times, Merlin was utterly remote, while on other days Merlin was warm, almost friendly, sometimes even showing flashes of a dry wit. "We are all fated to die one day," Balardi said. "I am prepared to stand here for the Maker and for our League and yield my life, but are my people also required to die? Many can find shelter among the Mid-World Powers or flee to other portions of Alantéa the Forerunner."

"On this day," came the thin, distant voice of Merlin, "they are safer within your walls than outside. Later, we shall see. Now, do I perceive that you are at less than full strength? Some test of power I sensed when you put forth your full strength as Master of Gravengate, but no tale of damage to you has come to me."

"I am wounded," Balardi said somberly. Lifting his arm like a weight of frozen dead flesh, he placed it before the device linking himself to Merlin. As though peering from several eyes, other devices surrounding the arm were activated: some made broad humming noises, while others shimmered with pale lights. Moments later, Balardi felt a tingling sensation, the first tremor in his dead arm since his encounter with Manassas.

"The power of these Enchanters is not unsubtle," came the faint, unemotional voice of Merlin. "It will be a few days before your wound is completely healed."

Balardi withdrew his damaged arm, massaging its cold and painful flesh with his left hand. "Healed or unhealed, the strength of these

Enchanters is too great for me alone: those approaching Gravengate number five, while I have only two untrained Adepts and an Elf-Mage of middle rank, who could not by himself counter the weakest of the Enchanters."

"The Enchanter Pentarchus has lingered far from Stone Mountain, and seems unlikely to present himself before Gravengate," came the thin, distant voice of Merlin. "The Seeress may know something of Pentarchus and his role. Have you spoken with her?"

"I have not. Until my encounter with Manassas, I had hoped that her slight talents might save us. Yet no matter how far her Sight may reach, she is still no Enchantress to stand beside me wielding a strength of battle magic."

"Consider her instead, as a catalyst, a mover of many significant forces. Wherever she passes, a tale of power travels beside her."

Balardi nodded and was silent for a moment, as though following Merlin's thoughts down complicated passageways. "I will speak with the Seeress, before seeking further counsel from you," Balardi said, and he withdrew from the alcove. Behind Balardi in the darkened alcove, all those strange, perverse shapes employed in communication crumbled into dust, then other equally strange shapes slowly formed to take their place.

· X ·

As the voice drew Sentauris through fields and orchards, a fatigue almost greater than exhaustion settled over her. Passing into a stand of tall, thick pines, she discovered a dark, quiet place, where all the usual flying creatures of midmorning had grown still and silent. Before her lay a makeshift bed of soft pine branches, a place that glowed briefly then grew as dark as an overcast, deep forest.

I am being summoned through gates of dreams, she thought, *and I am so tired.* She slipped down onto a resting place of soft branches and in the pace of ten heartbeats was fast asleep.

As before, she found herself standing in the temple of dreams chosen by Pallas Athena. The Goddess appeared before her, looming twice her height, though Pallas Athena no longer seemed remote and withdrawn; instead, she was visibly agitated, almost mortal in her tension.

"Wayward Daughter, what have you done to me?"

"Holy Mother," Sentauris said softly, "I could never seek your unhappiness. Yet when I sensed your hand guiding us through the enchanted passageways, I also found a second hand trying mightily to destroy us. Can you name this second force? Mordred has been named the coauthor of our ills, while this second, greater Power remains anonymous."

On the dais before Sentauris, Pallas Athena paced back and forth, deep in thought. "Yes, Mordred the Renegade is a being who will find his existence far less comfortable in the future. But this other, this unnamed Power, he was a greater Power than I am. Do you understand those words?"

Sentauris bowed her head, sensing the unhappiness of her proud patroness.

"I am both wary and angry," Pallas Athena continued. "Now I must shore up my realm against the onslaught of this particular God; such are the realities of power in the Mid-World of the Truce. Also, I loathe these Enchanters, so filled with the need to kill others, who have been armed by Mordred and this other Great God, while you, a heroine whom the Gods should favor, fight with weapons that will never harm your foes. Now, I will change that imbalance: beneath your bower, you will find six enchanted arrows that will have the power to destroy your enemies, be they Creatures Indomitable, or even Enchanters. Also...." The Goddess seemed to hesitate.

"Also, it may be that your Adepts have abandoned their Dragonfire somewhat too quickly."

Pallas Athena halted and looked down on Sentauris with a studied, remote benevolence. "Now, I have said too much, done too much, and I tremble at the edges of the Truce Terms. Sentauris, this is the last time I will speak to you; I cannot continue to give you aid, no matter how heroically you struggle. I must be done with you. Farewell, and may the God you have chosen reward you for your devotion."

Sentauris opened her mouth to offer profuse thanks, but instead, a remote ungovernable voice spoke through her lips: "Pallas Athena, Goddess, and Power of the Mid-World, you are infinitely resourceful, and you will find a way to speak to me again before I pass into Death's Dream Kingdom."

The Goddess stared down at an ashen faced Sentauris. "Do not apologize, daughter, for I recognize that specific tone of voice when your Farsight speaks, and so I will reconsider all these matters."

Sentauris woke with a start, rolling off her bed of soft fronds. While one hand wiped sleep from her eyes, a second fumbled beneath pine branches to discover a canister holding six slender arrows. Each was thin as a wand, shafts ebony-dark, narrow heads of tarnished silver, with rows of white feathers, bristly and thick. When she touched a shaft, her hand recoiled: images of falling Creatures Indomitable and shrieking Enchanters pushed their way into her mind.

Struggling not to touch any arrow directly, she tore strips of cloth from her cloak, and carefully wrapped each shaft so that none of the six would jostle against each other. With the canister strapped to her back, she turned and broke into a long, loping run that guided her back to Gravengate. Sentries met her at the outskirts of the great plain, offering her a swift steed.

·)(·

In less than an hour, Sentauris stood before Balardi and his chief advisors, consisting of the watch captains of Gravengate, and the Wizard's chief counselors. None of her mercenary captains had been summoned, while both Adepts and Elf-Mage still slept.

Sentauris listened closely to Balardi's voice, so filled with fulsome words, phrases that were undermined by an awkward uncertainty, as he glanced back and forth between Sentauris and the canister on her back that radiated such a strength of magic.

When Balardi had finished, she bowed low and said in soft tones, "My thanks for your kind words, Master of Gravengate. Even without my present fatigue, I could not hope to respond with your eloquence. I should soon join my comrades in sleep, but first, perhaps you might spare me two moments for a private audience." With a slight frown, Balardi dismissed his counselors.

When they had departed, Sentauris handed the Wizard the canister bearing those arrows forged by Pallas Athena. "These were intended as weapons for my use," she said in soft tones, as Balardi ran his fingers over each ebony-dark shaft, "though I will use them in accordance with your wishes as Lord of Gravengate."

The Wizard looked up at her as though waking from a long, troubled dream. "These are the deadliest Mid-World Weapons I have ever encountered," he murmured. "It is strange that before this moment, I looked only for survival and now, perhaps, I can dream of triumph."

·)(·

In the darkest part of a sleepless night, Sardonicus rose and dressed swiftly. On the pretext of checking the night watch, he climbed from the base of the innermost keep to its pinnacle, where he could view all sides of Gravengate's fortifications. To the east, where aid might come from Thorian, two Enchanters had made their camp, surrounded by war bands of Uraks. In the west, the remaining two Enchanters blocked aid from Merlin, with Vorrs prowling on the outskirts of their camp. North lay a diminished Army of the Undead, while the camp of their human legions serving the Enchanters lay to the south. Bonfires surged from the southern encampment, but in other directions, only pale lights glimmered.

Creatures of the Darkness were said to roam behind each sector, feasting on all the warm-blooded beings that they encountered.

More than a fortnight after the coming of the Enchanters, Gravengate was completely sealed; Sardonicus felt like an ant on a small cleft of sand in the middle of a stream, watching as grain by grain the sand forming that ant's support was swept away.

Fight and run, fight and run, always choosing your own place of battle, and if your foes threaten to encircle you, don't bother to fight, simply run. How did you manage to forget, Sardonicus, the first lessons of those who fight for gold?

Your skills brought gold, your good fortune brought glory, but now the payment of your life seems to be coming due. Do not waver, do not beg for mercy: this moment was foredoomed when you chose the hirelings' path.

Sardonicus stared up into overcast night skies through which only wispy pale patches of stars could be seen. He wondered, with great skepticism, if the Maker was as the Servants described: benevolent, understanding, forgiving. Nevertheless, it would not hurt to try.

Maker, he prayed, *Lord of the Universe, seldom have I traveled in paths set forth by you, and I come but late to your table, yet still in your mercy, I hope you will set a place for me.*

· ɤ ·

As Sardonicus offered his first prayer as a grown man, Sentauris was asleep, dreaming the dreams of a Seeress. Her Farsight took her first to the Saugus where the great river ran hard with the snowmelt of late spring. Then she seemed to drift north and west to the hidden place sheltering her uncle, Vlasoff. A smile slipped over her sleeping face.

As her dreaming mind drifted closer to Vlasoff that smile vanished. A hunting party was slipping through the night forest. A team of three Vorrs formed a vanguard, sniffing at the ground as they led the other hunters. Five Carags followed the Vorr sentries, armed with sabers, and one carried a heavy backpack filled with metal.

Uncle! — her dreaming mind shrieked. — Uncle, they are coming with torture tools! Get away!—

Nothing happened, except that her dreaming vision expanded: if Vorrs and Carags were not enough of a nightmare, their flanks were protected by Uraks. On each of their flanks seven Uraks, stalked cautiously through the forest. Holding drawn daggers, without heavy mail, clad only in leather, they passed soundlessly through the sleeping darkness.

A dreaming Sentauris twisted in the night. A death squad, a killing party! And I can do nothing!

Suddenly, the leading Vorr sighed and slumped to the ground. Two small shafts seemed to sprout from its eye sockets. Then the other two Vorrs were down, but incompletely dead, so that they thrashed and moaned. One Carag went down, then another.

A dreaming Sentauris stiffened in surprise. The hunters were themselves hunted — by Elven sentries!

More arrows swept from hidden places in the dark forest, and then the silent struggle grew louder. A score of Sidhe warriors emerged from the darkness. Armored by light chain mail, holding broadswords, they attacked leather clad Uraks and cut them down. Two Carags cast aside their human disguises and sought to flee on four legs, but arrows leaped out of the darkness so that every member of the death squad sent by Mordred lay dead in the night forest.

· Ж ·

Balardi paced back and forth as he spoke to Merlin from afar. "Three weeks have passed since the beginning of this siege, and now concentric rings of magic and men and monsters have formed about Gravengate like bands of steel. An Enchanter lies to the north, to the south, to the east, and to the west. I am surrounded by powers that I cannot match."

"These Enchanters," Merlin murmured, pausing before he continued. "Other, unknown challenges face the Enchanters, and so they have left Pentarchus behind to deal with those problems. Placing an Enchanter on four sides of Gravengate is merely an early show of force. Soon they will gather — to the north, I believe, to deal with those matters that confuse and divide them."

"And yet daily," Balardi said, voice rising in frustration, "daily and even hourly, we are assailed by archers and catapults, and after, a stormy tide of magic surges over us. In all, I have no time to build the greater spells required to counter our foes or cause them discomfort equal to my own."

"Against this distant force of magic could not an Adept or the Elf-Mage stand guard, and rouse you only at great need?"

Balardi frowned, unhappy with the direction of Merlin's thought. Candor forced him to reply, "That might well be possible."

"And as for the martial defense of Gravengate, you now have battle tested captains, or one of your own people might be raised to Captain General of Gravengate."

"Those mercenaries all look to Sentauris," Balardi said in hushed tones, "even my own watch captains seek her counsel." Merlin made no response. During the silence, Balardi could feel the great fortress shudder: huge stones were crashing into the unfinished west walls, battering at its already uneven edges.

"Indirectly," Balardi continued, struggling to contain his irritation, "you are suggesting that the Seeress become my battle leader. I had hoped for a more elegant solution."

"No simulacra," came the voice of Merlin, "or Sendings or magical servants might do as well as those beings now in your service."

With considerable difficulty Balardi kept his temper restrained, speaking measured words to Merlin before severing his connection with his brother Wizard. At this encounter, Merlin had again been completely remote and unsympathetic — though logical. As he stepped from the darkened alcove, a portion of Balardi's mind flared in anger, but another segment appreciated the dark irony of his next action: before nightfall, the Seeress, Sentauris would become Captain General of Gravengate.

· ✕ ·

Squint flapped his tired wings through the heavy night air until he found the distant, dark section of the upper ramparts where Whisper and Ghorm lay hidden. He kept one roasted duck's wing for himself while passing the other to Ghorm, who bit into it with a grunt of satisfaction. Ghorm was weary and Squint's shoulders ached from extended periods of flight, so both he and Ghorm ate in silence.

"Chomp, chomp, chomp," Whisper said.

"Easy for you," Ghorm muttered. "You seem to need only shadows to keep yourself going."

"He needs pools of darkness, pockets of magic, and a little moisture," Squint said. "You should hear Whisper grumble when everything gets too dry."

"I have no complaints," Whisper said softly, staring up where dark clouds passed in front of a full moon. "It's dark and moist, and I'm here with my fellow Familiars, celebrating everything we've accomplished. Look at how much things have changed in little more than three weeks."

Squint swallowed before speaking. "I never thought that the Wizard would listen to Sentauris. I asked you before, Ghorm, but you never replied. Did she give him some sort of magic potion?"

"Not a drop," Ghorm said. He took a piece of cloth from his pockets and wiped the duck grease from his mouth. "It seems that even a Wizard can change when death comes tapping on his door. What surprises me is what's happened to the Adepts — not long ago they were feeble, and now suddenly they're growing in power."

"The Elf-Mage Mír is still a greater force than either Wylar or Orantes," Squint said carefully, trying to slip cautiously around Ghorm's jealous feelings regarding the Adepts.

"At the beginning of this war," Ghorm muttered, "the Adepts were overshadowed by their predecessors, Hektor and Antéus. Now because of Wylar and Orantes, nobody will even remember the names of those old Adepts."

Whisper let his shadowy form rise slowly above the upper walls so that he could look down to the siege of Gravengate below where hundreds of watchfires ringed the fortress, and scattered moonlight beamed down over the machines of war manned by their foes. Trails of smoke were lifting into the air, and Whisper could still smell the burnt flesh from cooking fires. He shuddered to think what the Uraks had been feeding on, and he could see and sense that Vorrs still prowled through the darkness, seeking the flesh of any creatures still alive and unprotected on the surrounding Plain of Gravengate.

"Squint and I both feel your resentment," Whisper said in his soft Shade's voice, "and we have our own fears and discomforts. But look down to the fires and devices of our foes — in a short while, we may be destroyed by the depth of their hatred, and then all our hopes and worries and jealousies will be done forever."

·))(·

Sentauris stood staring skyward, waiting for cloud cover to part and reveal a full, glistening moon, one that shimmered with the land's new warmth. As Merlin had predicted, the Enchanters had gathered four leagues northeast of Gravengate, believing that the sullen quiet of the fortress was only a prelude to its forthcoming downfall. On this night — four weeks after her arrival at Gravengate — the Enchanters would learn otherwise.

As she stared into the night, the cloud cover thinned, then parted, like thick curtains transformed first into flimsy gauze then passing into nothingness. A full force of moonlight shimmered over their lightly armored horseriders.

"The gates," she murmured to Gallandus; her voice seemed closer to a sigh than a call to battle. Balardi had disdained the construction of sally ports, and so teams of men were forced to push aside the great rune-carved portals of the fortress. Out in the moonlight, prowling Vorrs lifted thick-furred heads and howled. A great gong rang out, but timidly, uncertainly.

A full half-tier of two hundred and fifty armed horseriders spilled from the gates. From his topmost tower, Balardi spoke words, releasing a thin, pale mist: as it coalesced, a lens formed above the Plain of Gravengate, so that the moonlight's strength was doubled. A strange light shimmered over the battlefield, like sunlight shining on some remote planet.

Farad and Sardonicus rode at the lead, bearing long lances, while Sentauris commanded their rearguard. As they picked up their pace, the fury of battle swept aside all their doubts and hesitations. Vorrs tore at their flanks, but outriders armed with sabers slashed them down. Sentauris shot three, saving her arrows forged by Athena for the greater battle to come.

Clusters of men, bands of Uraks were struck down as their sortie fought toward the siege engines facing west. In the brightest of moonlights, Vorrs howled, Uraks bellowed, and trumpet calls echoed over the plain. Signal fires flared to the south.

All around her, Sentauris could feel the rush of man, beast, and metal as they surged across Gravengate's Plain like an unbreakable wave. Only once did a Carag try to mingle with their ranks, posing as a straggler, but outriders marked him and left him bleeding and broken on the plain.

In the space of minutes, they reached the cluster of siege engines that had pounded the unfinished West Walls during the first four weeks of the siege. Those guarding their casting devices were overwhelmed by one swift charge; survivors fled into the night, though the enhanced moonlight left them without even a shield of darkness. Men of Gravengate dismounted, then drew axes and hewed at coils of rope, or battered at wooden machineries. Others brewed fire. Smoke rose from ruined devices then fire blossomed, adding a strange glow to the eerie, enchanted moonlight that filled the Plain with such bright light.

But other forces were shifting in the night. Sentauris stood, arrow notched, staring back toward Gravengate: their foes were rallying power to the gates so that all those left outside would be trapped on the Plain and destroyed before daybreak.

Adepts, she called with her mind. *Wylar, guard our backs. Orantes, a force of magic power comes to the gates. You two must hold our pathway to safety free.* The herald who had been forced to linger at her side sounded a reluctant trumpet call. Sardonicus and Farad called out loud, swift orders. Men remounted, with sergeants using harsh language to herd stragglers.

They made swift passage back to Gravengate, with the machineries of their foes all askew and ablaze behind them. But power was looming before the gates: the Undead figures of Murat and Fiüre. A force of sorcerous power had been grafted to their lifeless bodies, so the two dead things stood glowing with an unworldly light. And behind them loomed the strangely resurrected Creatures Indomitable, each born long ago with a strength of sorcery at its disposal.

And above them the glittering lens of Balardi was being challenged by the necromantic energies of the Enchanters — and as the Wizard's lens withered, a fog of dark energies was surging over the moon.

Their horses faltered and shied from the gates. Sentauris forced her way to the forefront, to stand beside Sardonicus and Farad. — *Adepts!* — her mind called out, and from above the gates, Wylar and Orantes lashed at the Undead servants of the Enchanters. As forces of magic surged back and forth, Sentauris led their half-tier sweeping left, then slid them through the gates along the eastern walls.

As the gates closed behind them, Sentauris called out into the night, "Destruction comes for your dead renegade souls. Tell your masters the Enchanters to depart from the League or be dead themselves forever!"

· X ·

"Shrieking hot dregs of dung!" Orantes cried out, then hurled the smoking metal band against a pillar. The ring shattered, spilling bits of hot metal over stone floors, while Orantes danced in pain and massaged his burned fingers. On the Adept's hands were several bands, three on his left, two on his right: each was gold or silver, inlaid with clusters of tiny gems.

"So close," Wylar murmured. He bent down and examined a fragment of ruined silver; on his own fingers also were five rings, devices that stored coils of Dragonfire, through which a fierce heat might be focused. Above them the high windows of the fortress filtered the last light of day. Then the light of several torches slowly filled the chamber as daylight diminished.

"Burn yourself, not me the next time," Orantes muttered, still rubbing his fingers, then he raised his head suddenly. "Is that...?"

Wylar drew on his cloak swiftly. "Come. The Seeress needs us again. She does not dare to call us directly for fear of angering Balardi, so she sighs, letting a whisper of her thoughts reach out to us."

"Then it's mediation, not magic required of me," Orantes said, stepping with swift dancing feet toward a side table where he poured wine into a battered goblet. As he followed Wylar, Orantes gulped down the wine with one quick motion, then with a second motion pitched the already battered cup over his left shoulder, so that it clattered on the floor beside broken bits of the Adepts' Dragonfire magic.

Mír waited for them outside the Wizard's council chamber, his pale, lean face showing a gloomy expression. Wordlessly, the three entered Balardi's chamber, where the Wizard broke off his argument with Sentauris to sneer at them.

"So, the Seeress has brought her flunkies and her ally to argue her case. Hear me!" The Wizard stood, pounding his council table with his newly healed right hand. "I had sooner surrender Gravengate openly to the

Enchanters than to have it subverted from me by an adventuress of the Mid-World."

Sentauris remained seated but turned to glance at the Adepts with raised eyebrows. "We disagree — again — but this is a small matter, and perhaps I should simply return to my chamber." She rose, but Wylar waved her back, then sat.

"If this were simply a 'small disagreement,'" the Adept said quietly, "you would not have sent for us." Wylar looked to Balardi. "Will you not sit, Lord? You are Master of Gravengate, and we will obey your commands, but as counselors and servants, perhaps we deserve a calmer hearing."

Balardi stared down at them, disbelief and mockery flashing over his bearded face. "How these worms have turned," he said softly, then sat. "Well, why not a parlay? We should send for wine, for your colleague's sober tongue is lickspittle dry." The Wizard signaled with his mind, and surprised porters in a far chamber scrambled into motion.

"So, as 'Master of Gravengate,'" the Wizard continued, "I have heard from the Seeress a suggested foray, one that would profit us little, and endanger the servants of the Adepts unduly. I have rejected her proposal, a decision that should have meant tale's end, yet here we sit."

They glanced at Sentauris, who sighed before speaking. "The Enchanters gather once again later this night. I foresee their summoning of Pentarchus. Whisper — properly prepared — may discover more of the nature of their alliance, and a chance exists that the Enchanters may name the second Mid-World Power who is author of our ills."

"Pus and cloud magic," the Wizard sneered and rose again to pace back and forth. "What does it matter that the Enchanters love one another or not, or whether some power is 'named'? They will still come with masses of men and a stormtide of magic to destroy me and my people."

"It may well matter," Mír said softly. "In spite of your great power, Master of Gravengate, your links to the Mid-World are questionable, and thus little news from beyond your borders reaches into the heart of your besieged kingdom. At will, I am linked to the Elf-Kindreds who dwell throughout Alantéa and have many embassies in the courts of Mid-World Powers.

"I can tell you that Mordred has been identified as the coauthor of your misery and is under pressure throughout the Mid-World. A watch has been set upon Mordred's place of power so that none pass within without being marked. Shapeshifting Carags are being purged by the Gods, with scores perishing each day. The Kindreds gather the carcasses of Vorrs into vast bonfires, while Taurag, the father of Trolls, has called for the heads of a thousand Uraks. If we 'name' a second Power, other miseries will flow to that God, for the Mid-World seems to detest alliances between Powers."

Balardi ceased to pace and sat back again in his place at Council's head. Cupbearers had placed wine before him, and he drank somberly. "So, this goal may be of worth, but what of the odds, which I discovered to be poor, and dangerous to the servants of the Adepts?"

"If you have cast a future upon it once," Wylar said, "then let us cast it a second time." The Wizard shrugged but drew from a pouch at his side two handfuls of ornamental figures, each no larger than a fingertip. Whispering soft words, the Wizard let the pieces fall lightly over his council table, where they whirled and spun then became motionless. All gathered about the Divination; Sentauris knew little of the Wizard's Divinations but saw that each piece held an image from *The Game of the Masters*.

"A jumble," muttered Orantes, "but in this pattern, we see the potential for damage to our servants, though such danger seems considerably short of doom."

"While in the larger pattern," Wylar added, "we see that the odds are far less than half that our Familiars will name the Power opposing us."

"But what is this?" Mír asked, pointing to a third section where the tiny figures seemed more densely clustered. "Doom lies over there, but doom for which side, dependent upon which events?"

"A jumble," Orantes repeated, shaking his head.

Sentauris sighed a third time. "Do not be angry with me, that my talents are specific to this field. Within a thousand frames of future chances, three hundred lead to the naming of this second power and the transformation of our struggle. In fifty of these thousand chances, Whisper or Squint is destroyed. In somewhat greater than four hundred, our actions provoke the Enchanters — untimely and less prepared — to battle."

"So that is the way of it," Balardi murmured, nodding his head. "We will go forward with your plan. I am not as stubborn as I showed myself, for sometimes it is wise to press hard to discover what forces are truly at work. Send for the Familiars."

· Ӿ ·

Hours later, Whisper fluttered swiftly through the night, cloaked in the Wizard's spells so that even his flimsy shadows were disguised. Above him, Squint soared, enchanted wings made powerful for this night so that even a hawk might not match his strength. If Vorrs sensed their passage, it was only as a vague feeling of unease, like a wisp of cloud passing across the moon.

Just as Whisper's speed had been trebled, his hearing had been equally increased, so that he could hear the desperate panting of a fox pursued by Vorrs, the distant rumbling sounds of Creatures Indomitable prowling through the night, and even the wingbeats of thousands of mosquitoes as they sought the harsh, bitter blood of Uraks.

As instructed, Whisper circled the Enchanters' camp, approaching it from the north, a direction from which the Enchanters anticipated reinforcements, not shadowy spies. Bored sentries sipped wine beside watchfires and were ignored. Several nonhuman guardians were easily bypassed. With the great command tent of the Enchanters looming before him, Whisper took the equivalent of a deep breath and sank beneath the ground, slipping easily through the earth's loam and clay until he settled under a far corner of the Enchanters' place of power.

Whisper rose through the soil with great caution, every sense alert. Muffled sounds slowly became words. Muted torchlight could be seen and sensed above him, and so he shifted toward a pool of shadows.

"...Grind, grind, grind," came the voice, a female voice, but one belonging to no soft maiden, "until we come to a deathly grip, then we tear their flesh and their souls to ribbons."

"Those words should be spoken to Pentarchus, not to me," a second voice said, softer and more subtle. Whisper reached through to the surface with soft lumps that doubled as eyes. The Enchanters stood back from a slight brazier that sent equally small amounts of flame and smoke into the tent's center. All four seemed larger than human, almost swollen. Was that because he viewed them from a strange angle? But no, other humans with normal sizes lingered at the fringes of the tent, struggling to control their uneasiness in the presence of their Enchanter warlords.

"Our old master is most anxious that we destroy Gravengate," said another of the Enchanters; his fair features were blotched with dark patches, and even from a distance he smelled faintly of Carag. "Does this incline us to rash acts? I consider otherwise, and yet...."

"Yet the being deep inside you calls for violence," said the dark-bearded, hawk-faced Enchanter, "and this is the same being that still greatly wishes to shed our forms and join itself together, so we should listen to this voice most carefully."

"This false war will not deceive our sponsors for long," the woman with a gaunt face muttered, then she sniffed the air. "Are we sealed? I sense onlookers." Muted words were spoken by four sets of lips; Whisper could feel the weight of a dark and heavy magic as it shifted into place. Alarmed, he sank from view, waiting for fifty of his slow pulses before resurfacing.

"...Pentarchus," one of the Carag Enchanters was saying.

"Likely, you sensed only the coming of Pentarchus," the other Carag said. The woman, the Witch Queen snarled something unintelligible then fell silent. The four Enchanters sat on one side of a broad table, though spaced apart so that none might reach out to touch another. Two vat-candles were set upon the table, providing the chambers of the tent with its only illumination; all other torches and braziers had been extinguished, and the Enchanters' human servants had departed.

Whisper shrank further back, willing his form to greater invisibility; but still, he watched, as in front of the Enchanters a panel seemed to form, showing events in a better lit portion of the League. The image of Pentarchus loomed before them, ghostly and vague at first, then sharper, more vibrant, until finally, it seemed as though Pentarchus himself was seated on one side of the broad rectangular table, facing the other four Enchanters.

"Well met," said the image of Pentarchus; his albino features held a slight, ironic smile. "I have much to report, but first I must tell you that a small voice whispers into my mind, and it says, 'you are not alone.' My brethren, you have an intruder."

The four Enchanters leaped to their feet, then turned as one being to stare at the pool of shadows harboring the eyes of that intruder. Wild with fear, Whisper sank down, outside of hearing and sight, fleeing for his life. As he sank, he activated the Wizard's device and Squint was revealed in the upper moonlit skies as a second spy, employed as a decoy to split the chase.

"Rather," Pentarchus continued serenely, "you had two intruders. But calm yourselves." Manassas had become thin and vague, sending portions of his substance into the soil in pursuit of Whisper, while Helcar's form sprouted great horned batwings, and his head turned to follow the progress of Squint as the Familiar raced back toward Gravengate.

"Calm yourselves," Pentarchus said again, raising his voice. "We have much to discuss, and the spies have fled to safety, so that rash pursuit will gain you nothing. Come!" Helcar and Manassas hesitated, hovering at the edge of transformation, then they reconstituted themselves and sat, struggling with an inner rage that seemed harder each day to control.

"This Wizard," spat out the Witch Queen, "has made his last move. The endgame follows, bringing the destruction of Gravengate."

"It may well be time," Pentarchus said quietly, "to claim our first victory. But let me set before you all that I have learned, then you four must sit in judgment and choose.

"First, this confession: I am unable to determine which of the four ancient powers we are bound with. Divinations, searches of past histories, devices of internal exploration, none of these reveal the sinister devices of the Great God Set. I have come to believe that Set discovered a mightily damaged though powerful Demon, and utterly transformed that Ancient Power before welding it to our forms.

"If I have failed to discover the nature of our ancient power, still I grow stronger, more powerful and integrated each day. You may wish to duplicate my efforts, so I will tell you directly that I am no longer a duality, but a triumvirate: within me lies the old Pentarchus, plus a fragment of this ancient power, and a third being that speaks in utterly soft tones to each of the other two. It was that voice that warned me of your intruder. You may call this third being an emissary, a messenger, or even an overlord, but I am accomplishing much that I never before thought possible.

"Now, let me speak briefly of our patrons of old. Messages have been sent to me, conveying the smoldering anger of Set, and the wild rage of Mordred. Why, they ask, with the power put at our disposal, why do the Wizards yet live? I have given them earnest promises but filled with bluster and bravado, to help them feel that we are uncertain of our own strength. Most interesting is the unhappiness of Mordred. Having been revealed as one of our sponsors, the Mid-World has turned upon him, with scores of Carags slain each day throughout Alantéa and the kingdoms of the Gods."

"So, our old master, Mordred, is filled with wrath," Manassas murmured. "I have no pity for this Renegade, who has betrayed us, though I will shelter any Carag who serves under our banner."

Pentarchus nodded solemnly. "So, I have said to the emissaries of Mordred. Yet this torment of one of our sponsoring Gods provides us with a weapon, strange as it may seem. I have crafted a spell, thus far left inactivated, a device that reveals the schemes of Set and his alliance with Mordred against the League. As masters of magic, we know that the Gods forbid such alliances, though how their bans are enforced remains a mystery. But if you agree, I will activate this magic, so that Set's designs will be revealed upon the deaths by violence of more than one of us. Thus, if Set betrays us, he will expose himself."

Helcar laughed softly. "A strange insurance," he said, "though only useful if Set knows of your device. How will you tell him?"

"His spies move among your ranks," Pentarchus replied, "just as Carags carry tales to Mordred. Also, the Emissaries of the Gods watch our every move, passing information throughout the Mid-World of the Truce. Through one of these channels, I will make certain that Set learns of our actions, but first is it your will that I proceed with this act of magic, our 'insurance' as Helcar calls it?"

"As I understand the Great God Set," the Witch Queen muttered, "our threat of revelation will not hinder him, but your thought is good, and you should proceed, bearing in mind that we may need more than one device to bind the Great God to our will." Helcar and Manassas nodded their agreement. Nairn was silent for a moment, wondering how great an error they had made by allowing Pentarchus to build so much power. His fellow Enchanter spoke softly now, but he was becoming more than a first among equals. Was there a way to restrain Pentarchus? No aspect of their present circumstances could be turned against his fellow Enchanter, and so Nairn nodded his head, imperceptibly, staring into the arctic blue eyes of the albino Enchanter.

"Now, as to Gravengate," Pentarchus continued. "We would seem to have the weight of power in this place, but Divinations and foretelling are blurred by a haze of uncertainty as though some Power has cast ashes over clear pools so that small light is reflected. Can it be that a third Power of the Mid-World has moved to counter Set and Mordred? I counsel delay; build your forces to an overwhelming mass until the future becomes more certain."

"Nonsense," the Witch Queen spat out. "This Wizard sets spies upon us, brews complex spells from an unreachable tower, speaks hidden words to his brethren in their places of strength, and trains his Adepts to become more powerful. We have been six weeks playing at war with Gravengate, and that is far too long. Enough." She glanced to the other Enchanters; all nodded, except for the albino Enchanter, who sat back, pursing his lips.

"I will not seek to dissuade you," Pentarchus said quietly. "Indeed, part of me, the old Pentarchus, agrees with you, while the 'fragment' sees an opportunity of some sort, and that portion which functions as overseer is undergoing a profound hesitation. For I must tell you that the fate of the Wizards, the crisis of their League, looms at Sea's Edge, and not at Gravengate."

"Thus," Nairn said slowly, "Gravengate may fall and the League, though weakened, still survives. And this means that Set cannot move against us, at least not yet."

"Thus," Pentarchus replied, "you should be extremely careful. Such confused auguries often indicate hidden or poorly understood forces."

"Grind, grind, grind," the Witch Queen repeated. "First, concentrate our siege, then bring a torrent of men at arms, then a fury of monstrosities, and last, a storm of magic. Gravengate will fall. What could be simpler?"

· X ·

Pentarchus sat quietly, alone in the stillness, with the greatest portions of his powerful intellect focused on the designs of Set, and their intersection with the fate of the League at Sea's Edge. Invisible servants no longer attended him, for the lesser portions of his mind brought objects and forces into play before his thoughts could crystallize.

Divination panels were framed on three sides so that a glance could tell Pentarchus of the progress of their war. On his left, the Divination showed Stone Mountain obscured by enchanted mists, as Thorian put forth his power to heal the shattered rock that formed the foundation of his stronghold.

The center panel held images of Gravengate, a fortress under siege. Massive stones were sent hurtling toward the battlements of Gravengate, then the stonecasts seemed to hover, to hesitate, as contending magics struggled to control their fall. Pentarchus shook his head in mild dismay:

as always, his fellow Enchanters had underestimated the Farsight of the Seeress; with their predictable battle plans, Sentauris was able to counter each of their attacks.

He glanced to the right, where the panel showed the Halls of Merlin at Sea's Edge, at the borders of an estuary bathed in remote, pale sunlight, with still waters barely lapping at the bay's shoreline. In that shadowed dwelling lurked the enigmatic Merlin, likely toiling — as did Pentarchus — to understand the strange intersection of forces that was yet to take place at Sea's Edge.

His eyes returned to the center panel with its images of war: the Seeress had planned yet another devious counterstroke, having hidden some device during recent night forays; and so, his fellow Enchanters would again encounter the unforeseen. Win or lose, though, it was good to divert their interest from their future struggle at Sea's Edge.

He stared at the center panel, where great forces were sliding into collision. The Enchanters had become most difficult to destroy, while the Adepts had powerfully reinforced themselves and joined with Mír to strongly shield the Seeress. A Wizard was nearly indestructible on his home ground, and so a stalemate with some damage sustained by each side seemed the most likely outcome.

Pentarchus glanced back to Sea's Edge with a frown. If the Enchanters were so powerful and so difficult to destroy, why did Sea's Edge present such danger? He had avoided telling them, but one of the main lines of fate emerging from that future confrontation at Sea's Edge involved the complete and utter destruction of each Enchanter.

·)(·

From a much greater distance, and with far different emotions, another watcher monitored the unfolding battle. As always, the Great God Wotan studied the affairs of the Wizards with conflicting emotions: the humiliation of the upstart Wizards was the source of considerable amusement, while the thought of their complete destruction generated a profound disquiet. Wotan understood the source of these conflicting thoughts and chose not to further investigate his inner conflict.

On the other hand, some of the servants of the Wizards, even from afar, seemed worthy of a God's regard. The renegade Elf-Mage Mír paced the northeast walls, feeling the approach of the Enchanters' might, while the strong, magical forces within him stirred to battle. The Adept Wylar stood fixed, resolute, on the battlements beneath the topmost keep, fingers thick with newly forged rings of power. Like the Elf-Mage, Wylar's flesh was prepared for battle, warded against weapons, and reinforced against the shock of great magic.

Yet only ten steps from Wylar stood Orantes; as this Adept watched the Enchanters approach, his flesh grew pale, while fear formed tiny beads of sweat on his forehead.

You were not meant for this conflict, Adept. Wotan's thoughts whispered to the mind of Orantes. **You were born with this fainthearted nature, a feast-loving human with the Gift, so I do not fault you, yet I do not think you will survive this war.**

Wotan turned to Sentauris, watching as the Seeress readied the fortress for battle. Siege weapons, armaments, forces magical, all things were at her command, and she dealt with them with a sharpness of mind that bordered on brilliance. The Seeress was beginning to understand, Wotan sensed, that this was the last battle that would employ the Armed Host and the Fortress; thereafter the conflict between the Wizards' League and the Enchanters would take a far different form, not to be resolved until a fateful collision of forces at Sea's Edge.

Watching the Seeress, the Great God felt his spirit stir: she was valiant and weaponed. Lashed to her back was a canister of enchanted shafts — these were greyish hued, crafted by Balardi, and yet somehow Wotan had looked for other, more powerful devices. Even so, Sentauris could not be aided by Wotan: Pallas Athena was her patroness, and he would never tamper with the servant of another God.

Also, with Sentauris was her small servant Ghorm. Wotan smiled with pleasure as he watched the slight Familiar, a creature with the body of a small goblin and the heart of a dragon. Ghorm was prepared to hurl himself at the Enchanters, but he also seethed with resentment: he was lugging a second canister, trailing behind Sentauris in the last moments before battle.

Wotan peered forward, recognizing God Power in the second canister, with its ebony-dark, powerfully enchanted shafts. Then the Great God leaned back and laughed aloud. Not only had the Wizard Balardi overcome his dislike of the Seeress, but the two of them had created a stratagem. The Wizard-forged grey-hued shafts were intended to deceive their foes. While powerful enough against so many of their adversaries, those grey arrows were no challenge for the Enchanters. But those ebony-dark arrows created by Pallas Athena were a deadly threat to any being less than a God.

· ꓮ ·

"A thousand other spear carriers could perform this errand," Ghorm's complaints rose over the cries of men and beast, and the grating sounds of siege weapons moving toward the gate's towers, and the hum of bowstrings, "not just this dimwitted hobgoblin." Sounds of defiance rang from the fortress, though the sweaty smell of fear also rose from the tiers ranged below the gates.

"Is it fire?" Farad called again up to Sentauris, and she willed them all to silence, retreating deeper into farsighted visions, reaching out into the mass of their foes as scores upon scores of Uraks and bullocks dragged siege platforms toward the gates facing the northern walls. Catapults with short arms and with broad launching pads loomed behind the siege platforms, ready to hurl destruction — perhaps fire — at the fortress. Sounds of oncoming battle beat upon her eardrums, but all sight and sound retreated as she reached....

Spell shields had been crafted for the servants of the Enchanters, but the main thrust of the Enchanters was directed at Gravengate. A great strength of sorcery reached for the fortress like a wispy grey mist forming an enormous, almost invisible hand. As the hand's fingers touched the stone of Gravengate, she felt the fortress tremble.

Wizard! She called out to Balardi. ***A Spell of Unmaking comes to Gravengate!***

This magic has the weight of a Great Spell, though not its sudden, destructive power. Yet by seeking to unmake this fortress, they will prevent Wizard, Mage, and Adepts from smashing the legions of the Enchanters into dust. Thus, I see battle before the walls — Murat and Fiüre, the dead things are their leaders! Die forever, renegades! And Creatures of the Darkness, both living and dead, are ready for a second thrust...all these things I have foreseen, but what is this carnage within our own walls? How will they penetrate this great fortress? I see the ladders leaning, the siege platforms, more than a few Vorrs within our gates, slashing and ripping

Ah...light! These short-armed catapults will not launch fire upon us, but they will cast unliving warriors! The Undead Murat and Fiüre led their foes, so what other tool would they select?

War cries and the noise of battle shattered her concentration; the greatest of the siege platforms had ranged itself against the left-hand tower beside the gates, just two hundred paces from her. Bellowing Uraks were springing to the fortress walls, while Vorrs snarled and leaped over them, their brutish fangs ripping at the mail and flesh of Gravengate's defenders.

"Seeress!" a voice called just ten paces from her. "What do I tell Sardonicus? Will these siege weapons cast fire?" Farad had climbed to stand on the upper walls of the fortress. His hand rested on Gravengate's stone bulwark, and as he touched it, the stonework crumbled, coming away in his fingers like rotten chalk.

"By the Maker..." he breathed.

"Let the Wizard counter their magic," Sentauris called to him. "We must deal with the coming battle. Listen closely. Their catapults will send not fire but the Undead. Watch!" As she spoke, a jumble of arms and legs and torsos came hurtling over the walls. The pale Undead lay for a few seconds in shattered, broken forms on the mustering grounds within the main walls; then their ruined bodies reknit, and the Undead rose to battle.

"Dregs of dung," Farad muttered, then he raced away, seeking Sardonicus. She turned back to the siege platform, where armed Uraks pressed and battered against forces captained by Gallandus. Pikemen held Uraks pinned, but the sheer bulk of the creatures was forcing the defenders back, and Urak war leaders were rising over their fallen to smash down at the defenders. Outside the walls, horse archers roamed freely, striking down the unwary and the unprotected on the upper walls. Men died in the tower press but could not fall. Flopping dead forms flew overhead, smashing down then rising to assail the defenders of Gravengate. And still the walls of the fortress trembled at the edge of destruction.

The first assault of the Enchanters was gaining ground. Sentauris glanced up to the Adepts. *Wylar! Orantes! Mír, add your strength to the Wizard's power!* Carefully she edged her way toward the siege platform. Arrows whistled overhead. She chose only her own unenchanted shafts and aimed as only she could aim, testing scores of future possibilities before launching each shaft. An arrow filled the eye socket of one Urak Warlord; another arrow intersected the neck of a second. Shielding from both metal and spells deflected her other casts, but a score of heavy, weighted javelins struck down the last three Urak captains, and the assault seemed to falter for a moment, like a strong wave being sucked back into the ocean just before a greater surge.

Whisper! she called to the hidden Familiar. ***Whisper, stand ready!*** Sentauris felt the stonework tremble then firm: Gravengate's strength was being renewed. She glanced up to the citadel, to the topmost keep, where Balardi stood godlike, like a statue of carved stone. On the lower battlements, Wylar and Mír and Orantes added a powerful measure of their own strength to the Wizard's.

Master of Gravengate! her mind called to Gravengate's pinnacle. ***Wizard, I was wrong! Wizard, this fortress, and the strength of magic within it doubles your own power, and I should never have doubted Merlin's wisdom!*** She turned back to the struggle within the fortress walls. Vorrs lay panting, bleeding, many of their bodies bristling shafts. As the Wizard and his allies put forth their strength, the Undead seemed to falter, to lose focus, and when they fell, the dead were no longer able to rise.

Gravengate comes alive, and the necromancy of the Enchanters must give way. Now, with the shifting tide of battle, comes our counter.

Whisper! Do not fail me! Whisper, light the fuse, and then flee back to me!

Beside her, Ghorm's complaints had trailed off, but his eyes still flashed resentment. "So, after Whisper explodes their siege weapons," the Familiar muttered, "I suppose Squint will drop one last destructive spell on the Enchanters, and our battle will be over."

"The blasting powder may still fail," she murmured, though her Farsight showed devastation. "Whisper!" she called as the Familiar rose from the stone. "Well done. Now tell Gallandus to fall back and form a shield-wall. Go!" She edged along the ramparts, counting under her breath. Just a day and a half ago they had planted blasting powder beneath the soil just to the left of the gate's tower — her Farsight had shown her where their siege platform would be placed. Now, the fuse was lit, and she counted.

"Help me search, Ghorm," she murmured. "We seek the siege masters, the Undead forms of Murat and Fiüre." She placed arrows beside her — two shafts of silver and grey. "And note that I am choosing the Wizard crafted shafts for this purpose. You will see —" Three heartbeats before its time, their blasting powder exploded, rocking the fortress. The great siege platform that had been ranged against Gravengate's strong walls collapsed into fragments, so that astonished attackers dropped helplessly through the air, to become a stricken mound of shattered beams and broken bodies at the base of the fortress walls.

With so many eyes staring, frozen, at the devastation, she leaped to her feet and found the renegade captains of the Undead, Murat and Fiüre. They stared back at Sentauris with eyes that glowed with a fearless sorcerous malice. A Wizard crafted arrow caught each of them, and their dead forms vanished in flashes of white fire.

· ϻ ·

As the siege-platform toppled, Set cried out in fury, sending his ghost-slaves gibbering in fear. From a great distance, waves of this thoughts washed over the Enchanters:

WHAT HAVE YOU DONE WITH THE POWER I ENTRUSTED TO YOU?!?

Somehow the minds of four Enchanters were shielded from him, while Pentarchus dithered elsewhere, hidden even from the Great God's sight. Set forced himself to become calmer, to watch in silence. After all, this opening phase of machineries and soldiery was truly a lesser thrust, negligible when compared to the power that was forming before Gravengate the Doomed.

Set subsided, sinking back to his throne, watching through his Vision Panel as the servants of the Enchanters — both living and unliving — drew back to clear a path for the misshapen Creatures Indomitable. The two Creatures of the Darkness that the Enchanters had raised from the dead were leading five other living, though malformed monstrosities as they crawled or thrashed or lurched their way toward the fortress. As they approached Gravengate, nine-tenths of the men manning the north walls and the gates fled to the inner keep, leaving only a handful of defenders.

Now, Seeress, Set's thoughts called to her in hidden, disguised tones that were drenched with malice. *How will you deal with this thrust? The Enchanters will hold your Adepts frozen in spell tests, then you alone must deal with seven Creatures Indomitable. Where is your cleverness now, you short-lived maggot-creature with the Sight?*

· X ·

With the failure of their first assault, the Enchanters redoubled their efforts to unmake Gravengate. Seams of dust began seeping from its bulwarks, and the fortress hummed as though some mighty engine bored into its foundations. Ghorm turned from the approaching monstrosities and glanced first to the Wizard, then to the Adepts.

Would that I had strength to add to the Adepts' magic! Ghorm's thoughts were forming something close to a prayer. *I should be calling upon mighty spells instead of Orantes — look how the fat Adept trembles under pressure, with sheets of perspiration pouring from pale, flabby flesh. Maker, why —*

Ghorm turned suddenly. Sentauris had drawn a Wizard crafted arrow and stood frozen, ready to strike at one of the resurrected Creatures Indomitable. On the far left-hand side of the Gate Towers, men serving Sardonicus were hauling up a huge siege weapon, a crossbow three times the length of a tall man.

"What are you doing?" Ghorm called. "Even I can sense that those will never work, not against these *things*."

"That is indeed the point," Sentauris breathed out. Her Wizard crafted shaft leaped at the chest of the foremost Undead monstrosity. Her arrow struck, blazing with sorcerous fire that staggered the Undead Creature, flaring with power until the white fire passed.

"After these, I will no longer be feared," Sentauris muttered. Other arrows flashed white light, burning themselves out against the enchanted flesh of Creatures Indomitable. Pain was delivered to the monsters, but only slight damage. Sentauris pulled back, sinking against the ramparts, and turning to watch Sardonicus.

"The Enchanters will know that I am weaponed," she murmured to Ghorm, "let them believe I am only lightly armed. Now, Sardonicus... just higher, to the left...." Standing several hundred paces from Sentauris, Sardonicus could not hope to hear the Seeress, but as though guided by her unseen hand his men launched the first huge crossbolt: one huge, misshapen Creature stood transfixed, staring down at the beam of wood that had appeared so suddenly in its lower torso.

"A nice cast," she cried. "Again, Sardonicus, for no being functions well with a bolt of steel and a wedge of wood in its guts!" Another shaft impaled a second Creature, and it stood howling, beating at its own chest. Yet as it raged, other monstrosities had reached the walls of Gravengate, and were smashing at them with huge fists, or pounding its stonework with broad tails, or lashing the fortress with other crude extremities.

Sentauris and Ghorm were forced from the walls as the mortar of the fortress began to crumble. Sardonicus released one last shaft, then he and his followers fled the outer ramparts. His last cast missed by a wide mark, thudding deep into the Plain of Gravengate. Grimly lugging his burden of dark arrows, Ghorm followed Sentauris to the base of the keep, then the Familiar turned to the left-hand tower by the gates, watching as Gravengate's great crossbow slid and toppled over the walls' far side and vanished. Everywhere, stonework shuddered, and at the gates, some monstrosity had shattered a crossbeam that supported one great rune-carved panel.

Ghorm glanced up to the Wizard, his Elf-Mage, and two Adepts: for what it was worth, all four stood strong as they intoned words of power, and even a haggard Orantes seemed more resolute. As their magic strengthened, the fortress no longer trembled with destructive sorcery; instead, it was simply being battered down by enormously powerful and misshapen Creatures Indomitable. Wordlessly, Ghorm lifted his canister of God forged arrows and offered them to Sentauris.

Instead, she turned from Gravengate's outer walls and looked up to its topmost peak. *Wylar! Orantes! As we agreed, release them, now!* The Adepts seemed not to heed Sentauris; they chanted on, and if their fingers twitched three times in unison, their motions were almost undetectable.

Columns of dust, pillars of flame, vortices of bright light, whirlwinds of blue water — all flashed from nothingness and swarmed toward Gravengate's assailants: turmoil ensued as Elementals and Creatures Indomitable fell to battle. Ghorm drew a deep breath. *And so, the Wizard has taught the Adepts well, even in this brief time. Am I doomed because I envy them so much?*

"Alas, our allies will not hold for long," Sentauris murmured, then she broke into a run that left Ghorm trailing behind her, panting as he struggled with his burden. Sentauris raced to a courtyard that was shielded from the outer walls. Within, Farad was calling out instructions, as a long-armed catapult was being drawn back. Sentauris led others in guiding the weapon's long arm, changing its cast a few degrees to the northeast.

"Just a hair's breadth more..." she murmured. "It will never reach them, but closer...now launch!" With a wrenching motion, the stone arced up into the sky, hurtling toward the Enchanters. A second stone was launched, with Sentauris muttering and snarling as though arguing with herself as she followed both the stone's flight and the movements of the distant Enchanters.

After a third stone was hurled, she turned briefly to Ghorm. "The Enchanters will deflect these casts, but their hold over our magic will falter. Two are scattering while the other two focus their power against the skyfall above. Come!" Again, she ran, this time to a place where she could see both the Adepts and the Elf-Mage on Gravengate's topmost tower, and the faltering outer bulwarks that crumbled beneath an onslaught of monstrosities.

Mír! Her mind cried out to the Elf-Mage. *Mír, free yourself and save Gravengate. Wizard, ready your powers!* As her mind reached to the Elf-Mage, more stonecasts arced overhead, creating further distractions for the Enchanters.

Mír stepped forward, a statue slipping from a trance. Light gathered to him, and a distant, haunting music came to life. Mír's ageless features spoke words of power that had been constructed long ago, his voice rising and falling, a melody of such power that Gravengate's defenders stood transfixed, weapons faltering. A stillness, an uneasy quiet began to replace the tumult of war. Even the monstrosities ceased their assault on the fortress, standing uncertain, baffled, and almost afraid.

Images and sounds flooded into Ghorm's mind: of seagulls crying aloud as they pursued the setting sun; of wavelets lapping at broad, sunlit, sandy beaches; of painted-winged blackbirds passing through emerald forests; of fawns with large eyes and shaky legs nibbling at the new growths of spring. Orchards glistened with pink and azure blossoms and hummed with the wingbeats of a thousand bees. And in the depths of night, fish with silver streaks leaped into the air above broad, swiftly flowing rivers, striving to catch glimpses of starlight.

Score upon score of the sights and smells and sounds of Alantéa the Forerunner gathered around the fortress. As all those powerful sensations coalesced, they leaped beyond Gravengate's walls — and grafted themselves to the twisted, demented minds of the Creatures of the Darkness.

Monstrosities howled in pain, then clubbed their own heads, or battered themselves against the ground. Some stumbled against Gravengate's crumbling walls, then lurched away in pain, while others turned and sped toward the farthest horizon, away from the battle, crying aloud, heedless of those in their path. Only two remained: those raised from the dead by the Enchanters, monstrosities that could no longer be touched even by the magical images of any living thing.

Both Undead Creatures gathered themselves and turned to the creaking, vulnerable, rune-carved gates of the fortress, and stepped with menace toward those gates.

But from Balardi came two casts of pure power — bolts of black death prepared for the Undead. Both misshapen Creatures toppled backward, smoking, and broken, never to rise again.

And so ended the second assault of the Enchanters on the shaken fortress of Gravengate.

·)(·

Watching from afar, the cool, emotionless Pentarchus was moved to both wonder and revulsion. Merlin was a master, moving with matchless subtlety against the Enchanters. Somehow, he had discovered that the Elf-Lords — collectively, a Power in their own right — had maintained mighty spells against the Creatures Indomitable. Obviously, Merlin had approached them saying, *Behold, we have destroyed more Creatures Indomitable than you might ever have had to face. If you allow your renegade servant, Mír, to acquire your counter to these creatures, we will so deplete their ranks that you will have peace for an age, time enough to create greater and more intricate magic.*

Merlin was an adversary worthy of respect.

On the other hand, Pentarchus recoiled from the great wastage of his fellow Enchanters: nearly all the power assembled by Set and Mordred was destroyed or dissolving in chaos. Creatures of the Darkness blundered about, while human figures scurried from their paths, with many humans fleeing north, passing from the Wizards and their League. Vorrs were skulking from the battlefield in twos and threes, and though the Uraks seemed unshaken, Pentarchus understood that many would slip away under cover of darkness. Only the Undead stood firm, yet these were sharply reduced in numbers and stared out in confusion as though their masters no longer guided them.

Pentarchus began to turn away in disgust, then he hesitated: the Enchanters themselves were coming forth to battle, abandoning all their broken tools, determined to destroy Gravengate with their own, unassisted might. Their power might well be great enough, yet it was ugly, unsubtle violence. And in the end, did it truly matter whether they prevailed?

Pentarchus — that old portion of Pentarchus the Sorcerer — turned back to his complex magic.

At that moment, the two other portions of his tripartite personality cried aloud, as though its own life was in danger.

The 'fragment' within him shrieked in anger and in fear.

And the third portion — governor, translator, mediator, emissary between the other two — this voice called out, "Watch! Watch! Watch! You must watch!"

Thoroughly alarmed, Pentarchus cleared away his other Divination Panels, so that he viewed Gravengate only, now in larger focus, with more detail. The Enchanter also shut down his previous, complicated magic, and began chanting. Power gathered to Pentarchus.

· Ж ·

"To the Fortress of the Keep!" Sentauris called to the remaining men-at-arms. "Protect yourselves within the Keep! Let the Wizard defend Gravengate!" As men fled from the gates and the northern walls, she turned and raced to the fortifications facing northeast. As she ran, she gathered a coil of thick rope, while Ghorm still trailed behind her, gasping with effort as he carried their God-forged weapons.

With her farsighted vision, she followed the Enchanters as they approached the crumbling fortress: Nairn and the Witch Queen were centermost, with Manassas on their western flank, and Helcar to their eastern. All four Enchanters loomed large, with distended, unhuman bodies. And as the two Carag Enchanters drew near, each began to mass in bulk, becoming more like giants, hulking, threatening. When one wounded Creature Indomitable with a spear in its guts rose to contest the passage of Manassas, that monstrosity was smashed back to the ground and trampled.

Sentauris reached the base of the northeast fortifications, breathing hard, senses filled with uncertainty and fear. She turned and waved Ghorm down; her Familiar skidded to a halt beside a cluster of fallen Undead bodies. The eyes of the fallen had seen many horrors, but now they stared lifelessly into the depths of eternity.

Suddenly, Nairn and the Witch Queen released a burst of such power that the gates were crushed into ruin, with unhinged, rune-carved center panels blown back into the heart of the fortress. Sentauris dodged to one side, shielding herself against a hailstorm of wood and stone fragments. Then she climbed swiftly, racing to the upper walls. Halfway up the fortification's stone steps, she turned to the Elf-Mage, a figure glowing again with the light of gathering magic.

Mír! Stand back, she called to the Elf-Mage glowing on the heights. ***This is the Wizard's time! Do noth*—** Four bolts of dark, necromantic fire lashed at the Elf-Mage. Mír stood frozen for a split second as though transformed by death. As he toppled from the heights, a Portal seemed to reach out and swallow Mír, and then their ally was gone.

"Mír..." she whispered, then shook herself free, and raced to the top of the stone battlements. She lashed her thick rope to an iron ring set into the stone, then used the rope to pull Ghorm to the upper walls. As she hauled, she heard power rumble through Gravengate: a Wizard stirring in wrath.

Balardi unleashed a storm of magic against Nairn and the Witch Queen, smashing down their shielding spells, battering their gaunt forms back. Trembling, shaking with fury, the two Enchanters struggled to their feet, then all four Enchanters again focused casts of great magic against the Wizard. Dark lightning smashed at Balardi. His own spells shattered into crystal fragments, and the Wizard sank back, gasping, with blood flowing from his ears and nostrils.

Orantes, hold! She called to the Adept, as a fear of death swept over Orantes.

Sentauris drew the first of her God-forged arrows, but a shaken Orantes released before time his own hidden magic: from the rings upon his fingers, eight concentric circles of force formed, then a beam of bright Dragonfire swept through, catching the looming, huge form of Manassas in one monstrous thigh. Manassas slumped, howling deafening sounds. The Enchanter struggled to transform himself, but his damaged essence was unable to respond.

Slowly, like horror in a dream, the three remaining Enchanters turned toward Orantes. Stumbling in fear, the Adept broke and fled, but a parting cast from Manassas shattered his shielding, then Helcar bathed Orantes in dark, necromantic lights. Orantes collapsed, blackened, with death groping for his life.

"Stop, Wylar!" Sentauris cried, and she strung her God-forged arrow. But Wylar, moved to rage, was calling forth his own Dragonfire. As Wylar sped toward Orantes, concentric rings of force focused beams of sorcerous fire at Helcar; the Enchanter toppled backward, smoking in ruin.

Blasts rocked the citadel where Wylar had stood, but the Adept was racing along the citadel's upper parapets. Wylar stumbled, fell, and rose in one motion, hurling a second burst of Dragonfire at Manassas, while the Carag Enchanter struggled to kneel. Gasping aloud, as though invoking his God, Mordred, Manassas toppled, shaking the earth underneath his bloated form.

And as the earth trembled, Sentauris found the Witch Queen's form and launched her first God-forged arrow. From across a great expanse, the Witch Queen read the deadly eyes and fierce features of Sentauris. A Portal flashed before Azüre; she leaped through, with the enchanted shaft in pursuit.

Sentauris launched a second shaft. Nairn stood in astonishment, staring at the hole in space where the Witch Queen had vanished. A God-forged arrow caught his tall gaunt form chest high. He stared down at the shaft, his lips sputtering spells: his form shook and shuddered with dark magic, but he could not transform himself from destruction. Diamond-ice surrounded him, but he could no longer shield himself.

Portal magic swirled around the Enchanter; Nairn seemed to implode, to collapse within himself, and so vanished from the battlefield.

Sentauris notched a third arrow and stood glancing back and forth between the twitching, smoking forms of Helcar and Manassas.

Then suddenly, Pentarchus burst onto the Plain of Gravengate. Sentauris wheeled from Helcar and hurled death toward Pentarchus. The great Enchanter raised his right hand and the ebony-black God-forged arrow of Sentauris exploded into grey dust.

On the left side of Pentarchus, the Witch Queen burst from her Portal and raced to shield the stricken Helcar. A second time, Sentauris launched death at the Witch Queen, but Pentarchus again raised a single hand, destroying the shaft in flight. As the Enchanter lowered his right hand, he pointed one lone finger from his left at Sentauris, staring at her with eyes that radiated a cold malice.

Sentauris grabbed Ghorm, and dropped from the walls, swinging down her coil of thick rope, pushing herself from the battlements above. The Enchanter's first thrust destroyed the last three of her God-forged arrows, while his second cast smashed the walls above her, sending shards of stone cascading all around her.

The two landed roughly. Seeress and Familiar struggled to their feet, racing toward the inner keep. As they sped from the wrath of Pentarchus, Balardi came to life, and Wylar rose from beside a stricken Orantes. Dragonfire raged at the Enchanter, but Pentarchus seemed to step lightly to one side. Balardi strove to grip the great Enchanter in spell test, but Pentarchus allowed himself to be grappled just long enough so that the Witch Queen had time to transfer the bloated and dying forms of the Carag Enchanters far from the Plain of Gravengate.

Then the remaining two Enchanters passed swiftly through Portals and vanished. Gravengate still stood, but it had taken a deadly wound; and within and without its walls lay broken stones and beams, discarded weapons, the bodies of men and horses, slain Vorrs and broken Uraks, dead Elementals and fatally wounded Creatures of the Darkness, all strewn about in patterns of destruction as though cast down by an immeasurably powerful celestial storm:

Deadfall.

Chapter Thirteen

The Healers and the Healed

I N THE AFTERMATH OF *battle, the Gates of Dreams were opened to her, and so in sleep Sentauris rode waves of light, luminous clouds that cast her back to the time when starlight had shone so brightly over The Weasel's Feast, then back to Tuvan the Citadel sparkling in daylight, and finally to the muted light cast over an earlier dreaming vision, when the Goddess, Pallas Athena had loomed so tall and brave before her.*

Sentauris stood as a third party, watching as her own form bowed low before the Goddess — yet now Pallas Athena seemed grim, almost haggard, where before she had stood remote and powerful. The Goddess finished speaking to her kneeling servant, then turned to Sentauris, the dream voyager. As one might sow a dandelion into the wind, the Goddess puffed air at Sentauris, and the Seeress was swept away.

She floated through clouded skies, then down through pools of darkness, until she found herself drawn again to an island of muted light, back to the place where Merlin stood leaning over his long gaming board, while The Game of the Masters showed its pieces passing through their enchanted paces.

This Merlin was the remote, unsympathetic Wizard she had dealt with before the Wild Time, a Merlin who did not even glance in her direction. Nor did Merlin look to the dim figure of Pentarchus that played the distant pieces opposite Merlin. Instead, both players stared at a third figure, an unidentifiable Power that loomed huge in the muted light.

Merlin's face remained frozen in concentration, as though by willpower he might unveil that obscured, powerful God, while Pentarchus nodded imperceptibly, as though saying to that Power, yes, I know you well, I have reason to fear you, yet I will no longer be swayed by your power to do me harm.

And the figure, a God moved to wrath, stared down with infinite malice directed at both Wizard and Enchanter, then with two mighty hands smashed down upon the great gaming board so that it collapsed, and all its many, intricately carved pieces flew as shattered fragments from the Game's wreckage. Sentauris felt herself sliding, slipping, falling free as though from a precipice, and she struggled desperately to wake.

Her eyes popped open, and she gasped for breath. Now, by all the Nine Billion Gods, what was that all about? She sat up in sudden alarm. Some crisis was upon them, a fateful moment that had nothing to do with her dream visions. Still exhausted, she had sought sleep early in the evening, little more than a day after the great, devastating battle before Gravengate. She glanced out of her chamber portal, watching as the last traces of dusk gave way to dark night. Her mind searched near and far. The walls were manned, with a treble guard on the mound of rubble that stood in place of the ruined gates. Their foes were leagues from Gravengate, struggling with deep, brutal wounds. Balardi lay in his place of power, connected in some strange fashion to a healing force from Sea's Edge. Mír had been gathered into the Mid-World to live or die as the Powers might ordain. Ghorm investigated the night, though his inner spirit still seethed with resentment at his small part in the great battle.

Wylar stood guard, watching for some sudden, unforeseen thrust of their foes, while Orantes lay heal —

She sat up with a sudden shiver. Orantes. They had pulled the Adept back from death, but now Orantes was retreating into himself, pushing aside, little by little, all the healing strength that Balardi and Wylar had gathered around him; in the morning he would be found dead, believed a victim of the necromantic powers of their foes.

Up now, and quickly. But what about my jealous chaperone, Ghorm? She drew on her cloak, then stared for a moment into the descending night. Ghorm, you are destined for some adventure, an event touched only lightly by the malice of our foes....

Drawing a deep breath, she fled her chamber, vaulting up the adjoining stairs two at a time, until she stood in front of Orantes' place of healing, where his lone guard lay slumped and snoring, cradling an empty flagon of wine. *That's somehow fitting*, she thought, and slipped inside, closing the door softly behind her. She stood silently in the darkness, letting her breathing subside.

"I knew you would come." The small voice of Orantes came from the far corner of the chamber. "Do not, I beg you, judge me too harshly. But I cannot stand against such power anymore. I cannot. It is simply not in me, no matter how I might wish for such strength. I was just not made for this struggle..." Orantes trailed off; she sensed that all the poison had passed from his flesh, but his mind still churned with dark venom.

"On the other hand," he whispered, "if I fled from here, where would I go? What would I think when I stared into the distance, thinking of you and Wylar and the others? I would look for cliffs or chasms. Yet now, if you will just let me be, just for a few more hours, I can exit gracefully, a casualty.... What are you doing?"

Sentauris had pulled off her cloak and quickly discarded her other night garments. She slid into bed beside Orantes and began pulling and tugging at his own clothing.

"No, wait," he murmured, "not like this, not from pity, not at the end."

"Hush, Orantes, it is time. I always knew we would one day be lovers, ever since that long ago evening at *The Weasel's Feast*."

It was astonishing how much love could be shared in one single night, even when one lover struggled with deep wounds.

·)(·

Wylar paced the upper ramparts of Gravengate, staring out into the moonless night sky. Beyond the outer walls, carrion deadfall still lay in grotesque, twisted positions. Already, scavengers feasted on the dead, though the foragers themselves were stalked by Vorrs that always prowled in the darkness. The night was warmer, Wylar's mind noted; soon he would no longer need his heavy, muffled cloak.

Wylar felt himself retreat even farther from his dreams; his own future happiness had vanished. He could sense that Sentauris had chosen Orantes and not himself. Such a choice was not surprising; they seemed destined for each other, each of them with a love of life that treated each day's experience as part of a perpetual feast. As for himself, he would grow into his role as Wylar the Dour, retreating always deeper into himself, a process he could only partly understand, and could not control.

He stared up into the moonless night sky with unblinking eyes; and if tears formed, they were absorbed by the inner portions of his mind.

Yet as he stared skyward, a winged motion caught his eye: Squint, his companion, coasting in over the warming air of spring to offer awkward though welcome comfort as his master paced the upper walls.

From below, Ghorm watched Adept and comforting Familiar, and all the pieces of the puzzle — both from the fears of his mind, and the evidence of his own senses — fell into place. His mind exploded into rage: *She chose the fat one! Even now she's lying with that dimwitted clown! Wylar I might understand, but Orantes the buffoon? Orantes the fat crybaby? Maker, what have you done to me? I have had enough....*

Ghorm drew a deep breath and glanced around. Whisper would be seeking him, but if he moved swiftly, taking only his dagger and grey cloak, passing over dark paths on a moonless night, and with the besieging armies in disarray, surely, he could make his way north undiscovered and unseen.

Anything to be far from Gravengate, where he was no more than a feeble, abandoned pawn.

He moved quickly from the walls, avoiding the guards. In the modest chamber he shared with Whisper, he strapped on his blade, drew on his grey cloak, and was out in the corridor in seconds. *Down, down, then beyond the walls, little Ghorm, the useless Goblin.*

The interior guards were lax; Ghorm was swift. He passed into the lower levels with only one sleepy-eyed human noticing him. As a creature of magic, Ghorm had been born into the Mid-World without the benefit of parents, though Familiars were much sought after and quickly adopted. His claim of Goblin heritage was a jest, a story he told about himself, though now, as he sought lower ground, he found himself comfortable in rough passageways that smelled of damp stone.

I will become a Seer among Goblins, telling tales on stormy nights of huge, blundering Creatures of the Darkness.

He searched for culverts with eyes that had grown accustomed to darkness, while at the same time he sniffed for the smell of carrion from airshafts that might lead to the battlefield outside Gravengate's walls. At last, he found a narrow passage where thousands of spiders had spun their webs for so many years, while water passed sluggishly over stones made slippery by mould.

Ghorm lit a candle as he moved forward, hunched over, using his sheathed dagger to beat aside the cobwebs. With every step from

Sentauris and her lover, a wild sense of freedom surged; but a sullen guilt was beginning to snarl back at him.

His candle sputtered and died. As the culvert narrowed and tilted up, he slipped and fell. Ghorm rose, cursing, but now he could smell more strongly the dead that lay scattered over the battlefield. Squirming up through narrow passageways, he forced his mind to dream of faraway places.

The culvert's top was obscured by an outcrop of stone and blocked by a metal grill. Moving with the caution of a long hunted creature, he used his dagger to force the rusted metal aside. At last, he was able to squirm through the opening, so that he could stand on the Plain of Gravengate, picking strands of spiderwebs from his head and shoulders.

Free! He glanced back to the fortress; even now a sense of love and longing was beginning to struggle against the wild anger that still raged inside him. But free to do what? His reverie was interrupted by the snuffling sounds of Vorrs that had discovered some new and most enticing scavenger. Ghorm drew his dagger and turned to meet them.

You always knew it would end like this, Ghorm, didn't you? Like a squirrel facing a wolf pack, you will become little more than a late at night snack.

Two Vorrs caught sight of Ghorm and his small blade; they snarled a deep throated growl that held more than a hint of laughter. They inched forward; Ghorm readied his slight magic, knowing that in its aftermath he would be completely defenseless.

One pace, two paces, the Vorrs advanced with deep throated sounds as though humming to themselves in expectation. Ghorm felt himself growing suddenly numb, and anger flared that his last moments were accompanied by panic. But the numbness was coming not from fear, but from a strangeness that separated him from all reality. As though watching their confrontation from outside of his own body, Ghorm saw both Vorrs drop their heads to the ground like puppies cringing before some powerful and angry master. Then Ghorm saw from a distance how his own body was embraced by a cocoon of luminous greyish silver light, then dropped through the earth like a stone cast into a deep, dark well.

Ghorm woke slowly, his mind only gradually understanding that he was not dead meat in the guts of Vorrs. Instead, he found himself seated on a slight stool, nodding and blinking, struggling to come completely awake. Lights fluttered at the edges of his vision, with large raven wings floating back and forth across a broad throne room, casting shadows over the stone walls of an immense cavern.

Ghorm glanced up, then bowed, suddenly and profoundly shaken: he was seated in the place of power of the All-Wise Father, great one-eyed Wotan, whose dark ravens sought the length and breadth of Alantéa for knowledge in aid of their God. Wotan was accounted one of the mightiest of the Mid-World Powers yet respected more than feared; for Wotan was known as a truth teller, and he did not play needless games with the lives of mortals.

"Hail, small servant of the League," Wotan spoke in soft tones, though it seemed to Ghorm that the God's voice had enough hidden strength to crush stone. With the jerky motions of the newly awakened, a bewildered Ghorm slipped from his stool and knelt before Wotan the All-Knowing.

"Why have I touched your life, Ghorm the Familiar, Ghorm the partial Adept? One eye only I may have, yet I am not blind to the heroism of your League, and not least in valor are your struggles, Ghorm, nor those of your mistress, Sentauris." Ghorm stiffened — Wotan was not going to help him escape.

"Many things I foresee, Ghorm, while others I can only sense. A strange intersection lies before your people, little servant." Ghorm glanced furtively to the throne of Wotan, all his feelings of awe giving way to the hot wrath blazing inside his mind: he was a lesser pawn, being forced back to the gaming board of the Powers. Ghorm's mouth curled in disdain and his mouth readied to speak angry words. But suddenly Wotan's hand gestured, flashing power; light blinded Ghorm and the fabric of matter all around him shuddered in transformation.

Blinking, Ghorm looked about him in wonder. The dimly lit throne room with its swirling ravens had vanished. He sat instead in the hut of some woodcutter or blacksmith. Across from Ghorm sat an older man with a white beard, dressed in ragged traveler's clothing, and yes, he had a dark patch over one eye, while the good eye was greyish, staring at the Familiar. Ghorm glanced down and saw that his own form had changed — he was a young man, a peasant, and indisputably human. Suddenly, his eyes filled with tears.

"I am not your enemy, Ghorm," the old man said, leaning across the table from the Familiar, "yet you were about to speak words that would make of me an unfriend forever. Thus, I have taken on a disguise, one that I wear when I wish to learn from the minds of mortals. To this form, you may speak words that might not be said to the Great God Wotan. And for this discussion, I have crafted for you the form you most desire, but which no Power could truly grant to you forever."

Ghorm glanced away. Daylight, the dim light of dusk, was slipping into the cottage through grimy windows. "Then, Lord, you know my heart's desire," he said in a small voice.

"To become human, a Magician of Adept rank, and become the great lover and defender of Sentauris." Wotan sat back, eyes filled with compassion. "None of these things lie within my power. Yet if you hold back your inner sorrow, I will speak to you of those things that might be done."

Ghorm nodded somberly, then the human figure of Wotan rose and paced. His hand casually flashed power, and flames sprang up from kindling and split logs in a stone fireplace.

"The Truce is nothing to you, Ghorm, but for the Gods, it governs almost all our actions. From you, the Truce Terms are hidden, yet I will tell you that the Terms forbid alliances of God with varying powers, to prevent a renewal of the Ancient Wars. Mordred has allied himself with a second, unknown Power and will be punished. Pallas Athena has intervened to preserve an estranged servant — Sentauris — and may have marked herself for retribution by the enemies of your League, though the Truce will not be called down against her.

"Now, Ghorm, if I aid you, no one will ever know of it, for the Gods, most importantly, the Greater Gods must remain subtle. Whatever you chose, you will lose memories of this moment, though you may well understand that some assistance was passed to you.

"Here are your two choices. Firstly, you may choose a destination in Alantéa or the Far Lands, there to emerge as a free being, though with no memory of our meeting. Deliberately, I have not studied your destiny in distant Far Avalon or Varaj, yet you must ask yourself whether you will later wish to return to your mistress when the hot wrath within you subsides. For after that change of heart, you would be forced to pass through many forbidding pathways over hundreds of leagues, perhaps even tracked by your foes, and by that time your friends and allies may no longer be on this side of life.

"Secondly, I can return you safely to your League. Ghorm, so many strange intersections lie before your peoples that I cannot predict their future or yours. But in one major future-chance, your mistress, her Adepts, and her Elf-Mage fight an unequal battle against a Power of the

Mid-World. Should that occur, I will grant you one fight; for one battle only, you will be yourself as a Mage or Adept, fully the equal of Wylar or Mír or Orantes. Ghorm, I must tell you that the Fates are Ice Maidens and will not be swayed by the hot fires that burn within you, and so your new strength may turn the tide of battle — or it may not. Yet after, you will lose those skills, and have no knowledge as to their source."

The figure of Wotan in human disguise ceased pacing and looked down to the young man seated before him. "Think now Ghorm, the Familiar. What will you choose?"

Ghorm looked away, struggling with his emotions. "Lord," he said softly, almost in a whisper, "you are mighty and just, yet you have crafted these choices to place me back in play as a lesser piece in a far greater game."

"Ghorm, you were born with a small measure of magic — I did not guide that event, nor did I cause you to love your mistress in a fashion that can never be fulfilled. And I did not make you valiant, worthy of a God's attention. All these things constitute your destiny, and you may now embrace your fate, or turn aside. Choose, Ghorm."

"Lord, I understand that I must return, and I thank —" Ghorm fell silent, for suddenly he found himself in the deepest foundations of Gravengate, mouth open, murmuring into the darkness. What was he saying? Speaking in the darkness to what creature? Some rodent? Was he imploring some perverse Rat God?

Though every memory of Wotan had vanished, he felt better, stronger. As his anger subsided, the rational portion of his mind understood that Sentauris was human; from time to time, she would need to be alone with another human, and it never lasted long. Also, might there still be a role for him to play in their struggle, even with his small store of magic?

He began climbing slowly back to the upper levels of the fortress, then stopped dead. *This sudden change of mood means that I have been tampered with by some strong hand. The touch of Balardi I would recognize, and Pallas Athena would surely nag and rebuke me, so it was some other force. But which Power?*

Lips curled into a sneer, Ghorm called down to the lower passages, "Thank you, most beloved Rat God, for your divine intervention."

· ☽ ·

Leagues from Ghorm, the Witch Queen stared out into the same dark night that had witnessed Ghorm's attempted escape. She stood guard, wondering whether Wizard or Mid-World Power would challenge them in their time of weakness. Inside their great command tent, Pentarchus tended Manassas and Helcar. Both lay submerged in a large vat of nutrients and dark magic, twitching and moaning as their bodies struggled to rebuild their broken and bodies and wounded souls.

More than an hour later, Pentarchus came to stand beside Azüre, though he cautiously avoided touching her, lest the Power within them struggle again for union with its separated components. Both Enchanters loomed gaunt and distorted, standing now two heads higher than a tall man. With the deepening night, a slight wind was picking and tugging at their cloaks.

"They will heal," Pentarchus said briefly.

The Witch Queen's eyes remained fixed on a far horizon. "And Nairn?"

"Nairn is far from us, and he will live unless Set is determined to destroy all of us."

"Yes, were I the Great God Set," Azüre said softly, "I might now destroy each of the five Enchanters, calling us rebels and madmen, thus concealing my own, failed plot."

Pentarchus nodded. "From afar I can feel the rage of Set, and although I believe it will be directed elsewhere, I am prepared for desperate flight."

"As I am. I will not yield to sleep until all five Enchanters stand once more together."

"We must watch, too, for other Gods. Those enchanted shafts were crafted by a Power beyond any Wizard's." Pentarchus sighed. "As our guiding force, I have watched for God-power rising to counter the Great God Set, though I looked for a more overt display, not a force as hidden or subtle as arming the Seeress."

"That woman will die a great death," murmured the Witch Queen. "Each Enchanter will possess her carnally, then as we watch, extracts of poisons will build and burst through her unbelieving, horror filled eyes."

Pentarchus laughed softly. "I do not normally indulge myself in such matters, though I, too, will take pleasure in that moment. Yet in the short term, our tasks have grown more complex — Merlin has vanished from Sea's Edge. The Wizards lack Portal Magic, so I must guess that some low-level God has drawn Merlin to its Mid-World haven. Search with me now, let us spy out this Wizard and his schemes."

The two gaunt creatures stood, leaning against a ragged, intermittent north wind, their powerfully enchanted minds searching intently though fruitlessly for signs of Merlin....

· ҉ ·

While far from Pentarchus, Mír stared up into Merlin's eyes. Mír's mind was floating on a gentle river that was leading to his own death; much of his body had already died, existing frozen in some trance state. At least in the last stages of death, all the pain and shock and terror of their struggle at Gravengate had subsided.

How we fought for your League, Wizard! Mír's mind tried to speak but no words came. Merlin nodded slowly, with enormous gentleness, then turned to bow before a second figure, one that dwarfed the Wizard.

Thoth, God of Wisdom, Mír's mind told him, *the bird faced Power of the Mid-World. The Kindreds have always been welcome at his courts. But why am I here? Or is this only a tale my mind tells me at the edge of an everlasting sleep?*

"Wizard, you presume on our acquaintance," Thoth said, staring down at the Wizard as though addressing some difficult and disobedient child. "You know that I will not aid you in your wars." Mír was able to turn his head just a fraction: he lay in some deep crib device, in an antechamber perhaps in the Halls of Thoth, Lord of Moonlight. Mír glanced back to Merlin.

The Wizard bowed again to Thoth, but he did not kneel before the Great God. "Lord, I know you will never come to battle before the *Time.* All I ask is your aid as a healer, for this valiant Elf-Mage lies near death, with deep wounds that are far beyond our own healing arts."

The bird face of Thoth loomed high over Mír, peering down at him with soft, unblinking eyes. "How did you come to my domain, Wizard?" the God grumbled. "By reputation, the Wizards have little Portal Magic." Then the God sniffed the air. "This moment reeks of Troll." Thoth turned to Merlin. "You have forged some link with Taurag, Father of Trolls, who is nothing like a God, but still a force within the Mid-World. That may be well for you, but I am part of no pact; I will not support this League of yours."

Merlin nodded and seemed to sigh. "I know that well, Lord. Yet just as you have healed maimed Creatures Indomitable, and broken Tanu, or shapeshifting Carags — all those creatures that found their way to your doorstep — so you might also save this Elf-Mage and let him return to a destiny you care nothing about, one way or another."

Thoth was silent for a moment. "Then let that be the way of it." The God raised his hands over Mír, bathing him in rays of light that sent the Elf-Mage tumbling into soft folds of enchanted sleep.

"To support the story of our confrontation," the God continued, staring down at the sleeping Mír, "I must now hurl you from my doorstep as an intruder. Yet before I 'hurl,' or send you back to your sanctuary at Sea's Edge, is there another small favor I might grant to you? Know that I remain a lesser friend to your peoples, though it is a wise policy that the Kindreds believe me unfriendly to your League."

Merlin bowed again, more deeply, then asked, "Where is Nairn? In his last convulsion before death, he transported himself back to his unnamed patron. If I could discover Nairn, I might also name the second and greater author of our misfortunes."

Thoth seemed to shrug. "I search endlessly, and casually for matters of interest in the Mid-World, and not always from my place of power. We will conveniently forget that you are at my side." The God's hands flashed power: Divination panels, scores of them, flared and faded, one by one, showing scores of Gods and their servants. Some sat wreathed in incense, attended by many hundreds of worshipers, while others conversed with powerful Mid-World servants, and many other Powers themselves stared at vision Portals showing far lands; and yet no Power could be seen attending a wounded human, the Enchanter Nairn....

While in a distant and remote kingdom of the Mid-World, Nairn stared up into the strangely remote and passive face of Dark-Souled Set. Something twisted and turned within Nairn's dying form, and he recognized that the 'fragment' within him wished to burst free from the confines of its human form and attack the Great God Set with all its might.

As he shook with torment, Nairn groaned aloud, closing his eyes until the pain subsided. With its lessening, he was able to stare again with clear eyes into Set's face. *All your choices are harsh, Set the Destroyer,* he thought, *carefully muting emotions inside his mind. If you do not heal us, we will fail, and in death, all your plots will be exposed. If we survive and destroy this League, we will shed your yoke, and then we will turn upon you, like five Basilisks ranged against a lone Griffin.*

Set turned and stepped quickly away before his inner fury caused him to destroy this damaged, dying Enchanter. He strode back into his place of power, still in a wild rage. Vision Portals flared into being then were smashed as Set stormed from panel to panel, crying aloud.

After a time of unrestrained destruction, Set began to set aside his anger: the stonework of his palace was beginning to seep dust, and all his servants had fled, knowing that to be near Set in his dark mood was to lose even their modest lives as feeble ghosts.

With one last smashing motion, the Great God sank back onto his throne and invoked the transforming miracle work that curbed his madness. Of what use was it to be a God, if that inner substance could not reincarnate, reinvent itself? Set became a creature of pure energy, a luminous silvery black haze, almost translucent, whose emotions were constrained through matrixes of pure reason. At last, the Great God's mind was able to form clear thoughts:

Of the five Enchanters, I might now destroy only those three that are damaged; for the other two are so poised for flight they might even escape my Spell of Unmaking. And after, tales would be spread of my involvement, with consequences that cannot be foreseen.

Though the Enchanters have suffered a great setback, they have not completely failed in their war against the League. They have taken great wounds while delivering substantial blows. In a matter of days, they may all be at full strength, prepared to struggle anew, and finally destroy the Wizards and their League.

That they have withheld their full strength suggests that they fear my devices, and so Pentarchus has been studying me from afar, while postponing full victory until the Enchanters are prepared to counter me.

Even so, the Spell of Unmaking will yet break apart the Enchanters with only ten words, and every aspect of my original designs may yet come to pass. Even Mordred may yet be used to absorb all blame when the Wizards are no more, and I destroy the Enchanters, then denounce their creator and patron, the Renegade Dark God Mordred.

And so, I will heal, and renew the Enchanters.

Yet some strange nexus of fate lies before them at Sea's Edge. Why did I not foresee this intersection, and why did I not understand the part to be played by the Seeress, and how her early death might have made all matters so much more simple?

Some aspect of destiny, some force of unknown potency lies hidden within this seemingly simple alliance of Wizards.

Yet I am the Great God Set, able to transform all these many futures to my liking, and now I will act. For Merlin sits at Sea's Edge like a small squat spider, his spiderweb of plots extended over Alantéa and the Mid-World. It is now time for a Sending of Sendings to smash him into pulp, thus destroying his League, and fulfilling the dark designs of the Great God Set....

Chapter Fourteen
Sea's Edge and the Wrath of Set

At daybreak Sentauris led a small war party outside Gravengate's walls, so they could guard her flanks while she picked among the dead. As she searched, droplets of fine mist fell over all the desolation and death that lay beyond the walls of Gravengate. Sentauris hoped to find hidden emblems or messages — anything that would enable her to name the second God who was seeking to destroy the League. If she could discover the identity of that Power, their struggle might very well be transformed by bringing the Mid-World of the Truce into play.

Behind her, closer to the makeshift, temporary gates of the fortress, thirty or so weary guardsmen were struggling to stay awake while dodging both large and small raindrops. But when Vorrs skulked too close to their search party, it was Sentauris who shot the foremost, neatly transfixing its neck as it leaped away in sudden flight. Other Vorrs sped from Gravengate's battleground, howling in fury.

She turned back to the careless, unthinking dead. Touching one rain-soaked man with matted grey hair, her Farsight found nothing but images of hard travel, grim death, and a hatred of those who sought freedom from the rule of Dark Gods. Of those Gods, the warrior knew almost nothing, and of the Enchanters, his dead mind had recorded only the vaguest and confusing images.

Sentauris looked up, staring into the distance, north, and west, to the place where the Enchanters had retreated. *The Enchanters...I cannot see them for my sight is blocked, yet so closely tuned to their devices have I become that I can sense their emotions, though their thoughts cannot yet be read. They have been checked, several of them deeply wounded, and still in a matter of days, they might again be at full strength and raise a torrent of power against our peoples. Still, now they radiate anxiety, hesitation, even resentment toward one another.*

She turned due west toward Sea's Edge, where Merlin ruled, casually and halfheartedly. Staring into the mists, Sentauris struggled with her Farsight to penetrate a distance of many leagues. *Merlin, your time of testing comes next. Death, the Dark Harvester, Death the Gleaner and Winnower, reaches for you at Sea's Edge — but the Enchanters will not be Death's agents. Merlin, defend yourself. Merlin, rise, and fight for our peoples!*

· ☿ ·

A warm and gentle rain swept the hills overlooking Sea's Edge, and as water cleansed the new growth of spring, the last decay of winter was finally washed away. Below the hills, down among the sandy dunes, scythe grasses, and scrub brush were bursting with slender, green, leafy shoots. Later in the summer, much of the hillside would turn dry and brittle, but now each petal and leaf seemed to take pleasure in the soft touch of warm rain.

The old man had always taken pleasure in the new growths of spring, though after more than two hundred spring seasons, his pilgrimage to the ocean shore revealed to him little that was new. The old man was cloaked, but his hood was pulled back, so that rain spattered down over his greyish white hair and beard. Old, but not stooped, Merlin passed from the estuary at Sea's Edge and climbed its overlooking hills without breathing hard. If a winter stiffness troubled his joints, his deeply enchanted body made all its required adjustments without transferring the least hint of discomfort to his mind.

When he reached the highest point of the overlooking hills, Merlin glanced down westward toward the ocean. A moment later he turned east to the foothills and to the estuary that lapped those still waters over his doorstep. All these images became fixed on the inner portions of his enchanted mind, like a frieze painted on a far wall in a sunlit courtyard.

Even as I stand here, Merlin thought, slowly shaking his head, *Stone Mountain is being restored by Thorian, just as Gravengate will one day be rebuilt — if our League survives. So why do I judge that my own stronghold at Sea's Edge will so quickly come to an end? Some inner portion of my mind needs to have these images be frozen forever, saying that soon I may regard them never again.*

The old man trudged down to the lower hills then passed through scrub brush, then into fields of scythe grasses, up hillocks, and down sandy dunes until he stood on the ocean shore, where waves pounded and foamed over the long, sandy beaches of Alantéa the Forerunner. Merlin studied the ocean for a time, then he closed his eyes and spoke soft words. Though he had not been born with the Farsighted reach of Sentauris, still there was much that subtle magic could show him from afar. Ocean sounds retreated as the Wizard's mind *reached....*

As though from a great height, Merlin watched the camp of the Enchanters, a place north and west of Gravengate, where two Enchanters stood uncovered and unattended in the drizzle and haze of the early morning. To come closer or to attempt to hear their words was to be barred from viewing them, so Merlin was content to view them from a distance.

The two gaunt figures stood apart from one another, speaking together in hushed tones, while a damp wind, as though investigating their strangeness, tugged at their long, dark cloaks. As the two conversed they were joined by a third Enchanter, one whose painful passage was marked by slow, hesitant steps.

Helcar heals first, having taken but one thrust of Dragonfire. Manassas will join him soon, with Nairn following, so that all five Enchanters will again stand together. But why have I continued to consider them human? It is obvious that they have become another race of beings, with their nonhuman portions providing much of their newfound power.

I have focused so strongly on the nature of the Gods opposing us, that I have neglected the furtive secrecy of these Enchanters. To what form of power have these beings — no longer human — been grafted? Are they now demigods? Who has created them, and can they be unmade? These are questions that the Seeress may also have considered. As Merlin shifted his vision, the noise of running surf intruded briefly on his hearing, then all the scents and sights and sounds again receded, as he reached for Sentauris.

The Seeress was beyond the walls of Gravengate, slipping through the mists, searching the dead bodies of their foes for clues as to the nature of their enemies. Ghorm was at her side, grumbling as always, but glad to be again in the presence of Sentauris. Now, sensing the mind of Merlin, she stood up swiftly, facing toward Sea's Edge where the great Wizard dwelt.

Merlin, her mind called across the distance. *Merlin, a storm of magic comes for you! Ready yourself*

I know this, daughter of the League. I know also that you and I tremble, our lips tremble, at the edge of naming the second Power who has attacked our

League. May those words come to us soon! Yet another mystery haunts this great struggle. What has transformed these Enchanters? What is the source of their newfound power?

Merlin, they consider themselves bound to fragments of an Ancient Power, and have thus obtained immort....

But here the image of Sentauris shuddered, sounds of her voice became throttled noises, then she vanished. From a great distance, Merlin's link was severed, and his hearing could only record the shore sounds of Sea's Edge.

The Wizard shook his head in gloomy contemplation. *I am surprised that I was permitted even that brief moment with the Seeress. Wizard and heroic allies have been and will be again, one of the great themes of this League, however long it may last. Also, I am glad that the Seeress is united once more with her small ally, for I sense that I will need both of them again in circumstances I cannot begin to understand. Why would I require both the Seeress and her Familiar? They have already preserved our fortresses, and so our struggle should proceed to a higher level, with greater powers moving to counter the Enchanters and the Gods supporting them. The tasks required of Sentauris and Ghorm should now be finished — but I sense they are not.*

Further, I will also need Mir, and our Adepts, who have risen to a higher level of power in this struggle. Yet how might these three be put into play against five Enchanters or the Powers of the Mid-World? And can our two Adepts still function together, with their rivalry for Sentauris, our Seeress, and great battle leader? Again, Merlin stared into the distance, mind reaching, and all the shoreline sounds receded....

"...strange as anything I might ever have imagined," Orantes was saying to Wylar. If the Adepts had become more powerful, they were still not able to sense Merlin's far-reaching intellect. "Somehow, all my days I have struggled to insulate myself from my own fears — through wine and laughter, lust and feasting — but fear of what? Fear of death, fear of rejection, of betrayal, of fear itself? Who can say, because no enchanted mirror seems able to show me clearly what lies within my own mind." Orantes was leaning over a parapet, with a goblet of wine to his left that the Adept had not yet touched. Vague mists spread tiny droplets over Orantes and Wylar as the two spoke in hushed voices.

"And so," Orantes continued, "for my love of Sentauris I was prepared to set all those old fears aside — whatever devils tormented me, they became only dusty scarecrows when I felt my love for her. I was transformed! But then she would not have me! She says that her own fate is strange, that she will never marry, that no distant, sunlit cottage will ever provide her with a fairytale ending. Certainly, if her fate is strange, then my own is equally bizarre."

"I do not understand, either," Wylar began, "but for both you and Sentaur —"

"No, be quiet just for a moment." Orantes straightened. "Enough nice, mealy-mouthed talk. If she has some affection for me, she cares equally for you. Sentauris is far too discrete to say these things openly, but I sensed that one day you, too, are destined to become her lover. Yet, in the end, she will choose neither of us nor does there exist some magnificent, enchanted hero waiting for her in the kingdoms of the Gods! She says she will never wed, that her fate lies elsewhere."

Orantes sipped wine, shook his head, then swept both goblet and wine off the parapet's edge. "Now you and I, my brother-in-arms, we may one day wed, but when we stare out into distant sunsets, we may not be thinking only of our wives."

Merlin pulled his mind away, faintly embarrassed, and troubled for the lives of his servants. Yet at least their alliance would not come to grief because of jealousy.... As before, when his mind returned from its enchanted voyage, ocean sounds returned, and as the Wizard looked down, he discovered that the tide had sent a crest of foam to lap at the tips of his boots. Merlin simply smiled and retreated to higher ground, so that he might look again upon the shore's coiled and pounding surf.

So, while great power moves against me and Sea's Edge, I have busied myself — for reasons I do not understand — with intermediate pieces like the Adepts, the Elf-Mage, and the Seeress. How might these possibly help us against a Greater God that so easily smashes aside The Game of the Masters? Who is this Power and why are the Enchanters turning against this God? From the posture of Pentarchus, I read fear mixed with defiance and determination.

At the beginning of this struggle, such a long time ago, Mordred and another Greater God conspired together, then opened a great war against us. Their first thrust consisted of Creatures Indomitable, Vorrs, Uraks, Carags, and many armed legions. When this onslaught was checked, the Enchanters were launched against us, and they now control most of our League. Yet they have not overcome even one of our strongholds, in part because they remain so overly cautious when dealing with their master and would-be allies....

Sea's Edge will be next; I can sense this unnamed Power preparing to move against me directly. So much is clear. But why cannot I discover the identity of this God-being And what form will its thrust take?

Merlin stared at the shore, lost in contemplation. Again, the lines of foam reached for him, but this time they fell short. *I have come to the sea because the answer to many of my questions lies beneath the waves. I have long sensed that some great mystery lies hidden deep within the ocean depths, though my search today is far different, more immediate. At this moment, some event transpires beneath the surface, and if I could only see beneath the sea's dark swells, or hear above the soft, muted sounds of its depths....*

Merlin's mind reached, but he could only sense the interlocking layers of dark, salted waters, where tendrils of green vegetation reached for pale, distant lights, and strands of dead seaweed sank down through the blackness; while in the depths, stones that were crusted with coral toppled over a sea-valley's edge, making low, grating sounds as they worked their way to the bottom of a jagged abyss.

·)X(·

Many hours after sunset, Set plunged through the depths, his enormous form churning through dark waters, stirring the many layers of silt that covered the sea's hidden treasures. Mordred had summoned him to a third meeting, using tones filled with threats that were only thinly veiled. It was rash and dangerous to attempt a third meeting in violation of the Truce, but a dark violence boiled in Set, and thoughts of battering and smashing Mordred filled Set with an inner fire that threatened to sear his own essence.

As Set thrashed through the ocean depths, the former rulers of dark waters fled — enormous squids scattered in panic, and the great whales that hunted them raced desperately toward the surface. For this underwater meeting, Set had taken the form of an enormous behemoth, the greatest monstrosity of the depths, a leviathan with the lines of a whale; but its body held scores of thick, stubby arms for grappling, and tusks were set in its jaws, ready to rip and tear.

Now, the behemoth's bulging eyes caught the first hint of light. In the distance a radiance of muted green and blue was glimmering, lights that shifted and swirled with the presence of another great beast: Mordred. Set surged forward, then suddenly brought his violent passage to a halt, coasting instead, slowly, toward the muted lights. Some force had been hidden from him, obscured from his senses — was he traveling toward some crude trap? What had Mordred devised, and how might he possibly hope to counter the Great God Set?

With all his powers focused on the impending confrontation, Set eased his way toward the muted lights that glowed so strangely on the ocean floor.

·)(·

As a transformed Set surged through dark waters, a sleeping Sentauris was passing through Gates of Dreams. She found herself in a dark forest before a small campfire where seven wolfhounds lay dozing or asleep. Suddenly aware, she turned to her right, where her uncle Vlasoff was staring into her eyes, his head nodding slowly.

She turned and embraced him. "Even if we only meet in dreams," she whispered, "it is still a wonderful moment for me. Uncle, you and I have fought so hard, and so strongly, for the League that you loved. You should be very proud of us."

Vlasoff smiled, hugging Sentauris in his strong arms. "I know, daughter of mine. The Goddess has shown me much. And we are meeting in something more than dreams, for the Goddess has been trying to heal me, though I am incompletely well. I am here to tell you that a great vision is coming into your dreaming mind, a vision you might otherwise discount. But you must listen very carefully to your own words, for the destiny of the League that we love is wrapped in those words. Listen to yourself, daughter of mine."

Sentauris stared into her uncle's eyes. "Is it possible that you or the Goddess might name the second and greater God of the Mid-World who assails us? If we could name that Power, so many things might become possible."

Vlasoff shook his head slowly. As he stared into his small campfire, his eyes lost their focus, and soft tears began to slip down his face. Her uncle wasn't able to respond; it seemed likely that he couldn't even understand her question.

Sentauris woke suddenly. Her night vision had been so powerful that she found herself on the floor, hurled from her bed. In the darkness, her mouth opened and spoke words that were strange, even to herself.

"Ten Words!" Then before she could even stand, her dry mouth opened again and said even louder. "The Great Dark God will speak only ten words — and the Enchanters will be completely unmade!"

·)(·

As Set approached cautiously, he saw that Mordred had also come prepared for battle: the Renegade Dark God had become a gigantic Carcharodon, a giant among giant sharks, with jagged teeth in treble rows, and fierce, glinting eyes. Set hung back at the outer circle of light, his great bulk partly obscured by shadowy dark waters.

"Ah, behold the Great God Set," Mordred called to him, eyes glinting with malice. "Come forward, Lord, and share your wisdom with me." The giant shark's tail betrayed Mordred's words, thrashing back and forth as though preparing to lunge at Set.

"Rash fool," Set replied quietly, though his own Leviathan's bulk shook with violence. "Each meeting brings an added risk. What have you to say that is so important?"

"Set, all your devices are laid bare. You intended to destroy the Wizards, then visit destruction upon your own creations, the Enchanters, and after, you planned to betray me to the Mid-World of the Truce so that I might become vanquished or exiled."

Mordred breathed scorn: turmoils of hot vapor bubbled from the depths. "Set, I will not be betrayed. Set, I defy you and declare myself your enemy forever. Come forward now, and deal with me, Power to Power, if you have real trust in your own might."

Set's form shuddered with violent impulses, but instead, he forced his own choked voice to speak. "First, we must meet elsewhere, far from this place. You seem far too assured here, beneath a mountain of dark waters."

Mordred laughed, taunting Set with rippling and lunging motions. Set's Leviathan form only backed further into the murky darkness beyond Mordred's circle of glimmering light.

Mordred seemed to shrug. A hesitation hung in the air, then a huge plate on the ocean floor grated to one side. A massive snake's head lifted out, as though some enormous serpent had lain coiled in the bowels of the earth, and now peered from its lair.

"Haeglin," Set breathed out, and behind Mordred's gigantic form, a rock shelf came to life, revealing enormous, crusted legs, and huge pincers, belonging to a bottom dweller as large in bulk as Set himself.

"Un-Maurag," Set spoke haltingly, backing from the light. Before him stood all three of the greatest of the Renegade Dark Gods; and the lineage of Un-Maurag was only a little less potent than Set's own. "But what of the Truce that forbids these alliances?" Set whispered, bubbles rising up through dark waters.

Mordred laughed aloud. "You, the truce breaker, dare to call upon this pact? Hear me, Set — the Renegade Dark Gods, or self-styled Dark Lords have never acknowledged this Truce. We are not foolish enough to raise our war standards together upon the shores of Alantéa or join with one another battling any other Power in the Mid-World kingdoms of the Gods. But we plot incessantly together, and we are your enemies forever, Set the betrayer." The three lunged at Set, and the Great God fled.

·)(·

"I can almost see them," Sentauris murmured into the darkness as she knelt upright. "I can almost hear them as they speak to one another...." On the floor of her dark bedchamber, her eyes closed, reaching. She cried out a single *word* in a language she had never before heard. Some distance from her, a cold, dark wind seemed to brush Balardi as he sat studying an ancient grimoire by candlelight, while many leagues from the fortress, four Enchanters woke suddenly in pain, as though their souls had been brushed by strands of hellfire.

A kneeling Sentauris toppled over. Only a dim moonlight penetrated the upper windows of her chamber as she whispered, "The Sight within me is blind again, for the moment. We must wait for Mír's return. Before that moment I must speak with Balardi. He and his brother Wizards must work ceaselessly in the next few days if any of our peoples are to survive."

· �X ·

Struggling with his own violence and fury, Set sought to transform himself into a being of reason, to become a remote Gods sealed within a throne room that lay upon the roof of the planet. As he fought with his inner rage, images of the Mid-World and of Alantéa the Forerunner flooded his mind; Set drew sustenance from numberless scenes of violence, predation, and brutal death. Gradually, the turmoil within his mind diminished, and Set became transformed.

Tendrils, filaments of power emerged from the throne room of Set, reaching out into the farthest reaches of his domain, strengthening, and sealing the foundations of his realm. Nairn was healing; Set increased his flow of power to the wounded Enchanter, though Nairn was not permitted to wake, not yet.

New servants were created to replace the old, demented ghostly beings that Set had so casually destroyed. These new creatures he made more powerful and vengeful — able to withstand his own wrath and visit it upon the many inhabitants of Alantéa and the Far Lands.

Set, a transformed God, glanced to the south of Alantéa, where Wizards and Enchanters busied themselves with lesser matters. The Elf-Mage Mír had not yet healed; it seemed fitting that the Mage and the far more powerful Enchanter Nairn should be returned at the same time, and so it would be arranged.

Set turned to Mordred, a Renegade Dark God struggling feverishly to shore up his own realm. Taken together, all three of the Renegade Dark Gods controlled only a small segment of the power of the Mid-World. If Fate ordained that these three alone suffered the full displeasure of the Truce...well, their mournful destiny was hardly worthy of pity. They might be enslaved or obliterated or merely exiled; it was impossible to know before judgment day, as no Power had yet aroused the full wrath of the Mid-World of the Truce.

Refreshed, Set again took upon himself his aspect as a mighty, but barely rational Dark God. His new servants bowed low before him. These beings were only twice the size of pitifully small humans and thus were forced to struggle with the great doors leading from his throne room. Pacing himself, Set followed his servants to his place of power, where these same lesser beings labored to open an alcove door leading to the Forge of Set.

Set stepped up to his Forge and grasped an enormous multifaceted crystal globe. One of Set's new servants might have stood upright within the device, though in Set's equally large hands the crystal was nothing more than a globe, although it was one that he was forced to hold with both hands.

The Great God spoke *words* and the globe shuddered with transforming energies. Then Set released it so that it floated in midair, spinning slowly like a small planet. Thousands of facets shimmered with the light of enchanted gems as it rotated. Set's servants knelt before their master's device, the Sending of all Sendings, now containing the souls of demonic servants — thousands of creatures created by the Wrath of Set — together with the destructive power of five Great Spells.

Set beheld his creation and was well pleased.

Yet more was needed. The Great God turned and dismissed his servants, so that they withdrew, backing and bowing to their lord and God. *It will be some time before I am accustomed to my new servants,* Set considered, *who if they are more capable than the old, are also far less entertaining. I can no longer indulge myself as I have in the past...except in this one matter, a task in which I must also **take** part while **standing** apart....*

Set paced around his revolving crystal, studying its interior. From the Forge of Set and from his other places of power, came flows of energy — both from his own stored potency and from forces drawn over centuries from the Mid-World. The air seemed to crackle with the threat of destruction, and within the globe, Set's ghosts came awake and began struggling for ascendancy among themselves.

In the fullness of his might, the Great God raised both his hands and called out *words* of power. Shuddering sounds rocked Set's empire, then suddenly the Great God stood as two beings: one being contained the Wrath of Set, the second, the Wisdom of Set. As Set's Wrath stepped forward to embrace the globe, the Wisdom of Set paced around its Avatar-Brother, calling down transforming miracle-work, cloaking Set's Wrath, so that it became disguised as a night-dark, gigantic Storm Giant, covered by the many layers of a huge black cloak.

The transformed Wrath of Set then gathered its globe, shielding it within the folds of its great cloak. Then, the disguised Avatar raised one hand and slipped downward, passing through the domain of Set, then through the root systems of power leading to the Mid-World, and from those lines of force into the soil of Alantéa the Forerunner.

Moving with great stealth, the Wrath of Set would require nearly two revolutions of the planet before it could pass through earth's core. Then it would assail Sea's Edge from an untraceable, undiscoverable base in the Far Lands.

No Power would ever discover how the Wrath of Set had destroyed the Wizard's lair. In the meantime, Set would let himself be seen, chastising errant servants, disrupting refugees that sought the League, waylaying lone Sidhe, setting sorcerous traps for inquisitive Elf-Mages, and all the other endeavors that filled the Dark God's day with mildly amusing diversions.

Strangely, Set looked forward to these tasks with little of his old enthusiasm.

· ✖ ·

As work on the rebuilding of Gravengate progressed, warm rains brought hints of summer. But when night embraced Gravengate, the mist and drizzle chilled the stonework of the fortress, so that its inhabitants felt as though they had fallen back to the early edge of spring.

Ghorm and Sentauris had changed into dry clothes and sat warming themselves beside a small fire. For several hours after nightfall, Sentauris sat speaking to Ghorm, telling him tales of heroes favored by the Gods. As she spoke, her own mind drifted. At times she heard her own voice as though a third person entertained both herself and Ghorm; both Seeress and Familiar were lingering at the edge of sleep. Suddenly, she shook herself awake — she had trailed off, lost the thread of her story, as though she was speaking again with Vlasoff — in dreams.

"Merlin lies sleeping beneath the hill," she heard her own voice whisper. "Though the Earth trembles at its core, still Merlin lies sleeping beneath the hill." Ghorm stood, staring at Sentauris with troubled eyes.

She stared into the fire and shook her head. "Let's not repeat those words, Ghorm. I can't tell whether they come from the past, or the future, or some hidden aspect of the present."

"You won't...."

"I won't go insane. At times, a thousand visions crowd each other in my mind, but they bring only confusion, not insanity." She stood and stretched. "Tale's end, Ghorm, though now I'm awake, curse it." Ghorm glanced away, biting his tongue. *So, off she goes with Orantes once again. Who are you to object, little Ghorm the Goblin?*

"It's better not to press, Ghorm," Sentauris said quietly. "Though on this night, I need only to walk. Moments ago, the Dreamways were calling to me, but now I am like a panther in a cage, ready to pace back and forth until I can find a way to slip through the iron bars of my prison." She pulled on a dark cloak, leaving Ghorm to seek sleep in his own chamber or to find companionship with other Familiars elsewhere in Gravengate.

Out in the corridor, she glanced to the upper landing that led to Mír's empty chamber. She and the Elf-Mage were quartered in the Tower of the West Wind, while Orantes and Wylar remained lodged in the Fortress of the Guard. Sentauris turned to face east, *reaching* for the Adepts: each lay awake, thinking dark thoughts on fate and grey, lifeless futures. She shook her head in discomfort. *The two of them would make for dreary company on a chilly night.* She shrugged and was down the tower's seven flights of stairs in seconds.

Out in the night, a moist darkness seemed to swallow sputtering watchfires so that fires gave off more smoke than light. Only werelight radiating from the Citadel of the Keep remained untouched by dampness.

Sentauris paced through the night, using her *sight* to avoid the night-watch. On the perimeter, both the inner and outer walls seemed well manned, and if damp guards huddled too closely together, their sloppy watch offered little danger to Gravengate.

She slipped beyond the Fortress of the Guard on swift steps, wary of the love-struck Orantes, and the soft, unspoken rebuke that lay behind Wylar's averted eyes. Her steps grew lighter, although she avoided running, not wishing to alert the guards. Rain pelted down harder, but the cold and the damp seemed to increase her awareness rather than incline her to sleep.

I am searching for something, but what? Or am I again being summoned? Her pace slowed as she neared the Citadel of the Keep. High above her, in his place of power, Balardi had become aware of her approach, curious about her swift movements late at night. Pretending to yawn, she passed a suddenly alert guard and entered the Keep.

Her feet had begun to choose their own path; they led her down three flights of stairs into a broad chamber where one of Gravengate's deep streams spilled endless tides of water over layers of fountains and basins. This water source was one of Gravengate's great siege-assets, but here the watch was more than sloppy: two young guards had fallen fast asleep, with both armor and spears leaning carelessly against torchlit walls. Far above Sentauris, the Wizard continued to follow her progress, and nothing she might do in the next few moments seemed likely to divert him.

She walked swiftly beyond the sleeping guards, eyes searching, every sense alert. There, on the far left-hand corner wall — were shadows twisting strangely in the torchlight, or were her eyes playing tricks on her? And beyond the shadows was that the outline of a door carved into stone, where no entrance had existed before?

Above her, the Wizard was massing power; she could feel the trembling as great magic prepared itself to repel any intrusion into Gravengate. But this Portal was intended for her, and it was a gateway, not a trap. She crossed to the chamber's far corner on swift feet and pushed the stone door open.

The way was open to a dark tunnel that led downward. She entered and closed the door behind her. But as she sealed herself from the light, the tunnel was assaulted by a force of magic, so that the dark passageway shuddered and shook all around her. She stumbled and fell. As the Master of Gravengate struggled with another Power, and the stonework of the fortress groaned and shook, Sentauris forced herself to her feet.

"Master of Gravengate!" she called out. "Hold back! Your foes lie outside of Gravengate and not inside!" She sensed the force of magic hesitate, as it studied her own presence and the nature of the stone passageway surrounding her. Then, suddenly, the magic called to Gravengate's defense died out, and she was left alone in a dark, enchanted passageway.

She edged forward, using her *Sight* to guide her through the darkness. All around her, stone walls shifted and trembled as she inched forward, though now in the distance, a dim light began to flicker. She quickened her pace, beginning to understand what lay before her.

The passage shuddered and shook with a strange harmony. Her own form began to shiver with an internal transformation; her body mass seemed to be lessening, growing smaller with each step. And her flesh was changing as she raced through the enchanted passageway. Her skin seemed to glow, its substance changed into heat, while her clothing passed from her as though shed in some effortless transformation.

I am becoming a being of light, a slender, brief fire. She could feel her form's heat warming the cold dark stone around her. *If there is an afterlife, perhaps it will be something like this — I will be reduced to sentient fire, no more than a hand's height tall.* She turned a corner and slowed. The passage was wider, opening into a broad chamber. Light filled the chamber, the majestic flames chosen by a Goddess revealing herself as a being of fire.

If I am garbed as a candle in the wind, then Pallas Athena emerges like a blazing torch, Sentauris thought. *Such is our relative strength.* Her flame-essence slipped forward into the chamber then bowed deeply before her Goddess and benefactor.

"Holy Mother," Sentauris said softly, her breath itself a whisper of flame.

"Mortal Daughter, I do not fault you, but these Wizards have become too powerful. I would not be troubled by the Master of Gravengate's strength, but other, lesser Gods, might find this Wizard difficult to overcome." Within the fire-essence that Sentauris had become, there seemed no tongue to bite, though she refrained from speaking.

"Yet perhaps," Pallas Athena continued, "the increasing power of Mortals is yet another jest created by the Maker. So many ages ago, I spoke with the Maker not just once, but several times, and though the First Fashioner restrained Himself from overwhelming me, I could sense an enormous power tempered by compassion. Perhaps He even foresaw this, our moment together."

The Goddess swirled flame and the chamber was suddenly changed: the two flame-beings stood before a great mirror so that both Goddess and Seeress could view their own essences, one beside the other. If the fires within Pallas Athena were far more radiant, higher, and majestic, many of the flaming patterns within Sentauris shone with intricate hues both subtle and brilliant.

"How I will miss you, mortal daughter," the Goddess murmured. "Even if you are a candle lit only for an evening, while I am starlight that never seems to age, and yet you do shine so brightly. Is it possible that to the Maker we are both candles?" The Goddess stared at Sentauris as though fixing her inner fires into memory.

Sentauris bowed. "Holy Mother," she murmured, "I have so much to thank you for, not least that you sent allies to keep Uncle Vlasoff from death at the hands of torturers."

Pallas Athena smiled. "For once it was not this Goddess intervening. I could name that other Power if I wished, though it is better that you do not know. Now, heed me, Seeress and Warrior Princess, for I have much to tell you. Firstly, I was astonished that the Enchanters withstood the weapons I crafted for you; so, I investigated the nature of these conjurors and the sources of their newfound powers. Each of these five beings is bound to some portion of an Ancient Adversary. This Adversary is a being I almost seem to recognize, a great force in the Ancient Wars, one that vanished during those many battles, for I do not believe that this Adversary passed into the Mid-World of the Truce.... I stood with the Spirit Lords then, and the Seraphs, supported by a few Gift Born humans, as we fought ceaselessly with the Demons, the Dragons, and the Creatures of the Darkness.

"I was then a Spirit Lord, yet now all is changed, for while the greatest part of me remains akin to Spirit Lords, the fires of Seraphs and Demons and Dragons are mingled within my inner core. Such is the sacrifice we made to preserve Earth's Gardens, and I do not regret the Mid-World of the Truce, a pact that embraces both good and evil, for otherwise, a desolation of grim, grey death would have gathered over this planet.

"So," Athena continued, "these Enchanters are bound to fragments of an Ancient Adversary, some being that remained outside the Mid-World of the Truce. Merlin has begun to understand the nature of the Enchanters; and to you, mortal daughter, have come the first of the words of power that may unmake, unbind these hybrid creatures. That such words exist, suggests that the unknown Great God who fashioned them, does not intend his Enchanters to survive beyond this struggle. Yet I fear that Pentarchus, the most powerful of the Enchanters, understands more of these matters than I do, and perhaps Merlin does also.

"A moment of destiny comes to Sea's Edge. First Merlin endures some great test — he may survive, or he may not. After, like the backlash of a powerful spell, Mír and Nairn are returned to your respective camps. Then, you must lead a force to Sea's Edge. Do not let the Wizards accompany you, for Powers not previously involved in this struggle will rise against them. Your League has sufficient foes without attracting others.

"For this moment of destiny, I have crafted new weapons for you, ones that are far more likely to destroy your foes. Use these with great caution, for they are deadly, powerful, and unrelenting. Mír will aid you, and your Adepts will modify their Dragonfire so that they again will have the power to damage your foes.

"Now go, daughter, whose essence is filled with destiny. Do not investigate the future and forecast that we will meet again, for I have searched these matters with my own powers. In many futures, you do not live beyond two more sunsets, while in a few others, you become old and grey, and the fires within you are reduced to the embers of coals. Then we will sit together, watching a bittersweet sunset and talk of parting until the End of Time. Farewell, my daughter."

Greater flames embraced a lesser fire. Their closeness held for a dozen heartbeats, then suddenly Sentauris was released. She found herself returned in human form to the entrance of an enchanted passageway. Her hands shook as she pulled the iron ring that opened the door made of stone and stepped into the lower gallery. There, she found herself in the presence of two score guardsmen, who watched her with anxious eyes.

The air was cold again; only her right hand remained warm. She glanced down and saw that her right hand held a dark canister containing seven arrows: each shaft was formed of bluish grey matter, the color of an angry sea, bristling with dark crimson feathers that seemed stirred by the anger of the Goddess.

·)(·

In the last hours of darkness, Merlin was engaged in a strange wizardry. He walked among the larger forms he had created; his own form was much smaller, and he stepped around them, pausing every now and again to engage them in dialogue. Sometimes the Enchanters' shapes responded, and sometimes they did not. These simulacra, constructs with the shapes and features of the Enchanters, stood almost three heads higher than the Wizard, and their eyes tended to lose focus when the Wizard was no longer engaged with them.

In the distant background could be heard soft sounds of lute and horn, as though the Wizard entertained a gathering of potent emissaries far beyond midnight. Outside the Halls of Merlin, masses of dark clouds had purged themselves of rain and were drifting north. A pale, listless moon hung overhead.

"Now, if you please," Merlin said to the larger of the Carag Enchanters, "tell me again why you would join this alliance, and allow yourself to be so completely transformed?"

"I wished to become mighty," the replica of Manassas said, staring down at the Wizard with gleaming dark eyes, "and because our master Mordred wished it so."

"Your master must have had great confidence in this second, greater power," Merlin murmured, "the Great God who made all you five Enchanters so mighty. And how is this Great God named?"

The mouth of the replicated Manassas muttered nonsense words and its eyes began to lose focus. Merlin only nodded gently, then turned away.

After studying the gaunt image of the Witch Queen, Merlin came to stand before the reconstructed form of Nairn, staring up into the dark bearded, hawk featured face of the Enchanter.

"We have all of us," Merlin began, "Wizard and Enchanter alike, studied the Powers of the Mid-World over so many years. Yet you have been closer to the Gods, entering their kingdoms to worship them or confide in their servants. What of their Emissaries, who flit and swirl about the League as they never dared when the Wizards held power? What role will these beings play?"

Nairn's eyes radiated scorn. "A great whale dies, and you wonder why scavenging seagulls flock to its carcass? Even should these Emissaries represent the Mid-World of the Truce, why should we fear them? Our patrons have never concerned themselves with these beings, so why should we?" Merlin was silent for a time, lost in distant thought, then he turned to Albino Enchanter, Pentarchus.

"So, you are now the greatest of the mortal or partly mortal conjurors," Merlin said. "To what form are you bound that you have become so mighty in such a brief time?"

The simulacrum of Pentarchus stared down at Merlin with arctic blue eyes. "Ancient Demon or Ancient Dragon, or so I have judged," Pentarchus replied, "and do not refer to me as the greatest of conjurors, for you, Merlin, may still be my equal. Yet our relative strength will never be known, for your doom comes with the dawn."

"Yes, my doom is upon me," Merlin said softly, "and when I am gone, the Enchanters will come to rule the League. Why do you not rejoice in this outcome?"

"When you pass, your League will falter and fail," Pentarchus said evenly. "We will focus on a second Wizard and that master of magic will join you in your everlasting sleep, followed by a third Wizard. Yet then our role is complete, and we may be dispensed with. Wizard, why do you think that I lingered so far from the battlefield? One spell of power exists that will unmake us. I seek to create another spell of power that will bind us forever and unify us with the being locked inside of us. I grow closer to that spell, and its words tremble upon my lips, but I cannot yet speak its words."

And so, I need to create a third spell, thought Merlin, *one that would protect our League and all our peoples.* In the last hours of darkness, Merlin walked among his replicated Enchanters, deepening his own understanding through discussion with his constructs, although a portion of his enchanted intellect understood that this process was only a final dance with the ghosts of his foes.

Night ended. The first beams of light slid toward Sea's Edge in shafts that glistened like magic daggers. Merlin sighed and waved away his ghostly Enchanters; they vanished without leaving even traces of smoke, or sighs of sorrow.

All of Merlin's human attendants had long since departed Sea's Edge; and now the Wizard called upon all his other servants, both visible and unseen, to flee the Halls of Merlin. Most vanished instantly. A few made brief testaments of undying loyalty before fleeing swiftly. Only one, the Sentinel, would not come within the Wizard's scope of power. This Sentinel, more powerful and determined than Merlin's other servants, sensed that doom was upon them and that its master might force it from Sea's Edge. Therefore, the Sentinel would not be called.

Sentinel, depart from Sea's Edge, the Wizard's mind called to his servant. *Survive to serve our League another day.*

Am I not the Sentinel, Wizard? Have I not become the Defender of Sea's Edge? Look to your own devices, Merlin my master.

Merlin peered into The Web of Fate and saw that his own doom had ensnared his Sentinel. As the first red rim of dawn peered over the horizon, a cool anger began building within the Wizard. Words slipped from his lips. Power rose from the deep wellsprings of Alantéa the Forerunner. Devices were activated, shielding the hills above Sea's Edge. Weapons, crafted long ago and hidden, woke from their slumber and gathered to their master's side.

A full third of the sun's orb glimmered from the east. The Sentinel raised itself high in the air, staring westward where darkness and cloud matter still ruled, and danger loomed. Still slight in the distance, a figure of doom was surging toward Sea's Edge.

I do not even have a God to pray to, thought the Sentinel. *Merlin, speak for me if there is any Power worth calling upon at the End of Time.*

Movements from the West became swifter. Clouds were battered and broken, as a gigantic creature strode across the ocean toward Sea's Edge. Their adversary came disguised as a cloaked and darkened Storm Giant, though the Sentinel understood that an essence of a God lay hidden within the oncoming form. And in both hands, the Giant held an enormous globe, a pulsing device, one that had become as great as Merlin's main hall.

Power lashed out from Sea's Edge: a storm of magic ripped and tore at the gigantic form. Dark and jagged lightning leaped from Merlin's Halls: the darkened Storm Giant was slowed but not stopped. More power, of a higher order, smashed at the enormous form, and now it seemed almost buffeted.

At this pulse beat of hesitation, the Sentinel formed itself into a bright lance, a beam of bright light, and launched itself at the darkened Storm Giant.

Retaining its disguise, the Wrath of Set recoiled. Its globe was left spinning in midair, radiating light, and pulsing dark energies. Raising both hands, the Wrath of Set gathered the Sentinel, crushed it, then pitched its broken form into the ocean depths.

The Wrath of Set gathered its Sending of all Sendings, took two mighty steps, then hurled the globe toward Sea's Edge.

Merlin called mighty **words** aloud, and all his crafted power raced to the defense of Sea's Edge. But the Sending burst upon the shoreline and all other magics were overwhelmed.

The foundations of the hills were blasted apart, sending avalanches of broken stones cascading down to the sea. Death swept over surrounding forests, leaving not even flames in their aftermath, but only mounds of greyish black dust. Sands boiled into glassy liquids. Pit Fiends slipped from the globe to attack every portion of the sorcerous energies that served the Wizard.

One last cast emerged from Sea's Edge, and this thrust caused the Wrath of Set to cry aloud. As though invoked by its master's cries, the Great Sending gathered itself around the Halls of Merlin. Never intended as a fortress or redoubt, the Wizard's place of power still gleamed with a silvery white radiance that withstood even the miracle work launched by Set.

Three times the Sending of Sendings surged against the Halls of Merlin, and three times the shaken Wizard within prevailed.

After the third test of strength, the Wrath of Set cried out in fury. Gliding over the turbulent waters, Set's Wrath strode toward the Halls of Merlin, crushing its central building with one blow of its gigantic foot.

Reaching within the Wizard's broken place of power, the Wrath of Set first drew out the two frozen and tiny forms of the Creatures of the Darkness preserved by Merlin. Set breathed life into them, so that they again grew large and monstrous, filled with all their ancient brute strength and hatred.

Yet in the gigantic hands of the Wrath of Set, the revived Creatures were only lesser beings. In his madness, the Wrath of Set tore each of them in half, then hurled their carcasses to the far hills. As the broken monstrosities hurtled from Sea's Edge, the Wrath of Set felt some strange sorcery quiver at its feet.

What was that?!? Set's Wrath recoiled — but nothing seemed to come from those strange pulses. Reaching again within the broken halls, Set's hand emerged with a tiny, writhing form — that of the Wizard, Merlin.

One hand crumpled the Wizard's form, squeezing and crushing it until the last drops of Merlin's lifeblood dripped down, spilling over his broken walls. A second motion of the hand hurled the ruined body of Merlin over the horizon. Then the Wrath of Set raised its blood-soaked hand as though to bathe it in the new light of day. Words of Power were spoken, sending more shudders over the shattered shoreline; then the Wrath of Set passed like dark smoke down through the ruin of Sea's Edge, into the soil of Alantéa, and so Set's Wrath vanished.

Chapter Fifteen

The Enchanters and

Their Deliverance

THE FOUR REMAINING ENCHANTERS sat in somber silence, though occasionally their eyes darted back and forth as though inviting speech. Within their enchanted bodies, the fragments of an Ancient Power stirred and seethed, agitated by the visions placed before it. Pentarchus had used his mastery of Divinations to recreate the destruction of Sea's Edge — a first, then a second time, followed by a third and final reenactment. Each vision was focused more closely on the death of Merlin, perhaps once the greatest of mortal magic wielders. Set had destroyed Merlin like a griffin crushing a mouse, and so the silence of the Enchanters was prolonged and filled with a profound disquiet.

Helcar glanced again to Manassas furtively mouthing the question *Nairn?*

Manassas merely shook his head, shrugged, then nodded to Pentarchus. The Albino Enchanter had turned his armchair to stare southwest toward Sea's Edge. All four sides of their great canvas pavilion had been raised so that a rising sun beamed in from their command pavilion's eastern side. It was only a brief time after a sunrise that had ushered the Wrath of Set and the destruction of Sea's Edge.

The Witch Queen finally interrupted their long, dark meditations. "If Nairn were present, even he would cease pursuing his own narrow interests — at least for this moment of crisis — and ask how we might all survive and triumph. Are there no other Dark Gods equal to our treacherous patron? Would no other Power accept our allegiance and shield us from the treachery of the Great God Set?"

Pentarchus turned and glanced at her with bushy eyebrows raised. "Mallegro...Arioch... Moloch...Ahriman...are any of these Set's equal? And would these other Dark Gods not consider a Spell of Annihilation to be a great jest? As for other Gods rivaling Set in power — Zôs, Wotan, Amon-Ra — what would those benevolent Powers make of our necromancy and its harvest of death?"

"And so?" Helcar prompted.

"And so, we wait, we ponder," Pentarchus said evenly. "I foresaw a climactic moment at Sea's Edge, but now Merlin is gone, and Pit Fiends are masters of his domain. In my earlier visions, we struggled for power in places of dark enchantments. Merlin was near, as was the Seeress and her lickspittle lackeys...words trembled upon my tongue...only a few words are contained within Set's Spell of Annihilation through which Set proposes to destroy us. When I know enough of those words, I will alter them to transform us into beings that can never be unmade."

The Witch Queen sat bolt upright. "One of Set's spellwords was spoken just one day past. Did you not feel its lash?"

"Flames searing our souls," Manassas agreed. "I looked for a God or Wizard as its source, but it was neither of those forces, it was another, a Giftless mortal."

"The Seeress," the Witch Queen hissed. "Who else has her strength of Farsight? Who else might discover this so-called Spell of Annihilation?"

"Sentauris, of course," Pentarchus agreed. "She was present, almost central, to visions of conflict at Sea's Edge, where our last, decisive struggle would have transformed or destroyed us."

The Witch Queen glared at Pentarchus with eyes that hung heavy with menace. "You said nothing about our possible destruction before."

"Yes, I did hesitate to discuss that possibility," Pentarchus said calmly. "Two futures lie before us. Either we reforge ourselves or we are utterly destroyed. If we triumph, the malice of Set and the treachery of Mordred would no longer be feared. However, that moment of decision has not yet arrived, and had there been a way to transform our destiny I myself would have acted, for do I not share the fate of the Enchanters? With Merlin's passing, however, matters become far simpler."

Pentarchus turned his chair to face the other three, then stared at them for a moment, favoring them with a rare, wintry smile. "The Seeress will still be drawn to this junction at Sea's Edge: the broken Halls of Merlin lie across an intersection, a nexus, a crossroads where the Fates separate the living from the dead. The Enchanters will greet her there, destroy her Adept flunkies, and the trifling Elf-Mage. After, we will each possess the Seeress, carnally and cruelly, so that the poisons seethe and surge within her. Then, at the last moments of her existence, we will control her Farsight and force the remaining unspoken words of Annihilation from her mind. With this knowledge, I will transform the Enchanters into beings that can never again be tampered with. The last two Wizards will be crushed, and after, we will turn upon our great malefactors, Set the Destroyer, and Mordred the Malignant."

Pentarchus spoke with authority; a new purpose seemed to rise within the Enchanters, though their faces hardened as they stared outside the pavilion to a place where the air rippled and shivered, forming an oval Portal to a distant Mid-World kingdom.

"Nairn is returning to us," the Witch Queen whispered, then she stood. "And so, we are prepared for our last great testing."

Balardi sat somberly at the head of his council table, staring into the distance. Every few minutes his eyes would glance at Wylar or Orantes, then flash to Sentauris, and after, the Wizard would shake his head in gloom.

"I will speak those same words for a third time," Sentauris said, "if only to break the silence. Merlin lies sleeping beneath the hill. I have not seen his sleeping form with my own inner visions, but those words whisper themselves into my mind over and over again in the tones always used by my Seer's Sight."

Wylar looked away with an unhappy, uncomfortable expression. Sentauris had spoken of Merlin's continued existence twice before, but nothing she could say could offset the vision of his own eyes. From afar, through the Wizard's power, they had viewed the destruction of Sea's Edge, and Wylar had seen the red gore spurting from the enormous dark hand of the Storm Giant — some enormously powerful Dark God in disguise. Now they sat in Gravengate's Council Chamber, listening to Sentauris as she spoke of forlorn hopes. Balardi stared out into space, face gaunt and drawn, feeling the work of a Wizard's long lifetime slipping from his hands.

"It is true," Orantes said hesitantly, "that Merlin at times seemed remote, while at other times he was far more human. Yet Wizards, too, are subject to moods."

"Besides, you speak of magic you do not understand," Balardi said, eyes still staring into the distance. "Simulacra — ghostly recreations — are one thing, but a complete, interchangeable replica is a thing no magician has ever succeeded in accomplishing. Also, Merlin would have spoken of this spellwork to Thorian and myself."

"Have you no devices," Sentauris shot back, "that would protect you at the edge of destruction? You may share matters of sorcery with your brother Wizards, but would you share one last great device that might save your life?" A startled Balardi glanced at Sentauris, wondering how much of her argument was based on guesswork, and how much on knowledge.

"And yet," Wylar added softly, "if we think back on our long struggle, the vision of Sentauris has never failed us. Also, Merlin was accounted the greatest of mortal magicians. When we consider the ruin of Sea's Edge, it seems almost too easy. The destruction and death of Merlin should have been far more difficult, more complex and protracted." Balardi shook his head, knowing something of the great miracle work that lay at the fingertips of the Gods.

"The Gods are mighty," Sentauris said, "and Alantéa the Forerunner is a land of many perils. But one major line of fate will take Merlin into the most remote and distant future, into the Far Lands on some strange tasks." Wylar's face again looked dubious, and conflicting emotions flashed over the face of his fellow Adept.

Come, Orantes, come, the Adept argued with himself. *Though this talk of Merlin alive is nothing but a fairytale for small children on dark nights, yet still you owe her this support and much, much more.* "I will go with you, Sentauris," Orantes said, after a pause. "Let us go together and discover what lies sleeping beneath the hill at Sea's Edge."

"And I, too, will journey with you to Sea's Edge," Wylar added. "Part of my mind says that Merlin is gone forever, while another portion whispers that you have never led us astray."

"Destiny will take us to Sea's Edge," Sentauris said. "You and Orantes, Ghorm and myself — and Mír. Balardi cannot join us, for the Gods would respond by breaking Mír's Portal magic and hurling us far from our destination."

"Not even our Familiars?" Wylar asked.

"Whisper and Squint would be destroyed in seconds," Sentauris said. "For strange reasons that I have not been permitted to understand, Ghorm must journey with us."

Balardi said nothing but pushed his chair back; it was time to communicate with Thorian. They would unfurl the Banner of the Maker, the God of Gods. Then they would make a stand, fighting one last brutal battle of magic before moving beyond death into the Long Sleep.

"Great Wizard," Wylar said softly, "our master, and pillar of the League, will you not wait for just a few moments? Recall how we once disagreed, sitting in this place nearly fifteen days ago. Then you cast a future on this very table and after, our choices grew far more clear. Can we not do the same at this intersection?"

"That was then," Balardi replied, "and this is now. Now is a time after the death of Merlin, the central force of our League."

"Cast a future," Orantes said, "if only to clarify matters for the rest of us. Then we will stand with you at the last stand, without confusion, without disagreement among ourselves." Orantes glanced to Sentauris, who sighed then nodded slowly.

Balardi rose, gathering the pouch at his side that contained small emblems fashioned of metal, each bearing an image of *The Game of the Masters*. With a gesture of defiance, he spilled his whole pouch over the council table, where all those emblems spun and whirled and settled into a stilled pattern. The Wizard gave the pattern one lone grim glance then turned to go.

"We are dead things," Wylar breathed out.

"The Wizard was right," Sentauris said softly. "My Sight has become a blind thing. How could I have been so far from the truth?"

And Orantes felt again the old fear that froze his loins and threatened to choke his heart.

But suddenly the emblems of the *Game* began to gleam with power. They rose above the table, each of them, as though touched by tiny invisible hands. Then they spun and whirled, flashing lights, twisting in midair until they resettled on the table.

"A new pattern!" Sentauris muttered. "See, Merlin lies sleeping beneath the hill, and just at this very moment, *The Game of the Masters* has learned this truth. Watch!" Before other eyes could read the pattern of the pieces, the emblems again rose, spun, and twisted, and danced, gleaming with power.

Finally, the pieces came to a halt, clustered, mounded, and clumped together in a dull and lifeless heap.

"There is no firm or complete pattern," Sentauris said, her voice dropping to a whisper. "So many forces and powers have been invoked that no clear future can emerge."

Astonished, still grim faced, Balardi turned suddenly to the far corner of the Council Chamber, where the air was beginning to shiver and pulse, becoming a great oval Portal-mouth. The Wizard stepped forward, speaking words of power so that the rippling motions in the air were held frozen.

Sentauris and the Adepts turned toward the frozen Portal, their hands reaching for weapons. A pause held them transfixed, then the Wizard murmured, "Mír is coming," and he waved aside his restraining magic. The oval formed and deepened, becoming a gateway to the halls of healing in the enchanted kingdoms of Thoth. Healed, and filled with an energy and purpose that radiated through the chamber, the Elf-Mage Mír stepped through, and the Portal vanished behind him.

"It may be hard for any of us to believe," the Elf-Mage said in a low, intense voice, "but Merlin *does* lie sleeping beneath the hill. Wizard, arm us mightily, for we must journey to Sea's Edge and draw Merlin from his place of deep slumber before the Enchanters find him first, and destroy him."

· ✗ ·

"Hold back, just for a moment, a brief time longer," Pentarchus spoke softly, though the others could feel energy surging within the Enchanter, like the last spurt that comes at the end of a great race. "Let our foes commit first to a Portal passage to Sea's Edge...." The Enchanter laughed aloud. "Why would they not transport one Wizard at least? They would have thus trebled their power, but they are sending only the Seeress, her Adepts, her Mage — and the little rat-like goblin that serves her! Such a small force is worth only one Enchanter and not all five, but still, we should hold back until they reach the ruined Halls of Merlin."

Behind Pentarchus, four impatient Enchanters stood apart from one another, tall and gaunt, ready to forge a Portal to Sea's Edge, then transform their destiny through swift and violent actions. Nairn tapped his feet, dancing with impatience, while the Carag Enchanters twitched with the urge to transform themselves. The Witch Queen struggled to remain calm by studying the features of Pentarchus, watching an unusual irritation flicker over the features of the Albino Enchanter.

"Again, it is Set or Mordred, or another brutal and stupid God Being!" Pentarchus raised his voice. "Let them through! Leave the Seeress alone! We, the Enchanters, will deal with them!" Like the others, the Witch Queen felt the tremors of distant Portal magic and she growled; some outside Power was tampering with the Portal formed by the Elf-Mage, preventing his party from slipping through enchanted passageways to Sea's Edge.

It was Set's doing! Set! Nairn's hatred boiled within both his mortal and immortal portions. *Set, how we yearn for your destruction! Yet your ruin must come very swiftly before the Mid-World of the Truce can come to your aid.* Then the cunning, calculating portion of Nairn's sorcerous mind made one last effort: *Wait, Nairn, wait. The Power within you cries aloud for a Great God's death, and your own soul seethes with rage. But are we, the Enchanters, truly prepared? Even Pentarchus has yielded at last to the impatient fragment within him, so none of the Enchanters regards the future with any caution. Nairn, the other Enchanters are so consumed by hatred that they —*

"The Seeress is through!" Pentarchus cried aloud. "And we are only a slight step behind them!" All Nairn's hesitations were swept aside as a great-arched Portal-mouth flashed open before the Enchanters, and they entered in order of power. Pentarchus was first, followed by Nairn and the Witch Queen, with the Carag Enchanters a half-step behind them.

"Stand fast!" Pentarchus called out. A force of sorcery hammered at their passage: the five found themselves in a tunnel that rocked and shook, struggling to cast the Enchanters from their feet. Winds howled and shrieked as though they had entered the center of a storm. Energies struck at them, mighty and malevolent, but the immortal Power within them would not be shaken.

The Enchanters held firm. Words of power were spoken, and their Portal was restored. Seconds later, all five stepped through, emerging into a sunlit wasteland. They found themselves on a glistening shore where melted sands still radiated heat. Great cracks and seams fractured a glassy surface where boulders had bounded down from broken hillsides. Above them lay the ruined Halls of Merlin, reduced to broken beams and shattered stone by the Wrath of Set. Lashed by wind, columns of soot were sweeping down from the hills. Ashes were cast into the dark, swollen waters that thrashed at the shoreline of Sea's Edge.

"Such is the charm of our new kingdom," Manassas murmured, "that even Vorrs and Uraks would not wish to live here...." The Enchanter trailed off: slight figures, four of them, emerged from the wreckage on the hillside above them. The two forces stared at one another across a ruined landscape, separated by distance, though each side fully recognized the nature of the other.

Then, slowly, deliberately, the Seeress notched an arrow and drew back her bow. Suddenly the power within the Enchanters shook and shuddered. Words leaped from their lips; Helcar and Manassas transformed themselves into beings formed of mist, while Portal mouths beckoned for Nairn and the Witch Queen Azúre, and the two readied for escape. Before Pentarchus, a wall of water four feet thick formed, shielding all five Enchanters from Sentauris with seething, soot-dark ocean water.

"It will not be as simple as we thought," Pentarchus said murmured. "The Power within us stared into the mouth of destruction and liked little of what it saw. The Seeress has again been weaponed by a powerful God. But we will approach this matter just a little differently, and the end of this final confrontation will come about as we wished."

· Ж ·

Sentauris lowered her bow, staring at the wall of water that obscured the Enchanters from her view. "They have been drawn here by my presence," she murmured. "They do not yet realize that Merlin still lives." The Adepts and Mír stood beside Sentauris. Ghorm was just a few paces away, sniffing at the strange odors emerging from the honeycombed tunnels beneath the hill. Each of them had been provided with enchanted weapons by Balardi, and yet their combined powers were in no way equal to those wielded by the Enchanters.

Orantes glanced up at the fissured hillside where dust, death, and devastation ruled. Then his eyes passed back down toward the shoreline where sunlight radiated strange light from cracked, glassy surfaces, and columns of dust swirled out to darkened ocean waters. *I am going to die here. I suppose it no longer matters, for I have learned enough of fear that I should meet death more easily. Yet still....* The Adept cried aloud: hands that radiated fire were reaching up from a fissure and had clutched both his ankles, searing the leather of his boots.

"Save your Dragonfire!" Sentauris called out. Wylar drew his enchanted blade and slashed down, severing two reddish pale gripping hands.

"Pit Fiends," Mír said, "the new rulers of Sea's Edge until the Enchanters come to power. Where is Merlin?" From beneath their feet came rumbles and shrieking noises as the Fiend struggled with its handless arms. Orantes danced about, the seared leather of his boots still smoking, while Sentauris with a calm deliberation, lashed together the shafts fashioned by Pallas Athena and unbound a second group of Wizard crafted arrows.

Ghorm knelt and poked at a severed hand: its reddish black substance was hot to the touch, and hard, as though Pit Fiends were formed of tendons that lacked a casing of soft flesh. The Familiar rose and drew his own long knife — like all their weapons it came from Balardi's armory and retained a measure of strength against beings of might and magic.

"Once, I could sense Merlin," Wylar said, "if the Wizard was within a half league or less, but now not even a trace of his old essence remains. Come, Sentauris, where are we to search?"

"Up, higher on the slopes, then down," Sentauris said softly, "down into the very heart of the hillside. To be completely hidden, Merlin would lie beneath a vault of stone so thick that all magic would be blocked. And his breathing would be slowed, so the Wizard would take one breath in a hundred...or a thousand. At least my mind tells me these things. Magic and Fate are struggling all around us, so my Sight is nearly blind." She drew a deep breath. "Somewhere on the hills above us, our destinies, life, or death lie on those upper slopes. Wylar and Orantes, the Enchanters are prepared only against your old Dragonfire; your reforged fire should not be revealed to them too quickly. Mír, you and the Adepts must shield one another. Ghorm, stay with them until your own part in this confused struggle becomes clear. Up now — let's go."

All drew weapons. Swords gleamed and glittered with enchantments: Sentauris held a scimitar that glistened with silver, while the Elf-Mage and the Adepts held swords that seemed made of white gold. Even Ghorm's long dagger radiated a shadow of green fire. Sentauris led them up the slope, setting a pace that was just at the edge of Orantes' endurance, and Ghorm's speed of foot.

As they climbed through the dust and the rubble, the new rulers of Sea's Edge rose to contest their passage. Fiends surged from seams in broken hills or leaped at them from behind clumps of rubble. Their bodies radiated heat and fire. Each stood as tall as Wylar or Mír, with the sharp features of wizened demons, but they were hunched like wingless, dark red gargoyles.

"Are the Enchanters not sufficient?" Orantes called out, hewing at the tall creature in front of him. His stroke went wide, but Ghorm scampered forward, lashing at the Fiend's shinbone. As it stumbled, Orantes dealt the creature a deathblow.

"Do we really need this gaggle of low-level monstrosities?" Orantes continued. As he wiped sweat from his brow, he noted that the others had neatly skewered their opponents and were not even breathing hard. *Some things never change,* he thought, *though Wylar's arm is singed, and Sentauris seems confused, almost to the point of uncertainty.*

They fought their way up the slope, leaving more than a score of dead Pit Fiends on the broken hillside. Not one Fiend, even in death, had spoken an intelligible word. None could respond to Ghorm's taunts with more than deep throated growls. But as their assaults failed, other Pit Fiends sought higher ground and hurled great stones downslope or toppled boulders so that they bounded down toward the intruders. A haze of dust and ash rose above the struggle, obscuring the sun, cloaking both humans and Fiends from the Enchanters. Sentauris led them from each rockfall, racing from point to point, deliberately conserving the magic of the Adepts for the last great testing, as they gradually fought their way to the upper slopes.

·)((·

"Their Wizard crafted weapons are insignificant," Pentarchus murmured, staring toward the cloud of ash that hovered over the hillside. As the haze built, their barrier of dark water had been allowed to wash away. "Now these God forged shafts, and the Farsight of the Seeress, these two things must be dealt with, while all fates still dance at the edge of an abyss.... Why is the future still so clouded? The force led by the Seeress is trivial compared to our own strength. Still, we must tread warily.

"Helcar, Manassas, you will become our guardians as we enter this honeycomb of tunnels — a hive formed for Pit Fiends by the Great God Set. Shield us from the unknown, then prepare to transform yourselves into Wylar and Orantes, so that we may capture the Seeress unharmed for our pleasure and our dark designs. Azüre, Nairn, call forth a great magic that will strip all the Farsight from the Seeress — transforming, wild magic that will yield a thousand unrestrained phantasms and differing futures. She will thus become blind — but wait until I have crafted a lesser magic that will strip from the Seeress all weapons that might possibly do us harm."

As the five Enchanters approached the hillside, three began chanting deep throated spell words that seemed to shudder in the sunlit air. The other two Enchanters grew in mass and density, so that when Pit Fiends attacked their party, Manassas easily crushed the life from all the creatures before him, while Helcar with casual backhand strokes, smashed them from the path of the Enchanters.

While their opponents struggled and fought their way to the upper slopes, the Enchanters passed cautiously into the lower portion of the hive of tunnels, less than a thousand paces from Sentauris and her allies.

· X ·

"Merlin," Sentauris whispered, then louder, "Merlin, come forth!" She passed deeper into a cleft in the rocks. Others in her party followed. As the tunnel's darkness deepened, werelight flashed from the Adepts' staffs, and a silver light radiated from Mír's outstretched hands. Though their way grew brighter, nothing could be seen except many other dark passages, and nothing could be scented except stale air, and a slight touch of burning acid given off by Pit Fiends. At two hundred paces into the hillside, with no hint of Merlin, the Adepts began to suspect a trap, and even Mír wavered.

"Thoth believed that Merlin still lived," the Elf-Mage murmured, "yet one Mid-World Power may be deceived by other, more powerful Gods." Sentauris remained silent, leading them forward into a dark maze, Ghorm at her side, the shining Elf-Mage a few steps behind her, and two uncertain Adepts at their rear.

As their small party passed further and deeper into dark passages, the glittering eyes of Pit Fiends followed them closely, waiting for the intruders to falter or separate, or enter a narrow passage where their magic weapons could no longer protect their pale, human flesh.

· X ·

One Pit Fiend watched the humans with an unusual intensity. This Fiend bulked larger than its brethren, and its eyes were bright and hard. Though its intellect would not yet provide it with speech, it had established dominance over the others by its bulk and bearing, and by delivering a brutal punishment to any potential rivals.

As this Fiend slipped from an upper crevice and began to pursue its human prey, a mighty hand seemed to clutch and hold it, then draw it back through a rock face that had become suddenly liquefied. The fiend shrieked and fought, filled with more rage than fear, but the hand holding the Fiend was unshaken.

Suddenly, the Fiend was released. It stood, pulsing with anger, in the presence of another pale, fleshy intruder. Yet the Fiend resisted its impulse to break and batter, for this human loomed larger than the other humans it had been tracking, with menace lurking in the shadows it cast on the cavern walls.

This pale creature made sounds that were unintelligible to the Fiend. Set's creation glanced warily about, preparing to flee, but then smoky fingers caressed its brow, and it stood frozen, with a thousand new thoughts thrusting through its mind.

"My first gifts," Pentarchus murmured, "intellect, awareness, and speech. Other gifts will follow."

"Nothing is given so easily," the Fiend hissed. "What do you wish from me?"

Pentarchus laughed softly. "Well spoken, Lord of the Dark Caverns — for that is what you will become if you listen closely to me. You have only to perform one simple task for me, and after, I will give you the power to be master of Sea's Edge forever, ruler of all those beings like yourself. Is this arrangement of interest to you? In fairness, I will choose another, should you decline."

The Fiend inclined its head and Pentarchus continued. "All I wish are these five slender shafts." Images sprang from the hand of Pentarchus, showing the God forged arrows carried by the tall Seeress. "A time of confusion, of wild magic, is about to come to this underground empire. Then you must seize these shafts and place them swiftly in this carrying device." The Enchanter passed over a cloth sack, one that pulsed with strange forces and was made with a fabric that would not burn even in the Fiend's hot fingers.

A fleeting smile flashed over the face of Pentarchus. "Take care not to touch the sharp points of those devices. Only bring them safely to me, and after, you will become mighty beyond the reach of your imagination."

·)(·

Merlin, the mind of Sentauris called out into the darkness. *Wizard, arise and defend your League!* She was probing in dark passages, moving twenty paces downslope while the others debated their next step, and Ghorm lashed at their hesitation with his sharp tongue.

Wizard! We dance with the Fates, and they are coldhearted Ice Maidens. You —

Suddenly, a great force of magic swept over them, and she cried aloud. Shapes flashed before her eyes then shriveled into dust. Stonework became fluid, rippling like grey rubber. Water surged downwards from upper passages. Pit Fiends slipped from side passages and stumbled toward her, making strange fearful noises. Sword held aside, she let them pass. Ghorm raced toward her but sudden shifts in the fluid rock blocked his path. Portals seemed to flash and flare all around her. Mír's voice rose above the spell-chants of Wylar and Orantes, but concussions echoed through stone passageways as their magic was hurled back at them.

Her senses shrieked. She turned and leaped from unseen peril — a half step too slow. Hands that radiated dark heat reached out and tore the powerful arsenal from her shoulders. A massive Pit Fiend raced from her, carrying a sack that held both her God-forged arrows and those made by Balardi. She leaped after the creature, but it slipped into a side passage, and the stone of the labyrinth closed behind it.

Portals, visions, transformations flared all around her. Passages opened and sealed themselves. Lights flared and died. Dust and noise obscured her senses, though from a distance she heard blasting sounds as Wylar and Orantes fought toward her; and passages trembled as Mír fought to control the transforming magic that surged all around them.

Sentauris set her bow aside and sheathed her sword. She then drew her slender dagger and slipped it beneath her Tanu-forged corselet, so that a single thrust could penetrate her heart's core.

I understand now, at the last. They will try to take me alive, and so to tear secrets from my dying Farsight. I will not yield to them. Maker forgive me, for I must die by my own hand. She paused at that moment, at first from reluctance to leave life, then because her Seer's Sight was sending wild signals into her mind.

From a far chamber, from a deep vault in the hills' stone roots, came a storm of counter spells, rising to contest the powerful sorcery of the Enchanters. And if the stone passageways still rippled with transformations, they were no longer completely under the Enchanter's control, nor were the visions and apparitions all around her those fashioned by Nairn and the Witch Queen.

She sheathed her dagger and drew her enchanted blade, senses reaching out.

I feel only dead magic, raised not by a live Wizard rising in wrath, but spells planted long ago, proof only that Merlin wished to protect this place, not that he lives. But still....

·)((·

Warfare of spell and counter spell raged both though ancient tunnel systems and those formed by the magic of Set. Deep in the hillside, the mind of the Pit Fiend bearing stolen weapons was filled with sudden doubts. If the weapons it carried were so powerful, why take them to the cold, pale fleshy human? Perhaps with these weapons, the Fiend itself might become a Power. After a one second's hesitation, the Fiend darted down a side passage, one that led him deeper into the hills' inner caverns, and farther from the Enchanters.

Seven hundred paces from the fleeing Fiend, Pentarchus cried out in rage and *reached* for the treacherous creature. Though now, with so many counter spells at war with the Enchanters' own powerful magic, Pentarchus found his reach lessened and the Pit Fiend was able to slip away.

Forget the others and seek the Seeress, his mind shouted to the other Enchanters. *Some secret lies hidden beneath these hills, and we must force that knowledge from her dying Farsight.*

·)((·

Sword drawn, she advanced through shifting corridors, where apparitions and visions flared and faltered. A shawled woman that might have once been her mother passed from one wall into the other without even glancing at Sentauris. Blind moles with white fur floated down from the ceiling and slipped easily through the stone passage at her feet. She *willed* them away, beginning to control her visions: transforming magics and counter spells were starting to form gateways for her own Farsight.

An abscess formed to her right, creating an alcove, a side chamber. She peered inside: Tallus stood before her, diminished by death, massive

Tanu head bowed in defeat, but then his image looked up to meet the eyes of Sentauris.

"Tallus! Why would your deathly image come to me at this time, at journey's end?"

"Recall only the cause of my death," the Tanu said, in the dry tones of the dead, "and the being that caused my downfall."

"A Creature of the Darkness. But those beings belong to the first portion of our tale. Now we must deal with the Enchanters — and the Gods!"

"You do not understand," Tallus whispered, then his Tanu eyes closed and Tallus vanished.

She turned, blundering into a Pit Fiend made mindless by fear. Her booted foot sent it fleeing blindly toward the Enchanters. Just ahead, light, the bright light of midday, spilled through a gap in the passageway. Swift steps took her to the opening of a great cavern, and she peered within. As though from a great height, she looked down on images of the Enchanters emerging from the Portal onto the glassy sands of Sea's Edge. The five stood gaunt, distended, monstrosities moving openly through bright sunlight.

Yes, I have known that the Enchanters were grafted to some Ancient Power, yet as I reach out to them, I discover neither Demon nor Dragon.... Sounds of battle raged behind her as Wylar and Orantes and Mír fought toward her. From a distance, she heard Nairn's laughter change to pain: the Enchanter had been countered by Wylar's reforged Dragonfire.

A shuddering sound echoed through the passageway before her; the broken, bleeding body of Orantes spilled from a left-hand crevice. Crying aloud, she raced to his side and knelt over Orantes, her Adept ally and lover.

"How I loved thee..." Orantes murmured through bloody lips, but his mouth was curled in malice. Her mind recoiled. Powerful, inhuman hands gripped her before she could respond.

"Manassas!" she shrieked. Arms pinned, she could wield neither sword nor dagger. But as she faced death, the second word of the Spell of Annihilation burst unbidden from her lips. At that shouted word, Manassas fell back, as though lashed by hellfire. Sentauris tore free, racing from the shaken Enchanter.

Down the corridor, more lights loomed, but these were muted, soft ones, spilling from a left-hand cavern. Warily, she approached and peered within — to discover her own form. She was seated in a lower chamber of Tuvan, speaking of the seed of Dragons, the Ancient Creatures Indomitable:

"And Creatures of the Darkness," she was saying, measuring the understanding of those around her, "mighty in sinew and sorcery, destroyed Seraphs and Demons, Spirit Lords and Dragons."

"What!?!" Gallandus rose. "A Creature of the Darkness greater than a God, greater than an Ancient Power? What dark of the night tale of horror is this?"

Sentauris recoiled from the scene and its revelation: the Enchanters had been joined, not to Demon or Dragon, but to a mighty Creature of the Darkness, one greater than many Gods! Shaken, she turned to find Wylar, hunched over, both hands struggling to contain a great wound in his lower abdomen. Thick red blood spurted through his fingers, as he stood in her path, not twenty paces distant.

"Sentauris, why did you choose another?" Wylar asked softly. "Tell me now, here at the end, why you did not seek me out, far beyond midnight, at the *Weasel's Feast?*" The tones were Wylar's, the form was Wylar's, and the thoughts may have been Wylar's, but this time Sentauris was not deceived.

"Helcar," she murmured. "Helcar, your Carag form is bound to a Creature Indomitable. Break free — seek deliverance from your fate, or you will die as a monster, not as a mortal being."

With a shrug, Helcar resumed his Enchanter's form. "Yes, deep down we have come to know this truth," Helcar said dreamily. Hands, invisible yet strong, reached out to grasp her. "It is fitting that thou, our greatest and most intimate of lovers, shouldst also know this truth." Invisible hands not only restrained her, but a second set also worked at the latches of her armor, and still others began the soft caressing of her thighs. Crooning sounds came as other Enchanters called to her.

"Sentauris, Sentauris, how we long for thee," Manassas called.

"The dark is favorable to us," Nairn sang out, "and filled with wild imaginings."

"You will know us all," Pentarchus murmured, "each of us in turn, for you have earned that right and much, much more."

"No other being will ever know such pleasure!" the Witch Queen cried out, her own body beginning to quiver in expectation. "Or such pain!"

As Helcar stepped toward her, the third word of the Spell of Annihilation burst from her lips. She broke free from shaken, invisible hands, racing beyond the stricken Helcar, slipping deeper and further down into a twisting tunnel system that shaped and reshaped itself in a struggle of transforming energies.

"Merlin!" she cried again. "You must rise and dance with destiny!" No answer came, except the faintest of stirrings, as though some ghostly creature stirred in the hills' deepest regions — and perhaps it was only some ancient troll or ogre. She raced on, vaguely aware that the Enchanters still pursued her, still certain of their prey.

As more magic trembled through the hillside, a great cavern formed to her left. She approached its entrance, every sense alert, watching as dark radiances poured from its mouth. When she glanced within, revelation was already radiating from her Seer's Sight.

Images of the Renegade Dark Gods lay to her left: Haeglin and Un-Maurag, who jeered and mocked at her forthcoming destruction. Mordred was absent, though he was second only to Un-Maurag in the hierarchies of the three Renegades. To the right stood an assembly of the great malevolent Gods — Powers who abided by the Truce, while working woe upon mortal and immortal peoples. Mallegro and Arioch stood with them, as did Moloch, and Ahriman, and Dis, and Kali, and several others, all of them jeering and mocking the Seeress, calling upon one another to behold her last moments of pain and death.

Notably absent was Set — just as Mordred had been missing from the smaller cluster of Renegades. And Set was accounted the most powerful of the Greater Dark Gods who loathed humankind. Suddenly, she *knew*. Images of Set and Mordred conspiring together in various guises flooded her mind.

She burst from the chamber and cried aloud: "Set, you are the author of our woes! All ye Gods and Powers of the Mid-World, know that Set and Mordred have conspired together outside the Truce. If I have discovered this truth, so also may the Gods with their far greater vision. Do not...." She fell silent, for now, a third force was entering the struggle of wild sorceries that raged underground. Set was extending his power into the battle.

As the Enchanters paused, she raced down, deeper into the hillside, calling, "Merlin, Merlin, save your people! Save the Wizards and your League!"

At last, a thought, sleep-filled and weary, reached out to her. *I am awake. I am standing. Is it time now to deal with Excalibur and the Grail?*

"No!" Sentauris cried. "Those things belong to a time so far in the future that the Gods have not even begun to dream of them! In this time, Set and Mordred have raised the Enchanters against you. Know now what I know." And she sent a torrent of thoughts, and visions, and her last three spoken Words of Power to the waking Wizard.

I come, Merlin's mind pulsed.

Sentauris turned from Merlin's voice back to the Enchanters. For Set had entered the struggle. Destiny would not wait for Merlin. Drawing her gleaming scimitar, knowing she was no match for her foes, she raced on swift feet back toward the Enchanters.

·)(·

As though forming a battleground for this final confrontation, the fluid rock had hardened, forming a great stone chamber. In its center stood the Enchanters, making strange croaking sounds, like basilisks speaking in the language of crows.

On the far wall, its stone surface had formed into the Mouth of Set. And Set's lips — huge, formed of fluid stone — spoke the first of ten Words. The Spell of Annihilation had begun. So powerful was Set's spell that each Word was delivered like a blow, smashing the Enchanters back.

At the third Word, the Enchanters rose in anger and fought with Set. Nairn and the Witch Queen struggled with magic that would freeze the rock, while the Carag Enchanters, growing in mass and bulk, tore stone slabs from the cavern floor and hurled them at the Mouth of Set.

Pentarchus, hands held aloft, began his own Spell of Reforging, twelve words that would seal the Enchanters to their inner Entity forever, and place them everlastingly beyond the reach of Set the Destroyer.

Each word of each spell struck Sentauris like a blow, but still, she fought her way toward the confrontation, sensing that she was too late. For as Set spoke his sixth Word, Pentarchus, hunched, drenched with sweat, could only manage his third.

She turned a corner so that sight and sound reached her: Enchanters battering with magic, wedges of rock crashing into the far wall, spell and counter spell still resonating through the stone. Now, from below, she heard a third spell, one of equal power, words thrusting upwards toward the Enchanters.

Sentauris barely paused. *Merlin's Magic...fourteen Words that will never be complete, unless....*

At the eighth word of the Spell of Annihilation, the Witch Queen merged her power with that of Nairn's, to focus a mighty thrust at the Mouth of Set. As the Mouth faltered, Manassas smashed at it with a huge wedge of rock, so that the Mouth misspoke the eighth Word and was forced to begin again with the first words of Set's Spell.

Snarling with rage, the Mouth of Set spoke again its first Word. But now Pentarchus stood tall, poised, and mighty, and he spoke his eighth Word. Though each Word required the force of a two-handed ax-blow, and though buffeted by Words from Set, and Words from Merlin, Pentarchus was Master. He spoke his ninth Word — of the twelve, three only were left.

Raging at her helplessness, Sentauris raced toward Pentarchus and hurled first her scimitar then her dagger at the Enchanter. Pentarchus barely paused, stepping easily from the flying metal...and the Enchanter spoke his tenth Word.

But from the chamber's far end, Orantes and Wylar slipped from a tunnel mouth and hurled focused, reforged Dragonfire at Pentarchus. As the Enchanter burned, his eleventh Word became a shriek. Shouting with rage, Helcar turned and lumbered toward the Adepts. Manassas, Azüre, and Nairn struggled again to halt the Mouth of Set.

In this turmoil of contending forces, Merlin's magic, the Spell of Unmaking, was completed first.

Suddenly, all was silent. The Mouth of Set stiffened as the power of Set withdrew, leaving only gnarled stone shaped like huge lips upon the cavern wall.

The Enchanters straightened, then were still. Their faces radiated wild panic, though their bodies froze like insects stilled by a spider's most potent venom. Great seams, running head to toe, appeared down the back and legs of each Enchanter.

Dark, pulpy, and moist substances emerged from the shells of humans and Carags. Drawn to one another like clumps of organic, black mercury, all five joined together, and the husks of their previous hosts were discarded. The Enchanters toppled, to lie broken, still, and lifeless.

Maker's Touch! thought Sentauris. *The Enchanters have been delivered, for they died as mortals, not as monstrosities.*

Chapter Sixteen

A Nightmare for Dark Gods

MAKER, GREAT GOD OF *all Gods,* Sentauris prayed, *what am I supposed to do now?*

The Enchanters had been destroyed, yet their hidden fragments had joined together to produce a horror beyond any nightmare. Before them, a subtle and mighty Creature of the Darkness stood more than three times human height. Even though it was hunchbacked, with one powerful set of arms to cope with matters of might, and a smaller set for the weaving of dark sorcery, the monster dominated the cavern. Its eyes were bulbous, like those of a goblin, though askew, twisted with one bulging eye sloped above its left brow, while a second hovered just to the right of a flattened nostril.

Sentauris was closest to the Creature. A sense of evil, of wrongness, hung throughout the caverns like a rancid cloud. The cavern was dark, though all things remained visible, lit by the dull glow left over by the underground collision of great magic. At the cavern's far end, she could see the forms of Mír and their Adept allies, slowly moving toward her, hugging the wall to her right as they climbed over shattered slabs of stone. Orantes held a stricken Ghorm carefully in his arms as they made their way toward the Seeress, all three of them staring at the Creature Indomitable with wary, haunted eyes.

Merlin, you are needed here! her mind called out.

As Sentauris backed away from it, the Creature looked up, suddenly aware of the Seeress and her Sight. Their eyes met. She glanced around for weapons, but there were none. She tensed, preparing to flee. Instead, the Creature turned to the fallen Enchanters, using its greater arms to break their bodies apart. Horror filled the cavern as the monster consumed their flesh and drank the dark, necromantic magic of the Enchanters. Only with Pentarchus did the Creature break apart his larger bones and consume the marrow of the dead Enchanter. With the cracking of bones and the nightmare of the monster's feast, Merlin was almost at her side before Sentauris was aware of him.

"Arm yourself," the Wizard murmured and passed to Sentauris both her abandoned bow and one set of arrows taken from her — those forged by Pallas Athena.

"Do not launch these weapons against the Spellweaver," Merlin continued, "unless it chooses to feed upon us. Your Farsight will guide you." Sentauris searched frames of confused, clouded futures, while the Creature rose from its feast and stared idly first at Mír and Wylar, then at Orantes, who held the exhausted body of Ghorm as though protecting an infant. The four had edged along the cavern wall, moving slowly toward Sentauris, and the Creature seemed to regard them as its next meal, and its smaller, sorcerous arms began reaching toward them. Sentauris, grim faced, notched an arrow.

"No, I think not," Merlin said quietly, then he raised his voice. "Spellweaver, I know of you from legend only, that you were second only to the Nameless among the Creatures Indomitable, and how you passed into legend during the Ancient Wars. Yet, you should use your might to regard us as we now are, not what you recall of mortals from long ago."

The hulking Spellweaver seemed to cock its head...and it peered at them with speckled, many-faceted, bulbous eyes.

"It sees us as we were at the beginning of the Ancient Wars," Sentauris whispered, "naked, herd like, gleaning fruit from trees...and it comes from nowhere, to feast on the strong and the weak.... But then, mighty defenders emerge — Seraphs and Spirit Lords, but the Spellweaver gives way only when five or more of the Ancient Powers rise against it....

"And now the Spellweaver regards the Enchanters, how subtle and mighty and dangerous they had become, even before the Spellweaver was grafted onto them. See, it tilts its head, and considers events should it choose to feed upon us. Ah, shock! Despite its power, the Creature sees that it might not survive that conflict. And turning his head somewhat further, it seems to understand that we will not pursue it should it pass from this place...."

"We are not your foes, Spellweaver, and Child of Dragons," Merlin called out. "You must know, at the core of your being that your own enemies are the Great God Set, and his ally, the Renegade Dark God, Mordred." The Wizard gestured, and Sentauris lowered her bow.

The hulking Spellweaver turned away from the enemies of its foes, for it perceived a strange confusion of destinies, in which the humans might still do damage to Set the Betrayer and to Set's ally, Mordred. Strength flooded the Spellweaver's form, and it allowed its own mass to increase so that it further dominated the cavern. It was mighty now, stronger than ever. Consuming the essences of all five Enchanters had substantially increased its natural strength so that only a few of those calling themselves Gods might stand against it — on neutral ground.

The Spellweaver peered deeply into the enchanted kingdoms of the Gods. Set was strengthening his realm, just as Mordred struggled feverishly to shore up his own defenses. To journey to those places was to die; for the jealous Powers would learn too much of the Spellweaver's own might and waylay it in the Mid-World as it passed through Portal passages.

Words, guttural and harsh, began spilling from the Spellweaver's gap jawed mouth. Power gathered to its body, both from the Mid-World and from long untapped and deep roots of Alantéa the Forerunner. Rushing sounds filled the cavern. Humans backed against cavern walls as dark magic swirled all around them. The Spellweaver's battle arms reached high toward the cavern's roof; its spell casting hands wove intricate patterns that only Merlin and Sentauris could follow.

Silence again filled the cavern. The Spellweaver's fingers made complex adjustments as though guiding distant magic. To the right of Sentauris watched Orantes, holding Ghorm, with Mír and Wylar beside him; the three stood, hunched down, backs against the cavern walls. Many varied, different forces of magic gathered to them, but they waited for a signal from Merlin.

"I can see so much more now," Sentauris said in a hushed voice. "All the bars to my Sight have been lifted. Though I cannot show you, Wizard, I can only describe what is happening:

"A storm of battle magic hurls itself into the Mid-World, and lashes at the enchanted empire of the Great God Set. Set's kingdom groans and its foundations tremble. Remote, almost forgotten realms of Set collapse into the stuff of ruined magic — air and light, traces of dust and water vapor. Is all the Mid-World made of so much magic with only traces of real matter? Set's Minions fall and abase themselves, for they must fear the End of Time and the Maker's Return.

"Set rises in wrath. Warfare rages as the Spellweaver's immense battle magic clashes with the miracle work of the Great God. Set's might is enormous. All the trembling motions that rock the pillars of his kingdom are slowly stilled. Like a storm rebuffed by a huge headland formed of granite, the Spellweaver's battle magic is forced from Set's domain. And how might it be otherwise, for is Set not among the mightiest of Mid-World Powers?

"Yet the Spellweaver is undaunted, unafraid. The same storm of battle magic turns to Mordred and hurls ruin at the Renegade's domain. Mordred's fortress shudders: his towers topple. Uraks are hurled into the air. They seek to fly, but no wings emerge from their heavy, dark forms. A contagion of madness runs through packs of Vorrs, and they rip and tear at one another. Carags are transformed into dead things that can no longer draw breath. Though Mordred counters frantically, a full third of his kingdom falls away, like a mountain's shelf sliding into a bottomless abyss...." Sentauris trailed off, eyes watching the Spellweaver carefully, knowing that it might still suddenly turn its might against those around it.

But with an abrupt shift in motion, the Spellweaver turned from the Wizard and his allies. Other Words of Power followed: a huge, arched Portal sprang into existence, leading to a grey, jagged, barren place, like a corridor leading to the far side of the moon. Into this strange passage slipped the hulking Spellweaver, passing forever from Alantéa, and from the Mid-World of the Truce.

· ☓ ·

Standing in his place of power, Set cried aloud. He had been driven beyond reason into a frenzy, and now, surrounded by dead servants, he struggled with his shame. Merlin and his Wizards still lived! Set had been named by the Seeress; other Powers would know of his treachery and his failure. At some point, the Truce would be called against him, unless....

And his kingdom had been attacked! The Spellweaver had slipped beyond his reach, but someone, something, some enemy must suffer. This outrage could not be borne; it would not be borne....

·)(·

While in his own place of power, Mordred shouted and raged, cursing the Maker and all his devices, and all the Maker's followers and their allies. With the ruin of his people, no servants remained to be destroyed; they were all dead or hidden, though within the outer reaches of his senses, he could hear the snarling, bloody madness that still ran riot among the Vorrs.

He had sacrificed his favored Carag Mages for nothing! A Renegade Dark God had embarked upon a great venture and had gained nothing but shame.

It could not be borne; it would not be borne....

·)(·

Magic and the sense of evil slipped slowly away from the caverns as Merlin led them upwards toward daylight. Two steps behind the Wizard, Sentauris heard a deep sigh of fatigue and regret that she never thought would ever pass from the lips of the great Wizard.

"Did you feel my fear, daughter of the League?" Merlin asked. "As I regarded the Spellweaver, could you feel my fear?"

Sentauris shook her head. "You have always been among the most difficult of mortals for me to sense, Merlin my master."

"I felt fear, fear that a great error had been made at quest's end. The Spellweaver might have turned upon us, yet what choice did I have? Had Set's Spell of Annihilation triumphed, the Enchanters and the hidden Spellweaver within them would have been destroyed. No trace of them would have been left upon Alantéa the Forerunner. After a time, Set would have renewed his war against a Wizard's League that was already reeling in defeat.

"Nor could I let the Enchanters triumph. The Spell of Transfiguration created by Pentarchus would have produced an abomination — reforged by Pentarchus, the Enchanters would have become immortal, each of them greater than many lesser Gods of the Mid-World. They would have become killing machines, destroying everything in front of them. The Enchanters would then have ruled what was left of our ruined League while waging an unwinnable, perpetual war against the Great God Set."

"Though you," Sentauris said, "as the greatest of mortal magic wielders, you might have survived."

Merlin shook his head. "I might have fled, but only a small chance remained for me. So, in the end, I had no choice, but still, at the moment of destiny when the Spellweaver watched us with hungry eyes, I felt great fear."

They emerged out into the bright light of late afternoon, though ocean winds still spread soot over beaches and blackened scrub brush. Orantes set Ghorm down, then Merlin knelt over a stricken Ghorm, whispering spell words. The little Familiar lay exhausted; as always, one burst of magic had left him depleted. Yet now, staring up into the eyes of the chanting Wizard, he felt his old strength returning. But it was all for nothing. Again, he had been useless, nothing more than unnecessary baggage, a mouse beside foxes fighting a battle against werewolves. *Why?!?*

Merlin gave no answer but rose and stared up into the afternoon skies as though studying star patterns that lay hidden beyond the blue skies of earth. Sighing, Merlin glanced back to the little Familiar, murmuring, "Ghorm, I have not truly 'healed' you — I have only borrowed heavily from your future, to restore you to the present. For reasons I do not yet understand, you and your allies must be at full strength for this day. In two weeks' time, you will require the better part of a month to rest. Rise now." Merlin turned to the others.

"Stand fast. Seek neither wine nor enchanted sleep. Many paths flow from this moment, and all too many of our destinies are filled with violence. If we have dared greatly and won great victories, surely now we deserve peace and surcease. But the Mid-World of the Truce seeks only tranquility for the Gods and has never brought us freedom from warfare. So, while seeking justice, we must look to...." The Wizard trailed off, turning to the east, slowly, as though haunted by the whispers of ghosts.

"As I feared," Merlin murmured, "the Great God Set emerges openly, preparing to destroy us, seeking out Thorian at Stone Mountain, farthest from us, so as later to contend that his war was separate from that of the Enchanters. Maker, guide us on this day."

From a pouch at his side, Merlin drew a slender, curled conch shell, and spoke into its opening: "Balardi, stand ready. I must transport us both to Stone Mountain, and there we must do battle with the Great God Set."

A second talisman was removed from the Wizard's pouch: this device was formed of metal, unadorned, large as both hands of the Wizard laid flat. It was shaped like a circle laid within a square, with both surrounded by a larger pentagram; but it seemed crude, unfinished, with each of the three figures fashioned of different metals. Merlin whispered Words over his talisman: it grew, not into a huge, arched Portal, but into a smallish seam in the air. Merlin slid through this gap and vanished, taking his Portal talisman with him.

"Wait, now wait," Mír muttered in disbelief. "It was always said that the three Wizards lacked Portal magic, indeed, that it had been forbidden them." Orantes found an outcrop that was streaked by soot, but otherwise clear. He slumped down and stared up at Sentauris, face filled with questions.

"The Wizards have been far craftier than I ever imagined," Sentauris said slowly, peering over the western horizon. "Merlin feared that some Power would seek to destroy him, and so crafted an alternate being, a copy of himself, one that might be easily sacrificed. Did that replica know its destiny? Did it feel terror and pain? Also, Merlin feared that the three Wizards would be isolated, and though they were barred from Portal magic, he sought this talisman...or bartered for it...that clumsy device was formed of three lesser ones, and not even one was crafted by a Wizard. I can see that...." Suddenly, her head jerked to the east, toward Stone Mountain.

"Set comes for them," she cried. "No longer concealed as a cloud walker, the Great God strides openly over the broad ocean toward Stone Mountain. Thorian awaits him, alone, on the pinnacle of his fortress. Now, all ye Gods and Powers of the Mid-World, where is this Truce? Why must...."

She lowered her voice. "But wait, a seam in the air is opening. Merlin and Balardi emerge — three Wizards are ranged against a Greater God. Somehow, the three are unafraid, as though they have long prepared for this moment...."

"Watch now, watch and wonder! Sky chariots await the Wizards: Elementals have shaped themselves into teams of blue phoenixes, and silver ravens, and whiteish gold eagles. The Wizards rise to give battle. They hurl powerful magic at Set the Destroyer. The Great God is astonished, and reels in confusion! Yet now his rage steadies him; battle is joined, and nothing is cert—"

She broke off, staring to a place not two hundred paces above the hillside, where a huge, arched Portal shimmered and flared, with magic challenged then countered.

"And now," Sentauris said in a completely small voice, "Mordred comes — for us."

· ✕ ·

Mordred strode through the Portal, garbed in his semblance as Ravager of Hillsides. Immense, clad in seamless black armor, the Renegade Dark God peered through a slit in his visor and laughed: Sea's Edge was completely ruined, a land that would never be restored.

As he stepped down the slope, small boulders were crushed beneath his feet. In his right hand, he held an orbed staff, with one ebony dark gem at its peak. He had come for the piddling meddlers who had too often interfered with the work of the Enchanters.

"Come forth!" Mordred called. "At least you can die beneath open skies!" They had hidden, of course; he might need to break the hills apart, a thought not unpleasing to his inner wrath.

Above him, Vision Portals flared: as always, when one Power moved openly over Alantéa the Forerunner, other Powers sought to observe, discreetly, from a distance. Mordred raised his great armored head and called to the watching Powers: "Behold! I care nothing for your Truce but see that I come alone, unaided by other Powers. I stand at Sea's Edge only for a brief hunt — I seek an extinction of vermin!"

At the edges of his awareness, Mordred could also sense a score of Emissaries, hovering near the shoreline, as though monitoring events on behalf of unseen Gods. He cared nothing for them; they were lesser beings who served distant, irrelevant masters. And this Truce that he had been taught to fear seemed nothing more than a construct of scrap paper, a thing that would be blown away by the first gusts of fierce winds.

Mordred looked again to the lower hillside, prepared to send a tide of destruction through the bolt holes honeycombing the slopes, but he found Mír standing less than a hundred paces away. The Elf-Mage was garbed in light, a slight figure standing less than a fifth of the Dark God's height, with less than one hundredths of the Dark Renegade's mass.

"Is this the Kindreds' last stand?" Mordred jeered. Power gathered to Mordred's staff. "Know that scores upon countless scores of Elves, and Tanu and Sidhe have died at my hands. None that have confronted me, though they were garbed in the brightest light, have ever survived."

"It has always been your war and not that of the Kindreds," Mír said softly. "And I will add that I stand here not for the Kindreds, but for the League." Mír's voice was raised, like a herald's call to battle. "And know this, Renegade Dark God: if you do not abandon your war against the League, your own life may be forfeit!"

Mordred leaned back and laughed. His staff flashed power at Mír: a white shield formed before the Elf-Mage, held for a moment, then began to fragment.

"Now the Adepts hurl their Dragonfire!" Mordred cried, voice dripping scorn. "Behold! I was born with Dragonfire flowing from my jaws!" From the right, Orantes emerged, focused fire flowing from his hands, and from the left came fire from Wylar. Rays lashed at Mordred, who suddenly cried aloud.

"What have you done!," the Dark God shrieked in pain, "to my ancient flames?" Blasts sent Orantes scurrying to shelter, while Wylar raced to a second strongpoint, hurling more fire. Mír dodged beyond his shattered shielding, calling upon the ground to snare the Renegade Dark God's metal shod feet.

As Mordred broke the clutches of earth, Sentauris rose from concealment just behind Mír. She drew back her bow and cast first one arrow then a second at the Dark God's armored form. One arrow scoured Mordred's armor and skipped away, whining and shrieking. The second was caught and held by Mordred's staff: both enchanted staff and sorcerous arrow groaned and fought until the spent arrow fell harmlessly to the ground.

Mordred turned to the skies, calling out, "Some being calling itself a God has armed these creatures! You have supplied insects with fire!" Mordred turned back to his tiny foes, who had scurried to new hiding places. "Ah, but see, all your hidden strength is revealed to me, little vermin, while I have not even begun to display my own might." Words of Power lifted from the Dark God's lips; torrents of energy flowed to Mordred; the ground trembled and thunder rumbled over clear, sunlit skies.

Orantes rose from hiding to hurl more Dragonfire at Mordred. Wylar aimed fire at the scoured portion of the Dark God's armor, while bolts of white force leaped from Mír's hands, assailing their foe. Mordred staggered a half step, but watched for Sentauris and her last three arrows, all the while gathering strength for one last moment of destruction.

I drink power, while the air whines all around me. I must end this matter so that the Renegade Dark Gods are never again challenged. In seconds.... Ah, but I am lashed from a fourth side! I feel pain, coming from behind — is this another Adept? But no, it must be the rat-goblin of the Seeress, useful for one, lesser thrust. Wait, now wait, the creature strikes again! And with power!

Astonished, Mordred staggered, lurched, then he turned. The being behind him was not Ghorm, but a slender, fair-featured Adept: the Great God Wotan's hidden gift had transformed the Familiar. The Dark God cried in anger, hurling destructive energies at the interloper. But shields formed before the slender Adept, and the intruder cast more magic at the Dark God, who staggered, lurched, attacked on four sides, his feet clutched by the ground, lashed by various magics, seared by Dragonfire, shaken by the strange sorcery of some unknown Adept.

Then suddenly Mordred turned toward Sentauris, staring at a flight of three God forged shafts, one heading for his visor, a second to the place where his heart might have been, and the third to the scoured surface where a previous arrow had broken the seal of his armor.

I am going to die, Mordred thought. *I am a dead God, staring at infinity and the Maker, at the End of Time....*

· ᙭ ·

As Set was driven back from Stone Mountain, battered clouds seemed to stream toward a deep red, setting sun. Elementals toppled from the Wizards' chariots, fading forms of eagles, ravens, and phoenixes who vanished into the air, only to be replaced by other Elementals.

Power lashed at Set, brutal and blinding. He skidded over the ocean, driven farther from the shore. The Great God in fury lashed back at Merlin, but the Wizard slipped again out of Set's reach, his chariot team of silver ravens speeding higher above the setting sun.

Set groaned aloud. He had come armed with nothing but his might and his wrath, while the Wizards had planned for this battle over scores of years. Some device of Merlin's was sapping his strength. Each discharge of energy somehow cost him more than twice the power spent. His own wrath had betrayed him.

Once again, he called forth those Creatures of the Darkness that were still bound to him: two only remained, lesser Creatures Indomitable, dazed, and bewildered, who toppled from hazy Portal mouths into the ocean. There they met the same fate as other Creatures Indomitable: scores of killer whales were waiting for them, smashing them in fury.

Every moment of this struggle seemed to encompass an age.

Earlier, after Set had stung Balardi, hammered at Thorian, the Great God had called forth a great flier, leather winged, sharpeyed, to rend the airborne chariots of the Wizards. But clouds of seahawks had driven it away from Stone Mountain. All his great, destructive arsenal, of transformations, of conjurations, of miracle work, of pure power — nothing seemed to function, as though the Wizards had studied him over scores of years and prepared against each of his weapons.

Set's rage had shifted slowly into a dull anger. It was time to depart; but Set's feet seemed bound, chained to the sea. *Then let me become again a Leviathan of the depths!* Set strove again to transform himself, but a score of devices, tendrils of magic, were clinging to his form.

He had stung two Wizards: Set could sense blood fluids flowing from Balardi and Thorian...though it only seemed to have driven Balardi into greater conjurations, and Thorian into a colder, calmer use of power.

Again, Set hurled destructive magic at the Wizard Merlin, but his Sending seemed to shiver in the air, to fade and slip downward like a wounded ghost. Once more, Set struggled to transform the ocean air into a substance that would no longer support flight. But his lips could not form the Words, and all miracle work was slipping through his fingers.

Battered from the ocean surrounding Stone Mountain, Set's retreat from the shore broke apart the low-lying clouds that radiated the deep red rays of a setting sun.

I cannot win this battle, thought Set. *I cannot even retreat from it. A deadly, final nightmare is upon me.*

Chapter Seventeen

A Gathering of Emissaries

Death came for Mordred, but it was halted inches from the armor of the Renegade Dark God. Hands flashed out of nothingness, three of them to each enchanted arrow, and the shafts were wrestled, whining and shrieking, from the air.

Nine hands in total struggled with three shafts. And each hand was different; one hand was gnarled, a second was fair, touched by a silvery sheen, another was covered by a grey beast-fur. The farthest hand from Mordred was fleshless, made of bone, while the one closest to Mordred's visor was talon-shaped, a claw. All the other "hands" were simply coils like the tails of powerful serpents.

Mordred glanced up: he was surrounded first by a score, then two scores of the Gods' greatest servants.

The Dark God's mind raced. *So here is a key portion of the Mid-World of the Truce: the Emissaries of the Gods — those serving both Gods of Light, and those of Darkness — are dispatched to deal with initial offenses; and so, they have haunted this struggle since its beginning. Thus, the Gods are not to be called until an ultimate battle. Yet never in a thousand-million casts of Fate might I have guessed that they would save me from death.*

Mordred smiled as he glanced at Sentauris, to Mír and the Adepts, and lastly to Ghorm, who had been restored to his slight Familiar's form. Each stood transfixed, held motionless by the power of the Emissaries of Gods.

Nor did I ever consider that the Truce might be called against my foes, and not against the Renegade Dark Gods! It is time to depart now, to snarl and scorn, and then to forsake Alantéa for a time, to lick my wounds in silence while I heal. Yet in the end, I will pass from this land undefeated and unyielding!

Mordred opened his mouth to bluster and threaten, but found that he, too, was frozen and could not speak. He was able to move, however: a huge Portal had formed, and he stumbled toward it in the company of his foes. Like Mordred, they did not seem to control their own bodies.

·) (·

Sentauris was held motionless, her senses blunted, frozen in some inner region where pain and strife no longer had any meaning. Yet still, she resisted, straining, reaching. *The Gods or the Gods' Servants have saved Mordred and delivered Set from his foes. They have taken us from Sea's Edge to Stone Mountain. Several scores perhaps hundreds of the Emissaries of the Gods have been dispatched at last to enforce the Truce, but at what cost to the people of the League?*

The forces that held her seemed to grip her more tightly. Her mind, with its powerful Seer's Sight, thrashed and fought. Dimly, she sensed that they stood on the limestone banks that formed a shelf above the dunes at Stone Mountain's shoreline. To the west the sun hovered, more red than gold, while at the water's edge the fate of the League — and all the people that she served — was being decided. Again, she struggled with her restraints.

Set remains unchained and stands defending himself before the Emissaries. Mordred as a Power has been freed, as has Merlin, as a principal mover in all this long struggle. Merlin is both a participant and a defendant in this perverse court. Yet perhaps I can at least watch some of this through the Wizard's mind.

Merlin stood upon the shore, arms folded, dwarfed by the towering figures that clustered on the shore. As Powers of the Mid-World, Set, and Mordred were more than three times the size of any single Emissary, while the slightest of Emissaries stood three heads taller than a tall human.

Though Merlin was insignificant in size and stood as a defendant before a tribunal of Mid-World Emissaries, the Wizard refused to stand like a supplicant. Instead, it seemed as though the Wizard was passing judgment upon the Mid-World of the Truce. Many Emissaries glared at the Wizard, while others would not meet his eyes, and a few glanced at Merlin with faces that acknowledged that their tribunal lacked justice.

Merlin watched closely as the Emissaries of the Gods struggled with one of their most powerful masters, the Great God Set. Surrounded by the Gods' most powerful servants, Set stood on the shoreline fabricating offenses of the League, thundering against those who would not abide by the will of the Gods, describing unlikely coincidences as Set and Mordred independently sought to chastise the League.

All these Emissaries are linked, Merlin thought. *They are bound to one another, and to their masters, the Gods. Thus, they are greater in strength even than their numbers, for the power of the Mid-World stands behind them. Their judgments are also linked: first one Emissary turns away from Set to stare into the sunset, then another turns, then a cluster of five. Five becomes a score, then three score. At the last, one reptile-faced Emissary abandons Set with a low hiss. It is so very strange that the Great God's lies are not more closely heeded.*

Set fell silent. All the Emissaries turned their backs on Set and stared seaward, some to the left and some to the right of the setting sun. Light sprang from the Emissaries, lancing out over the water, forming patterns, visions, and Set's conspiracy was laid bare.

Emissaries and their masters, the Gods, watched as Divination images showed Set and Mordred gathered together as cloud-beings in the Gangean Range. Lights shifted, refocused: Set and Mordred could be seen, in the fullness of Set's mockery, disguised as Seraphs, planning the creation of the Enchanters.

When lights formed new patterns, casting Set as a Leviathan of the depths, the Great God, at last, cried out, "Enough!" Lights spilling from the Divination faded, leaving only the red glow of the sun's last rays. Again, the Emissaries turned to confront Set.

"I stand condemned," Set murmured, face downcast. "Yet one day, I will stand again as a great pillar of the Mid-World of the Truce. Here is my penance: for three score circles of the sun, I will absent myself from Alantéa. My temples will decay, my followers desert me, my servants and priests will be abandoned. And after, it will be as though my eyes were forever blind to this League of Southern Alantéa, for I will heed it never again."

Lights seemed to flicker among the Emissaries as thoughts, messages, arguments, instructions passed between them and among the masters, the Gods. Then, one by one, the Emissaries bowed to Set. The Great God inclined his head, took two steps backward, and slipping through a seam in the air, Set vanished.

The Emissaries then turned to Mordred, who drew himself up, standing tall and haughty.

"I will depart," Mordred said, his voice filled with scorn, "though not in shame. Set's penance is not my way — I was never part of this Truce, and so the Mid-World must —" Lights had been flashing from Emissary to Emissary, brighter and hotter, intensifying in anger, and now more than a hundred Emissaries interrupted Mordred, speaking together in a great voice of doom:

"FOR THREE SCORE CIRCLES OF THE SUN SHALT THOU BE AS A ROCK SHELF IN THE HIGHEST OF MOUNTAINS. THE RAPTORS OF THE HEIGHTS SHALL DEFECATE UPON THEE, AND THE ICE SHALL STRIVE TO CHILL THEE AND FRACTURE THINE ESSENCE TO SEND THY SHATTERED FRAGMENTS CASCADING INTO THE GULF. THOU SHALT NEVER SLEEP BUT ENDURE ALL IN CONTEMPLATION OF THY TRANSGRESSIONS."

A profusion of energies lashed at Mordred, and in a single flash of bright light, the Renegade Dark God vanished.

The Mid-World of the Truce, Merlin's mind whispered, *is as powerful and dangerous as we have always feared — even when wielded by the Emissaries, and not the Gods Themselves.*

"Yet after," added one gaunt, spectral Emissary, "Mordred will be as he was, for if he has chosen not to behave as a deity, still he is made of the same substance as the Great Gods." This gaunt and spectral Emissary turned to Merlin. "Now, Wizard, we must deal, once and forever, with this League of yours."

"After this long war," the Wizard said, voice raised, "you will now stand in judgment over our people?" In answer, scores of Emissaries gathered closer to the Wizard, forming a staggered semi-circle. Lights flickered back and forth among the servants of the Gods, and their unseen masters.

"If you are going to judge my people," the Wizard said in more subdued tones, "at least free them." The Wizard gestured to the line of Wizards, and Adepts, to the Elf-Mage, the Seeress, and the lone Familiar who stood frozen in place on the limestone flats above the beach.

"There they stand," Merlin continued, "imprisoned like criminals guilty of the worst offenses. Yet what indeed have they done? We of the League were akin to a herd of deer feeding in a sunlit glade, assailed first by wolves, then by a tiger and a panther. Somehow this herd survived. Must it now be imprisoned for defending itself? Come now, is it not the business of the Gods to offer at least the appearance of justice?"

Irritation flashed over the foremost Emissary, passing in ripples over his spectral features and cold pale flesh, but lights flickered hesitantly among the Powers' other great servants. Suddenly, the Wizards were released. Thorian and Balardi stood still for a moment, eyes passing over the gathering of Emissaries on the broad beach in the last red glow of sunset. Then more lights flashed: Sentauris was released. She stood, speaking in hushed tones to the Wizards, telling them what she had understood of the fate of Mordred and Set. Other lights flashed: Ghorm was released, then Wylar and Orantes, and finally, Mír.

The Wizards, with their servants and allies, walked solemnly down from the limestone shelf to stand beside Merlin. Six humans, an Elf-Mage, and one Mid-World Familiar confronted more than seven score Emissaries — and beyond their greatest servants, the Gods of the Mid-World sat in judgment on the League.

As before, the spectral Emissary stood forward as spokesperson. "Behold, I speak the Will of the Gods: this League of South Alantéa is at an end. The Wizards may rule their fortresses and surrounding lands not more than five square leagues in total for each fortress. All other cities, towns, strong places, revert to a greater Alantéa."

"The Gods propose to punish us for defending ourselves," Merlin said, "and you truly believe that these terms represent the justice of the Mid-World. Are you prepared to defend yourselves before the Maker at the End of Time?"

No response, not even a flicker came, and Merlin sighed. "So, it has come to this. Will you allow us a time of transition, whereby our peoples and allies may depart to other destinations, to seek other destinies?

Lights flickered as thoughts flashed among the Emissaries. "One year," the gaunt Emissary replied, grudgingly.

Merlin turned to Thorian and Balardi; Thorian was tallest by a hand's breadth, while Balardi stood a half-head taller than Merlin. Yet none of those present could doubt that Merlin was chief among the three.

"Gravengate stands at the center of the League," Merlin said quietly. "The three of us will gather there. After our peoples are dispersed, we will arm ourselves mightily, then unfurl the banner of the Maker, the God of Gods. We will denounce the Mid-World of the Truce in the Maker's Name. Our destruction will follow, though who can say if the Maker has not left some bulwark of power to shore up his Servants within Alantéa the Forerunner? And on that day, I believe that many of the Ancient Secrets that lie smoldering within the Mid-World of the Truce will be at last revealed."

"You will not stand alone," Sentauris said. "I, for one, will not be 'dispersed.'"

"Nor will I depart," Orantes said quietly.

"Nor I," Mír added.

"Many of us will not depart," Wylar said. "We of the League will make a great stand."

"And not alone," Sentauris said, her voice lifting. "At least one of the Powers of the Mid-World will join us. We will create such a tumult of strife, that the Maker, who sits at the Heart of the Universe, at the Center of All Understanding, will surely take note of us."

Lights flickered among the Emissaries. The sun vanished down behind the Western Sea. With a snarl, the spectral Emissary turned and withdrew, fading into the press of beings that stood between the leaders of the League and its shoreline. A second Emissary stepped forward, and this servant was mounted on a dark stallion, a woman-warrior with streaming black hair and the wild eyes of a witch. Yet when she spoke, her voice was surprisingly gentle.

"You have offered rash thoughts and rash words to the Gods. Yet because of the wars waged against you in violation of the Truce, they withhold their just wrath. Wizard, the Gods might accept a return to the League as it was a year before, but how can this be accomplished? Soon all of Alantéa will be speaking of the League, how its Wizards and allies fought off first the Enchanters. And even after that astonishing victory, one of the greatest Gods of the Mid-World allied to a powerful Renegade sought to destroy you, and still, you prevailed."

"How can the people of Alantéa speak of things that never happened?" Merlin asked. "It is true that the League endured a time of strife. The Enchanters came upon us, masters of dark sorceries blended with cunning illusions. At the edge of defeat, they took upon themselves the guise of Gods and Powers, yet all their mastery of illusions failed them in the end. Let those who say otherwise come to us, to the Wizards' Strongholds and learn the truth of these matters."

Lights flickered as Emissaries flashed thoughts back and forth among themselves, then sought instructions from the Powers.

The Gods have lied about their origins, Sentauris thought to herself. *Perhaps they will make themselves comfortable with these fantastic fairy tales.*

"The Gods will monitor this 'new truth' most closely," said the dark-haired, mounted Emissary, then her voice grew stern. "The balance of our conditions will not be so easily met. First, your hidden alliances are at an end: no longer will the Kindreds lend you aid." Lights lashed out and suddenly Mír vanished.

"We are not cruel, Wizard," the Emissary continued. "This Mage has not joined Mordred in the Gangean Range, he has simply been returned to his peoples. Secondly, while three Wizards stand against the Will of the Gods, there will not be four or five: you will not be allowed to groom these Adepts to ever higher levels."

Merlin turned to Wylar and Orantes, as though inviting a reply.

Wylar took a deep breath and cleared his throat. "After this struggle, the Gods must understand much of the nature of the League — our alliance has three strong points, but no mobile forces. Orantes and I have become a reserve that can travel from place to place. Yet, to appease the Gods, we will dwell apart from the Wizards, and travel sparingly through the League. To the north and west of Sea's Edge lies a fair isle, and there Orantes and I will dwell, apart, though not exiled from our people."

More lights flickered among the Emissaries. "All this is so soft and easy." This time the spectral Emissary stood forward and once again spoke. "The Gods are not content that you should so readily tap into the wellsprings of power that lie within Alantéa the Forerunner. A drought of magic will lie over this League of yours: Elementals will weaken in your places of power and many of your invisible servants will be reduced to gusts of wind."

The wellsprings of power lie deep in Alantéa the Forerunner, Sentauris thought, *and the Wizards have set down deep tap roots, and thus will not be denied. Also, the Gods have overlooked the mercenary leaders who followed me to the League. If those are permitted to remain, the League will become a far greater military presence. And there are benefits to this "drought": the Gods will make of the League a place of little interest to the Mid-World of the Truce, and so the League's time of peace may last for scores of years.*

The spectral Emissary stood staring down at Sentauris for a moment as though reading her thoughts. "Also, we must deal with this mortal, this Seeress, your battle-leader, and inspiration. The Gods will not permit her to remain in this place, for some strange tale of power lies over her, some link to the future strength of the League, a connection that may only be severed by exile."

Merlin turned to Sentauris and said softly, "The Gods presume overmuch. Perhaps it is indeed time to raise the standard of the Maker and defy them."

Sentauris shook her head slowly. "Subtly and deliberately the Gods have restricted your alliance, but in doing so have allowed the people of the League a time of peace. As for myself, Wizard, you know how little of my own fate I am allowed to see; but here at this intersection, I understand that my future lies elsewhere in the Mid-World." She raised her voice: "I will come to the South of Alantéa never again as Sentauris the Seeress, and Captain-General of Gravengate. I will depart at daybreak. Let the peoples of the League make good use of their coming time of peace." She glanced for a moment into the face of a stricken Orantes, while Wylar bowed his head in sorrow.

Slowly, the lights flashing among the Gods' great servants flickered and died; silence and darkness reigned. On the beach, in fading light, one by one, the Emissaries called Portals to themselves and passed from the League, leaving only a small group of humans standing in the dusk, speaking in soft voices.

·)(·

At the first light of day, Sentauris rose and began preparing for their passage from the League. A subdued Ghorm busied himself beside her, part of his mind wondering if he would ever see Squint and Whisper again. When the first rays of sunlight slipped over their camp, the Adepts came to bid farewell to Sentauris, and Ghorm had the good grace to wait for Sentauris a few hundred paces away from them.

"I cannot believe," Sentauris said to the Adepts, struggling to control her voice, "that I will not be permitted to see either of you ever again. It would not be just, and at least some of the kind and benevolent Gods believe in justice."

Orantes tried to speak but found his voice choked with sorrow. In the distance, rays of bright sunlight had begun to brush Stone Mountain, and shorebirds were rising in flight. Orantes looked away, shaking his head. *This moment should have been bittersweet,* he thought, *but the hollow feeling inside me is going to swallow all joy forever.*

"The logical part of my mind understands," Wylar said, "that in any great struggle the strong must give their lives to defend those who are weaker. At least we're alive. But the part of my mind that *feels*, the part that loves you, says: this moment feels much more like defeat than victory."

"We are not defeated — we stand victorious against an incredible array of foes," Sentauris said. "But in victory, there has been a price. At least for this moment our joy and our pleasure have been pushed aside by the Mid-World of the Truce." She embraced Orantes, then Wylar, then each of them again.

"Now, listen to me for a moment." Her voice lowered, almost to a whisper. "Your League is now stronger than ever. Work hard to make it even more powerful. Accept the great love and gratitude of your peoples with good grace. Have builders work on your offshore retreat. But in the mornings as you prepare for your tasks, and in the long evenings as you ready for sleep, think about ways that we may meet again — places and times where our gatherings are neither brief nor furtive. I will do the same. Remember this: Creatures of the Darkness have not defeated us, nor have Dark Powers of the Mid-World. Even the Mid-World of the Truce was forced to change course by the words of Merlin. We may yet prevail."

After one last embrace, Sentauris walked from them with a heavy heart, ready to leave the League likely forever. She and Ghorm rode north from the coast, passing from the League in slow stages, riding from early morning until mid-afternoon, then halting in the outskirts of small villages. Most of the time they felt like ghosts passing through haunted valleys, because many of the townships were deserted, and almost all the farms and orchards and vineyards of the League lay in ruins. Other times, they felt the healing strength of sun and wind and water slide over the land, for spring was passing, and summer was coming. Only at Tuvan did the Enchanters' destructive power remain, waiting to be lifted by the Wizards' spell-work.

Images of Wylar and Orantes filled her thoughts, one memory yielding to another as she remembered their long struggle. Despite her brave words, she wondered if she would ever see them again. As she and Ghorm neared the League's border, she peered into the future, looking for images, visions, even hints. As always, her own future was mostly obscure; but slowly, grudgingly, images began to reach her mind.

Some creature had come for her in the darkness, while her Sight was blocked. As it sprang, Ghorm hurled magic at it, then collapsed. A dagger sliced out of the night, hurtling toward a slumping Ghorm, and her shield could almost reach the weapon.

She stood in the broad plaza of some Mid-World Power's enchanted domain. It was deep night, but bright moonlight poured down. Scores, perhaps hundreds of huge marble statues decorated the plaza, some depicting heroic matters, while others showed forms of frozen beauty. But danger approached under moonlit skies, and she scanned the shadows. At her side she could feel the strength of the blade — she was holding another Mid-World weapon! But now the shadows shifted to her right, from a direction where danger was not expected. A figure stepped forward into the moonlight and pulled aside his hood. Orantes!

She slipped through the sunlit glade, heart beating fast with a joy of anticipation. A Tanu guardian saluted her and waved her on. An Elf-maiden smiled and called to her charges. Suddenly, Sentauris was surrounded by children, ranging from tiny to mid-height, each of them calling out, "Mama! Mama! You are home!"

Maker's Touch! I am to be mother to a small tribe!

Astonished, she came to a halt. Revelation had come to her just at the borders of the League. In a few hours, she would pass, likely forever, from the Wizards' League.

"What was that about?" Ghorm muttered. "You see so much and share so little with me."

"Ghorm, I see so little of my own fate and control even less of it. But, I see, sometime in the future, I'm supposed to be a mother! Be happy, Ghorm, you will be an uncle to little ones that you love, and who love you."

Ghorm pushed himself away, dropped from the saddle, and turned his back on her, staring south. "It's not the offspring I would mind, it's the begetting of them. You have to understand that there's a limit to what I can endure."

Sighing, she dismounted. "Ghorm..." she trailed off, staring north and west, as another vision lanced through her mind. *Wylar! I am to meet you at the Weasel's Feast next spring, less than one full year from now! A respite — if I survive other dangers. Wylar, wait for me at the inn!*

"I caught some of that," Ghorm said darkly. He looked up to Sentauris, his small squat face twisted in grief. "One day you'll go with Wylar, just as you did with Orantes, away from me, to love him." Sentauris knelt beside her Familiar, embracing his small, squat form.

"Why was I placed into this world in this form," Ghorm choked between clenched teeth, the hot, bitter tears beginning to seep amber, touched by green from his weeping eyes, "to love you as I do, and never be with you as I wish."

"Ghorm..." Sentauris murmured, her own eyes brimming, "Ghorm..." but then the last portion of her vision reached into the core of her mind's eye. *Maker's Touch! Not only am I a shield of the League, but I'm a foremother to others who will serve the League in its next great moment of danger, sometime in the far future.... Images, features, words flooded into her mind. Khond, Cendro, Barak-Kor.... Yes, those too, but closer to home, one called... Galad, and another, Kalanin...and a third a youngling, a magician...Julian! Pillars in the night! Wylar, and Orantes and I formed one pillar, while Julian and Kalanin and Galad formed another! Struggling mightily for the League, they will learn far more of The Game of the Masters and the Mid-World of the Truce than I ever will. And they will never know of me, never!*

But to her weeping Familiar, she whispered, "Ghorm, all things are made perfect in the Maker's Mind. Behold, I see a distant valley in a faraway land, where the Maker permits us to choose our own forms. There, you and I walk arm in arm as humans, strolling beside still, clear waters that are graced with lily pads; and the birds sing forever all around us in voices that were never made for weeping."

Epilogue

More Than Eight Months Later

"**U**NCLE, YOU'RE AWAKE," SENTAURIS whispered. Beside the fire, Vlasoff's wolfhounds stirred, but then their eyes closed when they saw that it was only Sentauris leaning over their sleeping master.

"Uncle, sunrise is coming, and we're going away, just on a short journey, but we'll be back in a few days. Nothing will happen in that time, my Farsight can see that much. Do you remember everything I've been saying to you? Tell me what you remember."

"You won, you triumphed," Vlasoff said, eyes coming awake. "Whenever dark dreams crowd my mind, I speak those words."

"*We* won," Sentauris corrected him. "You, along with my parents were the first leaders of the League's resistance. The Wizards were willing to accept the slaughter of refugees as a price for their League, but we and others would not tolerate it."

"Wait, daughter of mine, wait," Vlasoff muttered, rubbing his face as his eyes faltered. "There was something I was supposed to tell you, but now I can't remember it. I've forgotten, again...."

"At night, uncle," Sentauris whispered, "sometimes an image comes to me, of an enormous owl, hovering over our farmhouse in the darkness."

"Yes, the owl," Vlasoff said, again coming to life, "an Emissary of Pallas Athena!"

"I know that the Goddess has been trying to help heal you."

Vlasoff nodded; with his motion, three sets of wolfhound eyes flashed open, glinting in the firelight. "Yes, but that's not all. My wonderful daughter, you are not to worry, but the Goddess is under siege. When she aided our League, other forces became aware of her. Now the Great Dark Gods have begun to attack her followers. Slowly, all her temples are being abandoned. She does not wish you to worry, she only wants you to know that there was a price and that she now pays it, not unwillingly."

Sentauris stared into the firelight and took a deep breath. "The Mid-World of the Truce may allow others to pressure her for a time, but the erratic memory of the Mid-World will not last for too many cycles of the sun. One day, Pallas Athena will stand as tall and strong as she ever did."

·)(·

Ghorm muttered to himself as they rode down the icy horse track toward the river: the farmhouse had been warm, and he had looked forward to a morning's sleep rich with dreams. Instead, they had risen early, and traveled all day, with few rest stops to offset his growing fatigue. Now, in the partial light of dusk, with their steed snorting icy vapor into the gloom, Ghorm felt the chill of the oncoming night.

"If I didn't need you, Ghorm," Sentauris reminded him quietly, "I would have left you behind. Besides, you should take heart — spring is coming." Ghorm snorted in disgust; just six nights ago, cracking, and groaning sounds had woken them as the ice jams in the upper Saugus had finally broken free, sending ice floes surging down the swift river out to a saltwater sea.

In the aftermath of the assault on the League, the South of Alantéa had endured the worst winter in its long memory, with shafts of ice plunging deep into the ground, and winter gales sweeping snowstorms over the land. Rivers were choked, roofs large and small were broken by heavy weights of snow, livestock and wild beasts devastated. But now, winter was over, and spring, even a reluctant, chilled spring, would be a welcome change.

They rode in silence for a time as the first glimpse of the lower Saugus, running grey and white, came into view. If Ghorm had become somewhat more gaunt, he seemed just a little wiser, with a touch of grey in his gnome like eyes. The appearance of Sentauris was unchanged, though she had become more assured, stronger, more confident and in greater control of events.

She and Ghorm had left the League in early summer, hoping for a time of peace after their struggles. Instead, warfare had burst over the borderlands. Rumors of the League's strength had drawn torrents of refugees southward, but then jealous Dark Gods had lashed at the fleeing humans with the violence of swords and spears and dark magic. Sentauris and others had fought back, providing armed guards for the refugees, ambushing larger raiding parties, then fighting pitched battles against even larger forces.

As Sentauris and her allies began to prevail, she became a focused target of the malice of Dark Gods. Sendings of great force were launched against her. When she ate in the company of so-called allies, dark potions were set before her. At night, supernatural entities stalked her dreams.

Yet as violence swirled around her, Sentauris discovered a strange truth: many of the Gods were reluctant to have her perish. Perhaps the Greater Gods were unwilling to make of her a martyr, and perhaps there was at least a little truth in the often quoted saying that the Gods loved a hero.

Twice, an Emissary of the Gods had deflected a fatal blow, and in one climactic struggle with a great supernatural entity, Ghorm had been restored to full Adept's strength. Completely astonished, Sentauris and Ghorm had turned on that powerful Sending and destroyed it. Sentauris thought she could name Ghorm's hidden patron, but she kept that thought carefully hidden in the farthest corners of her mind.

Now, as they rode down to the river at dusk, Sentauris could look forward to the coming spring as a time of something that might bring an end to constant warfare. That peace, Sentauris thought, was something that could easily be interrupted at any moment. As they neared the dark, swirling waters of the Saugus, the always suspicious but temporarily lulled mind of Ghorm came suddenly awake.

"Wait, now wait," Ghorm said. "Just a moment here. Isn't this the track that leads us to that place, *The Dead Rat's Gargle*, or whatever that stinking inn was called?"

"Yes, *The Weasel's Feast*. No harm in a decent meal and a brief night's rest, is there, Ghorm?"

The Familiar's first instinct was to yank on the reins of their horse. Instead, he made a swift count of seasons and days. "And this is a year, a full year since we met the Adepts at the inn, is it not?"

"Close," Sentauris said. "A year less a day."

"And so, you said nothing to me, you just arranged through one of your secret spies to meet the Adepts here, one year later, but you didn't say anything to me over all these months."

"You would have fussed and fumed at least three times every day. Besides, Squint and Whisper will be waiting for you."

Ghorm's squat face twisted in jealousy. "That doesn't balance sharing you with the Stoat and the Boar." After the Adept's heroic efforts, Ghorm had grudgingly promoted Orantes from a "Pig" to a "Boar."

"Ghorm, we have many allies in this wide world but few real friends. I have the Adepts and you have Squint and Whisper. Secondly, you always say to me 'Sweet talk, where's the gold?' But tonight, *take* the gold; there's a pouch for you in our saddle bag. Buy a roast pheasant for yourself and for Squint. As well, in a separate pouch are talismans of some potency. Find, if you can, appropriate gifts for your colleagues the Familiars."

"So, you've been planning this for months. You won't...."

"Think, Ghorm, about your contest of lies. Squint and Whisper will have been told about your Adept's strength in the battle with Mordred, but will they know how you suddenly rose in strength to fight against the great Sending?"

Ghorm took a deep breath and cleared his mind. Then the slightest of smiles formed on his face: perhaps in the next contest of lies he would understate his own role, he would be Ghorm the Humble. His fellow Familiars would have no idea how to react and the laughter that would follow....

And then they rode up over a rise along the horse track that snaked beside the riverbank. Above them, dusk was giving way to dark night, with stars beginning to flicker between gaps in the evening mists. To their left below them was the great river, ice floes thunking against one another in the fading light of dusk, and just to the river's right, they could see the gleaming lights of *The Weasel's Feast*, shimmering in the distance.

The Wild Time is the first of five books.
The Game of the Masters is the sequel.

Manufactured by Amazon.ca
Bolton, ON